# THE NAZAROVS

## by Markoosha Fischer

Author of *My Lives in Russia*

In *The Nazarovs*, Markoosha Fischer
has written a great human story, a living,
passionately felt novel of a Russian family
who spent their lives in a time of revolution, violent change, and the final betrayal
of the people.

Beginning about the time Czar Nicholas
II came to the throne, the novel sweeps
through half a century. Through the lives
of three generations of Nazarovs, it tells
the story of the years before the Revolution, the years of conspiracy, planning,
sacrifice, and exultant dedication to an
idea; of the coming of the Revolution and
the desperate, difficult, stirring years that
followed when a nation of people gave
its spirit and mind and body to making
that idea work; of the Purge and the
black, heartbreaking years of betrayal
when an idea was murdered, years of
heart-tightening fear and suspicion and
despair, when by ones and tens and hundreds, the people who had made the
Revolution were shot or exiled—or just
disappeared. And finally it pounds to a
climax with the coming of World War II
and the siege of Moscow, when a city
and a country gathered itself up for its
greatest effort.

There is no way to convey the beating
excitement of this story, which after all
is not the story of events but first, last,
and always the story of some people—
men, women, and children—who lived
these events, who made them and were
made by them.

Only in the novel form could a story
on such a vast scale be told—the whole
story of modern Russia. Covering a canvas
as large as Tolstoy's *War and Peace*, it is
the first novel to attempt a portrayal of
people's reactions to the entire course of
the Russian upheavals which started in
the last century and ended with the defense
of Moscow.

# THE
# NAZAROVS

*By the same author*

MY LIVES IN RUSSIA

# THE NAZAROVS

## By
## MARKOOSHA FISCHER

HARPER & BROTHERS
PUBLISHERS
NEW YORK AND LONDON

5-8

THE NAZAROVS

*Copyright, 1948, by Markoosha Fischer*
*Printed in the United States of America*

FIRST EDITION

D-X

# Table of Contents

PART I: 1892—1917

CHAPTER 1—*Olga* ................................................. 1

CHAPTER 2—*Vera* ................................................. 16

CHAPTER 3—*Czar Nicholas* ................................. 22

CHAPTER 4—*The Young Gavrilovs* .................... 25

CHAPTER 5—*Anton and Kseniya* ....................... 37

CHAPTER 6—*Vera* ................................................. 40

CHAPTER 7—*Anton* ............................................. 55

CHAPTER 8—*Fedor and Ludmilla* ...................... 60

CHAPTER 9—*1905* ............................................... 66

CHAPTER 10—*Anton and Maxim* ....................... 69

CHAPTER 11—*Igor* ............................................... 78

CHAPTER 12—*Anton and Kseniya* ..................... 88

CHAPTER 13—*Maxim* ........................................... 97

CHAPTER 14—*Natasha* ......................................... 99

PART II: 1917—1936

CHAPTER 15—*Revolution* ................................... 115

CHAPTER 16—*Kseniya* ......................................... 133

CHAPTER 17—*Vera* ............................................... 138

CHAPTER 18—*Natasha* ......................................... 145

CHAPTER 19—*Natasha and Peter* ....................... 161

CHAPTER 20—*Katya* ............................................. 167

CHAPTER 21—*Maxim and Kira* ........................... 170

CHAPTER 22—*Maxim and Kira* ........................... 179

CHAPTER 23—*Natasha and Peter* ....................... 198

CHAPTER 24—*Natasha* ......................................... 216

» v «

CHAPTER 25—*Fedor and Ludmilla*                 236
CHAPTER 26—*Katya and Gromov*                  247
CHAPTER 27—*Natasha and Peter*                 261
CHAPTER 28—*Maxim and Kira*                    280

PART III: 1936—1942
CHAPTER 29—*Maxim and Kira*                    301
CHAPTER 30—*Kira*                              318
CHAPTER 31—*Natasha and Peter*                 335
CHAPTER 32—*Natasha and Kira*                  352
CHAPTER 33—*War!*                              363

# THE
# NAZAROVS

# Part One

## 1892-1917

CHAPTER I

*Olga*

IT was the morning of May 5, 1892.

Singing the tune of the Polonaise from *Eugene Onegin*, Vera danced down the stairway. She threw a longing glance at the banister. Until last Monday, her twelfth birthday, she had always slid down. Since that memorable day, however, sliding down had been forbidden. She was a young lady now. Nevertheless, walking downstairs was boring. To make it more exciting she invented a game; at each step she was to look into the mirrors lining the walls of the stair well. She looked first at the sky-blue ribbon in her hair and at each step she looked a little lower. She had to be careful, though, for, according to the rules of the game, she was not to look at her slippers until she reached the very last step.

She was late for breakfast. The sun had been shining so beautifully on the golden dome of the Cathedral of the Saviour and the first buds on the chestnut tree in the yard had come out overnight. She had spent much too much time looking at them. Then there was last night's ballet program. She had had to read it over again and put it away in the little box on top of the cotillion ribbons from her birthday dance.

Something had gone wrong with her game; she had looked at her slippers four steps too soon. She jumped the last four steps, then stopped to compose herself before entering the dining room. Since last Monday she had tried hard to behave with the dignity and poise of her sisters.

She opened the door, an apology for being late on her lips. But there was no one to apologize to; the dining room was empty. This had happened before, mostly when father had made a "scandal." Usually, Mother and Olga and Zena lingered at the table after Father left. She suddenly remembered that while she had been busy with the chestnut tree and her souvenir box she had heard loud voices, hurried steps, and slammed doors. Vera danced around the table on tiptoes looking for signs of the scandal.

This time something really serious seemed to have happened. Father had just broken a roll in two when whatever made him furious occurred. In anger he had thrown his napkin to the floor, pushed his chair away, and rushed out of the room. He must have been in quite a temper. His chair was turned over and everything between his chair and the door bore signs of having been furiously kicked. Mother's plate was untouched, her napkin was still folded, and her chair had not been moved. She, too, must have left the room in a hurry. Her handkerchief and a glove were on the floor. Why should she have needed a glove so early in the morning? There was no sign that sister Olga had been in the room at all. Sister Zena's place was not set, of course, for she was still away visiting an aunt. Maxim and Igor's plates looked well cleaned. They must have finished eating before Father made the scandal.

From all the signs it was plain that what had happened that morning was more than an ordinary scandal. Vera's curiosity was at a fever pitch when the door opened and the old nursemaid, Nyanya, came in, a frail little figure in black. Nyanya had been with the family for three generations, and there were no secrets from her in the Nazarov household. Vera flew to her.

"Nyanya, Nyanya, what happened? Tell me, quick, quick!"

"What should have happened, little pigeon?" Nyanya asked. "What are you talking about? Did you have a bad dream?"

"A bad dream!" Vera said. "Who do you think I am? A little child? I am grown up now. Didn't you say so yourself on Monday? Quick, what happened?"

"Nothing unusual, darling," Nyanya said gently. "Father disliked something Mother said and he flew into one of his rages. What is there to be excited about? What do I see? My little angel hasn't eaten a thing yet!"

Vera, knowing it was useless to try to make Nyanya say something she did not want to say, ate her breakfast quickly and ran out of the room, determined to get to the root of the scandal.

Forgetting herself, she slid down the banister into the kitchen, where she vainly tried her luck with the cook and the kitchen help. She threw her "Tell me, quick, quick!" at the maids, the valets, the housemen, the laundresses, and the seamstresses. She pleaded even with Nikifor, the majestic doorman who, with his resplendent silver-braided uniform, huge build, and long reddish beard parted in two, was an outstanding landmark. Getting no satisfaction from any of them, she mounted the stairs to the upper floor. In the hall she heard her little brothers' voices coming from their classroom. They seemed to be alone there without their tutor. At any other time Vera would have flown noisily into their room, boxed their ears, and romped and laughed with them. But today she had more important things on her mind. Young as the boys were, they might have heard or noticed something. She found them sitting on the floor cutting out pictures from old magazines. Igor raised his pale thin face to his sister and showed no interest when she asked him:

"What happened? Were you there? What did they say?"

"Father screamed something at Mother . . . Better ask Maxim . . ."

Though only a year older, six-year-old Maxim was more responsive:

"I was just walking out of the door, and Mother said that Olga was going away, and she also said that Gregor was going away, and Father got awfully, awfully angry . . . Gregor came to say good-bye to us, and Olga too. . . . Why should they go away, and where are they going, Vera? And will we get another tutor? I don't want a new tutor, I want Gregor. I like Gregor, I like him very much . . ."

Vera was not interested in her brother's feelings about the tutor, and anyway he was nothing but a baby, really, and didn't understand anything. He must have mixed it all up. What would Olga have to do with a tutor?

Vera had little time left. The French governess, Mademoiselle Suzanne, was waiting in the study room. Slowly Vera passed her grandmother's door. Grandmother was never to be disturbed in the morning. And there was no use knocking at Mother or Olga's doors. They kept telling her that she was grown up now and must behave like a young lady, but they wouldn't think of treating her as other than a silly little girl and they would never tell her anything really interesting. For once Vera was not dancing or singing. With reluctant steps, still hoping that at the last moment a miracle might happen, she walked into the study room. Mademoiselle Suzanne said nothing. She only looked meaningly at the watch pinned over her heart and threw back the lace around her wrists. That meant: You are late, and I am ready for work. Vera slowly opened her books.

The night before, Olga had watched from her window as the carriage with her mother, father, and Vera drove off down the street. It was to drop her father at the Merchants' Club for a card game, then take her mother and Vera on to the ballet. Olga had begged off on the score of one of her frequent headaches. As the carriage disappeared from sight, Olga turned away and sought out her grandmother's sitting room. The big soft chair in which Grandmother now spent most of her time stood beneath a life-size painting of her as a young bride. Even at seventy-two, she made it easy to believe the legends about her former beauty, though the golden blond of her hair and the heavenly blue of her eyes were now gray. Gray also was the prevailing color in her clothes. She was dressed in a flowing gray silk negligee, with lace around her face, shoulders, and hands. A gray lacy shawl protected her against the evening chill.

Olga sat at her grandmother's feet on an embroidered velvet stool. With her clear white face, her black hair parted in the middle and braided around her head, her serious big black eyes and her plain dark dress, enlivened only by narrow white edgings on collar and cuffs, she looked almost austere next to her grandmother. Grandmother seemed surrounded by clouds of fine lace; her hair was piled high on her head in tiny curls, and her hands were covered with sparkling rings and bracelets.

They sat in silence for a while as they often did. Then Olga said:

"Grandmother, I am in love. I am going away to get married."

For Grandmother, the evening had been filled with the tranquillity of a sweet warm spring. Now a breath of icy air suddenly took the warmth away. She drew the shawl tighter around her shoulders and waited for Olga to continue. When Olga remained silent, she asked:

"But why must you go away from home to be married? Who is he?"

"Gregor Alekseich."

"Who?" asked Grandmother, unbelieving. "The boys' tutor?"

"Yes."

"But, Olga, you are out of you mind!" Grandmother's voice almost broke with agony. "Don't you know who he is? Don't you know where he comes from? Don't you know what your father will do?"

"I know, Grandmother, I know everything. But we are going away. Gregor will teach school in a village and I shall help him."

"You are sick, my child, you are very, very sick, and don't know what you are saying. Your headaches must have affected you. You cannot mean it, Olga. Oh, you are joking. Of course. You are joking. You wanted to see whether your old grandmother could take a joke. Yes, she can, dearest, she can. Now give her a nice big smile, and go to bed."

Grandmother hoped that her own painful little smile might chase the nightmare away.

"Grandmother, please," said Olga. "I cannot smile now. I am happy, I am very happy, but I cannot smile. I love Gregor. When I think that soon we shall be together every day of our lives until we die it is as if birds were singing in my heart. I never knew there was such happiness in the world. You never told me about it, and Mother never said anything."

Grandmother wasn't smiling now. She could not fool herself any longer. The horror was there to stay. She listened and her hand softly stroked Olga's dark head. When she spoke again, it was in a voice that had suddenly aged and become shaky. She said:

"Remember the other day your father came into the room when you were trying on those new French bonnets? He brushed them aside and said, 'Don't waste your time, my daughter, you will not find anything to fit your head among this junk. A crown, nothing less than a crown can fit my Olga.' 'My beautiful majestic Olga, my Greek goddess,' he calls you. He is right. You do look like a Greek goddess. Pah! A Greek goddess among filthy muzhiks!"

Grandmother's voice broke. Again the artificial smile, the painful smile came to her face.

"Olga, my love, my precious, don't go away. Think of us, please, please. A Nazarova cannot throw her life away on a muzhik, on a nameless muzhik at that. No love is worth it. Believe me, darling, believe me."

Grandmother was growing more miserable every minute, but Olga's big black eyes locked with hers as if she were demanding the answer to the question she had asked before.

"Why didn't you and Mother tell me anything about love? Never once did you talk to me about love. You remember that night when Mother found me crying over the story of Romeo and Juliet, and you all laughed at me, and Mother said, 'Don't ever believe what you read about love in books. They lie. It never happens like that in real life.' Grandmother, Grandmother, it does happen like that; I know it does; it happened to me."

More quietly Olga went on:

"Remember three months ago when Gregor walked in when we were having tea? He told Father that if the boys didn't behave properly he would have to look for another tutor. Father was speechless! Imagine, he, Anton Nazarov, being told by a servant—you know that anyone Father pays, even a teacher, is his servant—that his sons were no good. He started to fly into a rage but Gregor quietly left the room. The eight rubles a month he was getting was all the money in the world he possessed, but he would not sell his soul. Even father must have felt something of that because he called him back and it was decided that I should be present in the classroom and make the boys behave. I was annoyed. There were so many things I could do besides sitting there and being bored. But I was not bored long. When I listened to the stories Gregor was telling the boys I wasn't bored at all. He was telling them stories that sounded like children's fairy tales but he was saying things I had never heard before. None of the silly things Mademoiselle Suzanne or Miss Watson taught me. I felt ashamed. I, a Russian, who knew the name of every French and English king, knew hardly anything about Russia. He noticed that I was interested and talked sometimes for me. And I learned from him. I had always thought the czar was gentle and loved his people. But that isn't what Gregor says and I believe him. If you had heard him, Grandmother, you would have believed him too. The czar is suspicious and revengeful. The czar hates those who want Russia to be a free, a happy land . . ."

Grandmother was not interested in history or politics and she could not understand how Olga could talk about politics now when her life and the life of the whole family was at stake.

"Olga, listen . . . you had better tell me . . ."

But Olga did not listen. In a voice that sounded, Grandmother thought, as if she were making love, she went on:

"The czar hates education, science, everything that is good in Russia . . . Human lives mean nothing to him. The welfare of his people means nothing to him . . . And, Grandmother, Gregor says that the people are very tired of it, that they want a better life . . . Gregor brought me books to read, and he would sit with me and talk. It was good to listen to him, Grandmother, but . . ."

For the first time that evening a smile curled Olga's lips.

". . . it was even better to look at him. And suddenly everything else I did—parties, dinners, dress fittings, dancing—seemed so silly and such a waste of time. You remember the day Father said that the boys were behaving all right now and that I could be relieved of my unpleasant task? The only thought in my head all day and all night long was what could I do now. I knew I couldn't live without seeing Gregor. You know what I did? Next day I slipped a note into his hand and I met him in secret the same evening." Olga looked into her grandmother's face. "Well, Grandmother, why don't you say, 'Olga Nazarova threw herself at a muzhik'?"

But there was no anger or indignation on Grandmother's face. It had a faraway look. Olga was not sure that she was listening. She went on:

"That was the day my headaches started, and you all thought I was in my room and wasn't to be disturbed. I needed this time to be with him. Grandmother, I didn't know before but I know now that love can be stronger than father and mother, than walls and doors, than any obstacle in the whole world. When I read a book, his face is between me and the page; when I talk to someone, his face is between me and that person; when I walk in the street, his face is everywhere; when I'm in a crowd and he's not there, the world is empty and deserted;

when I see him, even if no one else is around, the world is filled with millions of people . . ."

The house had suddenly become alive. Doors opened and closed, bells rang, voices called, footsteps ran up and down the stairs.

"The masters have come home," Nyanya said outside Grandmother's door. Grandmother straightened herself, took a mirror, brought her curls, laces, and shawl into place. It was harder to bring to her face the friendly smile to which the family was accustomed. It was easier for Olga; she had become well used these last months to wearing a mask. Her mother and Vera came into the room.

"Why, Olga, you still up?" Kseniya asked with concern. "How could you let her, Mother, with her headache?"

Neither Grandmother nor Olga had need to answer, for Nyanya came in immediately with a tray of tea and cake. Vera was demonstrating the new pirouettes of her favorite ballerina. Her long white skirts twirling about her, her graceful little feet hardly touching the ground, she hummed the music softly, little disturbed by the lack of attention the others paid to her. Over her tea, Grandmother looked from Olga to Kseniya. In her deeply cut black velvet robe with a wide bustle and sweeping train, her chestnut hair falling in ringlets down her neck, her brown eyes animated and her cheeks pink with the excitement of the evening, Kseniya looked, Grandmother thought, rather like an older sister of Olga than her mother.

As soon as Vera had swallowed her last mouthful of cake, Grandmother sent her off to bed.

"You stay a minute," she said to Kseniya, who had put down her cup and was getting up from her chair. "There is something I want to tell you."

As soon as the door closed behind Vera, she said:

"Well, my dear, do not let us waste much time. Your husband may come in any minute now, and what we have to say had better be said before he comes."

In a few short sentences she told Kseniya Olga's story. Kseniya's face was gray and her eyes filled with terror.

"You know as well as I do," she said in a choking voice, "that this is impossible, thoroughly impossible. One does not go against the whole world. And even if I should permit it, Father would never let it happen. He would rather kill you, Olga."

Olga did not lose her calm. "Mother, dear, you don't seem to understand. There is no question of you or Father permitting or not permitting. I am going away. I could have gone away secretly. But I don't want to do it that way. I want everything about my life with Gregor to be open and truthful."

Olga took her trembling mother into her arms and tried to quiet her.

"O God, what words can I find to make you see that you mustn't do it?" cried Kseniya. "What words can I use to convince you that you cannot ruin all our lives because of love? Love isn't worth it! No man is worth it. Why can't I find the words to tell you that, why?"

Suddenly she turned to Grandmother and, with a fierceness Olga had never seen in her, cried out:

"Why don't you tell her that she cannot and must not do it? Why don't you tell her, why? Why don't you tell her that without her parents' blessing her life and the life of her children will be forever cursed? Why don't you tell her what you told me right here in this room twenty-three years ago? Tell her, tell her, why don't you? Break her heart the way you broke mine!"

Her last words were lost in wild sobs. Olga led her mother to a seat at Grandmother's feet. She sat down with her, gently stroking her hair as if she were the mother and not the daughter.

"I was waiting for that to come, Kseniya, and I am ready for it," said Grandmother slowly. "You told me your story, Olga; now you listen to me. You asked me why we've never told you anything about love. We couldn't tell you because we don't know much about it ourselves. In my time, girls didn't. My father chose my husband for me, and when your mother was ready for marriage, her father handled it in the same way. One day he simply told her that she was to marry Anton Nazarov, who was the chief clerk in the firm and whom he had picked to carry on the business. . . . That night your mother came into this room the way you came tonight, Olga. But you came to tell me what you were going to do; your mother came pleading with me to help her. She had fallen in love with another young man; she didn't want to marry Anton. . . . But how could I help her? I only knew that we women could never go against the will of our fathers and husbands. There was no law against their beating us to death if we would not obey. My father was still alive then. Even if I could have found the courage to speak to my husband, which I never could, I would rather have died a million deaths than oppose my father's will, and Anton was his choice too. There was nothing in the world I could do but cry with her. And you remember, Kseniya, I told you then that even if I could have helped you, I wouldn't do it. I didn't know any better then."

Grandmother stood up to her full height, leaning heavily on her cane.

"But I do know now. And I will not let anyone ruin Olga's life as I, in my ignorance, permitted yours to be ruined. Get up, Kseniya, pull yourself together, and for the sake of your daughter's happiness muster all your courage. Not that Anton will ever give Olga his blessing. I know that, but I don't think she will be the less happy for it. I have learned that too."

Olga bent low over her grandmother's hand and kissed it.

"We have been meek enough in our lives," continued the old woman. "We have done nothing but breed children, look pretty, and give orders to our servants. Providence once gave me the chance to be courageous and help my daughter. I missed it through my stupidity and cowardice. Kseniya, don't you too bend your neck in servility. It will be better for your soul if you fight and insist on your right to give Olga your blessing and let her know that she has a mother."

Olga's eyes were full of tears.

"Grandmother, darling Grandmother, I expected you to be angry and outraged, and instead you have been sweet and understanding. I will never forget it, never. Mother, please, Mother, don't cry. I'll be happy, don't worry about me."

"You dear little fool, she is not crying over you. She is crying over herself. She is crying because I found out too late about love. And now I need my rest. You need it too. We have troubled days ahead of us. I am afraid it is useless to wish any of us a peaceful night."

Grandmother made the sign of the cross over her daughter and granddaughter and pressed them close to her. "God bless you, my beloved ones. God bless you," she whispered.

The moment the door closed behind them, the door to the bedroom opened, and Nyanya appeared. Her eyes were red from crying and her whole little figure expressed anguish. The relationship of mistress and servant had disappeared long ago for Grandmother and Nyanya. For many years now she had spent her evenings with Grandmother in the sitting room, or when the family assembled, there, in the adjoining bedroom. Tonight, as usual, she had heard every word of the conversation. Grandmother knew it and she understood Nyanya's anguish.

For Gregor was the child who twenty-five years before had been sent to Moscow from their village to cover up the shame which Nyanya's daughter had brought upon her family. A married woman, she had given birth to a child a year and a half after her husband had been recruited into the army. The child was to have been left at the foundling asylum in Moscow and his existence forever forgotten. Nyanya had known well that this was the only thing to do in such a case. But there had been something in this child which had made her want to keep him. He had been so healthy, so friendly and bright. He had laughed at her, clung to her, and cried when she left the room. She had not been able to bring herself to let him disappear into an orphanage, where he would forget to smile forever. A family she knew had been ready to keep him for three rubles a month. Nyanya never forgot to thank God in her prayers for having given her the wisdom to keep the child. He had remained friendly, bright, and loving. She had set her heart on making something out of him, and with the help of charity organizations he had been sent to school. His teachers had discovered unusual abilities in him and prepared him to enter the university. A poorly paid tutorship here and there, a little gift from Nyanya on holidays had kept him alive, though often cold and hungry.

Last year when the master decided that a tutor would be better for his sons than a governess, he had entrusted them to Gregor. And now this. O God Almighty, Nyanya prayed, what would happen to her? She would be thrown out of the house, separated forever from everything and everybody she loved, forced to return to the village. The village which she hardly knew and which she feared. Wasn't God's revenge coming upon her now for having devoted her life and love to a strange family instead of her own? She had sent every one of her own four children back to the village as soon as she was through nursing them. She had sent them money and presents, and sometimes she visited them. But her heart really belonged to her master's family. Her own children were strangers to her. Nyanya felt confused and torn—torn between love and loyalty to her own kin and devotion to this family, to whom she really belonged. Yet her own people were nothing but filthy muzhiks to them. It was all wrong. She should be proud of her people. Hadn't they always toiled like serfs, every one of them, men, women, and children? And what had her masters ever done? Why should they be so proud of themselves? Why should they feel that the world had come to an end just because her grandson, her fine upright handsome Gregor wanted to marry their daughter?

But after one look at Grandmother's suffering face, Nyanya's doubts and confusion dissolved. Here was her place, the only place in the world, and her only task in life was to be around them, unnoticed when everything went well and ready to help when they needed her.

In silence, Nyanya got Grandmother ready for the night, and waited until she had settled her heavy body in bed before she left her. It was almost daylight before either of them found sleep.

Kseniya did not sleep at all that night. With terror in her heart, she waited for her husband to come home. When finally his feet sounded on the stairs, she felt so weak from her tears and anxiety that she decided to talk to him in the morning. He stumbled with heavy steps into his room, cursed the valet and threw himself into the bed muttering drunkenly. She knew he would fall asleep instantly. For twenty-three years she had lived with this man and often shared her bed with him. But she had never listened to his footsteps at night without apprehension. She never forgot their wedding night, the first time she had been alone with him.

And although she did not know it, neither was Anton ever able to forget. In unwary moments, the memory still persisted. He stood for the first time in their bedroom looking at her admiringly and with pride. She was beautiful and he was a lucky man to have got her, the daughter of the mighty Kanavsky. Kanavsky and Nazarov, the sign would read tomorrow, and some day it would be just Nazarov. The thought of this future gave him the courage he lacked, and he approached his wife. What did one say to a young bride? He did not know. They had hardly ever talked to each other before, except to say a few words about the weather or the food. Wordlessly, with fingers cold and rigid with nervousness, he had began roughly to undress her, clumsily pulling and tearing at buttons, ribbons and stays, pressing her to his body, sweating and shaking with embarrassment and excitement. Half fainting, she had struggled, but he was too strong.

He had left her almost immediately, unable to stand the silent reproach of the shaking prostrated little figure. There had been pity for her in his heart, there had been in his mind some disquieting thought that he might have behaved differently, that he might have been gentle. Her sobs and pleading had rung in his ears, and he had tried to drown them and his uncertainty in vodka.

Kseniya never knew how close she was that night to having her husband come back to her repentant and loving. He entered their bedroom in the early morning hours, his head blurred from drinking, his heart torn between fear and tenderness, fear of not asserting his masculinity, fear of losing his mastery, and fear of losing her love. Had there been anything in her eyes but horror and disgust of him, or had she known that there was as much terror in his heart as in hers, the disaster of their first night together might have been mended. But after his first quick look at her, he threw his clothes on the floor and fell beside her into a deep drunken sleep.

A little later a wretched pale Kseniya stood before her mother.

"I knew you would come, Kseniya," the older woman said gently. "Cry it out, little one; it has to come out; it will choke you otherwise. Cry it out, cry it out," she whispered tenderly, caressing Kseniya's hair.

"Mother, did you know what was going to happen to me?" Slowly the words came out amidst sobs.

Her mother said nothing, she only bent her head lower, and pity gave her fingers more softness and more tenderness.

"Why didn't you tell me? I would never, never have got married. I don't want to be married. I never want to see my husband again."

"Hush, hush, my child, don't ever say that. You are married to Anton. Nothing in the world can change that. You are a woman now and this is the way it always has been and is always going to be. Why didn't I tell you? A mother cannot talk to her daughter about these things before she is married. You will get used to Anton. We all had to get used to our husbands the hard way, believe me, my daughter. Obey him in everything, listen to every word he tells you, try to please him and never contradict him. He is your husband, you belong to him now. Remember that, my daughter. This is woman's fate. In it are plenty of tears but also joys. You will learn that. You will have children and you will love them. You will enjoy your beautiful clothes and jewels and horses. . . . Come, Kseniya, come now, my dear, dry your tears, wash your face with cold water. Put on your nicest dress. You order the dinner today, order rich food and plenty of wine. We will all eat and drink in good spirits. And remember this: many a woman has cried her eyes out on the first day and laughed the rest of her life. Go now, my Kseniya, make yourself beautiful."

Kseniya went. She ordered the dinner. She chose her nicest dress and emerged from her room a picture of young loveliness.

When Anton woke in the late afternoon, his valet told him that the family was assembling in the big dining room for dinner. "Also . . . Kseniya Nikolaevna?" She was also there, the valet told him.

Freshly washed and dressed, Anton appeared in the dining-room door. He looked at Kseniya. She was beautiful. One sign of forgiveness on her face, and he could forget forever all he had ever heard about ruling women with an iron hand and about showing them who was master. Kseniya did not know that. All she knew was the terror of the previous night and the counsel of obedience and submission her mother had given her. She was ready to be obedient and submissive. But not a flicker of feeling for him was in her eyes. They sat together at the table; they even kissed when the others drank their health. But he felt the icy cold beneath her forced kisses, and their future was sealed that evening. He remained the master, growing louder and louder the less sure he became that he wanted to be master. She was obedient and submissive to him day and night. Her mother was right. She got used to her new life. No one ever saw her tears, no one ever knew her terror when he approached her at night. She was a beautiful young wife, a good devoted mother, an excellent hostess.

She had little to say to her husband, whom she never learned to call by any name but the formal Anton Semenovich. Their conversation never ranged beyond everyday events. He gave orders and if he thought they were not being carried out properly or if something in the house was not according to his wishes he would fly into a rage, shout abuse, break dishes and furniture, get drunk and shout, "I'll show them who the master is!"

Now, for the first time in their twenty-three years together, Kseniya was going to say something to him which was not a mere everyday trifle. For the first time she was going to oppose her will to him. She spent the rest of the night crying and praying for strength.

Olga did not sleep much that night either. She went through her belongings and put aside what she wanted to take into her new life. There was not much. She did not want any of her clothing except a gray dress, a cloak, and a shawl which she had bought two years ago when they had gone on a pilgrimage to the Monastery. She added to it a few books, her diary, some underwear, and some family photographs. She opened the lacquered boxes in which she had kept her souvenirs, invitations, programs, cotillion prizes, ball carnets, and stuffed it all into the stove. She did not even open the boxes of plumes, ribbons, fans, laces, gloves; neither did she touch her jewel box. There would be no place for any of that in her future life. Her sisters would find use for it.

When she had finished she sat down on her favorite low window seat. The moon was paling, the first breath of morning woke the birds, and Olga was still sitting there lost in her dreams. She saw herself in a village dressed like a peasant, teaching children and adults. She would teach them what Gregor had taught her. They would listen to her, she was sure they would. And Gregor would be with her, always and forever with her. They would go far away, the two of them, just the two of them, together, always always together. . . .

She snuggled deeper into the seat and, smiling, passed from one world of dreams into another.

Vera danced for a while around her room, putting things away and softly humming to herself. Then, playing her usual bedtime game, she leaped high in the air and flew into her bed, laughing with joy. She pushed her doll out of the way. She was a young lady now, and young ladies didn't sleep with their dolls. Then, in sudden remorse, she pulled the doll to her, closed her eyes and slid into that half-dream world which was hers every night before she fell asleep.

"I am not Vera, no, I am not. I don't even know who she is, this Vera. I am Petitpas, the great ballerina Petitpas, the greatest ballerina in the whole world. I am Petitpas, and everybody is at my feet and everything around me is gold, sheer gold. I eat nothing but cake and drink nothing but lemonade, nothing else ever. And I have never in my life seen Miss Watson and Mademoiselle Suzanne. I don't even know who they are, I have never heard their names even. I am Petitpas, and I dance, I always dance, always, and I eat cake—"

Her doll pressed close to her, Vera was fast asleep.

Kseniya listened to the water carrier. He came early every morning, pushing the two-wheeled cart with its barrel, making a racket with the buckets, going in and out of the house, reporting all the night fires, robberies, and fights to the janitor, who was sweeping the sidewalk. Kseniya got dressed and slipped out of the house, her cape tight around her against the cool morning breeze from the river. In the little church to which she had gone since her childhood she sank to her knees in a dark corner. She remained there for two hours, pleading for guidance and strength. The sleepless night, the hours of crying and fervent praying had left her body weak and her face bloodless. But perhaps for the first time in her life she felt strong. Even if he were to kill her, she would not submit this time. She suddenly wanted him to rage and to rant as he had never raged and ranted before. A feverish passion seized her; she was ready for martyrdom; she wanted it.

Kseniya almost ran back home, breathlessly threw off her cape in the hall, and abruptly opened the door to the dining room. Her husband was reaching for his first breakfast roll. Maxim and Igor had just got up from the table. They stopped to kiss their mother as they left the room. Anton nodded to his wife and broke his roll in two. Kseniya did not sit down. Standing directly in front of Anton, she said in a voice unusually loud for her:

"Olga is getting married to Gregor Alekseich and is going away with him to live in a village and teach there."

"What? What did you say? Say it again!"

Anton's roar was heard all over the house. Nyanya had just brought Grandmother's breakfast to her room. Both women crossed themselves and their lips moved in prayer. Belowstairs, the servants shrugged their shoulders; the master was off again.

Olga jumped from the window seat on which she had been sleeping with the sun shining full on her face. She opened the door and heard her mother's voice loud but firm: "You heard what I said. Olga is getting married to Gregor Alekseich and is going away with him to live in a village, and I am giving her my maternal blessing." Then Olga heard the dining-room door open with a crash, heard her father's heavy footsteps and his voice breaking with fury:

"I have no daughter Olga, you hear me! I'll kill you with my own hands if you ever mention her name again! God's curse upon her and her children! May He turn your blessing into a curse too! I'll show you who is master here. I'll show you—" The sound of broken glass drowned his last words.

Heavy silence fell upon the house. Kseniya was near collapse. The big moment was gone. Nyanya, after comforting Grandmother with words and smelling salts, put Kseniya to bed. She made her swallow a little tea. Kseniya's teeth were chattering, her body was shaking, and only a large dose of Baldrian drops checked an attack of hysterics. She fell into a heavy sleep. She did not stir even when Olga knelt before her bed, kissed her hands, and whispered: "I am going away now, mother. I'll always love you, and I'll never forget what you did today. Good-by, mother dearest." Olga stood for a long time beside the bed, memorizing every feature of her mother's tortured face.

Her eyes were wet when she walked into the boys' classroom where she was to meet Gregor. He was there telling the boys that he was leaving. Igor looked unperturbed but Maxim's gray eyes were almost dark with excitement as he listened to Gregor.

"Don't forget what you heard from me," Gregor was saying gravely. "Think of it when you grow up . . ."

Maxim did not understand what was going on or what Olga had to do with Gregor's going away and why she should go away too, but he was excited because Gregor had shaken hands with him and was talking to him as if he were a grownup. And because she had something to do with Gregor, the hero whom Maxim had once heard say that he was not afraid of the police, this sister, who until then had been only one of those adults whose things he was not to touch and whose orders he was to obey, became close and a friend. And at this very moment she was kissing him good-by and her eyes were full of tears. Maxim, too, was ready to cry, but just then he saw Igor reach into his, Maxim's, pile of old magazines. Oh, no, that wouldn't do! Forgotten were Gregor, Olga, and the whole puzzling exciting situation. His hair tousled, his eyes flaming, Maxim flew to do battle with much more vigor than was necessary to rescue the magazines from his timid unresisting brother.

There was time for a few minutes with Grandmother and Nyanya, for a handkiss at Vera's door, for kisses and farewells in the kitchen; then, her eyes wet, with a small satchel in her hands, Olga stepped out of her parents' home.

At this very moment Vera came sauntering down the stairs.

CHAPTER 2

*Vera*

EXCITED whispering was going on in the kitchen. The servants realized that what had happened was not just another "scandal" to be gossiped about around the samovar. It was a serious matter, more serious than anything that had ever happened in this house, which to many of them had become a second home. It concerned them directly, for hadn't most of them come from that same village where Gregor was born? Weren't they all in some way responsible for what had happened? Suppose the master saw it that way? What then? As the doorman, Nikifor, put it:

"One of us dared raise his eyes to the master's daughter. The master's wrath will come down on our heads. God will make the whole flock suffer for the sins of one."

Stepan, the coachman, solemnly nodded his head. But Kseniya's personal maid was indignant. "What do you mean, one of us? One of who? You or me, or the dishwashers here? How do you like that, throwing us all together!" She threw a glance at the mirror to assure herself that her elegant little figure in its white starched dress had nothing in common with the uncouth dishwashers.

"Don't you give yourself airs just because the mistress lets you be near her. Any one of us could be in your place if only we licked the masters' boots as well as you do," came the angry voice of the chambermaid Mashenka.

"Hush, hush, you hussies," interrupted the cook. "Shut your mouths, both of you, and don't make things worse with your foul tongues. Now, listen to me, all of you. Go back to your work, don't let your eyes see or your ears hear anything. And remember, remember this well, don't say anything, anything at all; seal your lips tight. Who knows, with God's help, the storm may pass over our heads . . ."

Two long rings stopped all conversation. Stepan hastily wiped his mouth, got into his padded navy-blue overcoat, tied a wide red sash around his waist, and ran as fast as the heavy garment and his huge bulk permitted. He reached the carriage just as Anton came out of the house furiously slamming the front door. Carefully ignoring his master's disheveled air, his bloodshot eyes, and shivering hands, Stepan helped him into the carriage, spoke softly to the horses, and turned them in the direction of the Moscow embankment.

They stopped in front of a gloomy old building. Over the entrance a large sign read: . . . AND NAZAROV. TEXTILES. When old Kanavsky's name was taken off, they had forgotten to take off the "and" and no one had ever bothered to correct it. The clerks rushed out to greet Anton with bows and smiles. But the look on the master's face made them instantly and silently melt out of sight. Through dark corridors, between bales and boxes, Anton reached a door which he opened with his own key. He entered a dismal dark room. The furniture—a table, a chair, a couch, and a cupboard—was shabby and covered with dust. The shades were down. Anton did not raise them. He opened the cupboard, reached for a bottle and a glass, and sat down at the table.

This was the room to which he had fled twenty-three years before on his wedding night. He had thought of it then as the only place where he could hide. Since then it had become his refuge, a place were he tried to drown in vodka the doubts and regrets that tortured him.

He drank for a while in silence. The banging of his fist on the table at regular intervals was the only sound in the room for a long time. He opened his collar, unbuttoned his vest. His eyes were glazing and his tongue becoming heavy in his mouth.

So that was the end . . . No more Olga, no more crowns, no princes and counts in the Nazarov family . . . To hell with the princes and counts. Who wanted them when Olga, his pride, his goddess, was gone? And why was she gone? There was no need to ask himself; he well knew why. But why hadn't he spoken? Why hadn't he told her what he had in mind for her? If only he had told her, if only she had known the plans he had for her. She wouldn't have so much as cast a look at that bastard muzhik . . . Now, wait! Whom was he calling a bastard muzhik? Gregor? But hadn't he always thought him such a fine clever boy? There was not a thing wrong with him, really, not a thing. Hadn't his own grandfather been a muzhik? There was nothing wrong with a muzhik! No, no, no! It was all wrong! His Olga and a muzhik! If he had only talked, if he had only said one word! Why, why on earth couldn't he have gone to her and put his arm around her and said, Now listen, Kseniya, my dear . . . Kseniya—what was he thinking?

He tore his shirt wide open and gulped down another glass of vodka.

He was losing his mind. It was Olga he had meant, of course, Olga, my dear! Had he really? Wouldn't he have liked to put his arm around Kseniya and said, My dear! to her? Wouldn't he have given his right hand and his soul with it to let her know that he was a man, a real man in whose heart a fire burned, who was hungry for a touch of her hands, for a kiss from her lips, willingly given. O God, what was he thinking . . . ?

Hours later he opened his eyes, grabbed the bottle, drank a few mouthfuls, dipped his head into a bucket of cold water and said, "Well, and what now?" He threw the bottle into a corner, sat down on the chair, planted his elbows firmly on the table, and holding his head in both hands, plunged into unhappy bitter thinking. He was sober now, and the image of Kseniya did not torture him. He was sober and he could think.

That was that. And what now? There was Zena, a good handsome healthy girl. There was one who would never bring shame to the Nazarov name. But would she bring glory to it? No, she would bring healthy children, she would bring money . . . but who wanted more money? He had plenty of that now. Zena was a good girl, a very good girl, but she should have been born fifty years before. Then the firm had needed money. And that was what Zena's kind brought. So what was to be done? One couldn't go around dreaming beautiful dreams, then suddenly stop dreaming and go on making money and nothing but money. Of course, one could start dreaming other dreams. He could build a hospital, the biggest hospital that was ever built. And big gold letters would say: BUILT BY ANTON NAZAROV. Or he could build a church. That would be fine, very fine. But what about his daughter, a daughter who was to walk with her head high among the greatest of the great? What about the czar asking at a ball who that most beautiful of all women was? No, a hospital wouldn't do, neither would a church. Moscow had too many churches anyway.

Anton's thoughts turned to his sons. He had seen them before he left the house. The classroom door had been open and he had walked in. Igor hadn't even seemed to notice him, so absorbed was he in pasting up the pictures he had cut out. Maxim was racing around the room whistling and puffing.

"Look, look, I am an engine," he had triumphantly informed Anton, "I pull two thousand freight cars filled with the heaviest iron in the whole world!"

Why was it that Igor always chose the quietest games and that no game was ever noisy enough for Maxim? What would Maxim do with his energy when he grew up, that energy of which Igor seemed to have so little and Maxim enough for both? Ah, what was the use of thinking about it now? They were still too small to be of any help to him.

Anton pressed his fingers deeply into his temples as if he were trying to wring something out of his head. Suddenly he sank back in his chair.

Well, well, well. And why not? She was still a child but she was growing up quickly. Of course, she would never be a goddess. Yet why shouldn't she? Not all goddesses were majestic and dark. Couldn't there be a golden-haired one, dancing and laughing and making people happy?

Anton got up. He was in a hurry now. He washed his face again, straightened his clothes, and walked steadily through the dark halls filled with bales and boxes out to his carriage. He bade Stepan hurry, and in less than fifteen minutes he was at home.

He heard Vera's voice in the study room and walked in. She was having a lesson with Miss Watson. Brusquely, with no word of greeting, he ordered the governess from the room. She left, but showed in her rigid quick walk her indignation over the Russian barbarian's rudeness.

After her lessons with Mademoiselle Suzanne, Vera had continued her futile explorations of the morning's events. No one had given her any satisfaction until Grandmother called her in and told her what had happened.

"You are a big girl now," she finished, "and I have talked to you as to a big girl. Don't try to understand what you cannot understand at your age. Have a little patience. Go on as if nothing had happened and for God's sake don't torture your mother with questions and don't mention Olga's name in your father's presence. Better still, don't mention it in anyone's presence. Be good, be very good to your parents, their hearts are full of pain."

Grandmother's words came back to Vera now. She looked at her father with curiosity. How did a person look when his heart was full of pain? She felt uneasy. Father's look was so inquisitive. He had never looked at her this way. Was anything wrong with her face? She threw a quick look into the mirror. No, everything was all right. "Be very good to them," Grandmother had told her.

She put her arms around her father and pressed her face against him. Anton, with his violent outbreaks of temper, had not inspired many expressions of tenderness in his children. Vera's caress caught him unawares. He stood feeling clumsy and embarrassed, not knowing what to do. He was afraid to talk; he was not sure of his voice. He stroked her hair and smiled at her, searching for the right thing to say.

"Well, daughter," he finally recovered his voice, "suppose you and I go on a spree, just the two of us. Let us have a look at Moscow, just you and I. Right now. How about it?"

"Oh, yes, let us, let us, do let us!" Vera's excitement flamed. "I'll be ready in no time. I'll be quick, very quick!"

The last words she called back, running up the stairs to her room. She opened Grandmother's door and announced:

"Going with Father on a spree . . . I'll tell about it later . . ."

She dashed out like a whirlwind and did not notice the astonished faces of Grandmother, Kseniya, and Nyanya.

In her room, Vera changed her shoes and dress, retied her hair ribbon, and, cape and bonnet on her arm, dashed off again lest Father change his mind. No, he was there, waiting for her. Stepan lifted her into the carriage.

"Now," said Anton, "where do we start looking at Moscow? Want to go to the Sparrow Hills?"

"Oh, yes, father, yes. I've always wanted to go there. Let's go there, quick, quick!"

Vera's eyes and teeth sparkled, her bonnet kept falling back on her shoulders, letting her hair follow the wind. She bounced on the seat. She was often taken along in the carriage when her mother and sisters went shopping or for fresh air. But then she had to sit straight, her hands in her lap, neither laughing too loudly nor talking too much. Now she could laugh and talk as much and as loudly as she liked. And she could ask any questions she wanted to; Father knew all the answers. He knew the names of the churches and bridges; he knew when this or that house had been built; he even knew who lived in it. Vera had never been close to her father. One never knew what would make him angry and when he would fly into a rage. So she had followed the example of the others and had tried to keep as much out of his way as she could. Now suddenly it was different. He spoke softly and he looked at her with a tenderness she thought only her mother could have for her.

They came to the Sparrow Hills. Stepan brought them as far as the carriage could go. They walked up through the woods. For a long time they stood in silence, hand in hand, looking down on the hundreds of churches, the Kremlin walls, the palaces, the silvery ribbon of the river, and the rings of boulevards encircling the city.

It was a clear day, and the golden domes, the many-colored bulbs of St. Basil's and the white Kremlin walls shone intensely in the sun. The sun broke into a million sparkles in the softly flowing waters of the river.

Then Anton turned to Vera, pointing to something he was drawing in the sand:

"Look here, what do you see?"

"A ladder, father, and a very badly drawn ladder too." Vera broke into giggles.

But Anton was serious. "Now look well and listen well, my angel. On this ladder are all the people who live in the world. On every step of the ladder live different kinds of people. Way down here, on these steps, are just ordinary people, obscure people, the riffraff, infidels, Jews, muzhiks . . ." He swallowed deeply and forced away the burning ache that this word touched off. "See how black it is around them; there are millions of them living there in filth and squalor. Some of them are better off than the others. These begin to climb up the ladder. Your great-grandfather was one. He reached a few steps higher. His son climbed much higher, so did I. This is about where I am. See how few people have reached it. See how light it is here, how much space, how clean. But there are more steps to climb. Every man dreams of climbing as close to the top of the ladder as he can. I reached the highest step I was able to reach. I cannot reach higher, I never will reach higher. Not I!"

He put his arm around Vera, drew her close to him and almost shouted at her:

"Not I. But you! You can reach the top and you will!"

"I?" With fascination she had listened to him and followed the drawing of the ladder. Now she was caught by the passion and intensity of his voice. Her fingers tugged at Anton's sleeve and her eyes glistened with curiosity and impatience. "I? How could I? How?"

"Yes, little daughter, you. You will do it, you will be right there, on the very top! And this is how we will do it. Listen to me."

As if he were playing a game with her, he pictured her as a fairy princess, beautiful, graceful, exquisitely clothed, mistress of all the arts and all the virtues. And then who but a fairy prince, the most handsome and the most noble of all, one who was born right there on the top, would dare cast his eye on her and ask for her hand?

Vera listened to him and laughed happily. This was the best fairy tale she had ever heard.

"You think it is not possible? It is, I know it is. Just try. It isn't hard a bit. Let's start right away. Let's go home and tell Mother that little Vera made a bet with her father that she can in no time become a perfect young lady and that she wants to study dancing and music and painting and all those things perfect young ladies do. This is what we are going to tell her, and the rest we shall keep to our-selves . . ."

Vera nodded quickly. "Yes, oh, yes, I'll try, and I'll learn hard, real hard, you'll see!"

"And we will come here and we'll draw the ladder and see how far you have reached . . ."

"Yes, the more I learn the higher I'll reach. Oh, I'll learn quickly, and I'll go higher, and higher and higher. Oh, yes, father, we will do it! That's real fun!"

They did not tell Kseniya the whole story. But what they told her and what she saw in the months that followed was enough. She knew that Anton's hurt was not less than her own. Never since Olga's departure had he mentioned her name. But neither had he raged or shouted at anyone. He was lighter in spirit and friendlier than he had ever been. The reason was obviously Vera. He was finding solace in her, in her laughter and gaiety. And the bet about her becoming a "perfect young lady" she guessed to be Anton's way of saving Vera from Olga's fate. Whatever it was, Kseniya entered into the spirit of the game and found in it some distraction from her own sorrow. Soon Vera's days were crowded with dancing, reciting, singing, piano, painting, and riding lessons. An impoverished count was charged with initiating her into the social graces of fashionable drawing rooms.

## CHAPTER 3
## Czar Nicholas

WHEN Czar Alexander III died, the people's hopes turned to the young czar, Nicholas II. They were tired of a regime of violence, of bigotry and fear. In his first proclamation after his father's death he promised to seek the country's happiness. The people wondered what the promise implied and tried to translate it into personal terms. They did not have to wait long for an answer. The czar received representatives of the population. He made a speech. It was an angry scolding rather than a speech. The czar called the people's pleas for justice and more freedom "senseless dreams," and he made it clear to them that he was going to follow in his father's footsteps. He shouted hysterically. His wife, a former German princess, was present. She knew little Russian and did not understand what he was saying. "Qu'est-ce qu'il leur explique?" she asked her lady in waiting. "Il leur explique qu'ils sont des imbéciles," replied the lady in waiting.

The czar was young, weak and unintelligent. A few years earlier his father, worried about his heir's bad health, had called in a famous German physician. The doctor said that there was no hope for improvement unless the boy gave up his secret vices. The physician was honored by a resounding slap in the face from his Majesty's own hand. But when the future czar entered the path of his numerous adventures, his parents, remembering the doctor's words, were very tolerant. The young man's favorite companion in his escapades was his father's brother, Grand Duke Sergei, famous for his depravity. Their bacchanalian orgies were the talk of St. Petersburg. More than once the young czarevich was brought back to the royal palace dead drunk and behaving accordingly.

The people knew it and still they had turned to the young czar with their hopes, as they had always turned to a new ruler throughout their history. As other rulers had done, he promptly killed their hopes with his own words. Like his father, he turned the country over to the police. He surrounded himself with courtiers and ministers whose sole concern was to keep their powerful positions. They flattered him and lied to him, and ruled the country unscrupulously.

In 1896, two years after he came to the throne, his coronation took place in Moscow. According to custom, another proclamation had to be issued. Once more, the people's hopes came alive. Maybe now he would say something they wanted to hear.

The czar arrived in Moscow for the coronation with a pompous pageantry never surpassed before. Moscow, still hurt that Peter the Great had transferred the capital to St. Petersburg, consoled herself with the thought that at least she had remained the city of the czar's coronation. She was ready for the coronation now.

She had clothed every roof, every wall, and every lamppost with blue, red, and white; with velvet and silk; with golden and silver crests, insignia and eagles; with tinsel tassels and rosettes; with banners, streamers, pennants, and bunting; with wreaths, festoons, and garlands. Windows in shops, office buildings, and apartment houses were richly decorated and lighted. Moscow was riotous with color, a city of unheard-of magnificence and splendor. Hundreds of thousands of people crowded the streets day and night, a constantly surging human wave. Eyes already saturated with brilliance widened at the sight of the golden carriages carrying the Eastern dignitaries. Moscow ladies eyed with envy the Petersburg ladies, admired their chic and their elegant landaus and coachmen in red and gold, the smart attire of their escorts, guard officers and courtiers in tricorns covered with gold embroidery and plumes. The people's eyes feasted on all this magnificence and their hearts hoped for a word from the czar.

The word came. A proclamation was issued. The czar confirmed his intention of ruling in the spirit of his father. But many people were elated. Hadn't Little Father Czar in his proclamation promised them a grand popular feast on Khodynka? Hadn't he promised them rich amusement and rich gifts? Day and night preparations were going on. The populace of Moscow and of surrounding villages was watching them with great anticipation. Many looked forward to the exciting entertainment. But many, ragged and hungry, yearned for the promised presents, for something to cover their bodies and to fill their stomachs.

Finally, it was ready. Show tents for a circus, for puppet theaters, and for Roman wrestling had been built. Swings, merry-go-rounds, and a greasy pole had been erected; also platforms for acrobats, buffoons, animal trainers, singers, jongleurs, folk dancing, military bands, choruses. There were dozens of stands with the gifts. For the czar, a luxurious pavilion with a baldachin had been built.

On the eve of the festivities a mass pilgrimage started. Whole families with infants in arms, young children holding on to their mothers' skirts and the aged leaning on their canes moved slowly toward Khodynka. By midnight over half a million people thronged the field, and more were streaming to it in a compact solid mass. The teeming crowd stood closely packed together, body to body with no place for a needle to fall, with hardly any air to breathe. A depressing silence hung over the huge mass of people. Women and children began to suffocate. A few tried to break through the iron embrace of the crowd. Others understood this as a signal to get to the stands that held the gifts. Not human beings, but a crazed wild herd tore forward. Inhuman screams and desperate shouts for help filled the air.

The unscrupulous authorities responsible for the festivities, in their desire to pocket all the money possible, had granted consessions for stands without regard for the many old wells and ditches in the field. There were millions to spend for an unbroken line of soldiers to guard the czar's route from Petersburg to Moscow, for tens of thousands of spies and policemen to guard his every step day and night, for a Byzantine splendor to make the world marvel. But there was no money, not even a few miserable kopecks, for leveling the holes around the stands.

Thousands fell into the ditches, and the crowd, unable to stop, pushed by the hundreds of thousands behind them, trampled over them. Most of them were crushed to death under the stamping feet of the panicking mass. Wailing, weeping, cursing, praying, the people crashed into the stands and platforms. The czar's gifts, for which at least eight thousand people paid with their lives, lay scattered on the field. The czar's gifts—a cheap kerchief with a view of the Kremlin tied around a tin drinking cup marked with the date of the coronation and the czar's emblems, honey cookies, an apple, a few nuts, bread and sausage.

The news of the catastrophe spread over Moscow in an instant. Officialdom got busy. In a few hours the czar would be visiting Khodynka Field. Nothing must interfere with his Majesty's schedule. Moscow's authorities hurried to the field. Hundreds of fire wagons were sent to clear the place of the dead and injured. The bodies were thrown together. A few hours of feverish activity saw the tents and stands in place again. The ditches were filled with sand thrown over the bodies of the dead and of many still living. Great was the hurry to remove all signs of the tragedy before the arrival of the czar. Nothing must disturb the czar's peace of mind.

The Muscovites did not expect the czar to visit Khodynka. They thought he would cancel the rest of the coronation activities, that he would give orders to assist the bereaved and to punish the guilty. When the czar was told what had happened, he ordered all available military units to the Kremlin. He was afraid of the wrath of an outraged population. But the people were numb, and the czar relaxed. He continued with his coronation schedule as if nothing had happened. At three in the afternoon, a brilliant cortege of carriages and landaus moved along the road where the night before the crowd had streamed toward the crumbs that were thrown to them.

Khodynka was crowded again. New hundreds of thousands, eager for entertainment and gifts, greeted the czar. He and the czarina remained a few mintues in the pavilion for which so many thousands of rubles had been spent. They listened to the playing of the hymn and immediately returned to Moscow. In the evening, the czar spent several hours at the ball of the French ambassador, one of the most magnificent balls in a series of many magnificent balls. The czar danced and amused himself very well.

# CHAPTER 4
## The Young Gavrilovs

VERA was sixteen at the time of the coronation. Four years had passed since she had started the game of climbing the ladder. She had advanced quite a few steps since then. Her varied lessons had never ceased to be fun to her; they were part of a wonderful game. She had developed skill in many arts. Her natural beauty was brought out by careful grooming. Her silken blonde hair fell in curls around her shoulders, and there was an affinity between the glow in her hair and her velvety skin. Hers was not the fashionable beauty of the day: a languid pale face with eyes shyly cast down or timidly raised behind a fan. She was alive and vibrant; every waking moment her eyes and lips were ready to smile. When she laughed, her face seemed to open like a flower in full bloom. When she was pensive it closed. The perfect arch of her brows, the tender nostrils of her pert little nose, her lips—all would tighten and make her oval face look smaller and thinner. But she was not pensive often.

Her voice had always been clear; training had given it melody. Her dancing way of walking became even lighter. She still loved dancing above everything else, and spent hours before a mirror pirouetting and inventing new steps.

The last of the coronation festivities was the gala night at the theater. Never had the Bolshoi Theater seen such an array of beautiful women, magnificent clothes, sparkling jewels, medals, ribbons, stars, epaulets, shining bald heads. The red, blue, green, and orange of uniforms vied with the colorful silks and velvets of the women. On that night lorgnettes and opera glasses did not lie idle in the lap as a toy for bored hands. And it warmed Anton's heart to see how frequently they focused on his box in the balcony. Kseniya and Zena, with their round handsome faces set off by high jeweled boyar head-dresses, looked like sisters, and many a glance rested on them. But it was Vera who brought warm smiles to the faces. There was radiance in her slim figure, a constant play of emotion on her face, and grace and beauty in every one of her moves. She was not aware that people were looking at her. She was enthralled by the play, by the crowd, by the presence of the czar, by the very fact that she was there.

Anton was pleased. When Vera's time came she would look up, not down. Anton was also pleased by the stir in the opposite box. No one would have suspected him of the slightest interest, but nothing that went on there escaped him. He felt sorry for the owner of that box, his greatest but friendly rival in the textile world, Zakhar Gavrilov. Anton guessed that it was probably the first time in his life that anyone had been able to persuade old Zakhar to lay aside his old-fashioned, wide, tuniclike garment and squeeze himself into one of the tight modern creations. He looked as if he were suffocating; and he was. Under his asthmatic breathing, the heavy gold chain across his stomach rose and fell. He felt very uncomfortable in his absurd attire, and from time to time he tried to ease his tie. Also, he felt almost naked, because he had permitted his beard to be trimmed—something he had never done before.

With all due respect for the czar, Zakhar thought, was all this necessary? The czar certainly would not have minded his wearing proper clothes and letting his beard alone. But what was the use of fooling himself? Of course, the czar wouldn't have minded; and it hadn't been done for the czar at all. But couldn't a less tortuous way have been found to come to an agreement with Anton Nazarov? It could, if he had had his own way. But one couldn't have one's own

way with the young people today! "No, father, you can't show yourself this way . . . You know what kind of people the Nazarovs
are . . . They don't live the old-fashioned life you do . . ." His own
son, Pavel, had talked to him like that. Well, what was wrong with
the old-fashioned life? It had been good for hundreds of years, why
shouldn't it be good for another few hundred? Who in his day would
have thought of looking over a future bride! As if there were no
matchmakers to find out all it was necessary to find out.

It was ridiculous! What had the bride to do with his deal with
Nazarov? If he and Nazarov decided to merge their firms, Pavel and
Zena would marry. If not, they wouldn't. Who cared how the bride
looked? His own mind was made up and Nazarov seemed to be
ready too. It would be a fine thing if after all this bickering and
bargaining Pavel made difficulties! It was true, Pavel had been saying
all along that he would never marry a girl he didn't like. But what
if he had been saying that? He wouldn't dare oppose his father's will.
Other sons didn't. Just the same he wasn't too sure about Pavel. He
would feel better if Pavel liked the Nazarov girl. That must be the
one, the girl sitting next to Kseniya Nikolaevna. She didn't look bad
to him, not bad at all. Seemed to be healthy and strong. A good deal
was a good deal, but it never hurt to bring good blood into a family
too.

Zakhar began to feel quite happy. He whispered to his wife. "The
deal can be closed in a few days now," Pavel heard his father say.
Pavel deeply resented having his possible marriage treated as a "deal."
He had told his father so again and again, but he had agreed to have
a look at the girl. He had not promised anything. He was sure he
wouldn't like her. He had seen enough of these homespun, unpolished
daughters of his father's friends. But now that he had seen her, he
felt differently.

All evening long he had watched Zena and the movements of her
firm voluptuous body. She attracted him, she attracted him very
strongly. There was a quiet assurance about her which made one feel
that one could be very safe and peaceful with her. And she certainly
was not homespun and unpolished. She was well groomed and elegant;
so were her mother and little sister. She was well mannered, and
she looked intelligent. All this was important in his future wife. But
he wouldn't have thought of her as a future wife if he hadn't felt so
strongly her physical attraction. He looked at her and wondered how
it would feel to touch her skin and hair, to make her laugh, to put an
arm around her waist. Would her big clear eyes smile at him or scorn
him? Why had he always hated the idea of getting married? Really,

there seemed nothing wrong about being married, not to a girl like that. It even seemed like a good, a very good idea.

There was no whispering in the Nazarov box. Indeed, there was no one to whom Anton could whisper his satisfaction, for he had never mentioned his plans to either Kseniya or Zena. He had no idea that the principal concern of his women that evening was to catch an unobserved glimpse of the Gavrilov box. Over the grapevine of clerks and servants and through Nyanya, the women had long ago heard about the possible merger of the two firms. And who didn't know that when there were marriageable children such deals were sealed by a marriage?

With only an occasional quick glance at the Gavrilov box, Zena had nevertheless contrived to get a look at Pavel. She would have obeyed her father and married anyone he told her to marry, and she was ready to be a good wife to anyone he chose for her. But she was pleased to find young Gavrilov so attractive. She liked his dark hair and his small mustache and short trimmed beard. Once, when she was sure she was unobserved, she looked directly at him, and met his eyes. There was something in them which made her uncomfortable for the rest of the evening. She did not dare turn her head in his direction again.

She was very quiet when they arrived home, and went to bed immediately. She, the level headed, she, who always knew what to do and what to say, suddenly found herself uncertain. The dark eyes, saying something she did not understand, the powerful shoulders, the strong white teeth, which showed when he smiled, stayed persistently with her. She tried to get hold of her thoughts, to put them again on solid ground. She could not. Thinking of him brought him close to her; she felt his hands and his breath on her, and was suddenly weak. Then cold fear touched her. Suppose their fathers did not agree? She tossed restlessly in her bed and fell asleep only as the house began to come to life.

There was no long engagement. Both fathers were eager to get the wedding over with quickly and settle down to their real business. But short as the engagement was, it seemed long to Zena and Pavel, who spent their evenings together under the benevolent eyes of their families. They sat side by side, exchanged a word or two, and simply looked at each other. The first time they were left alone, Pavel without a word pressed his lips hungrily to Zena's throat. The caress left both of them trembling and speechless.

Moscow talked for a long time of the Nazarov-Gavrilov wedding. For three days the reception rooms of one of Moscow's largest hotels were open to guests; food and drinks were served day and night; and several orchestras played in turn. Large sums were distributed among the poor and thousands of them were fed during an entire week. Charitable institutions and churches were given generous donations. Anton Nazarov and Zakhar Gavrilov tried to outdo each other, and Moscow rejoiced in their rivalry.

The young Gavrilov marriage proved successful. Their home was pleasant; Zena and Pavel were hospitable; and their families liked to visit them. The old Gavrilovs' home was noisy and disorganized. Zakhar shouted and scolded at the women—it was the only way to teach them anything—and administered an occasional thrashing to children and servants. The servants were forever running around looking for keys, shawls or galoshes, answering calls, opening doors. The clocks were never right; meals were late; and everybody blamed everybody else for everything that went wrong. Any attempt by the younger people to bring some kind of order into the house was met by a stern reprimand from Zakhar: "What was good enough for my father and grandfather, is good enough for me!"

There was more order and poise in the Nazarov home. Things had their place; the servants were well trained; and meals had their fixed hours. But one never knew when Anton would start a row, and there was always a light cloud of sadness over the house, and a wistful look in Kseniya's big brown eyes. Even Vera's sunny laughter and gay chatter was not always able to break the mood of the house.

It was serene and light around the tea table at the young Gavrilovs'. At home Anton and Zakhar were both accustomed to having their own way in everything; when they talked, the others—and certainly their wives—listened and no one thought of contradicting them or opposing their wishes. At first both fathers had been shocked at the new order of things at the young Gavrilovs'. "How do you expect to have a real conversation with Zena talking right up as if she were a man?" "What do you mean Zena preferred a light carpet? You are the one to decide!" "Well, suppose Zena has a headache. That doesn't mean you can't go. What are you—a man or a washrag?" Zena and Pavel only laughed. The fathers gave up; there was nothing else to do. Some day Pavel would find out what trouble a wife could bring if you didn't hold her in check. Nevertheless, they came to enjoy it. The conversation was leisurely and usually about the same subjects: the firm, the food, the servants. The room, with its soft light, its rubber plants and oleanders, the green plush family album on the little round table, the open sewing basket in a corner on the floor, radiated peace and relaxation. Zakhar and Anton learned to tone down their thundering commanding voices.

Vera loved to go there. She and old Zakhar had become great

friends and they had many private jokes together. Occasionally Igor and Maxim also were taken along for an evening at Zena's. Igor would have preferred to stay home and play or read by himself but he went because he was too shy to say so. Maxim enjoyed the joking and teasing between Zakhar and Vera, and entered enthusiastically into word games which were sometimes played. As a rule, the conversation held little interest for him, and when he became too bored, he would make Vera interrupt it to play games. Vera always gladly obliged him because she too would get bored.

But when Zakhar's older son, Fedor, came home for a visit during the Christmas holidays, Maxim no longer wanted to play games, but listened eagerly to the talk of the adults. Fedor brought a change into the chitchat of the family gatherings. He was managing the firm's branch in Petersburg, and had recently married the daughter of an impoverished noble family. His Moscow relatives had looked forward with eagerness and some trepidation to meeting her. Not only had Ludmilla attended the Institute for the Daughters of Nobility, the Gavrilovs whispered, but also one of the women's colleges. The Gavrilovs had been flattered when their son married into the nobility, but the idea of his wife being one of those short-haired masculine-looking horrors who smoked cigarettes and talked against the czar was a frightening one.

Vera's impatience to meet Ludmilla had been greater than anyone else's. She had once seen a group of students in front of the university. The girls wore ugly clothing; some had men's caps on; and they spoke and laughed as noisily as men. When Vera tried to picture Ludmilla, she heard a rough loud voice and saw a man's cap pulled over messy short hair. All kinds of girls went to those colleges. You might even sit next to the daughter of a cook or a street cleaner! Worse still—Jewish girls were permitted to attend. She had once even heard of a Tartar girl who went to a university.

Consequently, Vera stared incredulously when she met Ludmilla for dinner at Zena's on her first evening in Moscow. Ludmilla was rather small, and gray eyed, with a delicate, pale face and long, ash-blonde hair parted in the middle and arranged in neat thick braids high on her head. Her dress was of light-gray taffeta, with ruffles around the neck and down the front. Her only ornament, besides her wedding ring, was a gold medallion on a black velvet ribbon. She blushed easily and talked very little in a voice which was soft and quiet.

Zakhar and his wife, the red-faced, massive Stepanida, were there too. Stepanida's face was wet with perspiration from too-tight corsets and too much food. She took no part in the conversation but nodded her approval when her husband spoke.

At first the conversation was slow and quiet. But Fedor, who had been away from Moscow long enough to forget his father's touchy spots and his temper, soon let loose a torrent by laughing at Moscow's old-fashioned horse cars and contrasting them to Petersburg's faster modern ones.

"And what do you want people to move faster for?" old Zakhar thundered. "Who wants to move faster anyway? Nowadays all you see people do is rush, run, push one another, shout at one another. Now even the store signs shout! We didn't use to have to impress the customers. Good merchandise and a good name were all we needed to get the customer in. And inside the store? What about praising the goods, what about bargaining with the customer, talking to him, convincing him, asking about his wife's health? Oh, no, the salesman stands there like a dummy, like a machine . . . All right, so there was no order in the store. So everything was not written down and accounted for. Who cared? The money was there, wasn't it?"

Zakhar's face was red. Pavel changed the subject and tactfully started to praise the luxurious new Moscow bathhouse, which was so much cleaner than the old one.

But the new bathhouse made Zakhar mad too.

"And what about the lice and flees in the old bathhouse? If God didn't want them to be with us, why did He create them? Who wants all these new things? And those new machines all the fools are buying from America and Germany—sewing machines, knitting machines, scales, typewriters even—who wants them? Let them keep their machines, I say—Russia is better off without them."

"But, father," protested Fedor, "isn't there anything good in what we have now? Don't you think it is safer now? Don't you think fewer people are robbed and killed now that we have gaslight and the streets are not pitch dark?"

"What did we want gaslight for?" Zakhar retorted. "Decent people stayed home after dark! What did they have to go out for? When evening came, they locked the gates, let the dogs out, and sat around till they fell asleep."

Everybody laughed and the women took this opportunity to fill the glasses with fresh tea and pile the plates anew with the cakes, jams, honey, homemade sweets, fruit, and nuts with which the table was laden.

Zena wanted to know from Ludmilla about the theaters and museums in Petersburg. But Zakhar let loose again:

"What do you have to go to such places for? Why must you always be amused and entertained? What makes you jump up the moment you sit down? Why can't you sit quiet, your hands folded in your lap, and just think or talk? No, you have to play cards or dominoes or some such foolishness. You have to run out into the night at a time when God meant good people to sleep and watch those good-for-nothing clowns . . . Am I right, friend Anton? Your father was as God-fearing and virtuous a man as my own, and you wouldn't say that their ways were not good enough for us to follow now, would you?"

"Of course, I wouldn't say that the old ways were wrong. Of course, I wouldn't say that," Anton carefully weighed his words. He did not want any more of Zakhar's outbursts. Ludmilla looked uncomfortable enough. But he didn't completely agree with Zakhar. "At the same time, why not try out some of these new things? After all, our fathers did not know about them; they might have liked them if they had."

Fedor and Pavel cheered. "Good for you, Anton Semenovich! Good for you!" Zena clapped her hands, and Vera blew him a kiss.

Zakhar was somewhat taken aback by Anton's unexpected support of the young. Blowing the hot tea in his saucer, he sipped it noisily.

Zena was worried lest Ludmilla think badly of their Moscow manners, but she could not do or say anything that would offend her father-in-law. She smiled at Zakhar and then turned to Ludmilla. "Let us show you Moscow tomorrow. We'll drive around the city and do some shopping, and then you will tell us what you think of us. Vera will be our guide; she knows Moscow well. Don't you, Vera?"

"Oh, that will be fun!" Vera's easy excitement flamed up. 'Now let's quickly go to bed so that tomorrow will come more quickly.' She danced eagerly around everybody to make sure that they did not take too long over their farewells.

When the women finished their shopping the next afternoon, they returned to the Nazarov house for tea. During the exchange of impressions of the day's drive, Ludmilla exclaimed over the luxurious displays in the store windows. Vera turned to her with lively interest.

"Why, don't you have all this in Petersburg?" she asked naïvely. "I thought everything was much richer there."

"Oh, I am sure . . . we have it . . . but . . . you see . . ." Then Ludmilla smiled and said very simply, "It is not so long that I have been able to afford luxuries. We were not rich at home. My father did not believe in my going to stores and just looking at things I couldn't buy. That's all. So don't be surprised if I still get a little excited over the beautiful things I see."

That Vera was nevertheless surprised was evident from the uncomprehending stare she gave Ludmilla. Kseniya, who was watching Ludmilla, thought she seemed a little uncomfortable under Vera's look, and when they had finished with tea, she invited Ludmilla to her room for a rest.

"Tell me about your family, Ludmilla. I know you have no mother. When did she die?"

Kseniya's voice was very gentle, and Ludmilla, instead of answering the question with a very few words, as she normally would, said:

"Do you really want to know? Everything? It's a long story, but I would love to tell it to you . . . I think you will understand . . ."

Kseniya only nodded.

Quietly, with few stops or pauses, the story came out. Her great-grandfather had been a rich man and a friend of the czar. But in spite of his friendship with the czar, he had been on the side of the people. And because he had fought for them and tried to bring a better government, he had been sent to Siberia. His wife had gone with him, and their son—Ludmilla's grandfather—had been born there. Of course, the family had lost its wealth, and by the time Ludmilla's father came of age there had been nothing for him to inherit but a rundown estate. Rather than live the life of an impoverished nobleman landowner, he had gone to St. Petersburg and taken a government job in the Finance Ministry, where he had fallen in love with the finance minister's daughter, and married her. Her family had welcomed him warmly. Young Voronsky was handsome and intelligent and was expected to make a brilliant career. He never did. As incorruptible as his grandfather had been, unwilling to bribe and flatter his way to the top, he had fought and exposed dishonesty and inefficiency wherever he found them—and had remained a minor official. If not for the Voronsky name and the influence of his wife's family, he would not have remained even that . . .

Ludmilla's quiet even voice stopped. It was Kseniya who broke the long silence.

"Please go on. What about your mother?"

"Mother knew that Father was not ambitious for wealth and position," Ludmilla said, "that he meant to work honestly and be useful to the people. She loved him and never tried to change him. But her family did! They made Father's life hell. They never stopped accusing him of having disgraced them—because in their world it was a disgrace to stay forever a minor official—and of ruining their daughter's life. They never let my parents alone! They tormented them until there was no peace in the house at all. Finally Mother began to plead with Father to give up his ideas and do things the way others did. But he wouldn't, and then Mother became ill. The doctors never knew what the matter was. Life was just going out of her body.

"The last blow came when it was time for me to enter school. Mother's family insisted that I should be sent to the Institute so that I would be brought up in a state proper for us. Father refused to let his daughter be brought up among rich girls under false pretenses. Mother had no strength to talk even, certainly not to fight. I once saw Father kissing her hands, and his eyes were full of tears. 'I may be a criminal,' he said, 'for not giving in. But it is against my conscience. I never did anything against my conscience. Please, please, understand me once more and forgive me!' But he finally did give in and I entered the Institute. Mother died two months later. Father locked himself into his room for weeks and didn't see a soul. The words that my grandmother and aunts said then were terrible words. They said . . . they said"—Ludmilla's voice had thinned to a whisper— "that Father killed her . . ."

She laced her fingers together tightly. "I felt so sorry for Mother. I would have cut off every one of my fingers for her. But I never thought that Father was wrong, never, never." She looked appealingly at Kseniya. "He is like my great-grandfather. After Mother died, I decided that I would try to be like that too, always honest and just, and useful to others, and not think only about myself. Mother's family has let us alone since she died. It is only on holidays that they remember us. I wish they forgot about us on holidays too. I don't want their presents . . . There was one more storm"—Kseniya caught the flicker of a smile—"that was when they heard I was to marry Fedor. They said it would be wrong, very wrong, to marry him. It would desecrate Mother's memory—he was not of a noble family. His father was a merchant and he was a merchant. The way they said that word 'merchant'! As if he were a murderer or a thief."

Ludmilla had finished. She felt almost as she had in the days when her mother was alive and she unburdened her heart to her. Kseniya's hand felt as gentle as her mother's, and she didn't say anything either. Like Ludmilla's mother, she comforted with an understanding smile and a caressing hand.

"Time to go home and dress for dinner," Zena called from downstairs.

Two hours later, walking through the parlor to the dining room on Fedor's arm, in a long white dress with little black bows, Ludmilla whispered to him:

"Please, dearest, don't get into any arguments tonight. Let's be peaceful. Let's be forgiving and indulgent and tenderhearted toward the whole world tonight!"

And entering the dining room she breathed into his ear: "I love you, darling! Don't fight with anybody!"

Fedor tried not to and patiently listened to what he later told Ludmilla was nothing but "preposterous nonsense." Only once did he let go. Zakhar was shouting about the "foreigners and infidels" who "polluted Holy Moscow." Anton joined him in this and Vera had her say too:

"They now have a new store on Kuznetsky, I saw it today for the first time, and to whom do you think it belongs? To Rap-po-port!" Pronouncing the name with a grimace and exaggerated inflection, she made it sound contemptible.

Ludmilla, innocent of the mirth around the table said quietly:

"We had a girl in college whose name was Rappoport too. She was brilliant, and graduated at the head of the class."

The silence that followed her words made her swallow with embarassment.

"How could your father," Anton said finally, turning to Ludmilla, "let you go to that kind of school?"

Ludmilla's pale face grew a little paler. Fedor answered for her quickly:

"What kind of school do you mean? A school where they teach something besides a little French chatter, curtsies, and false smiles? Where they find out that other people are as good as they are—whether they are rich or poor, Christian, Moslem, or Jewish, white, yellow, black? It was the very best thing Ludmilla's father could have done for her—to let her go among real people. He knew that whatever happened to her she would be prepared for life."

That was too much for Zakhar.

"And since when do you prepare girls for life? Their fathers and husbands take care of their lives. Anton is right. Those schools are no place for decent girls. It's all right for boys, but girls you keep home. Now, what's wrong with this chick? Look at her! Come, Vera, show us what you can do!"

"Yes, Vera, do show us!" Fedor was eager to have Ludmilla forget the incident.

Vera, nowise reluctant, obligingly and charmingly recited in French, sang, and danced. Then Pavel persuaded Zena to join Vera in a folk dance. After a moment, infected by their mood, Pavel joined them himself; then Fedor pulled Ludmilla in. Soon the table, samovar and all, was pushed aside, and young and old joined in a round dance. The high point was reached when Zakhar and Stepanida, panting and puffing, but with all the befitting gestures, danced the dance of the coquettish maiden and her pursuing young lover.

Maxim fell fast asleep in a corner while the dancing was going on. But earlier he had been wide awake. He had not missed a word that

Fedor said. He did not understand it all, but he was sure it was important. And what Fedor said about girls also going to school and preparing for life, Maxim had heard before. He had heard Gregor saying it to Olga. Maxim liked Fedor because he reminded him of Gregor.

Fedor liked Maxim too and had been conscious of the lively attention with which the boy had hung on his words. To Igor—shy, tense little Igor, so easily ignored—he scarcely gave a thought. But of Vera he was rapidly forming a very poor opinion. Later that night, when he and Ludmilla were alone in their room, he put that opinion into forceful language.

Ludmilla was distressed. "Oh, no, Fedor. Don't talk like that about her. After all, she is only a child, and such a joy to look at. When she laughs, it is as if the world were laughing. At times she is like my kitten—I want to pet her, she feels so soft and warm."

Fedor laughed. "What you are saying, my darling, in your own nice way, is exactly what I said. Vera is adorable to look at; she is amusing to have around. As you say, she is like your kitten—but has your kitten ever shown any interest in anyone, even in you, except when you feed her or pet her? There are no feelings inside Vera either. Have you seen her greet a servant or smile at a salesperson? She, who is so generous with her smiles?"

Ludmilla answered reluctantly. "You may be right. But she is so young yet. I wonder whether it isn't largely her father's fault. He wants her to be a sparkling butterfly and nothing else."

"I'm sure that's all she ever wants to be," Fedor said emphatically. "Try to talk to her about anything important, anything that comes from here, or here—" he touched his head and heart—"and she gets bored."

Ludmilla laughed. "I agree with you about the head, but she loves to talk about heart affairs."

"Heart affairs! Heart affairs! Oh, yes, that reminds me! I knew I had forgotten something." He drew her gently to him. "I love you, I love you, I love you!"

She turned her face to meet his lips, and there was no more talk of Vera or anyone else.

CHAPTER 5

*Anton and Kseniya*

WHEN the Petersburg visitors left Moscow, the old routine set in again. Stormy arguments rarely interrupted the slow flow of an evening around the tea table, and it was long since anyone had seen Anton in a rage. Then, about a week after Ludmilla and Fedor's departure, Vera unwittingly touched off an explosion.

"You'd never guess what Ludmilla told me," Vera said one evening when they were discussing Ludmilla's unconventional education. "Never! 'If I hadn't met Fedor,' she said, 'I'd have gone to live in a village and teach there—' "

Anton banged his fist on the table. Glasses and cups and spoons jumped and tinkled. His face was almost livid. "Stop it," he roared, "stop it! And never say it again, you hear me, never again!"

"Father, father, what have I said, what was wrong?" Vera was frightened.

Kseniya reached for Anton's glass to pour fresh tea. In doing it, she put her hand over his, and let it stay there. He instantly grew quiet and looked at her. She didn't say anything; she only nodded her head slightly. Anton said slowly, with great difficulty:

"Don't mind me, Vera. I am tired. I was up late."

He did not say a word for the rest of the evening. Vera quickly forgot the incident, as did the others, and the hum of talk swelled again.

Anton sat with closed eyes. It was a bitter cold January evening; outside the wind was howling. But Anton forgot it was winter. He smelled the breath of spring. It caressed him and enveloped him tenderly with two soft arms. It made him want to sit still and wait for something very pleasant to happen. He opened his eyes and shook his head. What crazy dreams! God, no, it wasn't a dream! Kseniya was looking at him, a friendly smile in her eyes.

So it was true. She, Kseniya, had a smile for him in her eyes, for him! No, it couldn't be; he was an old fool. Spring! Spring after twenty-eight years! But there was Kseniya's look and Kseniya's friendly smile. And again he sat very still. Waiting.

The party broke up soon. Anton sat and waited. Vera whirled

around him, teased him, and kissed him good night. Everybody was gone but he and Kseniya.

Now or never! Now or never! Talk to him! The voice in Kseniya was getting louder and louder, This "Talk to him!" had lived in her since that dreadful day almost five years before when Olga had left them and he had turned to Vera to save himself from despair. That day, for the first time in her life, Kseniya had seen love, real all-conquering love, in a woman's eyes; heard it in her voice. Was it only Anton's fault that she had never had it? She had carried in her heart nothing but bitterness. If she had been more forgiving and had tried —Maybe they were both to blame, not he alone.

Talk to him, talk to him! the voice inside was becoming insistent. But wasn't it too late? One couldn't go back a whole lifetime and start it all over again. No, one couldn't do that. But one could go ahead as if those bitter years had never been. She had thought always of her own unhappiness and never of how lonely and unhappy he might be. Only Olga had ever given him comfort. Vera? He got happiness out of giving her so much, not by getting anything from her. Vera did not give, Vera took. He had never got anything from anybody. She, Kseniya, had had her consolation in being wronged. But he?

His outburst tonight had made her think, Now or never! She had tried to tell him with her eyes. Had he understood? She thought he had. He was so still, and he hadn't left the room with his usual short "Good night." He might leave the room at any moment. Now or never, Kseniya! But no scenes. Make it quiet, very quiet.

Her voice sounded as calm as usual when she said, "Would you care for more tea? The samovar is still hot."

That was all she said. That was all she ever said. But Anton heard. There was more than an offer of tea in it. And when he answered carefully, "No, I don't think I want any; I am tired and ready for bed," she knew he was telling her that he had heard and that now he needed to be alone.

She prayed long and fervently that night. She found few words. She simply thanked God.

Vera was much too occupied with herself to notice the change in her parents. The change was subtle, and few except Grandmother and Nyanya saw it.

"It took them a long time to find out that there was no reason for them to be enemies," said Grandmother. Nyanya agreed.

To both Anton and Kseniya, the change brought a great inner peace, and for Anton the healing of another old wound. He was at home alone one evening, reading in his favorite armchair near the fireplace.

His eye was caught by a half-open drawer in a corner table. This was his personal drawer for cigarettes and tobacco. He opened the drawer and found it full of photographs and letters. He took them out and looked at them curiously; and the color left his face. It was Olga's handwriting. The photographs showed Olga, Gregor, and two dark-haired children. Their faces were stiff and frozen in the half-smile ordered by the photographer, but the artificiality of the pictures could not spoil Olga's proud clear look and beautiful features. Only in one picture did they look natural. She and Gregor were facing each other, and the adoration in Gregor's eyes almost reconciled Anton to him.

"I'd kill him with my own hands if he wouldn't kiss the ground she stands on," he muttered savagely.

The letters were sorted by date. The first had been written a few days after Olga left. She spoke of her deep love for her mother and father; she implored her mother to forgive her. Later letters described how they started their school in the village, how they had rebuilt the house themselves. The village showed no interest in the school. When Olga spoke of doing carpenter's work, plastering walls, scrubbing floors, helping repair the roof, it sounded as though she was serving God.

When they finally opened their school, at first no children came. Then one or two came, then more, and at length they all came. The parents were asked to come in the evenings. A few came out of curiosity, and stayed. Then so many came that the school was open from early morning till late at night. They had difficulties with the authorities. The priest fought them. Olga taught up to the time the children were born, and went back to school very soon afterwards, taking them along. And, of course, she had her household, her cow, and her vegetable garden.

"When I think of the past," she wrote, "I think only of Father, of you and the others in the family. I try to forget that I was ever a girl who ate and slept and spent money and danced without a thought in her head. But I was ignorant then and did not know that there could be such a rich life . . ."

Rich life indeed! thought Anton. She must be crazy, calling that poverty rich life! But she used those words—rich life—in all her letters. There was nothing she wanted in life but what she had—Gregor, the children, and the work.

She often mentioned Anton, and spoke of her concern for him. She loved him dearly, and she knew he could not have acted differently than he had.

"He does not belong to himself," she wrote. "He belongs to a whole class of people and he acts the way they do. Someday this will change.

They will find out that life is not confined to the four narrow walls within which they live."

Anton read and reread the letters till he heard the carriage stop outside the house. There was no time to put them back in the same order. But what did it matter? Kseniya had left them for him to read. He reached his bedroom before the house became lively with voices and noises, and undressed and went to bed in the dark. He heard Kseniya's voice calling good night to Grandmother, telling Vera to be quiet and not to disturb him. He heard her stop for a minute at his door. So she was concerned about him. She was concerned about how he felt after reading Olga's letters. Kseniya, Kseniya . . . Vera was his sunshine, his toy, but Olga and Kseniya held his heartstrings in their hands.

Kseniya, as he guessed, had found the drawer closed, the letters and photographs in disorder. She couldn't talk to him about it, but surely he heard her stop at his door. That would tell him. Tomorrow morning she would be up early, and when he came down she would be sitting at the table waiting for him and she would ask him whether he had slept well and whether he would be home early for dinner.

## CHAPTER 6
## *Vera*

WHEN Vera was sixteen, a French-woman fresh from a grand duke's palace was entrusted with imparting the final touch to her social graces. But beneath Vera's studied poise, she was still full of mischief. When the grownups were away in the evening, she flew like a firefly between the kitchen and the upper floors, shouting, singing, laughing, romping with her brothers.

But there were days when she was pensive and quiet. Questions to which she found no answers disturbed her. When, about two years earlier, she had first become interested in the connection between marriage and babies, she had come straight out with her whys and hows. Her first words had been interrupted by a shocked Kseniya—nice girls didn't talk about those things—and her father had turned away and mumbled something about her being too young. "When you get married, you will find out," Grandmother had said. Embarrassed giggles were all she had been able to get from the servants. She often lay awake trying to figure out the answers. She had thought of people she knew, and, putting two and two together, had got this much straight: when two people married, they moved to a new house with new furniture and then sometime later God sent them a baby. That part was clear. There still remained the question of how the baby got there. Well, she would find that out some other time; for the moment, she had been satisfied.

But that had been long long ago, two years ago; she had been only fourteen then. Now these questions demanded a complete answer. And there was something new that bothered her—that forbidden subject, love. No one would ever talk to her about it, and though in the pages of Pushkin, Turgenev, and Lermontov she found many passages about love, they did not answer her questions.

One evening when she opened the kitchen door she saw the house-man Kuzma sitting on a chair with Mashenka, the chambermaid, lying in his lap, his arms almost crushing her. Her eyes were closed, and their lips seemed never to want to separate. A light tremor shook Mashenka's body and Kuzma pressed her still closer.

When Vera thought of Kuzma and Mashenka, she felt hot and somehow ashamed of herself. Nevertheless, in the unadmitted hope of witnessing a similar scene, she lingered around the kitchen door in the evening. She saw a few playful kisses, but most of the time the servants, resting after the day's work, relaxed, drank tea, and talked and laughed and joked with one another. One evening, however, they were talking very quietly when Vera went down, and she stopped outside the closed door to listen.

"She wants to die, and who can blame her," the cook was saying. "You should have seen her. You wouldn't know it was our Dasha . . ."

Vera held her breath, to hear better. What could have happened to Dasha, the red-cheeked plump Dasha who always sang while ironing?

"Skin and bones she is, poor soul, her eyes swollen like pillows, and dry, burning dry. Not a tear left in them. All she keeps saying is 'I hope he dies and I die with him.' Well, she'll soon have her wish. She has no blanket for him, and he's lying in a box, blue with cold, filthy and skinny. She has no milk to nurse him and the woman says she will throw her out if she doesn't pay her. Pay her! For a corner in the stable where a dog wouldn't want to stay!"

"Serves her right." Vera heard the doorman's righteous voice. "A girl must watch herself and guard her honor."

"Oh, yes!" Mashenka burst out. "Is that what you men say when you turn a girl's heart upside down and promise her heaven on earth and marriage the very next day? And when you've got what you wanted, little you care if her life is hell or if she ends it in the river!" Mashenka broke into tears.

Vera couldn't see the furious look the cook threw at the indifferent Kuzma as she reached over to stroke Mashenka's hair, but she heard her say, "What do you expect, Mashenka? That's the way life is. That's woman's lot. Dasha knew Ivan wouldn't marry her. And why should he? The greengrocer promised him his daughter—"

"That wasn't what Ivan told Dasha! He promised her marriage, didn't he?"

"Yes, he promised," agreed the cook. "They all do, every one of them. And why shouldn't they? They don't lose anything. A girl can't force a man to marry her."

"And you say that this is right? Well, I don't. I don't, I don't . . ." Mashenka ran out of the kitchen, crying violently.

Vera returned to her room, more confused than before. Here was Dasha with no husband. Yet God had sent her a baby. But didn't only married people have children—or was it different with poor people? What was the answer?

Keeping eyes and ears open, it was possible to put some twos and twos together—not all of them, of course. Once she watched Pavel kissing Zena when they thought they were alone. She saw him press his lips to her breast, his fingers going up and down her body. Vera's knees felt so weak that she was afraid they would find her before she could move away. And once she had walked into her brothers' room when the tailor was there measuring them for their new school uniforms. He was starting to take the measurements for the trousers, and was down on his knees crawling around the boys and making mysterious signs on the floor with a piece of chalk.

"Don't forget," said Kseniya, "that they grow quickly. Leave them plenty of space for that."

Maxim laughed out loud when the tailor began to figure it out on him. It tickled him. When the tailor's fingers touched Igor's body, the boy stood tense and pale, biting his lips.

"Of course, of course. But you see, the instep . . ." The tailor threw a glance at Vera and stopped. "Well, if you want them to move freely . . . then this part here . . ." He looked again at Vera, made a helpless gesture, and stopped again.

"Oh, I see." Anton turned to Vera. "What are you doing around here? This is no place for you. Out with you!"

Vera waited for a while outside the door. But the tailor must have been explaining things with gestures because all she heard was:

"You see what happens if we take this in here. Now we could try it this way, see . . ."

Men, women, love, babies, marriage—they all somehow belonged together. But how? The circle turned and turned, and Vera found no way to make it stop.

Anton gave a ball for Vera's seventeenth birthday. He rented the big ballroom of the Metropole for the occasion, and spared no expense. Every important merchant family received an invitation, every prominent Muscovite he had ever met on a committee or in the organizations to which he belonged. There were artists, writers, university professors, a few military, and even a handful of prominent government officials. Ludmilla had sent him the names of a few friends of her family, members of the old nobility, and they were invited too.

The ball was a success, even beyond Anton's hope, and Vera lent it a special brilliance. In a cloud of white organdie with blue velvet bows the color of her eyes, with her lovely sunny looks and graceful charm, she won the approval of even the most aristocratic guests. As the center of attention and prodigal splendor, she enjoyed herself with her usual abandon. She ate with a hearty appetite, teased Zakhar about his tight vest, did not miss a single dance, curtsied when addressed by old ladies, and smiled happily on young and old, men and women. Busy as she was, from time to time she flew over to her father, squeezed his hand, kissed his cheek, and with an excited "Oh, I am so happy" flew off again.

The day after the ball Vera's social career began. A stream of invitations to balls, to theater parties, charity bazaars, dinners followed. Her parents, or sometimes Zena and Pavel, accompanied her, and afterwards all the details were always carefully interpreted in Grandmother's room. "All the details" meant what young men were present and how much attention they devoted to Vera. Of course, everybody showed a great deal of attention to Vera, but there existed an unwritten code of behavior about a particular kind of attention. And this was the only kind of attention in which the family, with the exception of Vera, was interested.

The troubled period when Vera had been preoccupied with love was over. In due course love would come to her, she told herself, but meanwhile she would enjoy this wonderful gay life. She loved to listen to compliments whispered during a dance, she loved to receive languid glances and know herself the cause of a sentimental sigh. She did not care who it was that sighed or whispered. She loved every one of them, but not one more than another.

Marriage brokers swarmed around Anton. He invariably said that his daughter was too young, that he was not interested in marriage for her. But he let them talk, and listened, and eliminated, one after another, the young men they had to offer.

The Nazarovs had always been one of the few chosen Moscow merchant families who were invited to state affairs. It was no novelty for them to attend balls and banquets given by the governor general or by the military command. But now Vera's triumphant success, which made her an asset to any party, and Anton's more than generous donations to churches, charities, museums, and anything else sponsored by people of importance, opened doors hitherto closed to them.

A sarcastic remark by Zakhar about his "hobnobbing with aristocrats" or a surprised look in a drawing room when he was introduced would come back to Anton in the stillness of the night and make him restless. Was he doing the right thing for Vera? Would he regret it? A few words in a letter from Olga were hard to forget. She wrote: "I wonder whether Father will not regret it some day. I would have preferred to see him come closer to our real people instead of trying so hard to be accepted by those who look down to him. And what will it do to Vera? Does she really belong there?"

No, no, Olga was wrong. He was doing the only right thing. Vera was a sparkling jewel and her father's duty was to get her the very best setting in this world. And where else could a setting worthy of her be found?

Nevertheless, two years after Vera's birthday ball no setting had yet been found. Of the many who had asked for her hand, not one had Anton even considered. There were some whom he might have considered if they had had serious intentions. But they danced and laughed with Vera, they sought her company—and became engaged to girls of their own class. Vera, surrounded by a never-ending stream of admirers, was indifferent to it. She forgot that all this had been conceived as a step to a brilliant marriage which would take her to the very top of that ladder. Reminded of that, she probably would have pleaded, "Oh, no, not yet, please. I am having such marvelous fun. No marriage could be better than this."

Life was indeed one great holiday for Vera. It was as if the whole world existed only to make it that holiday. Nothing had any reality unless it concerned her. Nobody had any interest for her unless they concerned themselves with her. Even members of her family were important only as they reflected her. Her triumphs made them happy and proud of her, and Vera loved them for it. She seldom failed to show herself before a party in her brothers' room, because Igor's eyes, adoring her beauty, added to her joy. She paid no attention to Maxim's scoffing remarks: "Ah, you big show-off!" or "Stop strutting like a peacock!" They fell on deaf ears. Nothing but admiration penetrated.

One day a broker reported a new prospect, a very special prospect, a young officer of a noble family—Anton was startled when he heard the name—which was in urgent and immediate need of money. (You understand, generations of extravagance—a venal estate manager—huge debts—ugly scandal threatening—exposure unthinkable—a matter of protecting the family honor.) The long and short of it was, young

Dolinin's family had sent him to Moscow to make a rich marriage and thus save them from the consequences of their folly. Very quickly—before the ugly rumors had time to spread. They would never before have thought of his marrying outside their circle—you understand, of course—but under the circumstances . . .

Of course, Anton understood. That was as it should be. One would not expect an aristocrat to marry the daughter of a merchant—even a girl like Vera—unless he needed her money. He would love her—Anton did not worry about that. A plan was worked out. They would meet at a ball in a few days, and if all went well, a reason could easily be found to set an early date for the marriage. The broker was emphatic about the early date. Unless he could lay hands on the money immediately, young Dolinin was not interested. He could not afford to waste any time.

Kseniya made especially elaborate preparations for the ball. New gowns were ordered in a hurry and seamstresses sat day and night working on exquisite creations in sheer white for Vera and wine color for Kseniya.

At the ball, their beauty, brought out to perfection by their jewels, fans, gloves, shawls, flowers, was startling, but for once Anton's eyes were not on his women. They wandered restlessly about the room. Then suddenly Anton turned to Kseniya: "That must be he." Behind her fan Kseniya slowly followed his eyes. A young officer they had never seen before was leaning against a column talking to the host but watching Vera, who was leading a mazurka. He seemed to be satisfied with what he saw. When he was introduced to Anton and Kseniya, he was courteous and attentive, and they talked easily about Petersburg. He showed interest at the mention of Fedor and Ludmilla. His family knew the Voronskys, he said.

Vera was brought back by her partner. Her face, in its frame of silken shining curls, was pink with the excitement of dancing and being admired, and her eyes sparkled. Smiling, she raised her eyes to the tall young officer. "Michel Pavlovich Dolinin." With a friendly nod she acknowledged the introduction. He asked for the next dance. It was a valse. She had promised it to a cadet. Gallantly, the youngster yielded the dance to his superior. Dolinin encircled Vera's tiny waist and took her hand in his, gently, very gently pressing it. He had to work fast. But he must be careful not to scare her. You never knew with these virgins. He must sweep her off her feet, switch on all his charm. These simple little geese fell easily; this shouldn't be hard for him. Her body felt soft under his fingers. He pressed her a little closer and looked deep into her eyes. He turned so that his mustache brushed her forehead. Just for a split second. He believed in the magic of this trick.

"You dance divinely. You like to dance?"

"Oh, I adore it. I could dance all day and all night. Don't you love to dance?"

"Of course, I do. And with a dancer like you I could dance to the end of the world."

He was wonderful to dance with. They must have a different way of dancing in Petersburg. He was really holding her close. Here the men hardly touched your waist with their fingers. It was pleasant to be held close. She liked it. His lips were so close to her ear that he was almost breathing into it. It was funny but she liked it. Was he saying anything or was he just breathing? That was funny. She laughed.

Michel laughed too, but he was disconcerted. When a girl laughed she was certainly not being swept off her feet. Perhaps he needed more time with her. But time was what he did not have. Well, he would give himself a week.

When the valse ended, they returned to her parents. She gave him two more dances. She promised him several for the next ball. He asked and received her parents' permission to take her skating. Kseniya invited him for dinner and a sleigh ride.

The courtship whirled to its conclusion with more dining, driving, and skating. He accompanied Kseniya and Vera shopping; Zena gave a dinner party for him; and in many touching and charming ways he showed them his appreciation. During a ball at the end of the week, Michel tested his success.

He held Vera close and spoke of the sadness that would envelop his life after he left Moscow. Vera did not laugh this time. She was sad too. It had been a wonderful week. She would miss him very much—more than she had ever missed any of her other admirers. His arm was wonderfully strong around her waist, and he was almost touching her cheeks with his lips. She tried to listen to him. But instead she listened to his fingers playing around her waist, very gently. Her head swam, and hot waves chased little shivers all through her—such enchanting shivers. She must not faint, she must pull herself together. She raised her head and looked into his eyes. No, no, that was even worse; she closed her eyes again. He had smiled, a triumphant smile, but all Vera saw was his eyes telling her something that made her delightfully dizzy. His fingers were playing again on her waist, a little higher now, and he was holding her so tightly that her breasts were touching him. Those enchanting shivers made her feel weak; and she wondered if it was possible to die of sheer bliss. Again she tried to listen to him.

" . . . the fragrance of your hair . . . touch of your fingers . . . I can't bear to go away . . ."

She bowed her head lower. She couldn't talk; she couldn't say anything. But he must guess how she felt. Or why did he press his lips on her fingers? The music stopped, and her hand lightly on his arm, Vera, quiet and unsmiling, returned to her parents. This was the end of the ball. He helped them into the sleigh. He wrapped Vera in furs, covered her feet with the bear rug and, protected by darkness, touched her cheek with his lips. "Till tomorrow."

In the carriage Vera said she had a headache. She sat silent with closed eyes, and when she reached home went straight to her room. She did not go to bed. She sat at the window, in the darkness, her hands crossed in her lap. Again and again she recalled every sensation of her last dance with Michel. So this was how love felt! But love meant marriage? . . . Even to think of this made her weak, delightfully, ecstatically weak. It almost hurt and it was heavenly sweet.

But would her father accept him? And did he want to marry her? He had loved her tonight, she was sure of that. But others had loved her too, and then married someone else. She had never minded before, but if Michel did, she would die. She knew why the others had done so, and she accepted the reason. Even though he loved her, he could not marry her if she was not acceptable to his family. What would she do then? Continue the life that had been interrupted tonight when he took her in his arms for that last dance? It had been a happy life, a wonderful, happy life. But it would not be a wonderful happy life any more. Not if he was not part of it. Not without him.

She was crying and her cheeks were wet, but she did not know it. Her hands remained quiet, crossed in her lap. The tears ran down her throat. What if she never saw him again? She sat still, crying, and her lips moved in a prayer.

"O God, dear God, I will always love You, I will always obey You, please, dear God, make him love me, make him want to marry me, make his family want him to marry me, make my father want him to marry me. Please, God, please . . ."

The quiet wedding little resembled the customary wedding in a rich merchant family. The ceremony took place in the small church near the Nazarovs instead of in the big cathedral. The food served at the wedding dinner was prepared with a view to quality rather than quantity. No one was drunk, no one was loud. Anton was at peace. Michel's behavior was perfect. He was friendly and respectful, and made them feel at ease among his aristocratic family. And he certainly was in love with Vera. No one could doubt that.

Vera was not the Vera of her birthday party. She smiled but not once did her voice rise in laughter. Her eyes shone, and they were of an intensity that made them almost dark. In a few hours nothing would stand between her and Michel. She was unable to swallow any food and when a toast was proposed she could do no more than wet her lips. She tried to listen to what people were saying to her, and answer. She could not. She would frame the words, Yes, she was looking forward to their trip, but when she opened her mouth to say them, the thought that she and Michel would be all alone in a few hours made her forget them.

In Michel's fervent ardor during their honeymoon Vera saw the expression of supreme love. In her ignorance, it did not occur to her that his passion was only the satisfaction of a healthy man's lust, which was aroused while he skillfully awakened her senses; that her exquisite young body could be more to a man than a tool for his hurried caresses. Michel had eyes for it only when he wanted her. When Vera danced into the room, whirling around to display a new dress or slippers or flowers, he would playfully tickle her silky throat or pink ear with his mustache, or let his fingers wander over the softness of her body. She thrilled to his play but soon, much too soon, he would crush her in his embrace and the game would be quickly over. She would have liked to play longer. And afterwards she would have liked to lie still and tell him what she felt, and have him gently caress her hair and hands as she wanted to caress his. But he immediately fell asleep.

Did it really matter? He loved her, she was sure of that. Otherwise would he kiss her so often and so passionately? And wasn't she endlessly happy to be his wife?

When they arrived at the Moscow station on their return from their honeymoon, she presented a picture of radiant happiness. After one glance at her, Anton warmly shook Michel's hand.

Several days passed in excitement over the reunion with the family and her new role as mistress of a house. The new house was gay and light, and her boudoir windows looked out into the same trees she had seen from her bedroom windows at home. Two of the servants, Dasha and Mashenka, had come from her mother's house.

In the activity of the first days Vera hardly noticed how little she saw of Michel. Some nights he came home very late. The first time he found Vera lying with wide-open eyes waiting for him he suppressed his irritation and gently rebuked her:

"Never do that, my angel. I really wouldn't like it. You know how it is. We can't leave the club before the generals do. It's a terrible bore but that's the way it is . . . You can't lie awake waiting for me. I want you to look beautiful. How are you to do it if you don't sleep enough? You want to be pretty for me, don't you?"

Of course, she wanted to be pretty for him; of course, she would go to sleep and not wait, she promised him. She would do anything to please him.

When Vera's new wardrobe was completed, they started their round of visits. The handsome young couple, both excellent dancers, gay and entertaining, were welcome everywhere. To the list of her old admirers, Vera added Michel's friends, charming them with her grace and quick smile and the way her face opened like a flower as she broke into contagious laughter.

When she danced with others she threw adoring looks at Michel. He answered them with a smile, and sentimental hearts fluttered over the romantic couple. Watching Vera in a ballroom, Michel felt grateful. He would have had to marry Nazarov's daughter or another rich merchant's daughter whoever she was. There had been no other way out. But to have got Vera was more than he deserved—and she deserved more than she was getting from him. But what could he do? He was not made to be a faithful, devoted husband—he could not change that—and he had no intention of giving up his new gypsy dancer. But he would try not to hurt Vera. He could not force love, but his feeling about her made it easier not to hurt her and it made it easier to imitate love.

When Vera was alone in the evening, she called in her parents or went over to visit them or the young Gavrilovs. She did not dress for these occasions, and with her hair cascading down, she was the child who delighted in teasing Zakhar, in mussing her father's hair, in devouring endless amounts of homemade sweets. There were also quiet hours at Grandmother's feet, with Mother and Nyanya.

"So he is wonderful, your Michel, is he?" was always Grandmother's first mocking question.

"Oh, yes, grandmother, he is . . . He is very wonderful. Don't ask me why; he's just wonderful, and that's all. But," she added wistfully one night, "I wish those generals wouldn't make him stay away from home so much. But he says he can't offend them . . ."

Grandmother and Kseniya exchanged a look. Nyanya pressed her lips close together.

". . . and he says that unless he pleases them he will never advance. And of course he wants to advance further and further until he is a general too. You can't blame him for it, can you? But you know what? If he did what I really want him to do he'd stay home every evening, even if he never advanced at all. Wouldn't that be funny?"

She laughed heartily.

"Oh, yes," Grandmother admitted readily, "that would be very funny."

She raised Vera's face and looked at her for a long time. Then she put her yellowish old hands on Vera's head and murmured: "God bless you, darling, now and forever, and don't let me live to see those eyes darkened by sorrow!"

Vera caught Grandmother's hands and pressed her warm lips to them.

The family knew well where Michel was spending his evenings. All they wanted was that Vera should not find out; let her continue to dance happily through life with everyone around her adoring and applauding. They had no word of blame for Michel. A young aristocrat marrying a merchant's daughter could not be expected to give up his mistresses and his gay life. Anyway, a man could live the way he wanted to live. No, there was nothing to reproach Michel with. He was careful not to hurt Vera. Nothing was wrong with him. The trouble was with Vera, the spoiled, protected child who knew nothing of life and had always lived in a world of make-believe.

Vera had been married a little over a year when she became pregnant. Uncomfortable in her tight corsets, and frightened by the jolting of the carriage on the cobbled Moscow streets, she gave up her social life and spent her days in flimsy frilly negligees lying on a cushion-covered couch. When the weather was good, Kseniya or Zena would walk with her in front of the house. A nurse was hired, and a midwife visited her every day. Vera's digestion, Vera's appetite or lack of it, Vera's sleep, Vera's every change in looks or mood were the only topics of conversation in the house.

Michel was genuinely concerned for her. A young Dolinin was on his way into the world—a child blessed with a name to be proud of and a fortune that would make his life a brilliant bed of roses. It had to be a boy and his name would be Pavel. For over two centuries there had never been any names but Pavel and Michel in the Dolinin family. But meanwhile his own life need not be neglected.

Vera had happily given up her dinners and parties—at last she would have those quiet evenings alone with Michel which she had always wanted. Instead, to her disappointment, he was now away more than ever. Important foreign dignitaries were coming to Moscow, and the governor general was expected to entertain them. Michel, it seemed, was on the committee that was planning the entertainment. They had endless conferences and always in the evening. When the dignitaries finally arrived, they seemed never to want to leave. He had so few free evenings, poor Michel. But he was very sweet about it. He was upset everytime he had to leave her. And he had been so thoughtful about moving into his own bedroom. He had hated to do it but he had been worried that he might disturb her when he came home late. He had kissed her and whispered into her hair, "It is agony for me . . . you understand . . . in your condition . . . just seeing you and nothing else . . . you understand . . . it is torture . . ." Sweet sweet Michel!

The youngest Dolinin was ushered into the world at sunrise. In the early evening the midwife had taken over the house. She who dared not sit down in the master's presence, had boldly pushed Michel and Anton out of the room, had shouted orders at Kseniya and Zena, had chased the servants up and down, demanding fresh towels, linen, and hot water, or just yelling at them for the fun of it. This was always a great moment in her humble life; every one of her words was law.

A last agonizing scream, a lusty yell, dead silence for a second—and bedlam had broken loose. Everybody cried, talked, laughed at the same time. The maid Mashenka ran into the kitchen for more water calling out:

"A boy, it's a boy, it's a boy!"

The cook, drying her hands on her apron, rushed out to add her voice to the general tumult. The coachman turned to the icon and crossed himself: "God bless him and give him a long happy life."

"Don't you worry, God will see to that. He always takes care of those who don't need His help." An angry bitter voice came from the corner where Dasha was ironing.

Mashenka put her arms around Dasha. "Please, just for today, Dasha, forget and be happy, please, please."

Dasha pushed her away. "And why should I, and why today? If I ever forgot, it certainly wouldn't be today, not today. But I won't forget. Neither today nor ever. And sure as I live, my Yasha shall know that his mother cursed him in her womb and that she begged God to rid her of him."

Dry sobs came out of her throat. Only yesterday she had seen him, her skinny rickety Yasha. Every kopeck she had she gave that woman. But the way he wolfed down the bun she brought him, he must be starving. She would give her last drop of blood for him. But what could she do, what could she do? She couldn't even cry. There were no more tears in her dried-out eyes and dried-out body.

Mashenka forgot about the new baby and the hot water in her concern for Dasha. It seemed such a short time ago that Dasha's laughter and red cheeks had made the Nazarov kitchen seem brighter. Why, why should it be this way? It had almost happened to her too . . . Someone shouted for the water. Mashenka got busy but her excitement over the new baby did not return. It didn't seem fair to be excited about it when Dasha was so miserable over her child.

The midwife remained for a while but her big hour was ended. When she was not busy with Vera she was relegated to the servants' quarters. There, almost purple in the face, she consumed incredible amounts of food and tea, and entertained her listeners with endless stories of her professional experiences, a subject which never tired them.

While her star was going into eclipse another one appeared in the firmament: a shy, embarrassed, healthy-looking young woman with full breasts and formidable hips, dressed in a colorful embroidered peasant costume with a high beaded headdress. The Nazarovs had unwillingly given in to Michel's insistence that a wet nurse should be found for the baby. A Dolinina did not nurse her child, he said.

Aksinya had been chosen only after a long and careful search. Anton's most trusted clerk had been sent down to Nyanya's village to investigate the field and had finally selected Aksinya after a doctor had examined several candidates as thoroughly as a peasant did a horse which he considered buying. Special food had been sent to the village for her, besides clothing, soap, and instructions concerning her behavior. Money was left to provide for her own baby when she was brought to Moscow.

With great ceremony the infant Pavel or Pavlik as the family called him was placed in her arms and put to her breast. He did not fumble at all; he did not turn his head away. No—not he. He knew exactly what was expected of him, and used his tiny tongue to help him get the nipple between his lips. As one long practiced, he got the food out of it and settled contentedly to his first meal. An adoring family sighed with relief.

Vera was showered with gifts. Her room was filled with the most exquisite flowers in Moscow's greenhouses; and her father-in-law sent a special messenger with a box of family jewels. These were the gems presented at the birth of the first child of the eldest son. Among them was a diamond diadem given only when the first child was a son.

When Vera began to go out again, she seemed to have an added radiance. Her figure was slightly fuller, but her soft dancing movements showed the same supple grace. With her new jewels and a new Paris wardrobe, ready again to dance and laugh, she quickly regained her place in Moscow's ballrooms. At home she spent hours watching Pavlik sleep and softly humming to him. He was going to be a handsome child. Already he showed the aquiline nose and elongated features of the Dolinins, but his coloring was Vera's. His eyes had the startling blueness of her eyes, his skin and hair her fairness.

Three times Aksinya was brought to Moscow to nurse Vera's children. After Pavlik, it was the dark-haired Kira, and two years later it was Katya, a miniature image of her mother. Each time Aksinya had to leave behind a baby who would be nursed by an unfamiliar breast and tended by unfamiliar hands. Each time she pressed to her heart a strange child and tried to make believe it was her own. Always there was the agony of knowing how easily her own forgot her, the pain of their indifference when she returned. How long it had taken her son to learn to call her Mother again.

Of course, it was a great privilege to have been chosen to nurse the master's children, and many a young village mother envied her. Look at Nyanya's children and grandchildren—didn't they have the best barns in the village, the best horses and cows? They didn't have to worry themselves to death when their roof went or a floor broke or a drought burned the fields. No, they wrote to Nyanya, and their worries were over. Now she, Aksinya, could do for her own family what Nyanya had done for hers.

So why did she cry when before a new departure she lay at night close to her husband or when she looked at her own children? She knew now what Nyanya had meant on that first dreadful day when she came to nurse Pavlik. "Now, Aksinya," Nyanya had said, "remember, think only of what your family will get; never, never, of what they miss or what you miss. Never listen to your heart, never." And Dasha had said, "Poor people must have no hearts. Then there will be nothing to break in them." But the reward was a rich one, and when Aksinya could make her heart keep still it seemed worth while.

Three times, after months of seclusion, Vera emerged with an added radiance, a fresh thirst for entertainment and excitement, and a new, extravagant wardrobe. Her figure, fuller after each birth, did not lose its soft grace. A round of visits announcing her reappearance preceded the never-ending whirl of dinner parties, horseback riding, balls, theaters, summer picnics, sleigh riding, skating. The whirl was the same, whether it was in Moscow or at the summer home in the pine woods, whether it was at the Crimean seashore or a Caucasian mountain resort.

Anton's old dream for her came true: she was presented at court, and was as successful in the sophisticated St. Petersburg society as in that of the more provincial Moscow. When she was at home she sang and danced with Pavlik and the two little girls, played games with them, and hummed them to sleep at night with soft lullabies. When the children cried or were fussy, she handed them over quickly to the nurses, who took them back to the nursery. The failing health of Grandmother or Nyanya gave her an occasional short moment of concern; and when old Zakhar Gavrilov died, she cried a little and then thought no more about it.

Michel was not much at home, but Vera became used to it and took it as lightly as everything else. When he was at home, he was an attentive husband and a devoted father, and Vera was completely happy. Going through the motions of a playful lover, he often caught fire, and Vera's belief in his never-dying love was strong. When he had to go out alone in the evening, she slept the sleep of the untroubled.

But one night she could not fall asleep. After dinner they had been sitting on the sofa together looking through the stereopticon slide at views of Yalta. They had been very close, his body pressed to hers, and she had felt warmly excited and happy. Suddenly he had looked at his watch and had said he must hurry—a meeting at the club. Vera had flushed hotly, and when he got up from the sofa she had felt an actual physical pain. In bed she tossed restlessly, and when she closed her eyes she felt him taking her in his arms.

It was long after midnight when she heard Michel's step in the hall. She waited tensely to see if he would stop at her door. She knew he would be angry if she ran out to meet him. She must be still, she must. But—oh, surely he couldn't mind her showing him how much she wanted him. But he did mind. Oh, how he did mind. He freed himself impatiently from her arms, and said in such a terrible cold voice, "You are not going to be vulgar, my dear!" and walked into his room, locking the door.

Vera stood still, drenched with hot shame. She did not know which had been worse—the way he had pushed her body away or the loud final click of his key in the lock. Or—and at the memory her face burned hotly again—the way his voice had sounded when he said "vulgar." "You vulgar little merchant girl! But what can one expect" was what he had meant. The cold contempt, that icy voice! Oh, no, not that again, never that again. She could not bear it. Somehow she got herself back in her room. The tears came now, and they burned her eyes. She could bear anything, she thought, if only he never again said "vulgar" in that voice; if only he never again looked at her as he had tonight. She would never let that happen again. He must never again say "vulgar" to her. Never! Never!

She knew what she must do. The old game was over and a new one would begin. This new game she would have to play alone; no one could know. There would be no more easy laughter or giving way to impulse. Carefully she would watch every one of her words and moves. She would be a model of perfection; every word and smile would be carefully weighed; every expression of endearment, every gesture properly measured. No one should know what she really felt. Just so long as Michel didn't call her vulgar again.

She greeted Michel charmingly the next day, and Michel smiled back in relief. The night before he had been worried that he might have behaved too rudely. But he had been taken unawares and had had no time to get hold of himself. And damn it, she needed to be taught a lesson. Other men did exactly what he did. And if there was a scandal, it was a polite quiet scandal. Nothing wrong in a polite quiet scandal. But Vera was different; he had to be careful. There could be no polite quiet scandal with her. Other wives knew what to expect when they married men like himself. But Vera had entered into marriage as if the doors of a fairyland had been opened to her. He and the children were never more than toys put into the fairyland to amuse her.

But thank God his fears had been unnecessary. She hadn't noticed a thing.

## CHAPTER 7
## *Anton*

ANTON was not well. He had the gout, the usual penalty of rich Moscovites for eating and drinking too much and too well. He often had to stay home from the office and the pain kept him awake at night. Time hung heavy on his hands. He was not a great reader. His newspaper and illustrated monthly were his only fare. Kseniya was around most of the time doing quietly and willingly whatever had to be done, but they did not talk much. A report from the firm and a visit from the children and grandchildren occasionally broke the monotony of the long empty days. He played solitaire endlessly, in order not to think too much.

The nights were worse than the days. During the day there were the familiar sounds to distract him and he could sit at the window. Theirs was a quiet street with little traffic, but there were always the street vendors to watch. It amused Anton to watch them quarrel for a good corner, pull a customer away from another vendor or run after a customer, clutching the strap of the box which held their apples, candy, shoelaces, or cigarettes.

But during the night there was no escape from his disturbing thoughts. They were always the same. What had he accomplished? He had given forty-two years to the firm, but the young Gavrilovs, now that Fedor had come back from Petersburg, had completely taken it over. They, with their new ways, with this new expensive machinery from England. He had fought against their getting it, but apparently they had been right. The new machines did produce more and had quickly paid for themselves. And he had fought against the new bookkeeper and his double Italian bookkeeping, whatever that was. But it seemed they had been right in that too. It didn't take much time now to figure things out. Every day before he went home the bookkeeper had it all in black and white. No, they really didn't need him at all to run the firm. Not any more.

He had his family, hadn't he? There was Kseniya, his dear gentle Kseniya. She was never cross, though at times, when he had a bad day, he knew he was anything but pleasant to take care of. But in the stillness of the night, the regrets for their wasted years twisted the sick man's soul in nightmarish misery.

The children? To think of Olga was like pressing a hand to an open wound. She was poor, very poor. But she sent back every penny her mother sent her, and she sounded in her letters as happy and contented as anyone he knew. For her, apparently, possessions, reputation, position had nothing to do with happiness. But if that was true, it meant that everything he had ever aspired to was wrong. What right had he to judge her life? What had he got from his own? Misery, pain, regrets.

He hadn't been wrong about Zena, had he? She was happy. But had this been his doing? Least of all had he been thinking of her happiness when he arranged her marriage. All he had wanted was to make the firm Nazarov-Gavrilov the biggest and richest in the field. It certainly had become the richest and the biggest in the field but he had little to do with it now. As soon as he closed his eyes, the Nazarov name would be dropped from it. Hadn't he done the same thing? It would have been much wiser to have married Zena to a little man and to have remained the master. Zena would have been contented with any husband. He had been unwise there too.

Vera . . . Well, Vera had filled his life with laughter and joy. And now she was all he had ever dreamed that she might be. Then why did the thought of her hurt? It wasn't because she had no time for him and hadn't even noticed that he was sick. That was as it should be. When one was on top of the ladder there wasn't much time. He didn't mind that. What really hurt was something else—her eyes, her laughter. Her eyes were too bright and her laughter too gay. She was hiding something. Well, it wasn't hard to guess what it was. That, too, had gone wrong.

Everything seemed to have been all right with the boys, in the beginning. They had had good teachers, had gone to good schools; he had sent them to church on Sundays. So why had they not turned out to be the sons he wanted them to be? Of course he wanted them to go into the firm straight from school. Why should there be only Gavrilovs in the firm? But Maxim had wanted to go to the university, and the entire family, especially the Gavrilovs, had sided with him. And he, Anton, had been made to feel that he would be a monster to refuse him. Even poor people, they had told him, sent their children to a university these days.

So Maxim was now a college student. He came and went as he liked, and talked back in a way that a few years ago would have made any father put a leather strap to good use. But, though the boy had been so eager to go to the university, he didn't seem to spend much time over his books. More often than not, Anton heard his voice in the kitchen. Well, he was young, a strong healthy boy, and the little kitchenmaid Dunya was not bad to look at. Better that than to be one of those students who walked in the streets singing godless songs and spitting at the czar's pictures. Better Dunya than that!

About Maxim, one at least knew that he was alive. His loud voice and laughter rang constantly through the house when he was at home. But his youngest, Igor, moved like a shadow through life. He never laughed loudly, never raised his voice. And he too had refused to go into the firm. He hadn't been insistent about it, the way Maxim had been. Pale, his eyes down, he had stood before Anton, had said almost in a whisper, "Oh, no, not that, never, father. I'd rather beg or starve, but not that." That was all. Anton had shouted and shaken his fists, but the boy had stood there white and trembling, saying no more. That was the last time Anton had shouted at anyone. That was before his first bad attack, which took all the sap out of him. The way the boy had stood there; the straight sandy hair falling over his forehead, the upturned freckled nose, the skinny boyish body shivering. It was the way Anton himself had stood before a stern father when he was sixteen. His father had shaken his fists right into his face. He hadn't minded the pain. He had only wanted his father to let him go, if only for a little while, to let him have a look at the world before he started counting bales of cloth and measuring yards of cotton. Day after day he had stood before his father, pleading, and day after day his father had thrashed him. Then one morning he had had no strength left to plead. He didn't have a look at the world, and he had started to count the bales and measure the yards that morning. He had gone to work early, he remembered; none of the clerks were in yet. A tiny kitten had come out of the yard and rubbed against his leg. He had bent down to fondle it, then straightened up. He would not pet it. He was not going to pet anyone, he was not going to love anyone. He had kicked at the kitten with his boot. It hurt him to hear it cry but he was not going to be soft to anyone. He was going to be as rude and mean as everyone else. Opening the office door he had stumbled over something. It was the office boy, scrubbing the floor. He had kicked him the way he had kicked the kitten. He had never done that before and, immediately ashamed, had been on the point of asking the boy to forgive him. But he had caught himself. He must not be soft, he must not. And as time went on and he grew older and the job bigger, there were more people he could kick.

That must not happen to his own son. Igor must not want to hurt people because someone, his own father, had hurt him. A few days later Anton said to Igor:

"Now, suppose I were to tell you that you don't have to go to work in the firm. What would you do? I am not saying anything, mind you, I am just asking."

The boy sat still, his gray melancholy eyes fixed hopefully on his father's face. "Father, would you, would you really?"

"Well, suppose I would, just suppose, what then?"

It wasn't easy for Igor to tell his father what he wanted to do. He wanted to be a poet. But that was something he couldn't talk to anyone about.

"All I want, father," he finally said in his quiet slow voice that so much resembled his mother's, "is to go out into the world, to see what the world is like. Will you let me, father, please, will you let me?"

The boy's voice shook with anguish. Anton's answer did not come for a long time. He sat with his head bent low and his hand covering his eyes. When he looked up again, his eyes and face were filled with pain.

"Maybe. But go now, my boy. Leave me alone."

With a weak gesture he motioned him out of the room. The boy grasped his father's hand, and what had always been an empty gesture learned in his childhood for the first time had meaning: he kissed the hand with fervor.

Anton heard him run up to his room. From his hand, a softness spread all over his body. Why, how easy it was to be happy!

The war with Japan brought Anton additional worries. All his life, he and the people he knew had been concerned only with their personal lives and business. The police, the government, foreign countries—of course, these had their proper place in conversation, but one didn't spend hours talking and worrying about them. Now all that was changed. What before had been the business of government officials and a few crackpots—politicians, old Zakhar used to call them—had now become, apparently, the business of everyone; even women had an opinion these days, it seemed. And the children! They raised their voices in the presence of adults as if they were equals. His own son, Maxim, laughed at him when he told him to shut his mouth and listen to his elders. The clerks and the servants talked. The salesmen and the street cleaners talked. Before, the students used to be the only ones to make real trouble. Now the workers had begun. They went out with the students and carried red flags and sang those shameless songs. He had seen a demonstration only the other day. They hadn't finished their songs. The Cossacks had ridden their horses right into the crowd, striking out right and left with their whips. It hadn't been a nice thing to watch. The lead in those whips must have been pretty heavy. The snow had been splashed red with blood.

Yes, people were very restless. Was it because of the war? Some said they shouldn't have gone to war at all. But the czar must have had a good reason to go to war. He wouldn't do anything that would harm his people. But what did they want in Japan? It was so very far away. Not that the firm could complain about the war. No merchant could. Money was rolling in as it never had before. But somehow it didn't seem right. Soldiers were dying there, their own flesh and blood, and the merchants pocketed money on it. The other day Kseniya had told him about the letter the cook had received from her village. All their young men went and some had come back already—without legs, arms, or eyes. But no one among Anton's friends was fighting. It wasn't hard for their kind to get out of military service. They even saw to it that none of their clerks went. But then Michel, who was an officer, hadn't gone either, and all his friends seemed to be around, doing something or other for the Ministry of Supply and doing very well for themselves indeed. Yes, what was tears for one was laughter for another.

Take anything—it was always one thing for one and something else for another. Now some people said that the czar started the war to take the people's minds off troubles at home; others said that the czar had shown great patience with the Japs but that he couldn't permit Russia's national honor to be dragged in the mud any longer. Some said that Russia's defeats were due to the incompetence, corruption, and greed of those who conducted the war. The way people who supplied the army made millions, it might well be so. But then, who knew, maybe the people were right who said that the army was weak because of those agitators who went around shouting against the war.

Now, take what they called "Bloody Sunday" in Petersburg. Most people would tell you that this was the way it had happened: a rebellious priest named Gapon, a man who they said looked more like a highway robber than a priest, had led a bunch of armed workers and students straight to the czar's palace. They had shouted and threatened and demanded to see the czar. Naturally, the palace guards shot them down. What else would you have expected them to do? That's why they were there—to protect the czar's sacred life. It sounded like a true story, and that's the way his paper had printed it.

But then along came Maxim and told him quite a different story. According to one of his classmates, who had been in Petersburg that day, that priest Gapon had wanted to help the workers get better living conditions. Gapon had tried this and that. Nothing had helped. So he had suggested that the workers march to the palace and tell their story to the czar. The czar loved his people, Gapon had assured them. The czar simply didn't know how they suffered; his ministers never told him the truth. If only he knew the truth he would help them. Gapon had told the workers· to take their wives and children, icons, church banners, and to carry in front of the procession a portrait of the czar. He would lead them, he had said. So one Sunday they had set out. Families had walked together dressed in their best. They had been singing patriotic songs and hymns. Father Gapon had led them in full priestly regalia, a large cross in his hands. Cossacks and soldiers had met them near the palace and they had stopped, and many had knelt in prayer. They had heard the order to charge but they hadn't believed it. When· the shooting had started, they had had to believe it. Men, women and children had fallen, and the icons, banners, and the czar's portraits had lain torn and broken on the blood-covered snow.

Four thousand people had been killed and wounded right in front of the palace. Maxim's classmate had gone there the next day and had seen the tree from which an eight-year-old boy, like other boys in other trees, had watched the demonstration. An officer had been standing beneath the tree, and the child had teased him, pointing to himself, "Look, your honor, here is a sparrow. Why don't you get him down?" The officer had got the little sparrow down. Maxim's friend had seen the red stains on the tree and a blood-soaked child's fur cap under it. If that was the truth, no wonder there was so much unrest about.

It might be the truth. Maxim might be noisy and forward, but he didn't tell lies and he wouldn't have repeated a lie. Anton's mind lingered on Maxim. Why, why, couldn't the boy go into the firm? Why did he think he had to go to the university? Well, someday, maybe, he would change his mind.

CHAPTER 8
*Fedor and Ludmilla*

IN the winter of 1904, as the war with Japan was drawing to an end, Fedor and Ludmilla gave their first big dinner in their new Moscow home. They had bought a white two-story house on the Tverskoi Boulevard, surrounded with old linden trees, and in the spring and summer the garden was filled with lilac, jasmine, and roses. For her dinner Ludmilla had hired a caterer from the Metropole Hotel, and had filled the rooms with hot-house flowers. The mass of flowers, the blazing light of the many crystal chandeliers, the excellent food and wines, and the combination of well-bred Petersburg elegance and warm Moscow hospitality made a pleasant impression on most of the guests, though some of the older ladies found the beautiful furniture which Ludmilla had inherited from her family too austere for their taste.

Vera came late and her entrance was spectacular. She was enveloped in a white velvet wrap with a hood covering her blonde curls. Her eyes and teeth shone, her cheeks were velvety pink. She was soon the center of a laughing and lively group, and watching her, Anton felt all his old pride in her, although, as always of late, he thought her gaiety exaggerated, her smile not genuine. Her eyes at times looked almost hard, and did not smile when her lips smiled. He wished he were mistaken, but he knew that he was not.

Vera and Michel had brought some of Michel's friends with them, among them an elderly colonel. Like most of the military people transferred from Petersburg to Moscow during the war, the colonel was connected with supply. But unlike the others, he seemed to be honestly devoted to the task of supplying the army instead of his own pocket. The colonel was silent while the conversation around the dinner table flipped gracefully from one topic to another, but he came to life when the small talk shifted into a more serious vein.

It started when one of the young officers launched a tirade against "traitors":

"How do you expect to win a war when your own people are traitors? When the students at our own Moscow university say that they are not supporting their own government, and that they hope Russia will lose and Japan will win? Our Little Father Czar is much too kindhearted. They ought to be hanged, these traitors, these rascals, every single one of them."

"You might not like the idea of hanging your host, but you may have to hang me too," laughed Fedor. "I don't think I would go as far as they do, but I do wonder whether a defeat wouldn't do us a lot of good. It might wake us up."

"I don't need to have anyone wake me," said Michel haughtily. "To me it is clear why we suffer defeats. How can you expect a country to win a war when its military class is treated the way it's treated in Russia? The Japanese worship their army, but here the civilians jeer at anyone in the uniform of an officer."

Ludmilla looked worried. The conversation was taking an unpleasant turn, but there seemed to be no way of stopping it. Fedor had the bit in his teeth.

"And did it ever occur to you," he asked too politely, "why that is so? How can people respect and love their army when the army is used against them whenever they speak up—"

"As every law-abiding citizen understands," put in the young officer who had started the argument, "our army is used only to put down revolts of traitors against our beloved czar. I am sure you don't call such traitorous conduct 'speaking up'?"

Fedor ignored him and went on, speaking directly to Michel:

"And did it ever occur to you that the people can't have much love and respect for the way military training is being knocked into the Russian soldier by flogging and cursing? How can you blame them for not loving the army?"

Unexpectedly, the elderly colonel came to Fedor's support.

"Yes," he said, "much blame for the tragedy is to be laid to the high military command, and some to all of us . . . Some of us knew that it was too early to provoke a battle. Some of our Far Eastern generals and admirals sent frantic appeals to wait till we were better prepared. Did the ignorant brass hats listen to them? No, they ordered them to fight when the fleet was spread out all over the seas. It was like a Sunday picnic for the Japs to sink our ships one after the other; and once the ships were gone, it was another picnic for them to move their troops against us. Those same Japs whom, we were told, we could beat by simply throwing our caps at them! Will we ever recover from this shame?"

"What should we have done, Colonel?" Michel asked sharply. "Presented the yellow devils with a platterful of the things they wanted, and bowed to them? Oh, please, do us a favor, help yourself, we are much too weak to resist you!"

"No need to be sarcastic, young man," the colonel answered with great seriousness. "This is a national catastrophe and there is no place for sarcasm. There are many ways of giving in without being weak. There is such a thing as proper timing, as brains, as diplomacy, as expediency. Oh, there is so much we could have done and did not do. We had generals who knew what to do, but theirs were voices crying in the wilderness. And now, when after all the criminal blunders and delays, some reserves have finally reached the front, when it looks as if we may still put up a fight and save our honor, these same brass hats are panicky and insist that it is too late and that we should lay down our arms. Now, when the time to fight has finally come, they scream, 'Peace, peace!' I wonder if they and those filthy speculators who fattened themselves on the war are ever disturbed in their sleep by the blood of our uselessly massacred sailors and soldiers!"

The colonel finished talking. Silence fell over the table. Maxim, who had hung on the colonel's lips, sighed deeply as if awakened from a dream. The majestic Metropole headwaiter hurried to the colonel. He lighted his cigarette, filled his wineglass, brought over a choice of dessert liqueurs, and showed his feelings in the only way a waiter was permitted to do. In his many years of serving at society dinners, this was the first time he ever heard anyone express sympathy for the plain people.

The silence was becoming awkwardly long. Ludmilla seemed to have forgotten her duties as a hostess completely, Vera thought. It would never do. This was not the way to start a salon and to introduce herself to society.

"Now, now, colonel." Vera smiled charmingly. "I am sure it isn't all as dark as you picture it. Those yellow midgets surely can't beat Russians. Don't you agree?"

She let her eyes wander around the table, inviting answers. She got them. Graceful light answers, the kind of answers that made for good dinner conversation: anecdotes about the Japanese, and about Red Cross nurses and their officer admirers; praise for the ladies who sacrificed so much of their time dancing for the war victims and rolling bandages; a pat on the shoulder for the magnanimous gifts the Moscow merchants had presented to war charities. Vera felt that she had saved Ludmilla's party. She was pleased with herself; and so was Michel. They exchanged a smile. Vera's was the right kind of smile. Michel approved of it. It contained none of the sentimental adoration he had always been supposed to answer with a deep look. It was the calm smile of a mature woman of the world. Yes, Vera had finally learned.

Although Ludmilla's salon was not the kind Vera considered proper, it was a very successful one. People came and went as they pleased. The discussions were loud and heated, and age and rank were of little consequence. A student contradicted his old professor and a lieutenant sharply argued with his superior. Nobody interrupted Maxim as they did at home when he had something to say. Guests were free to bring any number of friends. Actors and actresses, university professors, writers, liberal officers, merchants and industrialists, students and labor leaders found the doors of the white house on the Tverskoi Boulevard wide open to them. During the linden-blossom time, the evening tea table was set in the garden. In the summer, the scene merely shifted to the Gavrilovs' bungalow near the Moscow River, where the lively arguments continued, even while the guests swam, played croquet, or rowed in the moonlight.

During the winter evenings, the discussions went on around the large fireplace in Ludmilla's pleasant living room. A new play, a new book, a scientific discovery, a government order, every expression of popular mood, were argued out with equal interest and heat. Ludmilla's friendly but unobtrusive hospitality put at ease even those who had at first hesitated to come to the home of the young textile magnate whose wife bore one of the names of Russia's old nobility.

The dinners that Ludmilla gave at first for family and friends together soon had to be discontinued. As the political situation grew tenser, the discussions became too violent. Many of their friends, aware of Michel's obvious contempt and of his monarchist sympathies, would not come when he was to be there.

He managed to be there quite often. After Zakhar's death, Fedor and Pavel, with the help of foreign engineers, had modernized and mechanized the plants. When the unfamiliar newfangled machines had arrived from abroad and word of their installation spread, many an old Moscow manufacturer had crossed himself devoutly and whispered that the days of the Antichrist were approaching. When the first wave of workers' unrest shut plants and shops throughout the city, the Gavrilov plant remained open. Fedor and Pavel granted the workers' demands for more wages and shorter hours. When the workers demanded the right to organize a union, they agreed to that too. Later, during the general strike, when the strike committee ordered the workers at the Gavrilov plants out on a sympathy strike, the workers sent a delegation to the Gavrilovs to explain that they were going on strike not for themselves but for others. No one was punished; no wages were deducted.

Violently though Michel disapproved of all this, and much as he feared that the young Gavrilovs' methods would diminish the family fortune, he held himself in check, and was very careful not to provoke a serious quarrel. He was determined that nothing should interfere with his visits to Fedor and Ludmilla's house, with his knowing what they read, what they said, whom they saw, and what their friends were thinking. For Michel and many of his friends were members of the Black Band, that organization which, under the banner of devotion to czar and church, fought through its leaders with pen and words, but through its rank and file with any hot or cold weapon they could lay their hands on. If students or workers held a meeting; if Jews, Poles, Armenians, Tartars—but preferably Jews—were known to be getting together, whether for prayers, a funeral, or a wedding, the Black Band gave the signal and its lowest riffraff answered the call. The famous Okhotny Ryad, the Hunters' Row, a block in Moscow's theater section, not only provided Moscow gourmets with their choicest food, its shopkeepers and shopmen also provided the Black Band with its choicest, most vicious members. When there was work for them to do, the famous "Hunters' Row Men" would march—the greengrocers, the poultrymen, butchers, and fishmongers, armed with knives, clubs, whips, blackjacks. Their powerful bodies and their brutal faces, red from vodka and demagogic oratory supplied by their leaders, filled the hearts of the passers-by with fear and pity for their victims. What use to tell the police? Everybody knew that these men were the darlings of the police.

Michel, of course, had nothing to do with these activities of the Black Band. He was one of its leaders, and his activities were not among students or workers. It was among people like Fedor and his friends that Michel hunted for treason and disloyalty. When he could not be there, he learned through a spider web of espionage and servants' gossip of the dangerous thoughts expressed in Fedor's house. Of course, the Black Band had its problems. It was not all-powerful—not yet. To break up a secret meeting—and at the same time a few skulls—to waylay by night, beat up savagely a student or actor who had spoken disrespectfully of authority—that was simple enough. But there was not much the Black Band could do when respectable men, men of wealth and power, criticized authority.

"Don't think I like the idea of giving in to the workers," a leading manufacturer said to Fedor one evening. "Freedom of speech, freedom to hold meetings and go on strike—God alone knows what they will ask for next! But what are we to do? Whoever told the czar to shoot Father Gapon's peaceful demonstrators that Bloody Sunday dug his own grave and ours. I know that, many others know that, but do the czar's ministers know it? No, they have one answer to everything we say: no reforms under any circumstances! I hate reforms as much as they do, but if there is anything that can bring order into this blasted chaos it is reforms. And believe me or not, when I hear the workers say they are slaves of the czarist regime, I wonder whether we aren't too. Why can't we forge ahead here the way they do in Germany or in England? Because we aren't civilized and advanced enough to compete with the others abroad. And we can't increase our market at home because those tyrants on top—yes, yes, that's exactly what they are, tyrants—keep the people in poverty, filth, and stupidity!"

The owner of a Petersburg metallurgical plant was at Fedor's that night. On his swallow-tailed coat he wore a golden decoration bestowed on him not so much for his services in supplying the country with ammunition as for the iron fist with which he had handled his workers in the past. He gravely nodded in assent.

Words and nods were dutifully noted by Michel and registered with the Black Band. Of course, these men were out of their reach. But there was no harm in being vigilant. The day would come when the authorities would be grateful.

CHAPTER 9

*1905*

AFTER Petersburg's "Bloody Sunday" in January, 1905, strikes and unrest spread like a contagion throughout Russia. For months the country was convulsed until by October the disturbance culminated in a general strike which threatened to paralyze life. The government was finally convinced that something had to be done. The czar issued a manifesto—a beautiful manifesto, promising a constitution with freedom and civil rights. Prison doors were opened and some political prisoners freed. There was wild enthusiasm in the streets. Thousands marched with red banners and sang the "Marseillaise." Russia, silent throughout centuries, suddenly discovered that she had a voice and became alive and articulate. Everybody spoke. People who had never addressed an audience before made fiery speeches, spitting out their hatreds and hopes. These hatreds and hopes made them great orators.

The new constitution was hailed, and at the same time grudges against the government were openly aired. The workers did more airing than hailing. Instead of beautiful but vague promises for the future, they demanded immediate reforms, immediate free elections to a Constituent Assembly, and complete political amnesty. Many fighters for freedom were still languishing in jails and in Siberia. Their demands grew steadily louder and at times completely drowned out the hails. The peasants became restless too. They wanted bread; they could not fill their stomachs with promises. Burned estates and robbed granaries were the result. Encouraged by police and church, and infuriated by the sight of the red flags, Cossacks and Black Band men displayed increased ferocity, with Jews, students, or workers for their victims. The police stood by silently. The authorities wanted them to stand by silently—the more trouble the better. It was then possible to say, "See, the people really don't care for freedom; this is their way of saying so." The more trouble the more reason the government had to declare that reforms could be introduced only after the country was pacified. But the workers insisted on immediate action. No more fine-sounding phrases for them; only action would do. Their voices grew frighteningly loud.

Some fainthearted liberals, scared by these loud voices, by the peasant uprisings, by the Jewish pogroms, by the Black Band bloody terror, retired into their shells. They did not know how instrumental the authorities were in scaring them away. But many liberals, students, physicians, engineers, lawyers, teachers, writers, actors, used their voices and their pens in support of the workers. They too clamored for immediate action. And they got out of their literary salons and drawing rooms and worked with the people, in the open, at mass meetings, in the press, with strongly worded demands.

For several weeks they all, workers and intellectuals alike, talked and wrote, wrote and talked to their hearts' content. Universities, theaters, clubs, parks, restaurants, army baracks became meeting places where people made speeches, sang, and shouted. Life had moved from a dead point, whirled and rushed forward. It seemed as if czarism might be swept away in this powerful current. But one day the arrests began, arrests of the leaders, arrests of all those who had spoken, written, demanded. The diabolical game was over; the police's dragnet was full. The fighters for freedom had been decoyed out into the open. From the very day of the manifesto, their faces had been revealed for all to see, their names for all to know. A new song was sung in the prisons:

> The czar got very scared
> And issued a manifesto.
> The dead were given freedom,
> The living sent to jail.

The workers did not take it lying down. To their demands for the immediate introduction of the promised constitution, they added the demand that the arrests cease, and those arrested be released. More arrests followed. The workers persisted. Their demands were met with the iron fist of terror. The unarmed masses possessed one weapon only and they used it in Moscow in December 1905: a general strike was declared. The railroads were the first to stop. Only trains with soldiers returning from the war were permitted to move. Then, one after another, factories, printing plants, theaters, streetcars, stores, the post office, the telegraph joined the strike. There was no light, no water, no fuel, no food. Well-armed Cossacks and mounted dragoons patrolled the streets, dispersing crowds. Routed from one place, people assembled in another. At night the streets were empty. Arrests were made then and Black Band men roamed the city disposing of the strike leaders in their own sinister fashion. In the daytime, mounted guardians of order charged into street demonstrations and crowds, trampling the people and whipping them. Some soldiers refused to obey their officers, and some officers joined the demonstrators with their men. The strikers organized themselves into armed units and disarmed some of the police.

Barricades were built. Under the pretext that snipers had been shooting at them, the Cossacks and police fired volleys into houses and into crowds of curious onlookers. Many were killed and wounded. What years of revolutionary propaganda could not have done, the shooting and killing of women and children did. Muscovites of all classes took the side of the insurgents. They helped them build the barricades and invited them to their houses for a hot meal or a night's sleep; they hid them when necessary, and supplied their families with food and shelter. They treated the wounded. They were lavish with funds. For a whole week Moscow struck and fought. It was a long, bloody week. Without the sympathy and help of the population the uprising could not have lasted that long, for the workers were not yet strongly organized. This was their first appearance on the political scene as leaders of an armed revolt. The students were courageous as always and many of them, boys and girls, died during that week on the barricades. This was their curtain scene in Russia's revolutionary fight; from then on, the workers took the lead. But in December, 1905, they all had to give in. The government won. It won with the sheer might of arms and police and Black Band men. Bloody reprisals in Moscow and in the many cities and villages that had joined in the uprising followed the victory. Court-martials raged. Inhuman tortures were inflicted in prisons to force confessions. Many young people died under the tortures.

The backbone of the revolution was broken. The only weapon—the general strike—had failed. The defeat was costly and bitter, but the struggle went on. Not a spectacular struggle, with songs and red banners and marching columns cheered by spectators, but a perilous gallant underground fight. A fight led by men whose lives had no meaning for them unless they were dedicated to freeing Russia from czarist tyranny. Some went abroad, and their printed words of counsel and directive were smuggled over the border; others stayed in the country, took assumed names and disguises, and carried on their agitation against the regime. They were arrested and exiled. They escaped, and were again arrested and exiled, and escaped again. They, as well as those abroad, talked about historical materialism, dialectics, social democracy, surplus values, internationalism, Marxism, constitutional rights. Those might have seemed hard words for people with little education to understand, people who had to read or listen to them after twelve hours of backbreaking work, but decoded into terms of everyday life, those hard words meant food every day, warm clothing and a heated room, care for the infants, sick, and aged, schools, an end to corrupt authority and greedy priests, an end to their gnawing fear of the future.

The agitation and the preparation for the next revolt were conducted mostly among workers. However, few of those who led the fight were workers: Lenin, Trotsky, Radek, Alexandra Kollontai, Bukharin, Martov, Plekhanov—they were intellectuals, political thinkers, students of history, science, and economics. Some of them came from wealthy families. With their education and abilities, they could have had easy comfortable lives, but they chose the hard path of professional revolutionaries. They had an unshaken faith in the cause of freedom and in the ultimate victory.

Those who did not have this faith became disillusioned and felt lost. They tried to drown the bitterness of the failure and the realization of their helplessness in many ways—in scornful cynicism; in exaggerated preoccupation with their soul or with sex; in religion, in philosophy, and in mysticism—in any way that would ease their consciences for having turned their backs on the outside world.

## CHAPTER 10
## *Anton and Maxim*

ANTON was thoroughly disgusted. The revolution was over, and there was no reason life couldn't quiet down and be again what it had been in the past. But it wasn't. People were not the same. You used to know what people were like by the way they dressed and talked, by the carriages they rode in. But only the other day he'd heard about an aristocratic-looking young lady who had stepped out of an elegant landau in front of a jeweler's store on Petrovka. She slipped, they said, and a revolver and a package of illegal leaflets fell out of her sable muff! How could you live if you were all mixed up about people?

He could not even make out what was going on in his own family. Why did they have to tear Vera to pieces? What if she had helped out at the post office during the strike? All her friends had done the same thing. "Strikebreaker," Maxim had called her, and had turned away when she tried to kiss him. "I'll have nothing to do with you, ever!" he'd shouted at her. Strikebreaker! What a fancy word. What words would they invent next?

Now Michel and the young Gavrilovs were mortal enemies. Michel, Kseniya told him, had turned over to the police the names of some of Fedor's friends with reports of the things he'd heard them say. Of course, they'd no business talking like that. But it couldn't feel very good to have on your conscience friends sent to jail or Siberia. Fedor had not been the same since, and no wonder. Ludmilla seemed to feel just as bad too. Yesterday, when she'd come to sit with him for a while, all she'd talked about was the revolution.

"We are so tired, Anton Semenovich," she had said, "so very, very tired. . . . All this shooting, the wounded, the dying, our friends arrested, tortured, some of them dead—and all to no purpose. We're right back where we started. Only it is worse than that. Now we feel so hopeless and beaten . . . We have retired into our own lives . . ."

Now, why should she worry about it, a rich woman like her? It was of no concern to her. Why should she worry about people who were nothing to her? And she had avoided talking about Zena and Pavel at all—he had noticed that. Fedor and Pavel had always been inseparable, but now the revolution had come between them too. Zena had tried to explain it to him. During the strike, Fedor and Ludmilla had opened their house to everyone who wanted to come in, she said. And before long every nook in the house was full. So Fedor asked Pavel to take some people in, and Zena had definitely said no, and right she was. How can you let people from the streets into your house? Suppose they robbed you? Suppose your children caught some infectious disease? Zena certainly was right. But since then things had never been the same; Fedor and Pavel hardly saw each other now, outside of business. Neither did they see much of anyone else, even Fedor, whose house used to be like a railroad station, open to everyone.

"Retired into our own lives," had Ludmilla said? What had gotten into them all? That was exactly what Olga had written the other day, her first letter in a long time. They had had plenty of trouble in their village too. The peasants had set fire to the landlord's estate and some people had burned to death. The Cossacks had come then and several peasants had been shot and others sent to Siberia for hard labor. Gregor's school had been closed for a long while, and he was allowed to open it again only after he had promised to give up his adult classes and teach the children nothing but to read and write. So they had retired into their own lives, Olga had written, in order not to endanger the existence of the school.

Igor seemed to have done the same thing, not that he had ever had much to do with anyone else. But now they almost never saw him, except occasionally at meals, and he never opened his mouth unless to answer yes or no to a question. Nothing seemed to interest him. There was just no life in the boy at all. His pale face and body were nothing but skin and bones. Too bad Maxim couldn't give him some of his zest for life.

There was a boy who was not going to miss anything—not he. Imagine standing all night long to get a ticket to hear a man sing, even if his name was Chaliapin, or to see someone act! He could perfectly well get a box, as the rest of the family did when they went to the theater. But no, he'd rather stand all night with a bunch of other fools to get a seat in the gallery, where you could neither see nor hear. And the way they behaved there in the gallery was outrageous! At that play last week which praised the government they'd made such a racket with their boos and yells and catcalls that the management had had to close the play! And of course Maxim had had his hand in it. The way he boasted about it at home afterward, you'd think he'd saved a thousand people from death. The great hero!

Now that life was more or less orderly again, and there were no meetings for him to be running to all the time, it did seem that Maxim might forget his foolishness and remember that there were books to study. Anton snorted as he thought of those meetings. That was all you'd read about in the paper those days. Metallists, printers, textile workers, railroadmen, clerks, pharmacists, architects, barbers, masons, electricians, tailors, carpenters—who did they think was doing their work for them while they were jabbering away at their meetings? And the speakers they had! Nothing but people with Jewish names, or Georgians or Armenians or Tartars or Poles or Germans.

Anton spat in disgust; then, bored with his thoughts, began listening to the noises in the house. Kseniya was out shopping; the cook had gone to market; the maids were cleaning the rooms. From the kitchen came the clatter of dishes. That would be the kitchenmaid Dunya. Pretty girl, that Dunya. Maxim seemed to think so too. Spent half his time in the kitchen lately. Wasn't that his step now, going down the kitchen stairs?

Anton smiled. He might just as well listen to what was going on there. His pains weren't so bad now; a little walking would do him good. And if someone found him near the kitchen—well, it wasn't the first time he'd gone to look at the fish the cook brought from the market. Anton freed himself from the blanket Kseniya had tucked around his knees. He fastened the cord around his robe and reached for his cane, the one with the rubber end. He reached the kitchen door and smiled again as he heard Maxim's voice, eager and quick. Seemed to be working hard to convince the girl. That was good. A bad girl wouldn't have needed much convincing from the young master. Maxim's words came clearly through the door. Anton's smile changed suddenly to a frown.

"But the last speaker," Maxim was saying excitedly, "he was the best of all. 'Comrades,' he cried out, 'now or never! We have a chance to change our miserable hungry lives into decent happy lives. Are we going to miss this chance?' 'No! No!' we yelled so that the walls shook. 'Are we going to do it?' 'Yes! we will!' we yelled again. And then we sang. Oh, it was wonderful! You should have been there, Dunya. Ah, that's right, I forgot you had your meeting. How was it?"

"Ours surely wasn't anything like yours," Dunya said. "What could you expect? We have no educated people. One man, though, the way he spoke he certainly was educated. I didn't understand much of what he was saying. But the others, I understood them fine. They didn't make long speeches the way you do at your meetings. But we liked them a lot. One girl she only said: 'I am first up in the morning when it's dark and only when the last of them is in bed can I crawl under my coat on the kitchen floor.' After her an old woman got up and said: 'My masters, they wouldn't let me sleep in the kitchen. It spoils the air, they say. There is a trunk in the hall. That's where I sleep,' she said. And such an old woman too. And then another made a speech. 'I sleep with a sick child,' she said, 'and the child whines all night long, and don't think they let me off my feet all God's day long . . .'"

There was silence as if Dunya thought this could not be interesting for Maxim. Then she suddenly laughed.

"There was one girl, just like an actress. She kept changing her voice and sounded like the people she talked about. Just listen to this. She sleeps on the floor near the stairway. One night the master comes home late, stumbles over her, and almost falls. She showed us how he stumbled. Next morning she heard him say to the mistress, 'My dear, don't you think Zhenia—that's the girl's name—ought to sleep somewhere else? Why doesn't she sleep in the kitchen?' 'My dear, how can you suggest that? A servant sleeping where our food is being prepared! Fi donc!' 'How about the spare children's room, my dear?' 'How can you say that? Did you forget that our Hector sleeps there?' Hector is their dog. 'My dear, couldn't she sleep with Hector?' 'But, don't you know, my dear, that all servants have a bad odor, and you forget how delicate our Hector is. He couldn't sleep a wink with her in the room.' We were sick laughing at her and the 'my dear!'"

The door of the servants' entrance opened and Anton wondered whom it was that the two youngsters gave such a hearty welcome to. "Hello, you two!" said the newcomer in a loud cheerful voice. "I'm in a hurry, so let's hear it quick, Maxim! Hope you did it right!"

Anton listened unbelievingly. It was their former maid Dasha, the sour sulky Dasha, Dasha with her rickety hateful bastard! Neither Kseniya or later Vera had ever had the heart to send her away and Vera had been glad when she left of her own accord to work in a factory. Anton had seen her when she had come for her last wages. "Good-by, citizen Nazarov," she had had the impudence to say to him. He'd almost choked with rage. And now she was here and talking to his own son as if she could give him orders. And instead of shutting her off and showing her the door, listen to him!

"I wrote it all down, Dasha, the way you told me. Here it is. I hope you like it. If you think it's all right, I could help with the mimeographing. Dunya could help too."

Anton was furious; Maxim's voice sounded so anxious to please. He was fortunately spared the sight of his son's face. Maxim was looking at Dasha as if his very life depended on whether or not she liked what he had written.

"Let me hear it now, but go slowly, don't rush. You know that it takes time till those hard words go into my head . . . And you know what, Dunya, a cup of tea helps; it kind of makes my head lighter." Dasha laughed out loud. Anton had not heard her laugh for many years.

Maxim was reading:

"'The normal working day is never less than twelve hours, sometimes as much as sixteen . . . And what are we getting? Never more than a miserable fifteen to twenty rubles a month, sometimes as few as eight. . . . And how do the rich live? Strawberries in the middle of the winter! Champagne bought by the case! Hothouse grapes, raised and shipped especially for them. . . . Our children suffer from undernourishment; the children of the rich from overeating. Thousands of poor children die at birth. When we ask for shorter working hours, we are asked, What do you want more leisure for? You will only go to a saloon and get drunk. . . . We age early, much sooner than we should. When we get sick, our families starve, our wives and daughters sell themselves, our children die. . . . The foremen treat us like dirt, they bully us and they violate our women. . . . When we are injured at work, we are thrown out like garbage, and when we ask for safety devices, we are delivered to the police for rebelling. . . . Our women's hands are swollen and twisted from washing clothes in holes cut in the river's ice; when we ask to have water in the barracks, we are told to go look for work elsewhere. . . . How long are we going to stand our poverty so that the rich can grow fat on our sweat and our tears? . . . Comrades, brothers, there is strength in unity. Let us unite! Now is the moment for it! Don't let bayonets and bullets silence us. Death is better than the lives we live. They cannot kill all of us!'"

Maxim had finished. He was afraid to raise his eyes and hear Dasha's verdict. But a soft smile made Dasha's thin yellowish freckled face seem almost pretty.

"Good, good, Maxim, very good! For the son of a bloodsucker you do very well." Anton winced at the sound of Maxim's chuckle. "And to think that in a way I am responsible for it. If you hadn't found me that day crying my eyes out over my unlucky brat you might never have known what a miserable life the poor have. That was the day your eyes were opened. Keep them open. And now I must go. That's a good job you've done, Maxim. I'm sure the committee will approve."

Again Dasha laughed, and left the room with a light quick step that was very different from her former slow listless trudge.

Anton spat loudly. So meetings were still going on! Meetings, meetings, meetings! Like monsters, these meetings shadowed their lives. And now they had swallowed up his son, his own son, Maxim, whom he was sending to a university so that he should bring glory to the family with his education and refinement. And what happened? That slut, that tramp, that vermin, got him with her blasted committee and her workers and her meetings and worked him up against his own father. Bloodsucker, she called him, and Maxim laughed. He would crush her like a louse. He would set the dogs on her, if it weren't for that blasted constitution. But everybody talks about rights now! A father couldn't give his own son a sound thrashing and forbid him to go to meetings or have anything to do with the revolution! A master couldn't throw his former servant out of the house! . . . It wasn't right for Maxim to spend his time with a pretty healthy girl talking about workers and meetings! Did the constitution put water into a young man's blood?

Stifling his groans, Anton reached his room and, exhausted with pain and fury, sank into his chair.

On a few more occasions Anton heard Maxim's voice in the kitchen and listened at the door. He found out that Dasha was a member of the revolutionary committee and that Maxim was writing leaflets for them. They must have liked his leaflets, because Dasha came often and every time Maxim read a new leaflet to her. Once he had one on students. One of their girls had killed herself in prison, after being tortured. The students wanted to have a regular funeral service for her, but the police refused to permit it. Thousands of students demonstrated in the streets and demanded a decent funeral. They were shot at; some were killed, and many others wounded. Maxim certainly wrote it up beautifully. Anton, listening behind the door, had to admit it. He liked much less the one which Maxim read a few days later. One on the priests. It was true, all right, that the priests showed little saintliness, that they were more concerned with serving the police and filling their own pockets than with giving comfort to the people. But still a priest was a priest, and one had to respect him.

"What do the priests teach the people?" Maxim declaimed with feeling. " 'It is your own fault,' they say, 'that you are poor. Don't drink, don't smoke; work harder, go to church, respect the authorities!' That's what they tell us. But do they ever do anything for us? Have you ever heard of a priest who would do anything for you unless he was paid for it? . . . We believe in God, but can we worship God in church? What do we hear in church? That we should hate Jews, Poles, Tartars, and anybody else who worships God in a different way. Is that Christianity? The priests tell us to aspire to reach heaven, but do they mind our living in hell on earth? No, they want us to live like worms and never raise our heads. They know once we raise our heads—they will be the ones to suffer."

That was the last leaflet Anton heard Maxim read to Dasha. Soon afterward, in the spring of 1906, he suffered a stroke, and never again recovered the use of his legs. His former study was converted into a bedroom. The heavy bookcase was moved to another room and his bed, hidden behind a Japanese screen, took its place. Otherwise, little was changed. The cumbersome green-plush furniture, the oleanders, the heavy gilded frames of Repin's "Cossacks" and Vasnetzov's "Knights," the old, loud clock, the stuffed eagle over the door, the shelves with the bric-a-brac, remained where they had always been. During the day Anton grew tired of looking at them, but in the evening, when the lamps were lit, the familiar dull objects took on a new aspect. And in the evenings Kseniya was always there. All day Anton looked forward to the hour when the house would quiet down and the lamps would change the room and Kseniya would take her place at her embroidery frame. Evening after evening, they sat alone there, Kseniya never leaving the room except to spend a few minutes with Grandmother and Nyanya. Vera and Zena seldom came in the evening, and they never stayed long. Igor spent the evenings alone in his room, and Maxim was almost never at home. Occasionally Anton read aloud something that interested him in a paper or magazine, but otherwise they exchanged few words.

It was in this room that Anton consoled Kseniya when Grandmother died. Two weeks later Grandmother was followed by Nyanya, whose emaciated body could only have been kept alive by the miracle of her devotion to her old mistress. After that, Kseniya never left the room in the evening.

It was to this room too that one evening Maxim, now twenty-one, brought a resisting, tearful Dunya.

Maxim swallowed and made an effort to give his nervous voice steadiness:

"Father, Mother, Dunya and I are going to have a baby. . . . We are going to get married . . ."

Kseniya hurried over to Anton and took his hand. He should avoid all excitement, the doctor had warned.

"Maxim, for mercy's sake, you will kill your father!"

"Maxim, I told you so, please, let me go. . . . I didn't want it, Kseniya Nikolaevna, I didn't, Anton Semenovich, believe me . . ."

Stammering and crying, Dunya tried to free her hand from Maxim's grip. He would not let go. He cleared his voice for the next thrust: "And why should my marrying Dunya kill my father? What is wrong with her?"

"I beg you, son, have mercy on us," Kseniya implored him, "look at your father . . ."

A grayish shadow encircled Anton's sunken eyes. His lips moved, trying to form words. Kseniya bent close to his mouth. "Let him speak, Kseniya," he whispered.

Maxim was disheartened by his father's face. If Anton had raged and shouted as he used to years ago, it would have been easy to fight back. But how could he attack this helpless invalid? Finally he managed to get out the words he had rehearsed so many times since that day the week before when Dunya had told him that she was pregnant.

"What is wrong with her? There was nothing wrong with her when you chose her, was there? When the doctor examined her like a horse? When Mother told the other servants to give us opportunities to be alone? And suppose everything had gone the way you wanted it to when she first came here three years ago? A girl, as good as either one of my sisters would have been thrown out as thousands of others like her were. And why? Because your father and grandfather knew how to grab money and hers didn't! Well, your plan didn't work. I am not a scoundrel. I approached her as a decent man, after a long courtship, after I was sure we loved each other. If we didn't wait till we were married, it's only because we don't believe in priests. Priest or no priest, she is my wife. I know that in your eyes, and the eyes of the world you live in, the right thing to do is to sell and buy wives, and to make prostitutes and suicides out of decent girls like Dunya. But ours is a new world. In the world we are going to live in, there will be no rich and poor, no aristocrats being paid for their wives, no girls selling their womanhood for a piece of bread. You can turn us out of the house; we are not afraid. We are young and we can work. There are many like us. . . ."

"Enough now." Anton's voice was strong again. "You had your say. Mine will be shorter. No kitchenmaid is going to live in my house as my son's wife, and no bastards are going to be my grandchildren. Go now and make your choice, go!"

His arm around the crying Dunya, Maxim walked toward the door. The handle in his hands, he hesitated a moment. No, he must not look at them now. It would be too hard to take the next step if he did. He pushed the handle down and opened the door.

"Anton, Anton, I beseech you, don't let him go, don't drive our child out. . . . Maxim, don't go, Father doesn't mean it, he doesn't know what he is saying . . ." Kseniya was in agony, torn between fear for Anton's life and fear of losing her son.

The door had closed behind Maxim and Dunya. Sobbing, Kseniya ran after them. The sound of a broken glass stopped her. Reaching for his sedative Anton had overturned the water pitcher.

"My little son, my little son, wait, don't go, wait for me," Kseniya called.

She ran back to Anton. She couldn't leave him. He was pitiful to look at. His lips, pressed hard together, were a narrow bluish line. The muscles of his face twitched and quivered. He tried to stop it by pressing his lips so tightly that his face contorted into a terrible grimace. Beads of perspiration gave his skin a greenish corpselike shimmer and glued his thin hair to his skull. His eyes had almost disappeared in their dark hollows. Kseniya's heart cried out with pity. With shaking fingers, Anton fumbled and tugged at his covers. The water from the pitcher had soaked through the blankets and clothing and he was shivering with cold. Kseniya changed him and warmed him. Only when the sedative and the sleeping pills had wiped the tortured expression from his face, when he had relaxed and fallen into a slumber, did Kseniya let herself think of her son.

Her feet flew on the stairs. Maxim heard her calling and opened his door and took her gently in his arms. Dunya, squatting on the floor, was fastening a leather strap around Maxim's books. She left the room immediately. An open cardboard box held a few of their belongings. Then he was leaving!

Maxim led Kseniya to his bed and sat down with her, comforting her. Kseniya, with a sigh, rested her head on his shoulder and at length grew quiet. This was not the first time a child of hers had mothered and comforted her and made her feel the child instead of the mother. Fifteen years ago Olga had done it. There was nothing she had been able to do then because Anton had been so strong that she could not go against his will. And there was nothing she could do now, because Anton was so weak that going against his will might kill him.

"Mother, my little mother, my dear little mother," Maxim murmured. He kissed her hands and her face and tried hard to remember that he was a man, a husband.

"All right, son, it all will be all right, I am sure it all will be all right." She even had the strength now to give him a smile. "Get the icon down and call Dunya."

She blessed them both. She wanted to give them money but they would not take it.

"Please, Kseniya Nikolaevna, believe me, I don't want anything from Maxim, nothing at all, I assure you." Dunya's eyes, filled with tears, implored Kseniya to believe her. "I would go away alone, right now, if he would let me. But he won't. I will work, I will work hard, always. He can go on studying, I will never be in his way, never."

Kseniya pressed her to her heart. She could not fight with Anton now, she had to give in and let Maxim and Dunya leave the house. But she was not going to deprive herself of her son as she had of her daughter. He would belong to her, and so would Dunya. Dunya was not the little kitchenmaid now. She was a woman who had given her love to Maxim as a gift and not for a reward. When the child came, they would be ready to accept her help. Oh, yes, she would help them and she would have them in her life. She was not going to tear her heart out again.

After they left, Kseniya returned to Anton. He was still asleep. She sat with her needlework so that when he opened his eyes he wouldn't have to turn his head to look at her. She would be good to him, very good, but she was going to talk to him about Maxim as soon as he awakened. If she didn't do it at once, she might never be able to, and then it would be as it had been with Olga, whose name they had never mentioned. She would talk to him today, and she would not let him forbid her and the others to talk about Maxim.

When Anton woke, hours later, Kseniya put down the embroidery she was almost too tired to see and spoke at once. At her first words, the old Anton flared up. His face became frighteningly red and he pounded furiously on the floor with his cane. Kseniya went quietly on, her hand over his, gently smoothing back his stray wisps of hair. Slowly, Anton was subdued.

## CHAPTER 11
## Igor

IN this same room two years later, Anton and Kseniya were getting ready to settle for a quiet evening. Igor had not appeared for dinner. He was working on a literary magazine now and had irregular hours. Kseniya had just helped the cook prepare a tray for him of cold chicken, marinated mushrooms, cranberry jelly, cake, milk, and his favorite Antonovka apples. They were not expecting anyone that night. The night before they had had one of their now rare family reunions. Both young Gavrilovs with their wives, and the Dolinins had been there. There had not been much conversation. With Michel Dolinin around, words had to be carefully watched, and everybody tried to keep the talk on the weather and the horse races. But Vera, in her intense desire to identify herself completely with Michel's world, had said some things about "traitors to the czar" which made Fedor squirm. Anton did not mind her remarks—he was all for the czar. But he did not see why she had to be so superior about it. Did she think that one had to have her husband's blue blood to be a loyal servant of the throne?

Kseniya minded neither Vera's remarks nor her haughtiness. She did mind—and very much—something else. Maxim and Dunya might have come to the house now—Anton had finally agreed to that—if Vera had not objected. But Vera made her promise that Maxim should not put foot in his father's house, for she had been terrified that Michel's friends would get wind of the scandal.

Vera had had trouble enough with the mystery of her sister Olga. But society had long ago accepted her dramatic story of Olga's devotion to an eccentric old aunt. Vera had embroidered the story with great imagination. Olga had become a beautiful captive in a mysterious castle, where she sacrificed her life to the whim of an old woman possessed of an uncanny power over people. That at least was a good story and even an asset. But what could she make of a brother who insisted on marrying a kitchenmaid after he had made her pregnant? When Michel heard of it, he had said that they could not possibly stay in Moscow. He had even half jokingly hinted that a Dolinin could not be a member of a family which harbored a kitchenmaid. No, her efforts of years should not be destroyed by the caprice of a stupid youngster. If Maxim did not stay away from the family, she had warned, she would have to break with them, break openly, so that there could be no doubt in anyone's mind that she, Vera Dolinin, had nothing to do with the Nazarovs.

She had again made that clear to Kseniya only the night before, just as she was going upstairs to say good night to Igor. Thinking of it now, as she settled down to her knitting, Kseniya recalled Vera had stayed with Igor for quite a long while. She could hear the maid taking the tray up to Igor now. She sounded clumsy climbing the stairs, and Kseniya hoped she would not drop anything.

Anton watched Kseniya through half-closed eyes. She was sitting down now, spreading out her wide skirts. In a minute she would start knitting those socks for the poor. There, the knitting needles had begun to move.

A terrible scream rang through the house, followed by the noise of a falling tray. The house, which had seemed deserted an instant earlier, was suddenly full of people—running, crying, screaming. Anton recognized Kseniya's voice—a terrifying blood-curdling scream. He heard someone fall heavily. "Kseniya, Kseniya, what's happened, Kseniya!" he called. White and shaking, he knocked with his cane on the floor, the chair, the table, wherever he could reach. Nobody heard him.

Kseniya had left the door open when she ran upstairs. An apple, which had danced down step by step, rolled into the room, a large Antonovka apple. He heard Kseniya's voice again, closer. The servants led her into the room; they were almost carrying her. But that was not Kseniya, that could not be Kseniya. It was her dress, the blue velvet fur-trimmed robe she had been wearing a moment ago; those were her white fur slippers. But that crazed distorted face wasn't hers, the voice wasn't hers. Those hoarse cries couldn't be coming from her. Rocking her body back and forth, back and forth, she tugged at her hair. "No, no, no, no, it isn't true, it can't be, it can't be!" she kept screaming.

The cook was the first to think of Anton and to tell him what had happened. When the maid had opened the door, she had found Igor's body dangling in the air. He must have been dead for many hours. They thought he had not come home for dinner, but he had not left the house at all. All that time he had been hanging there. Anton sank back in his chair, trying to make himself smaller and smaller, as if by doing so he could disappear and remove himself from this horror. But there was Kseniya. It took an almost superhuman effort, but he finally found the strength to reach out his hand and touch her hair. But where was her hair? This moist hot stringy mass was not his Kseniya's hair. Where was Kseniya? Where was her hair? He pushed her away and screamed. Or so he thought. His hand slid off Kseniya's head and everything around became black.

After hours of stupor, prolonged by the doctor's injections, Anton opened his eyes. Ludmilla, her eyes red and swollen, was leaning over him.

"Ludmilla, what happened to you, why are you crying?" he asked feebly, reaching out for her hand to comfort her. "What is it? Tell me." Why was she crying? Anton looked around. Where was Kseniya? Why did Zena keep coming in and out of the room? She was crying too. Why were Fedor and Pavel there?

"Why are you and Zena crying, Ludmilla? Where is Kseniya? Please call Kseniya, I want Kseniya. Please, call her, and don't cry, please. Why are you crying?" A monstrous hairy beast was creeping closer and closer to him. He mustn't let it come. He knew it was bringing agony and hell. That monster mustn't come near him, mustn't come, mustn't come. But the monster did come and hell came with it. And the hell was Igor's body dangling in the air.

He heard raucous sounds coming out of his own throat. The monster must be taken away. Kseniya should make it go and leave him alone. He told Ludmilla all this in a loud voice and with gestures of his hands. But all anyone heard was those raucous sounds and all anyone saw was a faint twitching of his fingers.

Anton's feverish brain fought the monster that was teasing him with Igor's swaying body. He talked incessantly to the doctors, the nurses, Kseniya, Zena, Ludmilla, Vera, Fedor, Pavel, Maxim, whoever was around, telling them about the monster and imploring them to chase it away. It was many days later that the incoherent noises began to sound like words and that the burning wandering eyes were able to take notice of faces and objects. The monster was gone. But it did not take the image of Igor's hanging body with it. That was there to stay. That was real. It was in the black dresses and in the eyes of the women. And most of all it was in Kseniya, in his beloved Kseniya. Yes, that old woman was Kseniya. The slightly graying chestnut waves had become white and untidy, the youthful figure was bent, the smooth face wrinkled, and the agile walk heavy and slow.

When his mind cleared, Anton buried himself in long silences. Now that he was out of danger and recovering, the children no longer took turns at his bedside, although they came in occasionally for visits. Their visits, however, grew shorter and shorter, for the house, never too cheerful, was sunk in a depression which was hard to bear. Kseniya's grief was too deep to let her get comfort from anybody's presence. A somber silence reigned in the room. Nothing from the outside aroused any response in either Anton or Kseniya, not even their grandchildren. Staring into emptiness, Anton sat for hours without saying a word. When Kseniya was close to him he touched her hair or shoulders or hands and murmured, "Don't cry, Kseniya, don't cry, tears will not bring him back." When Kseniya tried to drown her unbearable suffering in physical pain, when she knocked her head against her chair or wrung her hands and cried out in agony, "Why, why, why did Igor do it? Didn't we love him enough? What did we fail to do? What? Why? Why?" Anton remained silent. That was what he was doing all the time: trying to answer the why.

Vera was the only one who knew the answer. When she had gone up to say good night to Igor the evening before his death, she had found him lying on the bed in his clothes, his body convulsed by sobs. When he saw her, he dried his tears and lay still, clutching something to his chest.

"Igor, Igor, what is the matter with you? I came to say good night to you. What is it?" Vera's voice had none of the affected brightness she had adopted in her new role. It was the sincerely troubled voice of a worried older sister. When he made no answer, she put her arms around him and made him lift his face. It was a tortured face with desperate lonely eyes. Vera bedded his head in her arms, she kissed him and murmured softly into his ear:

"Igor, my darling little brother, don't be unhappy; everything will work out, whatever it is; you will see. Nothing lasts long. Forget it. Someday we will laugh about it together, you and I, the way we used to laugh together, remember? Don't be unhappy, Igor, please. Please, my dear, what is it?"

Igor took a deep breath. "I am afraid, Vera, I am afraid," he finally whispered "Life is a terrible thing. . . . Oh, you wouldn't understand it . . . you have all you want. How can you know how it feels to be afraid of life?" He tried to free himself from Vera's arms but she wouldn't let him go.

"Afraid of life, you say? Is that what is the matter with you? Afraid of life?" She was not murmuring softly now. She was looking straight into his face.

He must be mistaken; it couldn't be fear he saw in her eyes. "Vera, are you afraid of life too? Vera, you, who have everything? You are afraid?"

"Yes, Igor, I am. I'm terribly afraid. Life horrifies me. It glitters only only on the surface, I found out. What goes on inside is horrible . . . I try never to think of it. We must not think of it, Igor, we must not . . ." Now it was Vera who hid her face in his arms.

"Vera, Vera too is afraid of life. Vera is afraid . . ." Igor repeated the words incredulously.

Vera was crying with relief. She had said it; she had said aloud something she had never admitted even to herself. For a little while they sat there, holding each other tightly. Suddenly Igor pushed Vera away fiercely.

"Go now, go, go, don't stay here, leave me, go away, don't touch me, don't dare to touch me, go, go . . ." He pushed her out of the room, carefully not to let her touch him. All the time he held clutched tightly in his hand a notebook in a gray paper cover.

After the first shock of Igor's death was over, Vera looked for the notebook. From the way he had held on to it, she thought, it must have been very important to him. She found it; it was his diary. He must have forgotten about it while preparing for death. He would not have left it for prying eyes.

". . . I heard them again . . . They think I am afraid to go home in the dark. They think this is why I stay there overnight . . . Last time I slept there they were quiet all night long. But yesterday I heard them well . . . They were talking and laughing afterwards. Zena never laughs like that during the day . . . I wish I were older; I wish I had the courage to try it . . . Grisha says he did it, and he is a year younger than I am, he is not fifteen yet . . .

"God, God Almighty, why did You let me, why didn't You warn me? . . . That dreadful, that hideous woman; she was reeking with stinking tobacco and vodka . . . what she was trying to do to me, O God, what she was trying to do to me. The way she laughed, the way the others laughed. How was I to know they were watching us behind the curtain? . . . And my spine gets cold when I think how I couldn't button my pants . . . Will I ever forget it? How can I go on living? . . .

"Three weeks have passed, but it is still as if it had just happened. Even in my sleep I feel her coarse hands on my body . . . Father was in a good mood yesterday; he offered me a sip of his vodka. I couldn't refuse, I touched the glass. I almost vomited right there over the table. I can't forget her smell . . .

". . . so much lying, always lying. I hate school. I hate the way they boast. I hate to listen to Grisha and Andrei. I wish I knew whether they were telling the truth. I never tell them the truth. At home I'm always lying too. I tell them I have a headache or homework to do, or that I have to go borrow a book from a school friend. I tell them any lie to be left alone, to get away from home. I take the skates and they think I go skating. I hate skating. I've never skated since the day I fell and that girl tripped and fell on top of me. I couldn't get up, and they thought I had broken something or fainted. My legs wouldn't hold me. She had touched my body . . . I couldn't let a woman touch my body; I will never let a woman touch my body, never. . . .

"Father will never know what he did for me today. I couldn't have gone to work in the firm. I would have killed myself if he had forced me. And I couldn't have gone to college. Why can't I be the way Maxim and the others are? They are healthy, they are not cursed. They don't have to think of this one thing all the time, all the time, all the time. . . . I look at my own mother with poisoned eyes. Could there be a greater sin than that? I look at her and I wonder about her body; I wonder about her and Father . . . I always have to think of their bodies when I look at women, even at very old women or little children. I cannot remember when it first started. When I was a little boy I always tried to watch Mother or Zena or Vera get dressed. I looked at them and it bothered me but I liked to look at them and I thought about it when I was in bed . . .

". . . I hate my bed. I hate my bed. It is soiled, not really soiled; I never forget the towel; it is soiled by my thinking. When I walked into the room yesterday, the maid was making the bed. She was leaning over it. All I saw of her was her legs spread wide apart . . . I almost lost my mind. I rushed out of the room . . . All night long I saw those legs in my bed . . .

"I went with Grisha last night. I think he knows now that I fooled him. He had a funny smile when I was telling him what a good time I had. The girls must have told him that I disappeared the moment he went upstairs. He wants me to join the League of Free Love. He says that's much better. The girls there aren't whores. They are students . . .

"I haven't written since I went with Grisha to the League of Free Love. He was right. The girls are different there. Most of them high school girls. No chairs in the room, only deep soft couches, and the floor is covered with a thick rug on which they throw cushions. In the big room they have a few candles. The shades are always down, during the day too. Over the shades they have dark-red velvet hangings. The world outside is shut out. Many words are prohibited. You can't mention words like newspapers, politics, work, duties, school, government, and many more. They have pictures on the walls, with nothing but naked bodies on them, naked men and naked women together . . . They have flowers, very dark flowers, and a heavy perfume in the air . . . The candles flicker over the bodies. Some of them naked all the time . . . It is very hard to write about it. But I must force myself. I don't want to go insane; I must get cured. And this might be the cure. To force myself to think about it quietly and to write about it . . . to write about Zoika . . . Zoika is more a snake than a girl. She has flaming red hair and her eyes are green and glittering. She wears a tight shimmering green dress. It clings to her like a snake's skin. She dances winding and twisting her body like a snake. When she takes off her dress her body keeps the green shimmer. When she first saw me, she looked at me for a long while, and said, 'Love is wonderful, come, I'll show you.' When she talks, her sharp little tongue moves like a snake's fangs. She kissed me. It wasn't really a kiss. Her tongue drank me. I fainted. When I opened my eyes, I was on a couch, her body was twined around mine like a snake's body . . . She wanted me to go into the other, the dark room . . . I ran away . . . Next day I went again. I told myself that I had to go because it would cure me. But I went because I had to see Zoika again. This time a blonde girl, Alyona, almost a child, with the face of an angel, dressed in a long white robe, her long hair falling below her waist called to me, 'Come, I am alone.' I wanted to run away. But Zoika saw me, and said I was hers. But I wouldn't go to the dark room with her . . .

"I go there every day. I can't stay away for one single day . . . I know now that it's not a cure, that it is a poison worse than all the other poisons . . . Zoika has never got me to the dark room, although she always tries . . . but she never will . . . Her kisses leave me drained . . . her fingers play with me and give me unbearable delight . . . I would give my life to be with her in that other room . . . to be with her the way the others are with the girls . . . I can't . . .

"Grisha told me that Alyona took poison. Alyona, the blonde child, pregnant and syphilitic. She is the third of the league girls to kill herself, and one boy did it. Now all the others have joined the Suicide Club. Are they right? Is this the only way out? . . .

"I am a patriot. I am a great Russian patriot . . . And I am drunk, I know I am drunk. But I am a hero. I help my country. Doesn't the government get all the profits from the vodka I drink? It is very patriotic to drink, very patriotic. I love my country, I make my country rich, I make it gloriously rich . . . I am a great patriot . . . I am very drunk . . .

"I am afraid to hope. I have hoped so often and always my hopes have turned to ashes. I am working; I am working like all normal people are working. How wonderful it sounds: 'I am preparing the poetry section in a literary magazine . . .' I go in the morning, like all people who work do, and stay there all day long. God, make this real, make me work hard, make me think of my work only, make me again write my own poetry and enjoy the poetry of others. . . .

"I still hope. Mother knows that something good is happening to me; she seems happy about it but she doesn't say anything. My heart feels warm because I am doing something that makes Mother happy. I wish I could talk to her. I wish I could talk to anyone. The other people who work here go out together in the evening; they laugh together and they discuss things. I try to be part of them, I really try it, I don't want to be an outsider. I try not to make them realize what a stranger I am in their midst. But I cannot talk to anyone about myself. . . .

"I went to the opera. I used to like music, and I thought it might help me. But that is false too. How can one sing when one is dying or announcing that dinner is served? And then in the intermission all came out, the dead ones too. It's all unreal. Lies everywhere, even in music. While the heroine was singing lustily on her deathbed, I was thinking about death. I very often think about death. Isn't it the best, the only way to end all misery? Why don't I do it? What makes me cling to life? Is it because of Mother? I don't know. Maybe I hope that someday it will straighten out. There is always time to die . . .

"I've fooled myself for a long time now. I've pretended there was still hope for me in my work. But there is no salvation for me, none anywhere. Could anything mean more to me than living with poetry? But it doesn't mean anything to me any more. I do it as I eat, as I put on my shoes, as I go to the toilet. Where else is there hope? I've sometimes thought a girl like Dunya could save me, a simple good girl. But such a girl would never come near me. What is left? Loneliness and secret vices . . . loneliness and pain and misery, everlasting mortifying misery. Loneliness, doesn't that mean to be alone? No, the worst loneliness, the one that eats your heart out with pain, is the one you know among people. . . .

"This is the end. I am very quiet, very peaceful now. I know this is the end of all misery. Tonight, for a short moment, I had hope again. It was Vera who gave me hope. I found out that she is afraid of life too. Nobody can be happy if even Vera is unhappy. That thought gave me hope. It meant that one can be unhappy inside and still live the way other people live and enjoy life. Vera enjoys life. I had hope again . . . And then, then the terrible thing happened . . . Vera, my sister Vera was not a sister. The touch of her arms, her body, was not that of a sister. Had she stayed another minute, she would have known it. I couldn't control myself. . . . I am the greatest sinner on earth. There is no hope for me."

Vera burned the diary. It certainly was not meant for anyone's eyes. She was horrified. Not because she thought she was the cause of Igor's death. His diary made it clear that he would have put an end to his life anyway. What horrified her was that such misery could exist in a person's life and that no one, not even those closest to him, should know anything about it. It was true, Igor had always been pale and silent and shy. They had thought him queer and teased him by calling him a poet and a genius. But that was all. Had anyone ever tried to find out why he was so silent and forlorn? Poor little brother! But unhappiness often lay behind smiles and indifferent looks, and no one the wiser. Did even Michel, the dearest and closest of all, know that when she talked to him questions, never stopping, hammered in her mind:

Where were you last night? With whom? What did you do? When did you come home? Where are you really going now? Where did you come from now? Were you with a woman . . .

Igor had several poems in his diary, his own and other poets'. Vera tore out one by Tiutchev.

Be silent, hidden and conceal
Whate'er you dread, whate'er you feel . . .
The heart was born dumb: who can sense
Its tremors, recondite?
And who can hear its silent cry?
A thought when spoken is a lie . . .*

Sitting at her parents' feet, Vera wondered as she had never wondered before about their lives, about Olga, Maxim, Zena. What did she know about them? She looked into the faces of servants and friends. What went on in their minds and hearts? What did they hide? Wearing a plain black dress, her hair combed straight back, without make-up, her studied brightness put aside, Vera for once in her life looked at others with interest and compassion.

But not for very long. The mourning wardrobe had to be attended to. The children wanted her. Michel could not be left to himself for too long. Of course, of course, she believed him when he said that he was lonely, that he missed her, that he needed her more than her parents did. He still played his part masterfully. She was not fooled by his playing any more, but it was better when she was not away from home.

Her whole life had to be rearranged, for the period of mourning had to be strictly observed. Balls, theaters, and horse races, big dinner parties were out. But one could always have a few friends for tea or for a small dinner. And there was nothing wrong about working at charity socials and bazaars, and they could be quite entertaining. At times she felt guilty about taking up her social life so soon after Igor's death and while her parents were still deeply enwrapped in their misery, but the horror of Igor's death, of his diary, faded quickly away. Tiutchev's poem was forgotten. The smooth sheltered walls closed in again around her. The cracks through which for a short moment she had tried to peer into other people's hearts disappeared. The shadow of the horror remained in appropriate words and gestures, in a very becoming black attire, and it was adroitly fitted into her role of Perfect Model of an Aristocratic Lady. The tragedy turned out well for Vera. Michel was proud of her. She might have lost her poise and overdone her affliction, as her parents did, but his own mother and sisters could not have behaved better. With little attentions and pleasant words he showed her how pleased he was with her. When he assured her that he preferred her in black, there was truth in it and his revived ardor was real. Under her deep mourning Vera was happy. Wasn't Michel's praise and love all she wanted?

* Translated by Babette Deutsch, and taken from *An Anthology of Russian Poetry*, edited by Avrahin Yarmolinsky.

KSENIYA awakened slowly to the life around her. She noticed that Vera's youngest child, Katya, had a cold; she said they must be careful. It was the first time since Igor's death that Kseniya had shown concern about her grandchildren. Soon she sent the second nurse away, declaring that she would herself help to take care of Anton, the way she used to. She would have to see that he ate better. The cook cried and kissed her mistress's hands when Kseniya walked into the kitchen. The last time she had sat at the kitchen table had been when she had helped prepare Igor's tray on that terrible day. No, she mustn't think of that. There were the living to think of. Anton, the other children. There was a letter to be written to Olga. And she must go to church. The church had not given Igor a proper funeral. A man who took his own life went against God, the priest had said. She must pray to God to forgive her son and let his soul rest in peace in heaven.

She went to church every morning, and came back shivering with cold and weak with hunger, but her soul was strengthened. Nothing could bring her son back, but she knew that her prayers would help him gain a peace he had never known when he was alive.

One morning as Kseniya was slowly walking out of the house on her way to church, Nikifor, the doorman, spoke to her.

"A boy is waiting for you, madam. He says he has a note and is to give it to no one but you."

Kseniya looked at the note and leaned against the doorjamb for support. Olga's handwriting! Olga in Moscow!

"Mother dear," the note read. "I came to help you and Father. My daughter Natasha is with me. We are waiting for you. Love you dearly. Olga."

The note clutched in her gloved hand, Kseniya walked toward the church. The doorman must think she had gone to church as usual. Out of sight of the house, she hailed a cab. The driver looked up sharply when the lady got into the cab without saying anything or bargaining about the price. He looked up even more sharply when she read him the address on Olga's note, then decided she must be one of the charity ladies visiting the poor. The name of the street had not meant anything to Kseniya. She knew few streets in Moscow outside her own neighborhood, the theater and shopping districts. They soon left these familiar streets. The cab fought its way through slush and mud. Four-story buildings gave way to two- and one-story dilapidated wooden houses. Passers-by stopped to look at the cab. This was not a neighborhood where people rode in cabs.

"Here we are, lady." The driver turned to Kseniya and pointed with his whip to the sign: MR. NIKIFOROV'S HOSTELRY FOR TRAVELERS. Kseniya looked at the slip with the address and the house; this couldn't be the right place. But the driver seemed sure. He opened the cover to let her out. A crowd gathered around them; doors and windows opened; and neighbors called to each other to come and see. In a daze, Kseniya stepped out of the cab and unbuttoned her coat to reach for her purse in the deep pocket of her dress. She handed the driver a ruble, and walked slowly toward the entrance of the house. Excited talk which she did not hear followed her.

"A ruble, did you see—a ruble!" "You must be crazy. Whoever heard of people throwing rubles around like that . . ." "But I saw . . ." "I saw it too, so help me God, with my own eyes I saw a ruble." . . .

Kseniya stood in the dark hallway. It was a nightmare from which she would soon awake. It couldn't be true. It couldn't be true that her Olga had anything to do with this awful street and this awful house. The smell was sickening. She pressed her handkerchief to her nose.

A door opened at the far end of the hall.

"Yes, yes, mother, I heard a door . . ." said a child's voice.

"Wait, Natasha, let me see . . ."

Kseniya's heart stood still for a second and then started to thump wildly. Olga's voice and Olga's step. In a moment Kseniya was standing in the middle of a room, holding Olga to her heart.

To Natasha it seemed an endless time till they released each other, pulled apart a little to look at each other wordlessly through eyes filled with tears. Then they embraced again, tightly.

Natasha waited patiently. They still had their hats, coats, and gloves on. Mother had been ready to go out when Grandmother came. Grandmother's black velvet hat was pushed to one side, despite its huge hatpins. Mother's gray bonnet had slipped down and caught on a hairpin and hung on it, dancing at each movement of her head. Grandmother had such nice waves in her hair. Mother's hair was combed back straight in a tight bun. Natasha wanted to be loyal to her mother but she couldn't help loving those nice waves. There were two beautiful pearls in her grandmother's ears. Mother had taken a long time shining her shoes but they did not seem shined at all compared to Grandmother's, which shone like mirrors. And Grandmother's gloves were velvety and soft.

Natasha had always thought that nobody in the world dressed better than her mother. But, then, there was no one like Grandmother in their village. Look at her coat! She could imagine a fairy princess wrapped in such a coat—but a real live woman and one's own grandmother at that! It was hard to believe. Natasha stretched out her hand and carefully touched the fur. It felt like a newborn baby rabbit! Mother's faded baggy coat suddenly looked ugly. Natasha's heart jumped. She was mean, mean! How could she think that way about her mother? Tears surged to her eyes. Mother, Mother, forgive me! I don't mind even a bit your faded coat and worn-out shoes. I love your coat and your hat and your shoes and your hair a million times more than Grandmother's. Natasha's qualms of conscience overcame her and she sobbed out loud.

The two women heard her. Olga tore herself away from Kseniya and took the child into her arms.

"Natasha, Natasha, my darling, what is it?"

Natasha looked at her mother, then at her grandmother. Her face was still wet with tears, but she burst out laughing.

Kseniya and Olga turned to each other with startled worried looks. The excitement had unsettled the child's mind. Suddenly, their eyes no longer blinded with tears, they saw themselves as Natasha saw them —hats awry, hair disheveled, faces smeared with tears—and they knew the cause of her mirth. After all, she was only a child! The almost unbearable poignancy of their meeting was broken.

They sat down on the bed, for the only chair in the room was filled with their coats and hats. First with her eyes and then with her hands, Natasha examined the softness of Grandmother's velvet-trimmed woolen dress, her rings and those beautiful earrings. For the first time since Igor's death, Kseniya smiled faintly, and drew the child close to her.

"How was the trip?" . . . "Aren't you hungry?" . . . "Don't you feel cold?" . . . "Could you sleep on the train?" . . . "Did you find your way here easily?" . . .

The words could have sounded trivial but they did not. They were the first words spoken between mother and daughter for seventeen years.

Then more words came, slowly and hesitantly at first:

"How could you get here so quickly?" . . . "You mustn't stay here another minute." . . . "How is Father? What will he say . . . How shall we tell the family?" . . . "How did you leave the other children?" . . .

But soon they came in a spate.

". . . this longing was forever eating at my heart . . . I so wanted to see you and Father. I had to keep it to myself. I couldn't tell Gregor;

he would not have understood it. He would have thought that he wasn't making me happy, which isn't true. And then something else, mother—this I was afraid to admit even to myself—I didn't mind the hardships, mother, believe me, I never did. But there were times when in my dreams I saw delicious meals in clean light rooms; music and paintings and new clothes and a comfortable bed with soft linen and blankets. The children would be well dressed, and playing in real rooms with real toys . . . Oh, mother, I am not fair to Gregor. I should have never said that. I wouldn't have given up the years with Gregor for anything in the world—but I am happy that I can talk to you and tell you of my dreams . . ."

"I don't know how to tell him, Olga. The doctor says to be very careful. He thinks it was a miracle he stood it . . . Your coming may be the one thing that will bring him out of his lethargy. There was not much life in him these last years anyway, you know. He just sat in his chair and brooded and brooded. But now he doesn't even brood; he just stares, with nothing alive in his eyes. Oh, Olga, my angel Olga, God bless you, you may bring him back to life."

At length, Kseniya got up. It was hard to leave them but she had to go. She had things to do. She must talk to Anton, prepare Olga's room, let the rest of the family know Olga was there. Kseniya stood erect, as she had not done for a long time.

She walked through the dreary muddy streets, not feeling the slush under her feet or the heavy weight of the soaked hems of her dress and coat. She walked for a long time before she found a cab.

First of all, she would call Zena. Zena always knew what should be done. If things didn't work out right with Anton, Olga and Natasha would have to stay at Zena's. They must not stay in that dreadful hole another night.

Then she must let Vera know. Kseniya winced at that thought. Would Vera make difficulties again? Would she again tell her mother to choose between her children? There would be no question this time. . . . Olga, Olga, Olga! She would not give up Olga a second time. Olga, beautiful even in her shabbiness and tiredness. The same Olga, with eyes which still didn't know what a lie was. If only Anton would open his heart and let Olga and Natasha in! Natasha looked like Olga, though she was not so dark; her eyes were livelier, her mouth wider. Anton couldn't resist her. Kseniya sent a swift prayer of gratitude to God; then her mind went on with its busy planning. She must get a message to Maxim somehow, and he must come immediately, whatever Vera might have to say about it. He had been at the house a great deal during the first weeks after the tragedy, but lately they had not seen him. Kseniya thought back: the last time had been that afternoon when Vera also had come in. She remembered now. Vera had gone over to Maxim and whispered angrily, and Maxim's face had become very red and he had left the room. No, he had not been back since then. Maxim, the only son left to them, should come freely to the house—and so should Dunya. Now wait, what had she heard them say about Dunya? Words she had heard but, in her grief over Igor, had not taken in, came back to her now. Maxim and Dunya had separated. That was it. Dunya had taken the baby and returned home to her parents. What else had they said? She must find out. Perhaps he needed help too. Perhaps Olga would be able to help him. Anton was asleep in his big chair when Kseniya arrived home, but he woke up as she came into the room. She crossed over and stood beside him.

"Kseniya, you?" His fingers made sure of it.

She stood with her back to the light. Better not let him see her face yet. Better let him have his luncheon first; the tray was untouched and he would need all his strength.

"Here, Anton, let me help you. First, the sandwich . . . I'll hold the milk for you . . ." When he had finished she put the tray on a side table, straightened the cover over his knees, and fluffed up the pillow at his back. Then she told him, her head bent down to his, her lips almost touching his ear.

"Anton, she is here, Olga, our Olga is here. Olga is in Moscow. I just saw her, her and Natasha . . . Natasha is nine years old, she looks like Olga as a child . . . Olga came because she wants to be with us. Anton, please, Anton, let her help us . . . please . . ."

Anton hurt her. She hadn't thought he had so much strength left. His fingers felt like iron rings around her hand, his nails pierced into her flesh. He didn't say anything. Kseniya went on. Quietly, slowly, so that he would hear well what she was saying. She told him everything: of the message, of the ride to the miserable house, of their meeting, what they had said, how Natasha had cried and then laughed, even what they were wearing. Gradually Anton's grip on her hand relaxed. His eyes closed. His fingers were cold and completely still.

"Well, Anton, I've told you everything. Which shall it be? More broken hearts, more wretchedness? Haven't we had enough of that in our lives? Now we have a chance for happiness, Anton, let's take that chance, please, let us take it. I want to be happy . . . Anton dear . . ."

Kseniya's head fell on Anton's chest, her arms went around his shoulders. Her tears came quietly.

After forty years, for the first time, Kseniya had called him "dear"; she had embraced him and begged for happiness. He had thought life was ended forever; nothing had remained but eternal mourning for the boy. And now Kseniya said, "We have a chance for happiness." Kseniya felt his hand on her hair. She had his answer.

In the afternoon Zena came and took charge. She inspected bedrooms, planned menus, gave orders to the maids, dispatched messages to the rest of the family, and sent Pavel for Olga and Natasha. From time to time she or Kseniya looked in on Anton to find out whether he needed anything, but his eyes were always closed.

He had fallen asleep even before Kseniya had left his room. When he finally awoke, the room was half dark; but he saw clearly the tall figure that moved swiftly across the room to his chair. His heart began to beat wildly and he stretched out his hands. No words were spoken. Her faint "Father, dear, dear father" was the merest breath.

Natasha, waiting behind the door with Zena, tugged at Zena's skirt. "Aunt Zena, I want to go in. I want to go to Mother. I want to see Grandfather. I have never seen my grandfather . . ."

The silence was broken. Kseniya lit the lamp. Anton and Olga looked at each other. Anton did not see the mature figure and tired face. He saw the beloved face and figure of the young Greek goddess. But Olga saw a weak shrunken shadow of the strongheaded tyrannical father she had always loved, and it hurt her.

"Call Natasha in," were the first words Anton said.

Kseniya opened the door, and Natasha ran over to Anton and threw her arms around him.

"Grandfather, grandfather, now I have a grandfather too! This morning I got a grandmother and now I have a grandfather. And I have an uncle and an aunt. And I am going to have some more uncles and aunts, Aunt Zena said, and cousins too. Cousins means children, grandfather. You know, grandfather, we never had any of them like other children have."

Mother had told her to be specially sweet to Grandfather because he was sick and sad. But Natasha did not find Grandfather sad at all. It was true, he was sick, he couldn't move. But he wasn't sad. When she tickled him with her pigtails the way she did to make her father smile, Grandfather smiled and hugged her. He loved her, she felt already that he loved her. And she loved him. She had to tell him.

"It's wonderful to have a real grandfather, and such a nice grandfather like you. Oh, I love you, grandfather, I will always love you. And I will be near you, and if you need something, you tell me, and I will get you everything you want. Everything. Yes, grandfather, yes? And if I am not in the room and you want something, whistle, like that . . ."

A shrill whistle, the like of which the walls of that room had never heard, pierced the air.

"Now, that's enough, Natasha," said Olga, "you will make Grandfather tired. Father, if you let her, you will never have a quiet moment. She will smother you with her attentions. . . . It is time for supper anyway, Aunt Zena says. Kiss Grandfather, Natasha, and come."

Natasha whispered into Olga's ear.

"Yes, yes," Olga said, "you may help bring him his supper and you may sit with him while he eats, if he wants you to."

"Sure, let her come," Anton said casually. But his eyes, wandering from Natasha to Olga to Kseniya, belied the forced indifference of his voice.

Supper was a festive affair. Zena had ordered delicacies she thought Olga probably had not eaten for many years and that Natasha might never have tasted. Caviar, many kinds of fish and cold meats, their cook's famous cooked herring salad, homemade rolls and pastries, sweet drinks, pineapple, Crimea grapes and apples, nuts, sugar-covered cranberries, and chocolate-coated cherries.

Kseniya's eyes, shining with happiness, showed no trace of the moment when amidst the excitement she had slipped into Igor's room and knelt at his bed:

"Forgive me, All-Merciful, for the joy in my heart. I have not forgotten my son, believe me. But I have found my daughter and her child, and I have seen my husband come back to life. Let me rejoice in them without sinning. Igor, do you hear me, Igor? Igor, my son, my very own, your mother is with you, even in her happiness . . ."

Throughout the meal Natasha kept exclaiming over the unaccustomed food. She could not get over the beauty of the china and silver and table linen. She had never seen anything like it. She was indignant when Olga urged her to use the napkin.

"Mother, you don't expect me to wipe my mouth on that?" she protested, and tenderly stroked the embroidered roses framing Kseniya's initials.

Answering Natasha's questions and laughing over her unreserved comments, the others felt no need to carry on a conversation, and thus slid easily through the first difficult hours. Natasha hardly ever stopped talking and was as excited and unrestrained when she was being fitted with her new clothes as she was when getting acquainted with Moscow or being introduced to all the new uncles, aunts, and cousins.

When she first met Vera's children she burst out laughing. Pavlik, her own age, nine years old, was dressed in a black velvet suit with a white frilled collar. Natasha had never seen a boy dressed in that fashion. Besides, he kept clicking his heels and bowing deeply to everyone who spoke to him. The girls were funny too. Both of them, Kira, who was eight years old, and the six-year-old Katya, opened their mouths only when someone asked them a question, and in Grandfather's room they never really talked; they whispered. They did not click their heels as their brother Pavlik did but they jumped up and down instead—curtsying, they called it. Katya was like a little doll, blue-eyed like her mother, all blonde curls and blue ribbons. Kira was very dark, her hair almost black and straight, her movements not so doll-like as her mother's or little sister's. Natasha would have liked to talk more to her, and she thought that Kira would have liked it too. She often caught Kira's eyes on her, and sometimes Kira smiled at her. But Kira was never alone. Either her mother or her governess was always near her and it seemed that they did not want Kira to talk to anyone.

Natasha enjoyed the company of the adults more than that of her cousins. Grownups could answer questions; they could tell stories. The cousins didn't seem to know a thing about Moscow; it was almost as if they lived somewhere else. And they didn't play real games—only dominoes and lotto. Where could one play real hide-and-seek or tug-of-war if not here with all these stairs and the many rooms? They said that one could not play here, that no noise was permitted in Grandfather's house. How silly! Who ever told them that?

For hours Natasha ran up and down the stairs, sliding down the banisters, playing mountain climbing, with the attic the mountain and the cellar the valley. She had never before lived in a house that had three floors and stairways. No one ever told her not to play. Only when Grandfather was asleep, she was not to make a noise. The cousins seemed to be afraid of Grandfather. They kissed his hand and whispered to him, instead of talking. Natasha could not understand why. Grandfather was so kind and friendly. And besides, Father had told her never to be afraid of anyone. One man was as good as another, Father always said. Mother told her not to mention Father unless she was asked about him, and then not to say much, only answer the questions. Why? There were so many whys in Natasha's life right then that the one about her father got quickly lost among the others.

In the late afternoon and after supper, Natasha liked to sit at Anton's feet and ask him questions. There was no end to his tales about the Moscow czars and churches and streets and warriors and monks. Olga and Kseniya would sit with their needlework, listening to the stories and Natasha's questions. They did not talk. The sound of Anton's voice, the smile on his face—what was there to say? Kseniya did not let clouds come near her.

When, on one of her visits, Vera took Kseniya aside with a worried look and started, "Mother, what shall I tell my . . ." Kseniya interrupted her with a quiet smile. "Tell your friends anything you want, Vera, anything at all, my daughter."

"But, mother, you don't understand . . . The story will get around . . ."

"And what if it does? Vera, Vera, can't you see how unimportant it is?"

"Unimportant? What are you saying, mother? How do you think Michel will feel about it? As if there weren't scandals enough in our family!"

"I cannot help you this time, my daughter. Do what you please, say what you please; nothing makes any difference. Olga is our daughter, and she belongs here. Whatever you and Michel feel about it." Kseniya repeated it slowly and very distinctly: "Whatever you and Michel feel about it . . . And something else, Vera; Maxim belongs here too and always will."

Maxim back too! Vera grew cold. Michel wouldn't stand for any more scandals. Suppose he made good his threat to step out of the Nazarov family if anything improper happened in it again? She would do anything to prevent that! But what could she do?

As a first step, she visited her parents' house as seldom as possible. No one noticed her absence, however, for the house was alive now, not only during the day, when Natasha made it her playground, but in the evenings as well, when Anton's room was filled with people and ringing with voices, eager, argumentative voices.

For the most part, Anton did not like what the voices were saying. Nothing the government did ever pleased any one of them. The czar must go; the people must rule themselves. "My little Bolshevik," Olga once called Maxim. She was joking, of course, because according to Anton's paper the Bolsheviks were only slightly less wicked than the devil himself. Olga did not agree with Maxim. She and Gregor, it appeared, belonged to the Social Revolutionary party, which believed that the salvation of the country lay in the Russian peasantry.

"You are always thinking of the city and the city workers," Olga said one evening. "You forget the peasant. But if the peasant is hungry, illiterate, enslaved, you'd better forget your hopes for a happier Russia. Unless you think of the peasant first, your road is the wrong road—"

Maxim almost jumped at her. "The city proletariat alone will save Russia," he shouted, "and the proletariat alone will save the whole world. Can you see the ignorant, backward peasant leading us forward?"

"I shouldn't be so sure the factory worker is the right leader," Pavel interposed. "He doesn't have too much education and culture either. Why do you ignore the natural leaders of the people, those who are educated, who think, the intelligentsia, the enlightened bourgeoisie?"

"And where will they lead us, pray?" Maxim retorted hotly. "Where do they lead us now? They have the Duma—yes, yes, I know. But the elections are controlled; its members are seldom true representatives of the people; and the czar dissolves one Duma after another. But why do you, the enlightened bourgeoisie, keep quiet about it? Why? The government will not kill you. They kill workers. They can let workers rot in jails and Siberia, but they wouldn't dare touch you, the 'enlightened bourgeoisie.' Stop talking and do something! What are you waiting for? For another manifesto, another fiendish lie to be presented to you on a silver platter? And while you are busy singing hosannas and kissing the bloody hand that gave it to you, thousands will pay with their very lives for it. You make me sick with your gibberish and whining and your timidity! Do something, for heaven's sake, do something, or stop sermonizing!"

"Well, well," laughed Fedor, "I understand now where comrade Maxim got his reputation of being a great orator. But don't you see, my young Cicero, by knocking your head on a stone wall you never get anywhere. The more of you are killed the fewer there are left to lead. Don't squander your forces. Can't you show some patience? You know, Maxim, that I want the same things you want. It may sound ridiculous, coming from me, the textile manufacturer Gavrilov, but it's a fact, and you know it. Would you otherwise come to me every time you need money or a good lawyer to get one of your friends out of jail or want a hideout for these same friends, who insist on sticking their heads out only to have them bashed in with a club?"

Anton was learning, listening to them. Fedor, one of the richest men in Moscow, was in sympathy with those who wanted to overthrow the czar! Ludmilla was right with him. It was very difficult for Anton to understand. Pavel seemed to be the most moderate of them, but he didn't want the czar either. Neither did Olga. And Maxim, his own son Maxim, was an active member of a revolutionary group. So Olga was not joking when she called him "my little Bolshevik." Well, at least he didn't have to put up with Dunya's opinions too. Anton had no regrets about the way that marriage had turned out.

## CHAPTER 13
## Maxim

MAXIM and Dunya had been very happy at first in their room on the outskirts of Moscow. Maxim had devoted much of his time to his revolutionary work, writing leaflets, instructing young workers and students, addressing secret meetings. A few hours of tutoring and an occasional job of editing or proofreading had provided what little money they needed to live in Moscow's humblest neighborhood. He had refused any help from his mother. Unless he lived the life of those around him, he had said, he could never become one of them, and how was he going to work among them if he was not one of them?

Their room was poor and its furniture scant, but it was clean and friendly, and that first year Maxim had enjoyed coming home. Dunya was always there, ready with a warm welcome, eager to prove herself Maxim's most devoted audience. She hung on his words when he read her his appeals and speeches, and nodded approvingly to everything he said. When the child came, Dunya managed quietly and well with little money and little space.

And then things had begun to change. Maxim wasn't clear about what had changed or how it had changed, but it wasn't the same any more. He found he did not mind staying late at committee meetings. He did not mind taking on tutoring in the evening hours, which he had avoided before. He preferred spending an evening in the rooms of his friends to having them come to his room.

The truth was that Maxim loved discussion, argument, hot sparks of thought flying back and forth. But Dunya, with the same adoring, enraptured look, invariably said yes to everything he said. He missed in her the response he got from his friends. He tired of the yes he knew in advance, and lost all pleasure in sharing his thoughts with her. Things he had never paid any attention to before began to irritate him. If he mentioned a dish he liked, she served it to him day after day until the mere thought of it made him sick. If he said that he liked a book or a person, she would, when that book or person was mentioned, repeat the exact words he had used with exactly the same fervor in her voice.

He began to watch her even in their lovemaking. Wouldn't she ever make a gesture of her own? Couldn't she even love in her own way? But in that, as in everything else, there was always the same unspoken yes to everything he did.

Dunya thought that Maxim was irritated and indifferent because he was overworked, that it was a mood which would soon pass. She became even more careful not to contradict him, to let him have his way in everything. But that, she soon found out, irritated him even more and made matters only worse. So she just kept quiet. Maxim, depressed by a feeling of guilt toward Dunya, tried honestly and hard. But his feeling was stronger than any good resolution he took. Dunya's forced little smile froze him.

He would have gone on. It was Dunya who forced the break. A day came when she understood that Maxim's mood was not temporary.

There was no anger in her, no bitterness toward him. The happiness she had had with him was a gift for which she would forever be thankful. She must go out of his way quietly, without disturbing him. She told him that in a few, simple words. She would go with the child back to her father. She had written to him and he expected her. It was the first time since Maxim had known her that Dunya had made her own decision, had used her own words instead of echoing his—and she had done it to say that she was going away. Perhaps they were making a mistake, Maxim suggested; perhaps they could well go on? No, Dunya did not think so. It was the end. They had both tried and it hadn't worked.

After Dunya left, Maxim threw himself even more fervently into his revolutionary work. The year after Igor's death, the family saw and heard nothing of him between his occasional visits.

CHAPTER 14
*Natasha*

"ANYTHING wrong, Kseniya?" Anton asked a few mornings later. Kseniya was helping him with his morning tea. She shook her head, but her fingers were not steady, and her eyes looked worried.

He asked again. Kseniya arose and in tears she told him.

"Olga has to go back; she can't stay any longer. What shall we do? How shall we live now? I can't face that dreadful emptiness again. That emptiness frightens me."

There was nothing he could say to console her. And there was nothing he could say to himself to relieve his sudden terrible chill. The chill must have reached his hands.

"Forgive me, Anton, I shouldn't have weakened so. Forgive me . . . I was thinking only of myself . . . You are cold all over . . . Your poor poor fingers . . ."

She blew on them, she rubbed them, she spread an extra blanket over his body.

Neither of them heard Olga when she opened the door, then quietly closed it again. In that one fleeting moment she realized the depth of her parents' unhappiness. How could she possibly leave them? Yet she couldn't stay away longer; she had not expected to be away even so long. But would she ever have another peaceful moment in her life, thinking of her parents as she had just seen them?

In the dining room, Natasha was gleefully planning the spending of her pocket money. But at the look on her mother's face, she broke off suddenly and said in a grave voice:

"Mother, you know what? I didn't realize till this very minute that all this money and buying and everything means we are going away —that we're leaving Moscow and Grandfather and Grandmother—"

Her eyes filled quickly with tears.

"Mother, is it very awful of me to feel so sorry about going away from here, when I am going back to Father and home? . . . But I can't help it . . . I can't help it. I feel so bad about going away from here . . . so bad . . ."

The tears couldn't be kept back any more. Her head hidden in Olga's lap, Natasha sobbed:

"I know, I know . . . I am terrible . . . to cry when I am going home to my own father, to my own brothers and sister . . . I will never forgive myself for this. But I so hate to go away from here . . . and to leave Grandfather and Grandmother. They will be sad again . . . and we came here so they shouldn't be sad any more. I can't think of leaving them all alone. We can't both go away."

Olga gently stroked Natasha's head. No, they couldn't both go away and plunge the house again into a dead silence. They might as well not have come at all. She should have thought about it before.

Olga lifted Natasha's wet face. "You are right, Natasha. Grandfather and Grandmother will be very sad if we both go away now. One of us must stay to see to it that they are not unhappy. It can't be me, you know that. I must go home. But you could stay if you wanted to. That would help them very much. What do you think, Natasha?"

"I'd like to stay, mother," Natasha said slowly. "I told you I am sorry to be going away. But now that I think of it . . . I'll miss Father so, and the others, and . . . Mother, that means I wouldn't see you. Oh, mother . . ."

Again Natasha hid her head in Olga's lap and her thin shoulders shook.

"Why, why can't one be in two places at once? Here and at home? I want so much, so much to stay here . . . and I must cry when I think of not seeing you."

Olga smiled. Well, that was Natasha. Cheers and tears, following each other like sunshine and rain. It would be very hard not to have her around. And what would Gregor say? Would he understand, and agree? It wasn't long till the summer; Natasha would come home in the summer and then they would see. But just now she must stay.

Olga intended to tell her parents their decision gradually and quietly.

But she had counted without Natasha. When Natasha saw her grandparents' distressed faces, her eyes filled with tears again. She ran over to them and blurted out between laughter and tears:

"I am staying, I am staying, I am staying with you. Yes, I am staying. It will be sad, it will be very sad not to see Father and Mother and not to be home . . . but I shall love it, to stay with you. You are glad too, aren't you? And you will not be sad anymore, will you?"

Olga was afraid Natasha would say too much.

"That's enough now, Natasha. Go and play till I am ready. I shall be ready soon and we'll go shopping."

"Is it true, Olga?" Kseniya asked anxiously. "Is it really true what the child said?"

Olga nodded. "Yes, she wants to stay with you. She is very happy about it, even if she sheds a few more tears about not seeing us. I shall miss her, there's no use denying it But I prefer it this way, and don't you worry about me. Are you pleased? And you, father?"

Anton pressed her hand and held her close when she bent down to kiss him. That would be her recompense, Olga thought, for not having Natasha at home.

Later in the day Olga talked things over with Kseniya. On one point she was firm. "Mother, you must see to it that Natasha stays the way she is now. She belongs to our life. She is not rich and never will be. She must stay modest and simple. She has everything she needs now, and will not need more for a long time to come. I don't want her to be dressed like a rich girl, and I don't want her to learn the ways of rich people. Let her stay the way she is. And, mother, I know this may be hard for you—I shall leave much happier if I know that Natasha can talk freely about her father . . . and she must write to him. Oh, yes—there is one more thing." Olga laughed, to help them shake off their serious mood. "Please, no paper curlers in my little girl's hair over night, and no corkscrews in the morning. And don't cheat me in that. Tight pigtails with a narrow ribbon. You heard me, mother? I said—narrow ribbon, and that doesn't mean a huge bow à la Kira and Katya. It means just that—pigtails with a tiny narrow ribbon!"

They both smiled, though Kseniya sincerely preferred huge bows to narrow ribbons.

They had arranged that Natasha was to go to a school where an acquaintance of Olga's taught. It was in a modest neighborhood, quite a distance from their house. Natasha would have to be taken in a carriage. Olga disliked the idea, but she wanted Natasha to be under that teacher's supervision; there were several other liberal teachers in the school, and the children were the kind that Olga wanted Natasha to be with.

On Olga's last morning, the whole family came to see her off, and they all had breakfast together. Olga slipped out of the room to say good-by to Anton.

"Thank you, Olga, thank you for everything," he said when she kissed his face and hands.

Her father, the formidable, fear-inspiring Anton Nazarov, humbly thanking her! And then he said, "Come again . . ." and she said, "I will, father, soon."

Life in the house centered around Natasha. The morning hours were quiet, for she was in school, but the household concerned itself with her nevertheless. The meals were discussed at great length, and Natasha's likes and dislikes considered. Anton and Kseniya never tired of recalling every word she had said the day before, every desire she had expressed. After the coachman's return in the mornings, he was called in, and his report on the trip to school was part of the regular morning routine. Letters from Olga were read and reread; replies composed; gifts for Natasha discussed.

Olga reminded Kseniya in every letter of her promise not to spoil Natasha. Kseniya kept her promise, but it was not easy. If only Natasha were at least going to one of the exclusive schools where they wore beautiful light-colored silk uniforms. But all Natasha wore was a drab brown uniform with a black pinafore. Some girls had silk pinafores for holidays, but Olga had forbidden even that. No silk for Natasha. And the hair ribbons, well, the hair ribbons were a constant source of chagrin to Kseniya. Those narrow brown or black strips couldn't honestly be called ribbons.

Kseniya deplored the enforced simplicity but it was a small price to pay for the joy of having Natasha. And besides, they could always think of little gifts which would not break the promise to Olga. A new penbox, for instance, and all the nice things that went in it: many-colored erasers, gay penwipers, pencils, pens and penholders of every shape and color. There were many things a schoolgirl could use—notebooks and rulers and colored chalks and water colors and transfers. A picture postcard album was a modest enough thing, and one could get new postcards every day. No one would call that spoiling a child. And though Natasha was not permitted to dress properly, Olga had never said a word about the dolls' wardrobes. So the dolls were dressed in all the finery that was forbidden to Natasha. Olga wanted Natasha to keep up her skating, and one could do many things with a skating outfit.

Never had Anton and Kseniya talked and smiled together as they did now in the pleasure of planning gifts for Natasha.

"Is there anything in the law to prohibit that?" Kseniya would ask and whirl in the air a tiny feather boa for a doll, and Anton would smile appreciatively.

The richest, the most wonderful hour of the day came in the early afternoon, when the carriage stopped at the door, and Natasha, her schoolbag dancing on her back, threw open the door and smothered her grandparents with kisses. Every day Kseniya pretended to remonstrate with her for not closing the doors and for letting the draft in, or for not taking off her coat and rubbers in the hall. Every day Anton made believe he didn't like to be so squeezed and crushed. And every day Natasha, having finished the hugging and kissing, poured out the events of her school day. She had her corner in Anton's room where she did her homework, played with her dolls, read, sorted her pictures, and otherwise amused herself. When Kseniya went for a walk with her on the boulevard, they returned from time to time to their street, so that Anton could see them from his window.

Never before had Anton and Kseniya dreaded the approach of summer. However, it had been understood all along that Natasha was to go home in the summer. Did that mean "in" the summer or "for" the summer? They did not ask about it in their letters. Olga was to come to fetch Natasha and would bring one of the other children with her.

When Olga came, she knew that her parents could not live without Natasha any more. To take her away would kill them. Gregor understood and agreed. He bore no grudge against Olga's parents. The world was made in a certain way and people acted in a certain way, accordingly. Gregor did not like the way the world was made. He wanted to change it and worked toward changing it. But as long as the world was as it was, people could not help behaving the way they did. Olga's parents were no different from others. They had behaved toward him as any one of their kind would have behaved. He missed Natasha badly. But Olga was the one who had thought it best so, and he was sure that any decision she made could only be right.

Natasha spent part of every summer and an occasional Christmas vacation with her parents. Gregor and Olga never ceased longing for her, but after a year or two they stopped worrying about her. They did worry at first that Natasha might grow up to be a stranger to them, a rich little girl who might someday be ashamed of them. But there was never any sign of that. Her grandparents kept their word. The books Natasha read were the kind of books they would have given her to read and she pitched in with the work at home and in the garden as if she had never been away. Her ties with her family and her village friends remained as close as ever. No, there was nothing to worry about with Natasha. If only there weren't that empty space in their house and in their hearts.

The summer of 1914 was a wonderful summer. Natasha spent the last part of it with her grandparents at Dubrovka, where they had a bungalow on a hill overlooking the Moscow River. At the end of a cool path between birches and pines was another bungalow hidden among trees. It belonged to Ludmilla and Fedor. There, wherever a patch had been cleared of trees, flowers bloomed. From early spring till the first frosty nights, Ludmilla's lilies-of-the-valley, her peonies, irises, lilac, jasmine, the gorgeous display of lilies and summer annuals, her roses, dahlias, chrysanthemums brought joy not only to her and the family, but to the whole neighborhood and nearby village, for Ludmilla was a generous gardener.

Natasha helped joyously with the gardening. Everything seemed good that summer: the plunge in the river in the morning, and the walk back with her wet hair blowing in the wind, a wet towel around her shoulders; breakfast on the veranda, with hot rolls and eggs— out of the henhouse not more than five minutes ago, the cook assured her every morning—and boiled sweet cream and ham and heavy yellow butter; the walks in the woods for basketfuls of mushrooms and berries; the afternoon swim; reading to Grandfather under the old oak where his armchair stood during the day; even helping Grandmother and cook with their preserving and pickling.

Once Vera came out with Kira and Katya. Vera raised an eyebrow when she looked at Natasha's bare feet, her sun-tanned face and arms, her simple cotton dress. Kira and Katya wore wide-brimmed hats to protect their faces from the sun, gloves, high brown shoes, and sheer white dresses with wide pink sashes. It was a hot afternoon, and Natasha was running down the path to the river for a swim when she heard quick steps behind her and someone calling her name. It was Kira.

"Can I go swimming with you, Natasha?" Kira asked.

"But what will your mother say?" Natasha wondered, looking at Kira's finery.

"Oh, let her say anything she wants . . . Can I go with you?" There was a daring in Kira's eyes which made Natasha believe that she really did not care what her mother might say.

Natasha helped Kira down the steep riverbank. With one quick motion of her hands Natasha pulled her dress over her head and stood naked, her white body, only slightly browned by the sun, in striking contrast to her darkly tanned face, legs, and arms. It took Kira many minutes to unbutton her dress and her shoes, to untie her many under-garments. Finally she emerged from her clothes, her body, though untouched by the sun, darker than Natasha's. Holding on to Natasha's hand, Kira stepped into the cool water. She had never bathed in a river before, and Natasha could not get her to move. She left her standing near the bank and, laughing and shouting, her brown arms glistening in the sun, swam away. Kira watched her with eyes full of admiration and envy. When Natasha returned from her swim the two girls splashed and played in the water together, and for the first time Natasha heard Kira's real voice and laughter, loud and gay, and saw her teeth flash in a wide happy smile. As they approached the house, Kira's smile disappeared and her voice grew quiet. She knew what awaited her. Her dress was damp and crushed, her hair wet and wild; ties and buttons, fastened in a hurry, gave her a strangely untidy appearance.

Vera could not control her anger. With a flushed face, she pulled and tugged at Kira's hair, dress and arms: "What is this? How could you so forget yourself? Do you think you are a little beggar? A muzhik?"

Vera took Kira into the house to put her clothes into order. Natasha could not hear Vera's words but her voice sounded like a serpent's hissing. The rest of the afternoon Vera did not let Kira leave her side. Kira was sullen, and not once could Natasha make her smile. They did not come out again that summer, though Natasha asked her grandmother several times to invite Kira. It was too bad for Kira, Natasha thought. She felt that Kira might have as wonderful a time there as she had herself.

Sometimes the evenings were almost better than the days—the enchanting still evenings, with the moon cutting silver ribbons on the river and the nightingales making one sad with happiness; and other evenings, loud evenings, noisy evenings, but also wonderful evenings, when Fedor came out and Maxim came out and neighbors dropped in, and they played games. And after the games they went for a night swim or for a boat ride, and laughed and sang.

And suddenly it was all over. Nobody felt like playing games, nobody was gay, and everybody talked of returning to town.

"The clouds are getting blacker every day. There is no escape . . . war is coming," said Fedor.

"Don't be ridiculous!" scoffed Maxim. "Who do you think fights wars? The people, the common people, the little people—that's who fights wars, and it is the same all over the world. Of course, the big shots want war. War means profits for them. War means conquests, new markets, more power in their hands. Why shouldn't they want war? They don't get killed. But the little fellow wins nothing from the war. Oh, no, don't you worry about a war coming. Look at this—" Natasha always marveled at the number of papers Maxim's pockets held—"read this and this too . . .

"See what it says here." Maxim's voice was triumphant. "The workers in Berlin and in Paris and in Vienna, everywhere, feel the same way. They are brothers, they belong together, they are not going to kill one another for their kings and emperors and capitalists. They have decided that when war is declared they will go on strike. How can the big fellows start a war if their cannon fodder is on strike? Just wait and see. On August fourth, it says here, workers' representatives will get together in Paris and announce that they will declare an international general strike the moment war is declared. So, don't worry."

"But, Maxim, don't you think that our national honor demands—"

"Don't make me laugh, Fedor. Though you are a capitalist, I always thought your brains worked the right way. National honor . . . national honor . . . Don't tell me you believe in that hocus-pocus. What do you want them to tell you? The truth? That all they want is to make the other powers weaker and grab for themselves as much as they can. O God, when will people understand that there are enough riches on this earth for everyone, without the killing and murdering and robbing that has gone on for centuries?" Maxim got up to go and Kseniya fussed around him.

"Must you go, Maxim, so late at night?" she worried. "We see you so seldom. Stay overnight . . . I am afraid, with all this talk about war . . ."

"Never worry about me, mother. There will be no war, don't you worry about that either. But there's a lot to do if we are to avoid it, namely, explaining to people who don't understand." Maxim threw a furious look at Fedor. "So I'd better be gone."

A few days later, on August 1, war was declared. The summer homes were quickly deserted; everybody returned to town.

Natasha could not forget Maxim's words. He had been so sure. An international general strike when war was declared! That's what the workers had decided. But why didn't they hear about it? Why instead, day and night, did they hear men marching to their mobilization centers, soldiers marching to the railroad stations? The papers were beginning to report the first encounters, the names of the killed and wounded. She wanted very much to ask Maxim about all this, but Maxim had disappeared again.

She put her confusion into a letter to her mother. Unfortunately, Olga explained in reply, the German Socialists, on whom they had mostly relied to lead the international protest, had declared as soon as the call for mobilization was issued that they were Germans first and Socialists second, and they had voted all the money the government asked for to carry on war. Only one or two, Olga wrote unhappily, had had the courage to vote against it. And in other countries the workers had felt the same way. Their own country came first, international solidarity was forgotten. Of course, there had been no meeting in Paris on the 4th. The borders between countries were closed.

Nearly everybody else, Natasha's aunts and uncles, cousins, teachers, schoolmates, the servants, seemed to be happy and excited about the war. No one said a word against it. The women knitted gloves, scarves, and socks for the soldiers; everybody was busy preparing bags with gifts for the front; everybody was visiting the wounded in hospitals. At school they were taught patriotic verses; patriotic battle scenes and pictures of hero-soldiers decorated the classroom walls. A colorful poster hung on the wall of the auditorium where they assembled for their morning prayers; it showed a fierce oversized Cossack armed to the teeth but so strong that he didn't have to have recourse to his arms. He simply swallowed one German soldier after another, twelve of them altogether. The same poster was plastered all over Moscow. When Natasha saw it first, it seemed familiar to her. Then one day she heard a man in the street say, as he pointed to the poster, "Hope he does a better job swallowing this time!" and she remembered the old poster in her grandmother's attic which showed this very same Cossack swallowing twelve tiny Japanese soldiers.

It was hard for Natasha to feel differently from the others and not to be carried away by the general patriotic spirit, but her parents' letters strengthened her. They had not been caught by the wave of patriotism and often wrote of their opposition to the war. Her final support came when Maxim suddenly reappeared two months after the beginning of the war. He dispelled her last doubts and waverings.

His meager meals at the workingmen's tearooms were never very filling, and his clothes showed the lack of feminine care. He looked thin and neglected, but his spirit was buoyant. He had a long conversation with Anton. From the very beginning of the war he had been torn between two possibilities: to go into the army and fight against the war in which he didn't believe, among the soldiers, or to stay outside and fight against it in civilian life. The party finally decided for him. He would be more useful, they told him, continuing his present work. A word by Anton to the right person, accompanied by the proper sum, would easily keep Maxim out of the army. However strong Anton's patriotic feelings, Maxim had no doubt that his father would be ready to do anything to help his son avoid the dangers of war.

The police were becoming ever more vigilant and punishments had increased in severity. It was not hard to tag an espionage case on any undesirable person. To protect himself, Maxim took a job on a highly patriotic evening newspaper, and did his party work under the cover of its respectability. To give authenticity to his role, he began to visit his parents frequently, and got himself decent clothes. With Natasha, he showed himself on the fashionable skating pond, and was seen at the theater and opera with the Gavrilovs.

The family of course knew that Maxim had not changed his opinions, and when no outsiders were around, the war was freely and heatedly discussed. Pavel was torn between his anticzarist feelings and his patriotism.

"I admit," he argued, "that a victory for us might mean a strengthening of czarism. I can assure you I don't want that. And still . . . I can't help it, I don't like the idea of the Germans defeating us."

"As long as a defeat will help destroy czarist tyranny, it doesn't matter what—"

"Oh, yes, Maxim, it does, it most certainly does, and I am not the only one to feel that way. There are others whom no one can accuse of too much loyalty to the czar, who say that we must fight and win. This is more than empty blind patriotism—"

"I think Pavel is right there," Fedor agreed. "The czarist regime is weak. After the war it won't require much of an effort to overthrow it. Let's finish the war; then we shall finish our enemies inside. If Germany wins, Germany, with her worship of militarism, it won't do Russia any good. I agree with Pavel on that. But I don't follow his ideas of conquest—"

"Of course," Pavel interrupted, "it sounds bad when you call it conquest. But I don't see what's wrong if Russia succeeds in fulfilling her historic aims."

This was too much for Maxim. "I saw it coming! Our centuries-old dreams of being masters of the Black Sea! The most sacred of all our sacred dreams—the Straits and Constantinople! Another sacred dream —to weaken the British lion and strengthen the paws of the Russian bear! And if our own Little Father Nicholas realizes these precious dreams for us, do you believe for one minute that we can overthrow him by the push of a finger? Go on, put your mind to sleep, suck at your pacifier! What a wonderful reason to fight and die for our beloved czar!"

"Maxim, Maxim," Ludmilla intervened, "you are being unfair now. You know there are lots of people—"

"All right," Maxim said, more quietly, "I know there are lots of people who dislike czarism and the idea of Russia's historic aims, and who still don't want the Germans to win the war. They'd prefer some other way of getting rid of the regime because they don't relish the idea of German soldiers on Russian soil. But"—and his voice began to get louder again—"we must begin to see people not as Germans or Russians or Chinese but as human beings. What's wrong with Germans?"

Zena was indignant. "Don't tell me, Maxim, that you've never heard of the Germans cutting off the fingers of Belgian babies and murdering whole villages by poisoning the wells?"

"Sure I've heard of it. How could I help hearing it? Aren't the papers full of it? But so are the German papers full of stories about the terrible things our soldiers, and the French and the Belgian and the British soldiers do to the Germans. You can't make decent people fight one another unless you feed them these horror tales.

"I hope to live to see the day when people stop thinking of one another as belonging to different countries, classes, races, religions! We are all human beings made exactly the same way, so why should we go on forever murdering and hating one another?"

As the war went on, the casualty lists grew alarmingly long; the streets were filled with bandaged, limping figures and the hospitals were overcrowded. Schools were taken over, sick and wounded lay on floors, in hallways and storage rooms. The price of the war was growing high and hard to bear. Patriotic fervor had to be constantly whipped up with demonstrations and martial music, with tales of the enemy's hair-raising atrocities, with poems and plays extolling Russia's glorious past and the heroes of that past, Alexander Nevsky, Alexander Donskoy, Suvorov, Kutuzov, Peter the Great.

"Those fools, those blasted fools, falling for this idiotic gibberish, these trashy slogans!" Maxim raged.

"As you have pointed out, our soldiers need an incentive to kill and to be killed," said Fedor wearily, "and that is their incentive—to suffer and die for the glory of the beloved fatherland as millions before them have died."

"But how about our intellectuals, our liberals?" Maxim demanded. "All you hear is Hurrah! Hurrah! and Hurrah! again. The Bolsheviks are the only ones who dare to say that this terrible slaughter is senseless. The blood of the people is being spilled so that the czar can get stronger, I tell you. We are fighting this war to strengthen his regime, even if it pleases the so-called democratic countries to call it a war for democracy. War for democracy, with the Russian czar on their side! War for democracy when an autocratic tyrant fights against a country that has free trade unions, over a hundred Socialists in the Reichstag, a free press . . . We must get out of this vicious circle, we must refuse to fight this war."

Since Maxim's visits to his parents were always sporadic, it was several days before anyone knew that he had been arrested. Kseniya kept the news from Anton, telling him only that Maxim had had to leave Moscow and had sent them word not to worry about him. She got permission from the police to send him a pillow and a blanket, food, cigarettes and money, and she was also permitted to visit him in prison. Sometimes she took Natasha with her. Maxim's political sympathies, his underground work, his sudden and mysterious disappearances and reappearances had always made him an exciting figure to Natasha; now, his arrest established him firmly as a hero in her eyes.

Maxim was in good spirits. Messages smuggled through bribed or sympathetic guards told him that others had taken the place of those who had been arrested when he was, and that the work was going on. One day Kseniya was told to bring him warm clothes. He was being sent to Siberia.

"Don't cry, mother," Maxim consoled her. "It won't be long till you see me again."

To Natasha, he said, "Don't let your brain go to sleep. Think, remember, and try to understand what I've told you."

Natasha needed these words, for the din of the patriotic drums was getting hard for a fifteen-year-old girl to resist. The thought of Maxim in Siberia helped her. While Kira and Katya, beautifully dressed, went with Vera to entertain the officers at their canteens and hospitals, Natasha, with her teacher and a few of her classmates, did war work in the filthy crowded hospitals where the common soldiers lay, as often as not, on mattresses on the floor. The soldiers' ignorance and lack of protection by the authorities made them easy targets of injustice and discrimination, and the girls helped them draft their complaints to the authorities, read to them, and wrote letters to their families for them.

Several times Kseniya took Natasha with her on a visit to an officers' hospital. The difference between the gay, friendly atmosphere and shining efficiency there and the crowded, understaffed, unfriendly conditions of the soldiers' hospitals gave Natasha a great deal to think about. So had many other things lately—her visits to Maxim's prison, for example, and certain things that happened in school.

There were, for instance, those days when tuition fees were collected in class. The names of those who were in arrears were called out in sharp reprimand. The girls whose names were called suffered agony, and Natasha suffered with them. But it was even worse when the names of those who paid no tuition because of their extreme poverty also were called out. Their classmates would look at them curiously but Natasha's head was always bent low; she would rather have died than looked at them.

One of the free students was a redheaded girl named Helen. She was, Natasha knew, the cleverest in the class, but somehow during each term there was discovered a fault in Helen's behavior which invariably prevented her from reaching the top of the class, the place which by right was hers. The fault was not hard to find: she was constantly criticized for not being neat in her appearance. It was true that Helen's dress was old and shabby, that her hands were rough and her fingernails broken and stained. And she was often late. But surely the teachers knew, Natasha thought, that Helen was doing all the housework at home and had a brood of motherless children to take care of in the morning before school.

The girls whose families were better off were treated differently. Often Natasha had committed, without punishment, the same little crimes for which Helen was invariably punished. Often she had failed by a hair in her examinations, and that hair was forgiven her—but not others.

Natasha pondered all this and was deeply disturbed. One night she poured out her thoughts to Anton.

". . . . Why is it all so unjust, Grandfather? Helen is the best, the very best of us. Why should it matter that her father is poor? She is good, isn't she? So why is life so cruel to her? What did I do to deserve what I have? Oh, Grandfather, life is so unjust . . . it hurts me so . . ."

Anton also was disturbed. He listened to Natasha with great sympathy, and from that day on she shared her thoughts with him. She had many to share. With several of her classmates who felt as she did, she decided that something must be done to change conditions. They knew that they couldn't do very much about changing real things, not right away, anyhow, but they thought they would make a start right there in their own school and in their own lives. After long exciting deliberations, they organized themselves in a group. "Reformists," they called themselves. When all the rules and plans were decided upon, Natasha wrote them out and read them to Anton.

"The alphabet must be changed. It is too complicated for children and also for adults . . .

"To give homework over Sundays and holidays is cruel and should be abolished . . .

"Teachers and parents must not always forbid and punish, but talk things over. That would be much better . . .

"And we pledge ourselves to be friends with all good people even if they are Jews or poor, and even if our parents don't permit us. We pledge ourselves to follow our conscience . . ."

"A bit strong this, isn't it?"

"No, grandfather, not at all. This is the right thing and we got together to do the right things, and we will. . . . Tell me, grandfather, would you refuse to be friends with a man who is good just because he is a Jew?"

After Natasha left him, Anton puzzled over what had made him answer her the way he had. What had made him tell her that lots of good innocent people suffered because of stupid prejudices? Was his own feeling about Jews, then, nothing but a stupid prejudice? Well, wasn't it, really? There was nothing wrong with any one of the Jews he knew. And there probably was nothing wrong with all the rest of them. It was just the way people around him talked about Jews, the way his paper talked about them. "A filthy anti-Semitic sheet," Maxim had once called it, and had added:

"I don't want to divide people into Jews and Gentiles, or into blondes and brunettes, or into white and black—only into who is exploiting and who is being exploited. A Jew who exploits his workers is as bad as a Gentile who does it . . ."

Natasha had one big secret from her grandparents. Once a week she and the other members of the Reformists club went to a place where a romantic-looking pale youth with long hair labored hard to explain to them the contents of pamphlets in red covers full of big hard words. This the girls were not supposed to mention to anyone. It was very exciting. Natasha wondered whether the others understood anything the young man said. She for one did not understand a single word. But she was proud and happy to "belong." She walked on clouds the day it came her turn to take one of the red pamphlets home to study and to report on it. She learned it all by heart and hoped that she would be permitted to recite it without being interrupted by questions. She need not have worried. Their study circle was dispersed before the meeting day, and the pale-faced youth arrested. Fortunately, the Reformists were warned in time and did not fall into the police trap. Natasha kept the pamphlet, which was called *Historic Materialism*, well hidden as a precious memento.

Natasha saw her cousin Pavlik almost never, since he was studying at the military academy, and Kira and Katya only rarely, when they made their short duty visits to their grandparents. Olga had not wanted her to see much of them, for she had not cared to have her exposed to their influence. Natasha had never liked to visit Vera's house, in any case, because the atmosphere of governesses and etiquette stifled her and because she knew she was not welcome there. Vera had created for her friends a romantic story about Natasha, but to her Natasha was a poor plainly dressed country girl who had taken her own place in her father's affection, and whose influence could only be bad for Kira and Katya. Although Natasha did not like to go there, she was always glad when Kira visited her grandparents. The two girls exchanged looks and smiles but Vera saw to it that they had little opportunity to talk with each other.

It was better at Zena's. It was gayer there, and Natasha was not made to feel an outsider. But there too it was very rich, and they talked mostly about things Natasha didn't understand or wasn't interested in. Pavel had given up social reforming, and with Zena had joined a group devoted to religious philosophy.

Anton began to wonder about Maxim's long silence. He had seldom been away for so long. Kseniya was considering telling him the truth and was waiting only for a suitable moment. He couldn't be too affected by it. Theirs was not the only family now that had a member in jail; the police were arresting many persons.

One evening the cook made mysterious signs to Kseniya. Following her into the kitchen, Kseniya found a peasant sitting at the table, sipping hot tea from a saucer. There was nothing unusual in that. The servants frequently had visitors from their villages. This one must have just arrived. His burlap sack, mittens, and stick were lying at his feet, which were shod in felt boots. His fur cap was on his knees and his thick reddish hair was cut in true peasant fashion in a straight line on his neck. He continued sipping his tea, making loud noises as he sucked the sugar. When he finished, he wiped his mouth with the back of his hand, made sure no drops were left on his beard, got up and bowed deeply to Kseniya. She still did not know why the cook had summoned her and looked inquiringly at her. The cook beamed all over her face. She turned the key in one kitchen door and stood at the other door holding the handle.

"Ready?" asked the peasant in an excitingly familiar voice. The cook nodded.

Carefully he took off his beard and wig.

"Sh-sh," he warned Kseniya. She suppressed her cry and fell into Maxim's arms.

Maxim had little time. They talked quickly. He had escaped; he had been lucky so far because his disguise was good, but he might be caught at any moment. The police surely kept an eye on the house but he had had to see her. Did his father know about him? Probably better not to see him—it would be too much for him.

What was Natasha doing? We wanted to see Natasha. They had only a few minutes, but they were long enough for Maxim to make sure that Natasha could be trusted with a message for the party. He said a few words and made her repeat them. She was not to write anything down, certainly not the address to which she was to deliver the message. And now he must disappear, he said. They would hear from him. They were not to worry about him.

"Are you sure you will be safe now?" Kseniya asked anxiously. "Wouldn't it have been safer, dear, if you had stayed in Siberia?"

"Will you never understand, mother?" Maxim laughed. "As if it were a question of safety! Who thinks of safety? Natasha, why don't you explain it to your grandmother? You understand, don't you?"

Natasha could not answer at first. She only nodded her head, her eyes shining like two stars, filled with the greatness of the moment, with worship of Maxim, with readiness to die for the Cause. Then she said, "Of course, I understand . . . I would do the same. I am not afraid of anything; I would do anything to help."

"See, mother? That is the right way to feel. Big things are in preparation . . . very big things . . . I couldn't stay away. They need every one of us."

Natasha's heart swelled with pride when she delivered her message. How unimportant their Reformists seemed now, and the red pamphlets, and all their talking and dreaming. Here it was, real danger, real work! She found courage to ask, "Is there anything I could do . . . ?"

The woman who received the message looked at her and understood the end of the sentence . . . "now that I have done this . . . now that I am part of you . . ."

"Yes, Natasha, I think you could. There are things that we can't do but that a little girl like you can do."

Frequently, thereafter, Natasha was sent into houses watched by police spies. Her music bag dangling from one arm, her bulging schoolbag from the other, she delivered leaflets and messages to men and women for whom the police had spread out nets all over the country. Who would suspect the slowly strolling pigtailed schoolgirl with big innocent eyes?

# Part Two
## 1917-1936

CHAPTER 15

*Revolution*

"THE czar has abdicated! . . . The czar has been arrested! . . . The czar has been killed! . . . The czar has disappeared! . . ." In February, 1917, Moscow buzzed with a thousand rumors. Whatever might happen, the czar was no more. The excitement was hard to bear; it was impossible to stay indoors. The streets were black with people, with men and women, laughing, weeping, embracing strangers under the very eyes of the police. The mighty guardians of law had suddenly lost their magic power to fill people with fear. But they continued to chant their time-honored "Break it up . . ." "Move on, move on, keep moving . . ." Nobody listened to them. People laughed right in their faces. The joy of laughing in a policeman's face! That was real freedom! People sang, shouted, and marched, marched, marched. They marched in all directions; processions met one another, joined together, arm in arm, shoulder to shoulder, strangers yesterday, brothers and sisters today.

Newspapers were eagerly torn from the hands of newsboys. Leaflets, appeals, posters appeared by the thousands. They were filled with exaltation, with words of hope which made the eyes fill with tears of joy. The monarchist press was silenced. Its adherents fumed and schemed behind closed doors but their voices, only yesterday arrogant and bloodthirsty, were not permitted in the open. Nothing disturbed the celebration. Prison doors were thrown open and prisoners were carried out on the shoulders of their comrades, into freedom. Political exiles returned from Siberia and foreign lands. Joy was in the air.

In the midst of the delirious celebrations, sober voices began to ask disturbing questions. Had the overthrow of the czar solved all problems? What about the war? What about the terrible casualties, the lack of shoes and guns for the soldiers? What about the lack of food, textiles, leather, seeds, metals, machinery, rolling stock, fuel, medicines? What about financial obligations, their obligations to their allies? What about the sky-rocketing prices? Ideas and plans foamed from a torrent of written and spoken words. As in 1905, Russia found her tongue again. Day and night, orators in meeting halls, in parks, and on street corners praised their own panaceas as the only possible solution. Day and night, crowds listened avidly to them. In the center of town, far from the workers' quarters and the slums, the listeners applauded speakers who promised a smooth and pleasant solution of all problems and who used fine words like patriotism, Russia's destiny, our brave allies, justice with the framework of law and order, respect for property. The listeners did not like their speakers to be interrupted by hecklers, especially when the hecklers wore rough clothes and used unrefined language. They had had such a lovely bloodless revolution. There was no sense upsetting things more than necessary. Nothing rough, nothing rude.

As soon as Maxim came out of hiding, he plunged completely into work for the party. There was little time to visit his parents, but he came one evening when the whole family was assembled in Anton's room. Vera was there too. She was subdued, her society queen manner much less marked. Michel was away on a mysterious mission. When Kseniya asked where he was, she answered curtly that he was visiting his father in Petrograd.

"Has he left his regiment?" asked Maxim.

"No. Why?"

"Oh, nothing special. I only thought it was a strange time to visit his family—when his regiment was in trouble. Don't you know that the officers of his regiment have refused to transfer their allegiance to the new government? Some have been arrested, some have fled. And he is visiting his father! How very touching!"

"He at least knows his duty toward his father. That's more than others do."

This skirmish between Vera and Maxim did not disturb Anton. Those two were always like cat and mouse. But he was disappointed in the general trend of the conversation. He was tired of disagreements and quarrels. Now that the czar was gone, why couldn't they all be happy and satisfied, and agree with one another? Wasn't that what they had all wanted except Vera? Now they'd got what they wanted and still they disagreed.

He had asked them in what he meant to be a light jovial tone:

"Are you finally pleased? You will get those democratic reforms you were always clamoring for. Are all of you for once pleased at the same time about the same thing?"

Pavel was the only one who agreed with him. "Yes, we'll get democratic reforms, and we'll get them in a peaceful democratic way. You see? It's what I've been saying all along. Our place was with the democracies. Fighting side by side with them bore fruit . . . We are going to be a civilized democracy . . ."

"I should be happier," said Fedor, "if I were sure that the rest of the country felt the way you do about a civilized democracy, that the workers agreed with you, and the peasants. Just now the peasants are dropping their guns or clutching them to their breast and running back to their villages so as not to miss the distribution of land. That worries me. The army shouldn't disintegrate now. Now that we are really fighting for democracy!"

"Ha-ha-ha! For democracy! Don't tell me, Fedor, that you seriously believe that bunk?" Maxim's tone was sharp and venomous.

Anton sank wearily deeper in his chair. The same thing again, the same old quarrels!

"You don't expect our peasants to fight for the British Empire or French bankers or our own landlords? Do you blame them for wanting to lay their hands on a piece of land of their own? And do you think our workers are willing to go on being exploited too? I imagine you'd like that . . . you would."

As usual, Ludmilla's sense of fairness was aroused. "Maxim, you ought to be ashamed of yourself . . . you ought to know better than to insult Fedor."

"Leave it be, Ludmilla," Fedor said. "I have heard more abuse lately from my workers than ever before. Even the czarist police knew that I was on the side of the people but you Bolsheviks don't. You don't know the difference between your enemies and people like Pavel and me. You throw us on the same pile with the sharks who skinned the workers."

For a while the conversation quieted down. It flared up again when Vera remarked:

"Why do you keep talking about workers and peasants? Who are they to know anything? Why are they to be consulted? You push aside nice decent people and you turn to the mob for advice."

Maxim looked as if he could have choked her. "You . . . you . . . you . . . with your nice decent people. Who? Your husband? Your husband, who . . ." Kseniya put her hand on his lips, and he swallowed his remark. "Who? The czar? That moron, that driveling coward, that spineless shadow of a man? Who? The czarina? The czarina who indulged in orgies with Rasputin, the czarina who despises the Russian people? Who? The ministers, that spying, betraying, intriguing, stealing, corrupted bunch of criminals? Did it ever occur to you that the mob you speak of consists of tens of millions of people who have made up their minds to start living like human beings and not like animals, as they always did and as you would want them to go on living? And they have arms in their hands."

Vera answered with a mocking smile. They couldn't scare her with those filthy foul-smelling muzhiks. She knew better . . . Michel and his friends were not asleep.

The conversation went back to the war. The provisional government which succeeded the czar's was desperately trying to launch an offensive, and to persuade the people that its pledge to the Allies had to be carried out, that the war against Germany had to be won before anything else.

Fedor and Pavel agreed with that.

"It will be an eternal blot on our national honor if we refuse to fight," Pavel said.

"Do you think, Maxim," asked Fedor, "that when the Kaiser sees our army turning its back to him, he will hurry and recall his own army? Don't you think rather that he'll invade Russia and make us pay a hard price for his victory?"

"If I were you, Fedor, I'd put my trust in the German people . . . They were ready to fight the czar but they will never raise their arms against the Russian people."

"If you're so sure of that, Maxim, why do you insist on the soldiers keeping their arms? I've heard your orators demand it."

"Don't you see why? Our fight is far from won yet . . . It has only started. This is no time to relax, to put down arms. Our enemies— and I don't mean the Germans, I mean our own enemies in Russia— are very much alive; they have not accepted their defeat. And how about their friends abroad? Don't they expect help from them? Ask my dear sister; she may know something about it. Where do you think her husband is right now? With whom do you think our czarist generals are negotiating at this very moment? With the Russian people? Oh, no, with foreign powers."

"You are right in that," Fedor agreed. "Our enemies are far from dead. They'd join with the devil if only they could kill the revolution. But doesn't the thought of a civil war frighten you? A Russian spilling the blood of his brother Russian?"

"What brother Russian?" Maxim demanded. "My brother-in-law Michel? The Black Band? Isn't a German worker who refuses to shoot a Russian worker closer to us than this kind of brother Russian? No, too much of the old system is still around to put down our arms—"

"I would shoot everyone who plots against the revolution," Natasha broke in excitedly, "I—"

"No, no, my pet," Maxim rebuked her gently. "No use killing individuals. It's the system that has to be destroyed, not individual people. Killing a few men will not solve anything."

"That's right," said Pavel. "And it's true there's too much of the old system left. But the measures you propose, Maxim, are so undemocratic. You want to ignore the Duma. After all, the Duma is our Parliament, our National Congress . . ."

Maxim threw up his arms in despair.

"Pavel, Pavel, you are hopeless! Completely hopeless! You are still betting on this anemic cadaverous talking machine. Will you never learn anything?"

"I could ask you the same question! What have you learned? Words, words, words. You are all so eloquent, you Bolsheviks! Why don't you explain to your brother-soldiers that their first sacred patriotic duty is to finish the Germans?"

"Why don't you explain it to them? You believe it, I don't. All the peasant dreams about is a piece of land. His forefathers have dreamed about it for generations. And now he hears that the large estates are going to be divided among the landless peasants. To hell with national honor and allies and whatever else your orators tempt him with to persuade him to give his life. If he can get a ride on the roof of a train or on a peasant's cart, it's all right. If not, he walks, he walks home. Millions walk away from the front to that dream of land. You call this lack of patriotism, desertion? It is the strongest urge he's ever felt in his life . . . Try to make him turn back, and fight the Germans so that the Russian capitalists can divide the German markets with other capitalist sharks."

By summer the food situation had become catastrophic. Prices reached unheard-of heights. Long lines of mutinous hungry women appeared all over the city. A handful of speculators flourished; the rest of the population suffered. The Bolsheviks said that the provisional government was unable to cope with the situation, and that the People's Soviets should take over the government. The provisional government replied with stern measures against the Bolsheviks. Some were arrested; Lenin and a few other leaders went into hiding; but the party work continued without letup. They issued fiery appeals against the government, which they printed underground; they insisted that they were the only friends of the masses and they gained rapidly in strength. The hopeless economic situation, the inability of the provisional government to improve the situation and to unite the people, its readiness to co-operate with enemies of the revolution, the desperate desire of the soldiers for peace brought millions into the Bolshevik camp.

Socialist and liberal parties protested against Bolshevik methods—crude and undemocratic, they called them—but there was not much they could do to oppose the Bolsheviks' growing power. The anti-Bolsheviks were split into numerous factions and groups, each holding grimly to its own particular brand of salvation. They had one thing, only one, in common—hatred and fear of the Bolsheviks. They were fiercely opposed to one another on almost every other point. Some of the differences between like-thinking groups seemed infinitesimal, but they clung to them stubbornly. There was unity only in the Bolshevik ranks.

Maxim survived the wave of Bolshevik arrests in July but again he had to disguise himself and change his sleeping quarters every night. In the late fall of 1917, the Bolshevik menace grew dark and there were persistent rumors that they were getting ready to take over the power. They began to come out from underground and agitate openly for the overthrow of the provisional government.

Maxim too discarded his disguise, and one evening found time to spend an hour with his parents. Unfortunately, it again happened to be one of those rare evenings when Vera also was there. There was open hatred in the looks Maxim and Vera exchanged. To Maxim, Vera's husband and his kind were mortal enemies. To Vera, Maxim was the embodiment of all the ugliness and brutality that had destroyed her comfort and peace. With the others, Vera thought, even though they had overthrown the czar, it would be possible to find some common language. The refinements of life would be left. Money would retain its importance. The servants wouldn't be disobedient and rebellious. That was what Vera's friends were saying. It was only the Bolsheviks, the rowdy vulgar Bolsheviks, who wanted to take it all away from them, and make them live in misery and degradation. Everybody should be equal, the Bolsheviks said. Her blood boiled at the thought of it. Now, smiling defiantly, she asked:

"Is it true, Maxim, that under the Bolsheviks everybody will be equal?"

"Certainly."

"Do you mean to say that I shall have to consider as my equal a man who uses no handkerchief to blow his nose?" Her laughter was hysterical.

"Oh, no, don't you fool yourself!" Maxim shouted. "No decent human being would want to consider himself your equal . . . You wench . . . you bought a husband . . ."

Anton's hands were tearing at his blanket, he breathed heavily. Kseniya hurried to his side. Full of anxiety she turned to her children:

"Maxim, I implore you . . . don't say any more . . . Think of us; you are both our children. And you, Vera, it might be better if you went now . . . it's Father I am worrying about . . ."

Vera's face was distorted with fury. She jumped up.

"All right, all right . . . order me out of my father's house! Because of him, of this . . . worthless rascal . . . this murderer . . . this bandit . . ."

"Listen to our grand lady forgetting her dainty manners!" Maxim's provoking voice pursued her in the hallway. "Trying to compete with a marketwoman."

Vera's departure did not make the atmosphere in the room much more peaceful.

"So you are ready to destroy the revolution?" Pavel's usually self-possessed quiet voice was almost shrill. "After decades of waiting we have reached our goal, and because a few crackpots are drunk with the desire for power, we have to see our hopes crash."

"For you this was the goal, the end," said Maxim, "for us Bolsheviks it is only the beginning."

"That means you seriously expect the masses to take over." Fedor's voice too was sharper than usual. "Who? Mutinous soldier deserters, workers who never before had any responsibilities, peasants who have no idea of what's going on around them as long as they get land? And you think you can manage with this human material, without us, without the educated people, the brains of the country?"

"If you want to go along with us, and help the people—it's all right. If not, we'll take over without you. Yes, we will!" Maxim's eyes burned with exalted faith. "You think we can't do it alone? We can! You think we'll destroy everything in our ignorance? We shall not! We can't promise you that it will all go smoothly in the beginning. There are hard times ahead. But did it go so well under the czars? They had hundreds of years to learn! It will not take us so long. If only you would believe in the people! If you knew the wisdom and strength and courage and talents that sleep in our people. Give us a few years, a few short years, years of peace, years of hard toil . . . It may even be better that you aren't coming with us! It will be better if we do it alone, with our own strength. Only then will victory be complete. Only then shall we be sure that no one will come to us and make us go fight for capitalism and imperialism, for Persian oil, for the Dardanelles and profits."

"Don't tell me Bolsheviks aren't interested in profits." Zena tried to hide her anger with sarcasm.

"No, they are not! You hear me, they are not!" Maxim shouted. Kseniya, concerned for Anton, was making signs to Maxim but he paid no attention to her. "Personal profits never—you hear me, never!—enter a Bolshevik's mind . . . nothing ever for himself. All for the people, for the party, for the common goal."

Passions rose higher, voices mounted. Kseniya cherished the rare moments she had her son with her, but this had to stop. Anton looked alarmingly exhausted. So did Maxim. It must have been long since he had had a full night's sleep. His eyes were red rimmed, his cheeks sunken. Kseniya put her arms around him.

"Maxim, my boy, don't you think you'd better stop? Lie down, relax, have some rest."

"Rest, mother? Wait till we win, first here, afterwards all over the world. Then we'll relax, then we'll take a rest, a real rest, a beautiful rest. Oh, what a rest I shall take then! I shall sleep, mother, for a whole month; day and night I'll sleep then!"

Before Maxim left, he pulled Natasha's braids and whispered under his breath:

"Good for you, child, good for you! Keep it up . . . don't weaken."

So Maxim knew that she was helping them. Natasha blushed with pleasure but she hardly needed his encouragement to keep up her spirit. Her heart belonged to the Cause and she was in a continuous ecstatic state of readiness to sacrifice her life for it. Besides, there was so much excitement in it.

Young people had a marvelous time. They led their own class war. They were organized in gangs. They marched, some with the slogans, "War to a Victorious End," "Forward, with Our Brave Allies to Victory"; others with "Down with the War," "Peace without Annexations and Contributions," "All Power to the Soviets!" Two columns would meet and engage in lusty verbal fights which more often than not ended in fist fights. Natasha was good with words as well as fists. The Bolsheviks instructed their youth not to make speeches—who would listen to them? But they were taught to play the "simpleton" and under the cover of childish ignorance ask embarrassing questions. Natasha, with her honest naïve face, excelled in confusing anti-Bolshevik speakers and making the audience laugh.

Her honest naïve face also made her grandparents believe the tales she told them about the many hours she spent away from home, and the excuses she gave them for coming home so late in such troubled times.

In the beginning it was hard for Natasha to lie. But Maxim once told her:

"This isn't lying, Natasha. It's for the Cause. I don't like lying. But there are times when for the sake of the work we are doing we must lie. We also have to lie to protect the feeling of those we love. Why worry your grandparents?"

The grandparents were not worrying about Natasha. They believed her. But many other things worried them. Life had become disturbingly unfamiliar; there was little left of the old well-established pattern. The servants, for instance. They had always been as much a part of the house as the old oak cupboard or the drawing-room furniture; they had always been devoted and obedient, and had never minded anything the masters did. But now they minded very much what the masters did, and they showed it. Some of the servants left them; they hurried back to their villages for the land distribution, or they stayed in town and looked for another kind of work. They showed no regrets in leaving their masters, as good servants should. One even said:

"Enough now . . . Long enough you have trampled us under your feet . . . Long enough we were your slaves . . . We are going to be the masters now."

The servants who stayed lost no opportunity to show Kseniya that she should be grateful to them. She was. She knew she could not have managed without them. The stores were empty, and what little got into them was snatched up instantly by the hundreds who stood in line day and night. The servants always argued about the queues. They were supposed to work now not more than eight hours, and they refused to stand in line one minute after their eight hours' work was finished. Who had ever heard of servants keeping hours? Kseniya had to pacify them with expensive presents, with dresses, with shoes. They wanted no money. What was money good for? Kseniya was bewildered. Money—that mainstay of life, that rock on which their very existence was built—money had become the least important thing on earth. A loaf of bread, a lump of sugar, a pat of butter, a chicken—these had become more important than money. And it was the servants who procured these riches for her, by standing in line or by illicit deals. Without them, the family would starve to death.

It was much worse at Vera's. Kseniya did not quarrel with her servants; she cried when one of them was unfriendly. But Vera quarreled constantly with hers; she stamped her foot at them and refused all their demands for less work and greater freedom. Kira tried to intervene and offered to help with the housework, but Vera would not hear of that. She continued quarreling with the servants until finally every one of them had left with the exception of the old cook. The cook stood in line, laundered, scrubbed, cooked, with seldom a sign of appreciation from Vera or Katya, who shared her mother's attitude toward servants. Kira was the only one to appreciate the cook's devotion.

Zena had solved the problem by taking the family to the Crimea. Crimea had food; and money still counted there.

Throughout the fall of 1917, passionate, violent arguments went on between the Bolsheviks and the other parties, and among the Bolsheviks. Had the time come for an insurrection to seize power and install Soviets? After endless conferences lasting days and nights without interruption, with speakers, dizzy from sleepless nights and foodless days, appealing, imploring, threatening, wrangling, arguing for and against—the Bolshevik answer was Yes. The Bolsheviks were moved by a fanatical conviction that no other party could liberate the country from the exploitation of capitalists and imperialists.

The die was cast. The civil war was on. Anti-Bolsheviks of all shades and colors from deep black to light pink gathered their forces. The Bolsheviks appealed in strong, easy words to the people, to workers, peasants, soldiers, sailors. Bread for all, land for all, peace! What could be easier to understand? "War to the Palaces, Peace to the Huts!" That too was easy to understand. All sides wrestled for the heart and the soul of the Russian people, and most of all for able-bodied men to defend their cause with a gun.

In October, the Bolsheviks seized power, proclaiming, "All Power to the Soviets!" To the Soviets of Workers, Soldiers, Peasants! The other side had the brains of the country, its army, the experience in government and industry, besides the keys to the treasury and bank coffers, to secret government files and production formulas. The Bolshevik leaders were well versed in hairsplitting ideological arguments with political opponents, in the art of escaping from czarist prisons and deceiving the czarist secret police. But how to open a safe? How to run a railroad? How to get food? Fuel? How make the telegraph work? The telephones? The factories?

Their opponents sneered at them. The Bolsheviks couldn't last! It needed education, refinement, wisdom, to govern. Where would those rowdies, those illiterates get that! While the leaders of anti-Bolshevik forces were getting ready to fight the Bolsheviks with guns, the lesser fry fought in their own way. Telephone girls turned up their noses and walked out when the Bolsheviks took over the telephone building. Bank employees refused to disclose safe combinations. Government clerks feigned complete ignorance about files, secret documents, ciphers, budgets, funds. The mighty railway workers' organization joined the anti-Bolshevik opposition and refused to run the railways. Guns and sabotage faced the Bolsheviks. Iron discipline in their ranks had always been the cornerstone of their organization. Now, when victory was at stake, no measures seemed too stern to fight any weakening of discipline or to force a way through the wall of opposition.

Their less hardy adherents could not help having qualms about some of the measures. Seventeen-year-old Natasha was one of them. She was not, at that age, a member of the party, but she had enthusiastically offered her services and had been assigned to a minor job in the reception room of the Central Soviet. She did not mind the rough language and crude manners of the people around her. She did not mind the rarely cleaned and never aired rooms; the bread and sausage handed to her by unwashed hands; the stench of cheap tobacco and sweating human flesh. She did not mind walking over bodies of sleeping workers and soldiers who straight from the front staggered into the conference and office rooms to fall asleep on the floor. When she could afford an hour's sleep, she did not mind lying down amidst that snoring smelling humanity.

She did not mind and did not feel the physical discomfort. But she rebelled against the ruthlessness toward human beings which she saw displayed on all sides.

One day Natasha saw Maxim in the building. She hardly recognized him. His eyes were inflamed, his fur cap seemed to be glued to his hair—he had taken off neither cap nor sheepskin coat for days—and his cheeks were covered with dirty-looking reddish growth. The Bolsheviks did not have many people like Maxim. Most of those familiar with letters and figures were on the other side of the barricades. The few who were not could not permit themselves the luxury of a pause in their work. Maxim looked at Natasha, he talked to her but he hardly seemed awake. Suddenly he began to listen carefully, and what he heard made him straighten his shoulders and throw back his head in a gesture familiar to those who knew him. What was it she was saying?

". . . must it be so cruel, Maxim? Can't it be done without hurting people unnecessarily, innocent people?"

"Natasha, my little Natasha, what are you talking about? Do you belong to us or to them? We move mountains, we change the world, and you are worried because somebody might get hurt. Lots of people will get hurt, lots of innocents will get hurt! Is this the time to think about it? Let them get hurt, let thousands of innocents die, as long as we win!"

He looked at her with concern. She must snap out of it. It would be a great pity if she was to turn against the revolution. They needed young people like Natasha, honest devoted young people with good education. He looked around for a place where he could sit down and talk to her. The hall was full of people, coming, going, running. In a corner some soldiers were holding a meeting. A young infantry-man, his face dark with mud and fatigue, his voice ringing with feeling, was addressing them:

"My life, my very life I am ready to give . . ."

Maxim led Natasha closer to the speaker.

". . . ready to give this very moment so that an officer shall never again lift his hand against a soldier, that rich people shall never, never anywhere in the world, tread the poor under their feet; that no child shall ever be hungry anywhere in the world; that no one in pain shall ever cry in vain for help; that no one in the whole big wide world shall ever suffer need. That's what we are fighting for . . . and you talk about not having enough to eat or about not being treated kindly enough! Aren't you ashamed of yourselves, aren't you ashamed to think about it now? This is no time to think of anything except victory and our future. Think with your hearts, not with your stomachs. And remember! The revolution not only casts aside those who resist it; it sweeps out of its path those who lose faith, who doubt, who waver . . ."

Natasha kissed Maxim's unshaven cheek, and Maxim threw a thankful look at the soldier. The soldier had saved him the job!

Natasha returned to her work. People were waiting and several hands stretched out papers to her.

"How about fixing me up, daughter? Three days, three nights I trudge around in this godless Babylon," complained an old peasant, "and do you think that one soul would help me? Our church burned down, to the very ground it burned down, and they laugh at me here, they use a shameless language." He spat on the floor in disgust. "Here . . . here it is . . . they wrote it all out . . . I am telling you the holy truth . . ."

Out of his sack he pulled a loaf of bread, a chunk of salt pork and a herring; under it, wrapped in a handkerchief, was the precious paper.

"Here it is, read it, daughter . . . God punished me, I can't read . . . but you can . . . Read it."

Natasha couldn't help the old man. She wished she could at least save him from being laughed at. But they did laugh at him and pushed him rudely away from her table.

A young soldier was waving a paper under her eyes: "Little sister, little sister, you listen to me now. Where do I go? Whom do I show this to?"

The paper said that the regiment was in need of felt boots. The next man was a delegate from a metallurgical plant. They had found an engineer, a Bolshevik, who had taken over; they could start turning out guns right away; they needed raw material.

An appeal by Trotsky to the soldiers was handed to her to be multigraphed. A group of political exiles had arrived from abroad; rooms and food must be provided for them. A famous safecracker was brought in from jail. Reliable men had to be picked to go with him to open a bank vault. Unable to make herself heard above the din of voices, Natasha pointed out to each the room he was to go to.

"Miss . . . may I ask you for your kind attention . . . if you will be so good . . ." The voice, polite and soft spoken, sounded out of place here. The old professor's house had been searched—oh, that was all right; he didn't come to complain about that. Oh, no! He understood that—but his manuscripts had been disturbed, pages were missing. Could she, could anyone, please, help him?

"You see, miss . . . it's my lifework . . . When finished it may prove of great help to humanity. Please, miss, please . . ."

Voices in the crowd checked him! "There are no misses around here . . . Forget about that . . . We are all comrades . . . Forget the misters and misses . . ."

"Please, citizeness, help me." Natasha didn't have any hope of recovering the missing pages; they had probably been used long since for cigarette paper. But she would try, she told him.

"I object, I object, I object . . ." as rude and loud as the voice was the red face of the screaming woman who brusquely elbowed her way to Natasha's table, followed by an embarrassed militiaman and by the putrid stench of rotten fish.

"Do you see anything wrong in this? Smell it, smell it!" She pushed the basket with the smelling fish under Natasha's nose. "For thirty years I have been selling fish, and no one has ever dared to do that to me. And he . . . this here . . ."

The fishwoman threw a contemptuous look at the little militiaman in his ragged civilian clothes. "This blunderhead here . . . this idiot . . . this nobody . . . dares to tell me what kind of fish I can and can't sell. Have you ever heard of such a nerve?"

She turned to the crowd for understanding and protection, but found no sympathy there. Instead, threatening fists quickly sobered her and stopped her outraged screaming. She would gladly have forgotten about her basket and her fish, and disappeared. But they wouldn't let her go. At least not before they told her a few things:

"We've had enough now of your kind . . . forget about the past, forget about your fish. If ever we catch you selling that stinking rot you call fish, better say a quick prayer; there won't be much time left for anything else. Plenty of times we and our children have got sick eating your fish . . . We couldn't lay our hands on you then. You had bought the police, you had bought the so-called health inspector . . . you had bought everyone. It's finished now, little mother, finished, finished for you forever . . . It's our government now, not yours. Our government can't be bought . . . our government protects us. Our militiamen have no shining uniforms and no big bellies but they wouldn't let anyone harm a hair on our heads. You can thank God they won't let us take the law into our hands. Ah, what I wouldn't like to do to you."

The last threat came from a young worker whose clenched fists were right under the fishwoman's chin. She evaded them and, screaming with fear, fought her way out of the hall.

"Good-by, little mother," yelled the young worker, "here is a present for you!"

Her many petticoats were little protection against his heavy boot.

When Natasha left the building a little later, the fresh air almost overcame her. While she had been working she had not noticed the reek of cheap tobacco and human sweat. Neither had she realized how hungry and tired she was. Now she leaned against the wall of the building and wondered if her legs would hold out for the hour's walk home. After a few minutes she decided to do what she had done once or twice before—to stop at Ludmilla's house, halfway between the Central Soviet and home. She might get a bite there.

There was no longer any luxury in the once-luxurious home of Ludmilla and Fedor Gavrilov. Like all other Muscovites, they had installed in their room a primitive iron stove with a pipe going out through a window. They heated it with whatever fuel they could lay their hands on, usually books or furniture. All the food they had was the sickeningly sweetish frozen vegetables or ossified dried fish that the rest of the population ate. Electric light was a luxury permitted only for an hour or two a day, and candles had to be used sparingly; they were hard to get. Gas had disappeared entirely, and so had soap. Water could be had only at the price of hauling it in buckets from wherever there still was any. Every drop of it was precious. There was a constant inner struggle over whether to wash clothes or dishes, brew the tasteless carrot tea or indulge in the extravagance of washing oneself. Life was full of such nasty worrying details, and Ludmilla was spared them no more than anyone else.

By the time Natasha reached Ludmilla's house, every step had become a conscious effort. Ludmilla heard her and opened the door.

"Well, Natasha dear, come right in." Ludmilla welcomed her as warmly as she had welcomed her guests in the days of her lavish parties. "Quick, take off your shoes, they are soaking wet; here, take Fedor's slippers. You sit, don't get up, let me help you."

Ludmilla made Natasha eat a boiled potato and a few mouthfuls of cabbage. The moment Natasha finished, she fell soundly asleep in the chair, her head on the table, her arms as a pillow. Ludmilla blew out the candle; there was no use wasting it. She sat in the darkness, listening to Natasha's breathing, and waiting for Fedor to come home. Soon she was asleep too. Her day was never an easy day either. The little food and fuel they had was the result of many hours in many lines, of much scheming, bargaining, and bartering.

Even in her sleep, Ludmilla did not miss Fedor's step. When he came into the room, the candle was lit and a smiling Ludmilla stretched out her hands to him. The half-dark chilly room, Natasha's pathetic childish pose of exhaustion, Ludmilla's hands, rough from work and cold, the miserable food on the expensive china plate, gave Fedor a sense of unreality. He sat down, a look of despair on his face.

"Any decision?"

"No, my dear, nothing. They can't make up their minds. Now they say Lenin has to decide it. Can you understand it? I've offered to teach them everything I know about the plant—and there is little I don't know about it; I helped build it; Pavel and I ordered every piece of machinery in it. I don't care that the plant doesn't belong to us now; I want it to belong to the people. But I want to see it running again! I want to see it alive! I've told them I wouldn't keep a thing back, that I'd show them everything. They could start running it tomorrow morning! But no; they have to verify this, and they have to verify that. They call in my own workers to confirm what I say in case I intend to sabotage them. Now, what do the workers know? Only what each of them used to do, one tiny part of the whole. They have no idea how to run the plant. I've pleaded with them to call in our old engineers. No, they say, they don't trust the engineers. They don't say it about me but I know they don't trust me."

"Can you blame them, Fedor? How many have behaved the way you have? What do the others do? They supply money to every scoundrel who is ready to betray Russia, just so long as the Bolsheviks are destroyed. They bribe their former engineers and workers to sabotage, to destroy machinery, to falsify records, formulas. How can the government help being suspicious and distrustful?"

"That's true, Ludmilla, I understand that, and that's why I don't give up. But how long can it last? For weeks now I've begged them to let me put the plant in shape. What more can I do? Maybe I am all wrong, Ludmilla. Maybe I'm a daydreamer, a castle builder, a plain damned fool. Maybe I should do what the others did, what my brother Pavel did. Take you, take our valuables, and go abroad, live a quiet life, in cleanliness and comfort. We don't have to live in this filth and darkness . . . we don't . . . Ludmilla, what do you say? It is not too late."

"Fedor dear, you know you don't mean it. We decided to stick to the revolution and we will. We knew it wasn't going to be easy for us and that we would have to sacrifice much. Remember, Fedor, how you said that we might have to pay for the sins others have committed?

And you said then that it was all right with you and that you were ready for it. Eat now, my dear, eat, and go to sleep. After a rest it will all seem different."

A few days later Fedor was told that Lenin had approved his offer and had appointed him chief engineer of his own former plant. Lenin wrote him a personal letter, saying how handicapped they were by the shortage of experts, how much easier their task would be if more skilled men would give their services.

Fedor worked with even greater zeal than he had when the plant was his own. The eighteen-hour day and the seven-day week did not seem too long. He didn't feel tired; he couldn't afford to be tired. But the machines lacked his human enthusiasm; they were getting tired and there was no cure for them. There were no spare parts, no way to replace the worn-out hearts, lungs, and limbs of the machines. Transport was crippled. Raw material didn't reach the plant.

Most of the men workers had left. The front needed them, the revolution was in danger. Many of their experienced women workers left too, for Moscow was desperately hungry. The women took their families and went back to the villages, where there was still some food. Unskilled fingers mishandled the weakened machines, damaged the precious textiles. To run the plant was a Herculean task. And always Fedor felt the breath of the secret police on his neck. A machine went out of order, the output fell—was it unavoidable or was it the chief engineer's subtle way of sabotaging and fighting the workers' revolution?

Neither was there much relaxation during the few hours he spent with Ludmilla at home. Moscow's living space had been redistributed. No one could have more than the few square feet which the government had decided was sufficient for a person to live in. Fedor was permitted to keep two rooms. The rest of the house—ten rooms—was given to eight families. They sounded like eighty to Fedor. The halls were full of the trunks, baskets, baby carriages, furniture which found no place in the crowded rooms. Their peaceful beautiful home looked like a market place. The kitchen was a bedlam, and with tears in her eyes Ludmilla would serve him cold unappetizing food. "I couldn't . . . I simply couldn't go into the kitchen today."

This was going on all over Moscow. From the slums on the outskirts of the city, from damp basements and windowless attics, families moved to airy sunny apartments with wide windows and parquet floors, with bathrooms and toilets and large kitchens.

Dasha, Maxim's early mentor, was put in charge of assigning the living space in the neighborhood where she had worked as a servant, first in Kseniya's household, then in Vera's. The revolution, to which she had given every beat of her heart, had released the fires of pity and hatred in her. She burned with pity for all those who had been beaten by life, who had suffered as she had. And she burned with hatred for the rich, the smug, the selfish, heartless rich. Now she could do something about both her pity and her hatred. And she did. She worked tirelessly and selflessly. It was the right job for her. She had been given charts, plans, figures, but she couldn't be bothered with them. She didn't understand them. She left that to her more educated assistants. Instead, she walked from house to house and made her own mysterious signs and marks on a piece of paper. The largest families, the palest children, the sick and the miserable got the sunniest, the largest rooms. She hated all rich people, but a very special hatred, a hatred she nursed and fanned, was reserved for Vera. She once said to Maxim:

"What is true is true. Your mother, Kseniya, was always good to me; I never had anything but kindness from her. But that sister of yours . . . wait till I get my hands on her."

The day came when the rooms in Vera's house were assigned. Vera and her three children, Pavlik, Kira, and Katya, were permitted to keep two. Michel was not counted as a member of the family; he had disappeared after the Bolshevik revolution. With the servants' quarters, there were fourteen other rooms to be occupied. Dasha was well prepared. She had reserved for Vera's house the largest and noisiest families, families who had never seen anything but city slums or village huts; who had never seen running water or a flush toilet.

When workers moved into the houses of the very rich, Dasha preached them a sermon:

"Don't you dare trifle with the honor of a workingman. Behave with dignity and with pride. Show them who the real aristocrats are. They, selfish brutes who are only interested in filling their bellies and their pockets, or you, who would want everybody in this world to have a good life. Don't you do any grabbing. Only touch what's yours. What's not yours is poison to you. And don't you let your children show themselves with running noses or wet pants. Don't ask me why—but this to them seems to be the biggest sin on earth. Worse than stealing or murdering. And be clean, very clean. I know what I am talking about. Give them an excuse, and they will make you feel little, they will trample all over you. That will hurt you like hell and that's exactly what they want." She would tell them: "Be proud. Walk into the kitchen with your head up. Don't let them know you never saw a gas stove. Come, let me show you."

She would show them how to work a kitchen stove, how to use the bathroom, how to clean their room.

She did not preach her usual sermon and she did not show anything to the families who moved into Vera's house. She did come for her regular inspections. But, whereas in other houses she scolded the women for a poorly scrubbed floor or for using the bathtub for laundry, she walked through Vera's untidy neglected house with a sly smile on her lips, saying nothing.

"Believe me," she told a friend, "I am not really mean, sore inside maybe, but not mean. But when I am there, in that house, near that woman, I am a devil. All I think of is to pay back my hurts . . . and to pay the full bitter price."

When the rooms in Anton's house were assigned, Natasha was permitted to keep her old room.

"But mind you," Dasha warned her, "as soon as he dies," she pointed to Anton's room, "you can't have it. You'll move in with your grandmother. Her room is plenty big for the two of you. I don't think he will last long."

"Dasha, please, not so loud, the door is open, he might hear you."

"What if he does? He knows it. Look at him. Fit for the coffin. He is of no earthly use to anyone. Only takes up space and eats food which would do more good to others."

"Dasha, Dasha, how can you be so heartless?"

"Heartless, me? Oh, no, Natasha, my girl, I am not heartless. But we plain people are simple about things. What's wrong if a very old paralyzed man dies? Then why not say so? And isn't it true that when babies are starving to death because their mothers' breasts are dry, it's a sin to waste food on useless lives? All right, kid, don't take it so tragically. Learn to face things as they are, true and naked, without your fancy frills and big words. Now, let's get busy."

Together they went through the house, and Dasha made her dots and crosses. A week later the new tenants were installed. A house committee was elected, with Natasha a member of it. She was made responsible for the cleanliness of the house and the observance of house rules. She was delighted. She loved few things in life as much as being among people and knowing about their affairs.

KSENIYA was lost. She did not know how to live in a world where the servants had disappeared, where their business was taken away from them, where food and all the necessities of life were gone, where their money was frozen in the bank. And now this—their house full of strangers, children crying, noisy women in her own kitchen. Anton was slowly dying. Zena gone—no one knew whether she was in the Crimea or abroad. Vera, left alone with the children, had become bitter even against her own parents. No letters from Olga.

Maxim had no time for his parents either. But at least he was safe. He, as a Bolshevik, was on top now. Couldn't he really help them? He said he couldn't. When the nurse left because of a new law forbidding nurses to work for private patients, Kseniya had begged Maxim to get another nurse for his father.

"Don't ask me, mother," he had said. "I will not do it, not even for Father. I have always fought against privileges for a few . . ."

And he used the same words again when she implored him to help her get his father some food; he couldn't digest the cabbage, it was killing him, and that was all they had.

"I would give you my own food, if I had any," he added, "but none of us gets anything special. We are all equal in hunger."

Even Natasha wasn't the same. They hardly ever saw her. Kseniya didn't approve of a young girl, almost a child, spending her days and evenings among filthy smoking swearing men, but there was nothing she could do about it. Natasha helped them as much as she could; she felt sorry for them, Kseniya knew. Yet at the same time she was friendly and nice to those disgusting people who had moved into the house. She acted as if something wonderful had happened. To Kseniya, it was a hurricane that had passed over their lives and destroyed them completely. If only they could die, she and Anton, both of them at the same time.

Kseniya's wish was not fulfilled. Anton died without her. There was little life left in him; she hardly noticed when he stopped breathing one morning.

She was alone when he died. Natasha would not be back till late in the evening. There was no one to send to Vera and no way to reach

Maxim. Only strangers around, godless people who could not be expected to know what should be done. Kseniya put copper coins on Anton's eyes; she folded his hands, and sat close to him on the chair on which she had been sitting close to him for the past ten years. Natasha found her there when she came home late that night, tears running down her cheeks, whispering softly to herself.

Natasha's grief was deep, but at the moment her grandmother's need came first; she had to be taken care of. And something had to be done about Grandfather. With a pitifully quivering face, Natasha went to find the neighbors. The neighbors would know; they would help.

They did know. They came and they helped, those new friends of Natasha's. Kseniya was put to bed with a hot-water bottle at her feet. An old woman sat with her and fed her hot tea with dried raspberries. Murmuring prayers, two other women washed and dressed Anton. Someone brought a precious candle and put it at his head. Natasha cried herself to sleep. Kseniya lay with eyes wide open, comfortable and warm. Friendly hands had seen to that. Twice during the night the door opened and a dark figure slipped in to relieve another dark figure at Anton's bed. Not for one moment was Anton left without a prayer for his soul.

In the morning a priest came to comfort Kseniya and to talk about the funeral service. Neighbors came in and asked for his blessing. Vera arrived, her face drawn and her eyes tragic, all in black. She was still an impressive-looking figure, even as she knelt by her father's body. She hardly waited for the priest and the neighbors to leave the room to ask icily:

"Mother, who are those terrible people? What are they doing in your room? Why do you let them in? Where is our priest? Why did you get this filthy ordinary priest? For Father! What would he have said? And where is Natasha? Couldn't she have stayed home for one day? And she was supposed to be Father's darling! Is she afraid the Bolshevik card house will crumble an hour earlier if she stays home?"

"Vera, please," Kseniya pleaded feebly, "don't be so harsh. Father is lying here . . . The priest was kind to me . . . A neighbor called him in; he had been her priest for many years. Vera, they are not bad people. I thought they were bad, too, before I knew them. They are not godless, and they have good hearts. They brought a candle and gave us water to wash Father. Vera dear, I am very tired now . . . don't be harsh . . . please."

Not more than a dozen people followed Anton Nazarov's plain birch coffin. The neighbors who had given a helpful hand, and the family. Not even the whole family; Maxim was not with them.

"Please, mother, understand me," he begged Kseniya when the

body was being brought out of the house, "if there were no priest, I would come. But I can't, in my position, I can't take part in a religious ceremony. My heart is with you, mother, but I must leave you now. I must not be seen with a priest even if it is my own father's funeral."

When they returned home from the funeral, Anton's bed was not in the room any more. Neither were his wheelchair and the medicine table. The furniture had been rearranged to fill up the empty spaces. The samovar was ready and the table set for a memorial repast. Warmed-up dry bread, sugarless plum jam, a piece of hard goat cheese, cabbage soup with slices of salt pork in it, a bottle of vodka—it was not a rich meal but the neighbors had dug deep in their treasure chests to produce it.

Kseniya sat between Natasha and Manilov, an elderly man with kind young eyes under bushy eyebrows and a friendly mouth hidden by a profuse gray beard. Kseniya was overcome by the attention and kindness of people with whom only a few days ago she would have nothing to do. They had thought of everything to ease her grief; they had even known that it would have tormented her not to have had a memorial repast for Anton. She was ashamed, she felt guilty before them. She tried to say it.

"I am so grateful to you. Believe me, I don't deserve it . . . I don't deserve it from you . . ."

Manilov patted her hand.

"Forget it, Kseniya Nikolaevna, forget it. We understand how you felt. People don't like strangers in their homes. Don't feel bad about it. Now that you know that we don't eat people alive, that some of us even kissed the priest's hand—unfortunately not me, I am a sinner, my soul is lost—now everything will change. We will get along fine together. Don't you worry."

"A fine funeral it was, everything as it should be, everything proper, befitting. It couldn't have been better," a woman said. The others nodded approvingly.

Natasha threw an anxious look at Kseniya. Was Grandmother going to say something? She hoped not. Natasha had heard Kseniya last night asking God to forgive her for not giving her husband a proper funeral, for letting Anton go to Him in such an unbecoming way. But Kseniya did not say anything now. She bowed her head and sighed.

Kseniya cried throughout the night. The emptiness around her gnawed at her heart; it made her pace the room aimlessly, clutch desperately at a piece of furniture; it made her praying sound like an angry muttering. She didn't want Natasha's consolation and sent her out of the room. Only toward morning did she fall asleep.

Natasha too cried that night. She cried for her grandfather. He had been so good to her, and she had loved him so dearly. He had even made it easy for her to be without her parents. When she thought of her parents, Natasha's loneliness deepened. Were they alive? Constant fighting was reported from around their region. Their village was changing hands all the time. Had they survived the fighting and the terror? There had been no letters for so long. Mother . . . Mother . . . nothing must happen to Mother. How Mother would feel when she heard of Grandfather's death! Grandmother . . . what would happen to Grandmother without Grandfather? The pillow was getting wetter and wetter.

"He is of no earthly use to anyone . . . Learn to face things as they are, true and naked . . ." That was what Dasha had said. Dasha was a good Bolshevik; she was trusted by the party. What Dasha said couldn't be wrong. Dasha had said that Grandfather was only taking away the food younger people needed.

These days one could not long think of anything, not even of one's dead grandfather, without returning to the formidable matters of food, soap, fuel, candles. Natasha could not hide it from herself—it would be much easier to take care of all that with grandfather gone. He's had to be washed every so often; he'd had to be kept warm, and he couldn't be left in a dark room. The grandparents did not know that she could never have provided all those extras if the neighbors hadn't helped out. And of course she had been grateful and glad to help their children with their homework, and sit with their babies in her free time. But that wouldn't be necessary now. For just Grandmother and herself, she wouldn't have to work so hard. She would have more time for her studies. Life would be much easier. Natasha forced herself not to shrink away from her thoughts, even though they seemed terrible to her. "Learn to face things as they are, true and naked . . ." Life was going to be easier without Grandfather; that was the naked truth and she, like real Bolsheviks, must not shrink away from unpleasant truths.

Natasha tossed restlessly in her bed. She wanted to be a good Bolshevik, but it was hard to make herself think of Grandfather's death as something she should be pleased about.

During the day Natasha forgot the thoughts that had troubled her mind before sleep closed in on her. But as she walked home in the evening they came back to her. She walked quickly, without looking to right or left, without drinking in with curious eyes the life around her, as she always did. She rehearsed what she was going to say to Grandmother. She would try to make Grandmother see why she shouldn't be so miserable over Grandfather's death, and at the end she would say:

"It is all true, grandmother, isn't it? Then why be afraid to say it? Let us learn to face life as it is."

The trip home seemed very short; she was almost running. At the door she stopped. Somebody was talking in Grandmother's room. A familiar voice. Manilov! What was he doing in Grandmother's room?

". . . so you see, dear Kseniya Nikolaevna, it really amounts to this. When a situation arises people shouldn't knock their heads against a stone wall. They only get hurt and they can't go through the wall anyway. Now, take your own case. You lost your husband. There is no denying, this is a very sad thing to have happened. But then again— think of how he had suffered; he got practically nothing out of his life any more. And what about you? Will it do him any good if you do nothing but mourn for him? You are a believer, aren't you? So let's take your own, religious arguments. Did Christ spend His days mourning over His own troubles? Did He close His eyes and His heart to the troubles of His fellow men? You are His follower, aren't you? Then why don't you follow Him? Look around; there is plenty for you to do, there is plenty of trouble all around you . . ."

Behind the door Natasha held her breath waiting for Grandmother to say something.

"Give me a little time . . ."

How weak and thin Grandmother's voice sounded! Now she wouldn't have to make the speech she had prepared. The old, wise Manilov was taking care of Grandmother much better than she ever could.

That night Natasha moved into Grandmother's room. A new tenant, with a written order from the Housing Department, presented himself for Natasha's room. The department kept close watch over deaths and marriages and did not waste any time.

During the next days Natasha always found one of the neighbors with Grandmother. It was as if they were taking turns in order not to leave her alone. Grandmother gradually learned to know all of them, their children, their occupations.

One day Natasha heard her telling a neighbor—and her voice sounded proud telling it—that her son was a Bolshevik, that he had been in Siberia and escaped, and was now an important man in the government. She had never talked about it before. Kseniya could never free herself of the feeling that Maxim's prison term was something to be ashamed of. That evening Natasha climbed into Grandmother's bed and nestled close to her.

"Grandmother darling, I heard you—I heard you being proud of Maxim. Grandmother, I love you for it. Grandmother, I know it is hard for you to feel the way we do. You are not young, you have lived the kind of life that makes it hard for you to understand what has happened. But try, please try to understand. All you have to do is not to think of what the revolution has done to you, to your family. Think of what it has done for those who were all far down in life, who never went to school, who never could get out of the rot into which they were born. Think of them . . . And think why my mother, Maxim, Manilov, and so many other good people gave up comfortable lives. Why did they do it? Because they couldn't stand it, thinking of the others who lived in hopeless misery. And now, grandmother, everybody is going to live comfortable lives, everybody is going to schools, everybody is getting the same chance in life. Everybody!"

CHAPTER 17
## Vera

VERA was smiling. That strong beautiful odor. It was the smell of horses. Michel's smell when he came to her straight from the stables. The smell was getting closer and closer. Soon she would be in his arms . . . in Michel's arms . . . He was saying something. What was he saying? Why was his voice getting so loud? Vera was sliding out of her sleep. She fought against it. The horse smell was disappearing. She didn't want it to disappear. She wanted Michel . . . The horse smell was changing into that other smell which she didn't like. She didn't want to wake up. The other smell was getting stronger; the voice was getting louder and louder, and, of course, it wasn't Michel's voice at all. . . . Wearily Vera gave up, and opened her eyes. To wake up in the morning, to return to reality from a happy dream was sheer horror every day.

How could she, even in a dream, have mistaken that stench of rotten cabbage mixed with soiled diapers, human sweat, and a defective toilet for the smell of healthy clean horses? And the voices? The coarse quarreling voices, how could she have heard Michel's voice in that? Vera did not want to get up. She knew that if she stayed in bed the disasters of the past two years would come back to her in all their horror. But anything, even reliving that terror, was better than getting out of bed and starting the day.

Inexorably, past events marched toward her; she couldn't stop them. First—it was always first—that day in November, soon after the Bolshevik revolution. She had been standing at the window in the darkened room. It was not yet evening, but the sky was heavy and low. The room had been cold, and she had on her coat and boots. There were a few pieces of wood left, but she hadn't wanted to use them till Pavlik came home. Or Michel . . . There had been no word from him since his regiment had retired from the Petrograd front. But why wasn't Pavlik home yet? It was no time for a boy of seventeen to be away from home. She had heard that they were sending young boys into battle. They shouldn't do that! Not even though the boys were to be future officers. Pavlik was only a child.

The shooting sounded very close. Where was Pavlik? They should have sent the boys home the moment the shooting started. It was shameful! And it was all the fault of those Bolsheviks, those bandits! Well, they couldn't last much longer.

Then a woman passed under the windows. She saw Vera and shouted to her:

"Why don't you go and get your bastard?" Her voice was rude and full of hate. Vera recognized her as a woman who used to help on washdays. What had she said? What bastard?

Then the door opened and the old cook came in, tears streaming down her face.

"Mistress, Vera Antonovna . . . you better come . . . our young master . . . our Pavlik . . ."

For several days, the Junkers, pupils of the officers' schools, together with a group of high school students, had been fighting the Bolsheviks. It was a lost battle. Most of them had died. The shooting Vera had heard had been the last desperate attempt of a few survivors to shoot their way out to safety. Pavlik had almost succeeded. A bullet caught up with him a few steps from his home. He lay sprawled on the pavement. Someone had closed his eyes but had not wiped his tears. He had died crying for his mother. His face was round and childish under its coat of pallor and dirt. With an unhuman scream, Vera fell over his body.

The cook cried and begged for a long time before she found people to help her bring the boy and Vera into the house. One of the men whispered to her:

"Don't think I am one of those godless ones . . . Don't think I don't feel sorry . . . But you know how it is these days. You show mercy to the wrong people and—before you know it—you are one of the wrong people yourself. Not that you can blame them . . ."

Many months later, before Vera had recovered from the blow of Pavlik's death and while she was still deaf and blind to everything around her, a piece of folded brown wrapping paper shook her out of her torpor. The paper was suddenly lying there on the floor near the door. How it got there no one knew. All the cook could remember was that a beggar had been seen around the kitchen that day. The paper contained a note from Michel. He was safe, he wrote, but he could not tell her where he was. He asked her not to lose hope. They were assembling their strength and the final victorious battle would soon be fought. Friends from outside were helping them.

Several months later, as suddenly and as mysteriously as the first, a second note appeared. They were all to join him soon. A reliable friend would take care of them when the time came. They were to be ready to leave at a moment's notice, but were not to take much with them, only what they could easily carry without arousing suspicion, and they were to dress inconspicuously. A few jewels could be safely hidden in a shoe heel or in a loaf of bread; the rest were to be put away in a safe place until they returned home.

Didn't any news from Moscow reach him where he was? Didn't he know that most of their valuables had been taken away from them? Vera divided the few jewels she had left in two parts. Her nails breaking, her hands bleeding, she lifted floor boards, made holes in icon and family portrait frames, and hid one part there. Those to be taken along she sewed in a belt buckle and in her velvet coat buttons, and hid in holes screwed into shoe heels. What would Michel say when they arrived without Pavlik? But not even the thought of her dead son could take away from Vera the excitement of getting ready to be with Michel again. She had to be careful not to show her feelings. Kira and Katya would wonder about the change in her, and they mustn't know anything yet. Time enough to tell them when she received word to be ready. She had carefully selected the dresses they were to wear, the coats, hats, shoes, rubbers, gloves. The things to be taken along she packed in a marketing bag. They would walk out of the house as if they were going to market.

For many months Vera waited for a word from the "reliable friend." The first excitement of anticipation wore off. Uncontrollable nervousness took its place. She jumped and paled at every step near her door, and steps were heard near her door twenty-four hours a day. To leave the room became agony. Returning to it, she would throw herself on the floor looking for a note.

One morning, her half-opened eyes noticed a piece of folded brown wrapping paper. With the agility of a young animal, she leaped to the floor and grabbed up the paper. "Yes, yes, yes, Michel!" she murmured, tearing the paper open with fingers which wouldn't obey. She read the note again and again. A great silence enveloped her.

"I have the sad task," the note said, "of informing you that your husband was killed in a skirmish with a Bolshevik band. I was with him up to the last minute. He spoke of you and the children, and regretted not having made you come earlier. He hoped that you would help one another to survive and to get along till the day of victory came. Don't try to find me—it will endanger me and yourself."

Vera sat still and looked at the broken board under the door, the board which to her had been the symbol of the misery of their present lives. Through this crack children threw rubbish into the room, the noises from the outside came in freely. Through this crack the note had come. She read the note again. She lifted herself with difficulty from the floor. Her hair was stringy and unkempt; her silk nightgown, now faded and unevenly stretched, trailed behind her and hindered her steps. With eyes wide open, staring straight ahead, she walked through the room. She unpacked the marketing bag. She put away the clothes she had prepared for the trip. Then she sat down, her hands folded in her lap. A light tremor started to shake her body from the roots of her hair to her toes. Her teeth chattered. Like a horse galloping, she thought inanely.

There was no pain in her heart. There was no heart because there was no more life.

"I am not alive any more, I am dead," she said in a loud voice, "it is good to be dead, I am dead . . ."

"Mother, what are you saying, what are you talking about? What is the matter, mother?" Kira and Katya stood in the room.

"Father is dead . . ."

Katya's blue eyes filled with quick tears. She dropped to her knees beside Vera and kissed her hands and cried bitterly. Vera did not move; she did not see and did not feel anything. Kira pulled Katya to her feet and whispered to her:

"Go quick, tell Grandmother. But first of all, try to find cook; ask the neighbors, they will know where to find her . . . Quick."

Vera's hand opened and the note fell to the floor. She did not move when Kira picked it up and read it. So Father had been fighting against the Bolsheviks, and Mother had been in touch with him. And they had all been going to join him! How little her mother understood to think that she, Kira, would have gone with her to join the White Army. But there was no point in thinking about that now!

Big and strong as she was, Kira managed to dress Vera's inert heavy body only with great effort. It was unpleasant to the touch in its limp flabbiness. Not wanting to use the bathtub which everybody in the house used, Vera had neglected herself and her body showed it. It seemed such a short time ago, Kira thought—why it was less than three years ago—that her mother had moved in a cloud of fragrant aroma, her body well bathed and massaged, her skin smooth and lovely. Kira combed her hair, getting the comb through the tangles with difficulty. Again she remembered the soft blonde curls which she had so admired as a child, she with her straight black hair which yielded to no curlers.

If only Katya was able to find cook. She always knew how to treat Vera, how to take her abuse and whims. But she had left the week before, with tears and regrets.

"I would have stayed, honey, believe me, I would have stayed," she cried, kissing Kira good-by, "I want to stay . . . I have nowhere to go . . . I have always worked with masters . . . But I can't stay; they laugh at me; they point their fingers at me. 'Serf' they call me and worse names than that too . . . Work in a factory, they say, work anywhere, but not for masters, they say . . ."

Well, who else could help? Kira wondered. Grandmother would not be much help; Mother did not get along with her at all. Mother couldn't forgive her for not raving and raging about the Bolsheviks the way she did herself. Mother really didn't get along with anybody, Kira thought. She resented everybody. She even resented her own daughters because they didn't feel that the world had come to an end . . . Someone came in. Thank God, it was cook!

Vera saw her too and slowly said: "The master is dead . . . and I am going to die too."

"No, no, no! Don't say that!" The cook threw up her arms in terror. "It's a sin, it's a deadly sin to say that, don't you know? Every one of us will die, but only when He wants us to. You don't go against His holy will. You have your daughters to live for—you have your prayers to say for your son's soul and now for the dear master's soul. Come now, come, Vera Antonovna, let us all have some tea."

To Kira's relief, the cook again took possession of the family. She tied an apron around her dress and armed with tea utensils sailed out into the kitchen to prepare her remedy for all human ills.

A few minutes later Katya peeped fearfully into the room. The sight of her mother sitting dressed on a chair and of Kira quietly paging a book reassured her. If only she could be like Kira! But she never could. She always needed someone to guide her; she needed a strong hand in which she could put hers. She whispered to Kira:

"Grandmother wasn't in. They'll tell her to come here . . . I asked the neighbors about cook . . ."

Kira whispered back: "Cook came; she's in the kitchen, making tea."

Both smiled. Nothing ever happened in the family without cook's brewing tea to help the situation.

The cook brought in the steaming teakettle and sat down with them. She had never done it before, but she had suddenly assumed a role of the greatest importance, and she was aware of it. To Kira, the few days without her had seemed like a nightmare. Neither her mother nor Katya was able or willing to scrub floors or carry wood or bring home their rations of potatoes, or do the thousand and one things that required strong arms and strong nerves. Besides, her mother flatly refused to go into the kitchen, to rub shoulders with the women there. Katya did not know how to cook or how to do any other housework, and Kira knew she could not have carried the whole load much longer. Would cook stay? Or had she come only to help out with their mother today? As if to answer this, cook, red and perspiring from the boiling-hot tea, pushed her cup away and, fully aware of the importance of the moment, announced:

"Let them say what they want. Let them call me names, let them laugh at me. My ears are closed to them. I am staying here. Stupid old woman that I was! As if at my age one starts life anew! Here I belong and here I stay. Vera Antonovna! Kira! Katya!" She got up and solemnly bowed to each of them. "Forgive the old fool for having deserted you."

As the girls left the room, the last words they heard were: "Vera Antonovna, dear, cry, try hard to cry. Nothing helps as much as tears. Cry, dear!"

But what they heard a while later from the adjoining room were not tears but their mother's wild voice:

"You hated him, you always hated him, I know . . ." Her voice sounded hardly human. "Are you happy now, are you? He is dead, dead, dead! Go, run, tell it to Maxim, to Natasha. Spread the happy news! Why don't you go? They will dance with joy. You love them, don't you? You love them, and you hated him . . . and you hated Pavlik . . . and you hate me and you hate Kira and Katya. Your only love is for the murderers of my son and of my husband, for the butchers . . . for the monsters . . . for . . ."

Vera began to choke. It was a terrible sound, and Katya clung in fear to Kira's arm.

"What is it, Kira? What is it? Is Mother dying?"

"No, no, Katya," said Kira calmly. "It's just as well for her to get this out; it must have been choking her long enough."

Soon the terrifying choking stopped and only dry convulsive sobs came from their mother's room. Close together, the two sisters sat in silence. Kira, her large gray almond-shaped eyes lost in thought, closed her arms in protection around Katya.

Their father was dead and they weren't crying for him. Even Katya's, the soft little kitten's tears, were not for him. She was crying out of excitement and some pity for her mother. And she, Kira, herself? She felt nothing at all but a heavy responsibility on her for the three of them.

Father, her handsome dashing father, who had always had a smile on his full red lips, who had always been on the lookout for pleasure and fun, had been a stranger to her. He had rocked her on his knees, he had tickled her with his silken mustache, he had brought her huge boxes of chocolate, taken her to horse races and to expensive restaurants, showered her with presents on her birthdays and on holidays. But he had always remained a stranger. So had her mother. Much of her mother's time had been given to her and Katya. But it had been given at hairdressers' and dressmakers' and furriers' and in novelty shops. It had been given to make well-dressed dolls of them, decorous young ladies fit for the drawing-room life of curtsies and politesse. Governesses and teachers had helped her in that.

But Kira knew about other things too. She had often heard her mother cry. She had seen her come out of Father's room when he was away, dazed and white faced. Once she had followed her and watched her through the keyhole. She had seen her go through Father's pockets and desk drawers. She had seen her read a letter, smell his clothes, and cry heartbreakingly. Kira had learned early not to trust smiles and polite words. Even as a child she had been drawn to Natasha, to Maxim, to Ludmilla. She trusted their smiles and their words. They did not sound false to her, and when she understood the words they were saying, she believed them rather than her parents'.

Grandmother was talking to her:

". . . will be all right now. I think she will fall asleep; she has cried long enough." Grandmother's eyes were red from crying too. "Take care of her. I don't think I can be much good to her now. Maybe she will be less bitter later. You will tell me how she is . . . and tell me if you need anything. You know I love you, you and Katya . . . your mother isn't fair to me . . ." Grandmother's soft crying touched Kira.

"I know, grandmother, I know . . . don't worry about that." The girl of seventeen put her arms around the old woman with the same gesture of tender protection she had for her young sister.

Vera did not fall asleep easily. She cried till no more tears were left in her. When she woke up, her eyes were dry; everything in her was dry. In a very few days her voice, her gestures, her walk had acquired a stony hardness which terrified her daughters. Every morning she went to church to pray for Michel. For the first time she performed household chores which did not require her being in the kitchen; she sewed and ironed, set and cleared the table, and even at times took cook's place in a line at the food store. Kira could devote all her time to her library job during the day and to her evening courses at night. Katya had lessons with a private tutor who taught pupils whose parents wouldn't let them mingle with the common people who had filled the Soviet schools.

Dead though Vera seemed to be to everything else, she intended that her daughters should be prepared to take their rightful place in society when the present nightmare of life was over. That it soon would be over, Vera never doubted. For that day, she had hidden decent clothes, a few valuable pieces of china and crystal, and she refused to sell any of the furniture that cluttered their two over-crowded rooms. The girls' hands must not get rough and their manners must not be allowed to suffer from contact with the present political masters. This was hard in Kira's case. Kira had to work; if no one in the family worked, they would be deprived even of the few miserable crumbs now thrown to them. Besides, Vera had never nursed too high a hope that Kira would shine in society. Kira was too tall and her movements too impulsive and quick to present the proper figure in a ballroom. When she talked, she opened her mouth too wide; when she laughed, her laughter was much too loud. And though Kira had never contradicted her mother's wild outbursts against the Bolsheviks, Vera suspected her of not hating them as much as she should. There was not much Vera could do about Kira. But Katya must be saved, Katya with her lovely beauty and her docile softness. As for herself, she did not matter; she was dead. A kerchief tied around her hair in the house, a big shawl over her head in the street—this saved combing it daily—in a faded dress, an old coat with buttons missing, and unshined shoes, she moved through life with a stony look in her eyes, her lips pressed together, with never a smile and seldom a word. She constantly rubbed her hands, as if trying to wipe off the touch of a life that disgusted her.

CHAPTER 18

## Natasha

NATASHA could have slept on and on. She was tired. It was true, there were no household duties to hurry her out of bed—Grandmother took care of those now; and anyway there was so little to shop for, to cook, to eat, that this took very little time. But there were many other tasks, for which no day ever was long enough.

First, there was her new job. It was much better than the job she had had four years before at the reception desk in the Central Soviet, and infinitely better than being in the Finance Commissariat, to which she had next been sent. Her work there on long columns of figures had bored her, and the people had been mostly oldish people. They'd kept moving their lips even when they weren't working, as if, she thought, they were forever adding figures. They hadn't wanted to let her go; there were so few people who were literate who could also be trusted, they'd said. And it was against the law to leave a job without permission.

One day Natasha read something Lenin had said about young people. Their task was to liquidate illiteracy in Russia; they must give all their strength, all their work to that cause. The Bolsheviks, Lenin had said, must transform Russia from a poor and miserable land into a rich land. And literacy was the first step. She had copied his words and had pasted them above her bed. She felt that he had meant them for her. Let others add up figures, make speeches, work at a lathe, bang on a typewriter; she was going to open to people the Wonderland of the Written Word. The Finance Commissariat was obliged to release her. The task of liquidating illiteracy had priority over even the pressing job of resolving the country's cata-strophic financial confusion.

Half her working day Natasha spent teaching classes for adults; during the other half she attended the university. Into the remaining few hours she crammed a host of activities. She had joined the Com-somol, the Young Communists organization, and had been assigned the leadership of two Pioneer groups in her district, groups of school children to be trained in the Communist spirit. Busy as this kept her, she seldom wasted the free theater, lecture, and concert tickets which, in her triple capacity of trade union member, Comsomol member, and student, she was getting plentifully.

Her duties as a member of the House Committee also took much of her time. Some of these duties were anything but pleasant. She had to plead with the chairman of the House Committee for every electric bulb, for every bit of wood, every nail, every hour of the handyman's time. Some of the tenants were unco-operative and even mean. They cheated or refused to do their share in taking out the garbage, in cleaning and guarding the house. But all that mattered little when she could satisfy her insatiable curiosity about people. She often sat in a room and talked long after the business she had come about was forgotten. There were rooms in which she especially liked to linger—Manilov's, for instance, where neighbors had a habit of dropping in for a minute and staying till long after midnight.

The familiar noises in the apartment, as well as an alarm clock, reminded her that it was time to get up. Every morning, exactly as Natasha was about to get out of bed, one of the old women started a quarrel in the kitchen with anyone she could find. Every morning it was over something different—a broken plate, a mislaid knife, some spilled water. It wasn't hard to pick a fight. The crowded rooms, the crowded kitchen; the difficulty of feeding a hungry family when there was nothing to feed them with, of replacing garments and shoes worn to shreds when there was nothing to replace them with, had made everybody tired and edgy. The children in the room below began to scream—another reminder of the time—while their parents fought it out in angry hissing whispers. They were all angry, because they were exhausted, hungry, because their nerves were worn thin.

A great tenderness for all of them swept over Natasha. She jumped out of bed. The harder she worked, the harder they all worked, the quicker they would reach their goal, the sooner they would get out of the crowded noisy holes into beautiful homes, into sunshine and light and gardens, with enough food for all, with enough of everything for all. She combed her hair straight back, but always one tiny curl after another got out of line till her face was framed in an aureole of soft ringlets. In her plain dark dress without frill or ornament, she had something of Olga's austerity, but the seriousness of her face was lighted with vitality; it sparkled and glowed as Olga's never had.

Kseniya had a cup of carrot tea and a slice of bread with jam ready for her granddaughter. There wasn't time to sit down. Natasha pulled on her coat and tied her shawl while drinking the tea, munching the bread, and cheering Kseniya:

"Take it easy today, grandmother, rest well and gather your strength! For tonight is the night of nights! It's ration day! Have all the pots and pans ready for the grand feast. One for the carrots, and one for the beets, and one for the buckwheat, and one for the herring, and one for the oil—I hope, I hope, I hope!"

With a kiss and a laugh she was gone.

Kseniya went over to the window. There she was, almost running in her hurry, but waving back and smiling. What would life have been without Natasha? Kseniya sat down by the window where Anton had spent the last years of his life looking out on that same street. There would have been so much more for him to see now. Their quiet little street was as busy as a big thoroughfare. Building and paving was going on all over the city and trucks and carts filled with lumber, cement, bricks, glass, roofing material passed under their windows all day long. And there were so many new people. The one-family houses in which the same families had lived for generations were occupied now by ten, fifteen, twenty families. In the old days, she had known every member of the neighborhood families, every one of their servants and visitors; now she hardly knew all the people in her own house. The street was always full of children playing. The old families wouldn't have thought of letting their children play in the street.

Kseniya opened her sewing basket. Frayed collars on Natasha's blouses had to be turned; threadbare elbows on a dress mended; stockings darned over and over again. Yes, life was bewildering, and if not for Natasha it would have been unbearable. She missed Anton but thank God he had been spared the distress of living in this new world. Maybe for those who were young now, life would again be good someday and would run as a life should run—regularly, orderly, neatly, day by day, hour by hour. People would again live in their own homes by themselves. Children would again be brought up properly to respect their elders; meals would be real meals and served at the same hours. Stores would be stores and sell goods to people. God would again come back to His children. But she would not live to see it.

What made it even more bewildering for Kseniya was that no day was ever like another. Every day brought new regulations, new instructions changing those of the day before, upsetting things even more. How was she to remember everything? And if she didn't remember, they called her to the House Committee. And there a boy who could have been her grandson made her stand for hours on her aching feet waiting in a long line; then he shouted at her and threatened her. When she once told him that he should be ashamed to treat an old woman that way, he almost threw her out of the room.

"You should thank us for letting you stay here . . . you bourgeois, you exploiter!" he yelled. "If it weren't for Natasha, there'd be no trace of you around here."

Kseniya's back got tired when she sewed and her fingers hurt. She had to sew without a thimble. She had lost hers and there was none to be bought. Her eyes hurt too. She needed new glasses. There was a place where one could get glasses, but the government ran it, and Natasha could not get permission to buy a pair there for her grandmother, the wife of a former capitalist. Kseniya leaned back in her chair and closed her eyes, listening to the voices in the hall and in the kitchen. She knew most of her neighbors well now. Sometimes during the day she took her sewing into their rooms or asked them into her room. They were the wives, the mothers, the grandmothers, whose lives were the lives of their husbands and their children. Rich or poor, educated or illiterate, their cares and interests were all the same. Life had leveled them out and erased whatever differences there had been in their past. They at least spoke a language she understood. Everybody else nowadays used too many new words and talked about things she'd never heard of. Who would ever have thought that she, Kseniya, would go to a theater and not understand a thing that went on on the stage? But that had happened to her not long before. Natasha had been after her for a long time to go to the theater with her.

"You always liked the theater . . . you used to go a lot to theaters. Why don't you want to go now? We have wonderful theaters now! Do come with me, grandmother," Natasha urged.

"All right, all right," Kseniya had finally agreed. "Let's go . . . But if you don't mind, let's go to an opera or to a ballet."

"Opera? Ballet?" Natasha had been horrified. "Forget about them, grandmother! They're old-fashioned, czarist, bourgeois; they have to be thrown out! Oh, no, we'll go to a new theater; you will see the new art, the simple art, the art which all people can understand and not only a chosen few."

They had gone to Natasha's favorite theater, the Meyerhold. Natasha had loved the play and had applauded enthusiastically. But why it was called theater was a puzzle to Kseniya, who had never seen a stage without a curtain and the audience watching the workers change the scenery, if you could call it scenery. Nothing but stairs, ladders, and wheels. And you couldn't tell when the stage hands had finished and the actors had begun. They had all been dressed alike; every one of them, men and women, wore blue overalls. The only difference was that the stage workers had behaved like normal human beings while the actors had jumped, climbed stairs, turned somersaults, screamed. To show love or anger, they'd climbed and jumped faster, and the wheel had turned furiously. When the actors' love or anger cooled off, they and the wheels moved more slowly. Their words had been lost—at least to Kseniya—in the continuous jumping and turning, but the audience had approved wholeheartedly.

Unless she could see a regular theater, with curtains and a proper stage and actors decently dressed, and words sung or spoken so that she could understand them, Kseniya was done with the theater forever. Laboratories of Art, the young people called them. Laboratories! Those nasty places where they cut up rabbits and rats. What on earth had that got to do with theaters?

Kseniya's back felt rested and she returned to her sewing. She had an easy day today—nothing but the sewing to do. There wasn't a crumb in the house except dry bread and jam, so there was nothing to cook. There was some washing to do, but she'd better wait till Natasha brought home her ration; there might be soap in it. Last time she had washed with sand the way the neighbors did. It rubbed the laundry clean all right but it also rubbed her skin off. The brick she used to clean the pots also rubbed her skin off. Kseniya was hungry but the thought of eating bread and jam again made her feel sick. She hoped Natasha would bring some food.

Natasha did bring food in the evening: potatoes, turnips, beets, half a pound of sausage, a pound of cereal, a pound of frozen fish, and even a little oil. It wasn't anything to make a feast with but it was something one could cook and eat hot. Some of the other families got their rations too, and the air in the kitchen was hot with steam.

After supper they went into Manilov's room.

In consideration of his many years in czarist prisons, Manilov was given a pension, and in order to restore his health he received luxuries usually reserved for children, nursing mothers, and worthy invalids, such as milk, sugar, white bread, an occasional ration of meat. He had the best room in the house, Kseniya's former drawing room. He lived quietly with his wife, not actively participating in political life, but interested in current problems and willingly discussing them, preferably with young people. He had gone into his first exile as a young student and after that had been out of prison hardly more than two months at a time. His many years of exile and imprisonment had been spent in reading and discussing not only Marxist theories, labor movements, and revolutionary methods, but also philosophy, religion, and the intricacies of the human mind, and he had retained a rare youthfulness of spirit. In the Bolshevik revolution he saw the torch that was showing humanity the road toward the final victory over poverty and injustice, toward the triumph of good over evil. When young people came to him, as they did, with their confused minds and troubled hearts, he did not pretend to have the answers but he shared with them his reflections on life. They looked at his serene face, made unbelievably young despite its frame of gray hair by the childish innocent look of his blue eyes; they listened to his voice, deep and slow and careful, and the burden of their heroic but harassed lives seemed to lighten. It was peaceful in Manilov's room, even though at times tempers were aroused and voices were loud.

Tonight they had one of those hot arguments. Manilov did not speak much. He was as much at a loss to know right from wrong as the young people were. It was spring, 1921, and they argued angrily and passionately about the New Economic Policy, which was just being introduced. Private trade again permitted! Russia's natural resources again opened to exploitation by foreign capitalists! When short of arguments, either side quoted Lenin.

Like the Bible, thought Manilov, Lenin is always good for a quotation.

Manilov felt as they did about Lenin. For him too Lenin's words were law. But what Lenin was now saying was contrary to what he had said before.

". . . no, no, and definitely no! Never any deals with capitalists, our own or foreign—"

". . . but Lenin says it is impossible to go on now."

". . . but didn't he say before that if you make one concession to the bourgeoisie, they will swallow you head and tail?"

"He said that in nineteen-nineteen and nineteen-twenty, the period of War Communism. Then our slogan was 'All for the War! All for Victory!' Now we have to begin to build for the peace. During the war we made the peasant give us every bit of grain he harvested. But he's not going to work indefinitely for nothing. If we don't give him something, he will starve us all to death! And what have we to give him? The factories produce hardly anything. You see, peace requires a different approach."

"But weren't we told that the abolition of private property was the basis of our new system? And now we introduce private property again! Doesn't that mean we're abolishing our new system? That we're liquidating the revolution?"

"Lenin says that our aim should be not to stop the development of capitalism but to lead it into the channel of state capitalism—"

"But aren't the foreign bourgeoisie, the sharks, the bloodsuckers, the exploiters, our worst enemies? Can we let them overrun our country? I'd rather not live than see capitalism in Russia again."

"And you think I like it? You think it was this I wanted when I froze my legs fighting in the swamps? But if Lenin says that at times we are forced to take a step backwards so as to move forward more quickly later—we must do it and that's all there is to it!"

That was the way Manilov felt. He was very unhappy over the New Economic Policy, with its private trade, profits, and foreign exploiters. But he trusted Lenin. If Lenin said so, it was right and had to be done.

Until recently, Kseniya had not worried about marriage for Natasha. On the contrary, she had prayed and hoped that Natasha would not rush into one of those short-lived marriages—if you could call those godless ceremonies marriages—as most girls were doing. And why shouldn't they? All they or their husbands had to do to get out of it and try their luck again was to send a postcard to the Divorce Bureau. Sex had never ceased to arouse Kseniya's disgust, and today's marriages seemed to be nothing but sex. Disgraceful as it was for a girl to remain unmarried, Kseniya would have preferred this shame for Natasha to the shame of one of the modern marriages.

But times had changed. This was 1923—and Natasha was twenty-three years old. Two years of the New Economic Policy—NEP, as it was called—had brought into the light a different kind of husband, the Nepmen, men with real businesses, with an apartment, with money to buy good clothes and good food. Some of them were vulgar but at least they could provide for a young wife and did not make her earn a living as the Bolshevik husbands did. But Kseniya doubted whether Natasha would want a Nepman for a husband; she had never been one to be interested in money, and now as a young Comsomol she seemed less than ever to be interested in anything but her revolution.

Kseniya was right. Nothing was further from Natasha's mind than to marry a Nepman. To her the NEP and the Nepmen were an evil which deep in her heart she still thought should have been avoided somehow. Life wasn't the same any more. Moscow wasn't the same city. The Nepmen had changed the face of it, the very spirit of it. On her way to work Natasha passed one of the new bakeries with piles of pure-white bread, cakes, and pastries. Their smell and the tantalizing displays were sickening to an empty stomach. But it was not alone the sight of the hungry beggars outside the store that bothered Natasha. They had all, every one of them, been hungry enough these years.

But now, Natasha thought bitterly, only they were hungry, they who continued to work and to sacrifice for the revolution, while the Nepmen and those who served them gorged themselves with food and wallowed in luxuries. Shop windows which had been boarded up since the revolution suddenly blossomed out with fineries the existence of which had almost been forgotten—lacy underwear, silk stockings, gowns, shoes, leather bags, hats, gloves. Natasha hated it all!

The revolution had first needed heroes to fight and die for it. Now it needed Nepmen and that bitter enemy of yesterday, the foreign capitalist, to run the shops and carry on the trade. And they demanded rich food, gambling clubs, bright lights, pretty clothes for their women. The party said that the country was devastated and that its industries had to be rebuilt. But was the only way to do it through the same people whom they had been fighting with guns only a short while before?

Did everything again have to be measured in terms of money? Several of their adult schools had had to close; there was no money for them. There was no money now for the colorful trains and boats which had covered the country with posters, books, illustrated newspapers, and theatrical shows, bringing light and new ideas into the most godforsaken corners of the land; for theatrical studios and art schools for proletarian youth; for the workers' faculties at universities, where young workers who had had no education could catch up with the children of the rich; for libraries, newspapers, theaters, factory schools, even elementary schools. Now the art and music schools were filled with Nepmen's children. They could pay the new high fees; the others couldn't, of course. Many old teachers, rejected by the revolution, came back. The Nepmen preferred their notions about life, history, and human behavior.

Natasha faithfully carried out the orders of the party but she couldn't force herself to stop doubting the wisdom of the party. If she thought something was wrong, how could she tell herself that it was right? There was that time when the papers were full of pictures from the Genoa Conference in the spring of 1922, and one of them showed Chicherin, the Soviet foreign commissar, in a high silk hat shaking hands with the Italian king before having lunch with him. Natasha had been miserable about that picture. Couldn't they see how wrong it was? The Soviet delegate, the representative of the Soviet republic, dressed up like a scarecrow, bowing to the king like a capitalist diplomat. Shouldn't the Soviet representative show by his simple and modest appearance that he was different from the others, that he represented the common people, not the landlords and bankers? They had laughed at her for saying that. These were unimportant details, they'd said. "If you live among wolves, you howl with the wolves." But to her they were important, very important. How was the world going to understand them if they didn't show what they really were?

There were many other questions that troubled her but it was some help to know that she was not the only one who questioned and doubted. Morals was the problem that disturbed the young people most. They had rejected the old concept of morals but were not sure what should take its place. They went to hear Trotsky, Bukharin, and other revolutionary leaders who concerned themselves with youth problems. With fiery words, the leaders appealed to youth to be strong and pure, to have faith and patience, and not give up the struggle for the ideals of the revolution. The appeals had been easier to follow when they had called upon them to sacrifice and die. It was hard to be heroic at a typewriter, lathe, cash register or kitchen stove, with easy money around, with gypsy restaurants, alluring women, warm clothes and warm rooms to be got for money. Some felt they had sacrificed enough, that if the government was again permitting luxuries and personal profits they should enjoy them too. Others, like Natasha, felt that no one should enjoy luxuries unless everyone could enjoy them.

Manilov felt sorry for his young friends. They were so tempestuous; they insisted that life moves forward very fast in a straight line. The introduction of the NEP had disturbed him too. But Lenin had promised that it was only for a short while, and what were a few years in the life of a nation, in the life of a revolution? But he did not blame youth for their impatience.

"You are right, Natasha," he once replied to her complaints about the low morals of Soviet youth. "I agree with you that morals are low. We shouldn't have permitted youth to become demoralized, you say. We should have thought of it earlier, we should have prevented it, you say. How? When? Have you forgotten, dear? Was there time to think of anything besides guns and bullets in the midst of our death struggle? Could we have talked then of the new family, of new sex morals, of respect for the new Soviet woman? Have you forgotten the iron ring around us? We could think of nothing then except of how to get out of the deadly embrace. . . . Well, we have broken through it but our victory left us exhausted, naked, hungry. Now, only now, could we start thinking of our personal problems. No one can teach us how to do it; nobody before us has done it. We have nothing to learn from the bourgeoisie, with their rotten morals, their hypocrisy, and their discrimination against human beings. We must work out our own morals."

"Why do you keep saying 'morals'?" one of Manilov's listeners objected. "That's a bourgeois word."

"You don't like the word? A word is not important, my friend. Call it anything you want, call it 'rules of life,' if you like that better. Call it 'Commandments,' as Bukharin suggests. Never be afraid of words. Truth, justice, goodness, beauty, humaneness, feelings, decency, respect, they are all fine words, though many sneer at them now."

Manilov never tired of holding the future, their own radiant future, before them.

"In the future we won't need any moral teachings at all. In our future society a human being will grow up with the new revolutionary morals. What is moral, you ask? First of all, it is respect for human personality, for the dignity of man. All men are born equal, as a good American once said, and before him Christ, the very first Communist on earth. It is never to fail to reach out a helping hand to the weak and defenseless. Never to be selfish and greedy. We will build a new life, and we will live the morals we teach. Instead of slavery, we shall have a truly free human activity; instead of obedience under pressure—free thought; instead of greediness and selfish grabbing—a just division of the earth's riches; instead of a blind belief in God—an intelligent understanding of the laws of nature; instead of each for himself—all of us together, for a common goal, for a common cause. Can you see it? Can you follow it?"

They could—for a while. They could while Manilov held the vision of the future before their eyes. But life threw too many shadows on the vision and it was hard to fight the shadows.

"Why do you think I drink?" complained one youth. "It's because of too much preaching. In the Comsomol they preach. When I go home, Father preaches. The newspapers preach. The teachers preach. I am dead bored with always being preached at. When I drink I forget it. If only there were less preaching in our lives and more excitement. Believe me, I hate the sight of the Nepmen but I wonder whether there isn't more excitement in their lives. Our life is empty."

"What? Our lives empty?" came the outraged voice of another youth. "Our life is rich, brimming rich! If you were a good Communist . . ."

"They tell us that to be a good Communist means to carry out all party instructions, never to miss a party meeting, and most important of all—never, but never forget to carry your membership card with you. It isn't enough for me. I envy you if it is for you."

"Yes, it is enough for me! To you it's preaching, empty, dead words. I put life into it, into these same words and preachings. This very morning, for instance, I saw near the post office a house, a good house, but a dilapidated, a sad-looking house. It needs cleaning and fresh paint to bring it back to life. On Sunday we will go out, all of us, the girls too, and we will give the house a gay bright coat of paint and in the evening the house will be fresh and young again. Don't you feel that this is poetry, that it could make one weep with happiness? One after another our houses, our gardens, our villages, and our cities will become fresh and young again and our whole country will be bright and gay. I don't believe you, you can't help feeling it."

"I wish I could dance or weep with joy because somebody paints a house or sweeps a street. But I can't, I need more than that to be satisfied. Don't you think I am right?" He turned to Manilov.

"You are, my boy."

The second youth was shocked. "Comrade Manilov, you don't mean to say that I am wrong?"

"Of course, you are not."

"But we can't both be right."

"Oh, yes, you can. You are two different human beings, so you react differently to the same things. You can't squeeze everybody into the same pattern and say: only this and this, and nothing else, should give you joy, and only this and this, and nothing else, should make you feel bad. It isn't so easy to say who is wrong and who is right, and who is good and who is bad. For instance, do you think that all the people on our side of the barricades were angels, and on the other side they were all devils? No, some of our own people were not good people at all and some on the other side were good and believed as honestly in their cause as we did in ours."

"Now you say, comrade Manilov," Natasha argued, "that it is not natural that all people should feel the same way about the same things. The party insists that we do. We are told that we all want the same things—food, shelter, schools, care in sickness, care in old age, entertainment. The party wants us to concentrate all our efforts to achieve them."

"Of course, my child, everybody wants those things. But there is such a variety of foods, shelters and clothing and entertainments and schools and even hospitals, I can't see how you can make millions of people all feel the same way about them. I don't see how you can make all people behave in one way. Our characters are too various for that, our tastes and our emotions. Even in one family, as we all well know, you can't force all the members to like the same food, books, clothes. If we try to force them to do so, what do we get? Twisted human beings, insincerity, frustration, hatreds, often insanity. Read Ostrovski, read Dostoevski, Tolstoi, Balzac, Dickens, Zola, read any writer who knew anything about human beings. He will tell you the same thing. People go out of bounds if you tamper with their personalities. Murderers, tyrants, madmen are mostly the tragic results of it. If we want a healthy human race, a normal happy world, we must give people freedom to develop their personalities within a world of law and justice, and this law and justice should be decided by the people themselves."

"But," Natasha protested, "what about the chaos the party says will result if some of us have our own ways and thoughts?"

"With all respect for the party I would much rather see a few of us get out of line than force everybody into bonds."

Natasha had thought the revolution would solve all human problems, and most of all, the problem of personal relations. She had dreamed of a world in which there would be no unhappy marriages, no tensions, no quarrels. To her, the new relationship between sexes meant truth and equality between man and woman; only real love and respect as the basis for marriage; freedom to end the relationship when love and respect were gone. What troubled her was that so many did not share her ideas on the new perfect marriage. She often heard:

"Who wants it? Why not have some fun in life?" . . . "Look at all the girls who want to be loved? Why limit yourself to one?" . . . "Don't we have freedom now? Aren't we free to love as many as we want to?" . . . "Aren't girls here so that we can enjoy them?" . .

It was easy for men to talk. They could flit from one woman to another, their lives undisturbed. But a woman was left behind with a broken heart, or with a child to take care of. "Nobody forced her. She knew what she was doing. And how do I know I was the man? . . . We are free now, aren't we?" was the usual refrain.

Law gave women equal rights, the government encouraged them to study, to go ahead, to take their rightful place at the side of men. All Natasha read and heard at meetings sounded very good, and many women had reached the front ranks, she knew. But many more were still used by men, husbands and lovers. It was hard for girls, she thought. To resist a man meant to be old-fashioned, to be out of tune with the time, not to have accepted the revolution, to be bourgeois. To be called "bourgeois" was worst of all. Girls submitted rather than be exposed to that. Girls tried to be tough, to drink and swear with the men. And why not? Didn't even some of the leaders encourage them to behave that way? Alexandra Kollontai, the old Bolshevik, the woman Lenin had entrusted with a high post in the government, came out for free love without any restrictions whatever. "Satisfaction of instincts," she said, "is as natural as drinking a glass of water." "And can't more than one person drink water from the same glass?" the public quickly added to it. "Come, let's have a drink of water," men called to women. "Give me a drink of water" was written with chalk on the walls.

Fewer remembered Lenin's reply to Kollontai. "Will a normal person," he asked, "under normal conditions drink from a glass with a rim greasy from many lips?" Natasha never forgot it. It gave her strength. She knew she was right if Lenin said so.

If a man's arm went around her waist, if a man tried to kiss her, she recoiled in disgust. Nothing could make Natasha feel that she was wrong, that it was her "bourgeois bringing up." She would let a man do anything to her body if she loved him. But never if she did not! Nothing could make her give up her deep belief that the revolution would finally remake people, make them cleaner, freer, and better. She believed what Trotsky, Bukharin, Koltsov, Lunacharski were saying: that Soviet youth was to give humanity an example of what a revolution does to human beings.

Natasha found support in Dasha. One could not accuse the former maid, Dasha, of a "bourgeois bringing up," and Dasha too was fighting for a new relationship in marriage, for purity between the sexes, for normal families. Dasha had been transferred from her job with the Housing Commission to the Women's Department of the party. All day long she rushed from one factory and house to another, wherever women worked and lived. Thin and quick, a red kerchief with a hammer and sickle tight around her hair, summer and winter wearing the same cotton dress and leather jacket, she was a familiar and welcome sight to the Moscow workingwomen. Her "Women, listen to me!" always promised something important and interesting. Birth control, family washing, utilization of food remnants, faithless, drunken, or abusive husbands, women's political activity, bringing up children—everything she was talking about was their very life.

Once Dasha took Natasha along to a workers' meeting on family problems. She was uneasy about the meeting. "Six years after the revolution, and men still resent having a woman speak to them. If our government weren't so strict in enforcing women's rights, we'd be today the same slaves we were before the revolution. Most men hate to treat us as equals."

The hall was filled with men and women. They were already in the thick of the discussion when Dasha and Natasha took their seats.

". . . equality, equality, you keep talking about equality," a woman was saying. "But who of you men will help scrub the floors or wash the diapers?"

"You want to know how family discord arises?" An elderly Communist was speaking now. "The husband wants his wife to stay home and work for him. So he advances in life and his wife stays behind, forever bound to her stove and washtub. She is cut off from the world, she doesn't go along with the times; she refuses, for instance, to remove the icons. If he is a party member, he has trouble on account of that. He doesn't want the children to be christened or to go to church. She insists. They quarrel . . ."

"And you think it is better if both work and are politically active?" asked another man. "You come home; it is cold and unfriendly, no real home at all. Something has to be done about it. But what?"

There was silence. Nobody had an answer.

"What would you want?" asked a woman. "Have the wife stay home forever? Is that why we made the revolution? Don't you think that she too wants to get out into the world? She has waited long enough for her chance to live a full life."

"I have an idea, I have an excellent idea!" exclaimed a young worker. "I read about it. The ancient Greeks had two kinds of women—one was the wife, the mother of his children; she stayed home and kept house for him. The other was the pleasure giver. Something like the geishas, only classier. Now wouldn't that be something for us? One wife for the home, one for the outside."

There was an explosion of laughter. Dasha slowly got up.

"Don't hurry," she said quietly, "don't hurry at all. Take your time, laugh, laugh as long as you like. We have so much cause for laughter. We haven't lost any of our brothers, sons, husbands, fathers fighting for you and your women. We haven't seen our children's bodies swollen from hunger and blue with cold. Go on, why don't you laugh? Women are such a good subject to laugh about. Women who have watched over every waking moment of your lives, who have shared your privations and dangers. Laugh at them, laugh at them because they too want a ray of the sun which begins to shine over our lives . . . Don't you know what to do about it? I will tell you! Schools must be built, thousands and thousands of schools, where children can spend their days from morning to night, studying and playing and making music and seeing shows and getting strong and healthy through sports and games. Nurseries must be built, kindergartens to take care of all our children. Communal laundries must be built, communal kitchens, communal sewing shops, in every city block, in every village. Unharness the woman, deliver the woman from her everyday slavery and drudgery; make her free for our new wonderful life. Then she will find time to be your friend and comrade, to have a cozy friendly home in which happy children will get a healthy start in life."

Natasha heard tears in Dasha's voice when she spoke of the "happy children" and the "healthy start" in life. It must be true, as she had always suspected, that something was wrong with Dasha's son. But hadn't the revolution opened wide the doors for his kind of social outcast? Dasha, always outspoken, never mincing words or keeping back her thoughts on anything, never said more than "He is all right" when Natasha asked her about Yasha.

Walking home after the meeting, Natasha listened to Dasha. Dasha was pleased with the results of the meeting. A resolution had been passed urging help for women to go to schools, to lighten their burden of housework, and encouraging their participation in political and social activities. Dasha laughed recalling some of the funny moments. Natasha's sudden question, "Dasha, how is Yasha, what is he doing?" caught her in a relaxed mood. Natasha felt her fingers tighten on her arm. She stroked her fingers gently and asked again: "How is he? Tell me about him, Dasha."

"What is there to tell? There isn't much to tell." Dasha's voice was reluctant at first, then the words rushed out:

"It's a very short story. What other story was to be expected from such a childhood? Unwanted even by his own mother, sick, ugly, despised by everybody. At fifteen he was in jail for petty thievery. That was the first time, but there were many times after that for burglary. The revolution came too late for my poor boy. I never intended leaving the housing job; I was forced to leave it. Yasha heard me talk about empty attics and deserted cellars, and that's where he and his gang hid their stolen goods. A trunk with furs was found in my own attic . . . if not for the party's trust in me, I'd have been in jail today. He is free right now but I wish he were in prison. Oh, Natasha, I wish he were dead! My son is a Nepman. He is rich now.

He rides in autos; he has mistresses dressed in silks and furs. I signed a paper renouncing him as my son. Otherwise I would have had to leave the party, and if I'd had to leave the party I would have killed myself . . . Yasha, my unlucky Yasha! What chance did he ever have in life? You understand now why I talk so much about mothers and children? What good would the revolution have been if we couldn't build a world safe for mothers and their children?"

Natasha never tired in her searching curiosity about human lives. Riding in a streetcar, she scrutinized people's faces. She peeped into basement and ground-floor windows, snatching a sight of people quarreling, eating, embracing, crying, reading. She couldn't at times keep from listening at the doors in her house, or glancing quickly through them if they stood ajar.

One evening as she passed through the hall she heard someone groaning and stopped outside the door. Ilya Gromov, a member of the Cheka, the secret police, was recovering after a nervous breakdown. Some people in the house, even Communists, avoided him. Natasha was not sure about her own feelings. Wasn't the Cheka the guardian, the faithful watchdog of the revolution? Who knew whether the revolution could have been saved without them? But the tales of tortures in the Cheka prisons were so horrible.

Natasha had never been in Gromov's room but his moans finally made her knock at his door. There was no answer. She knocked louder, then opened the door. Gromov was lying dressed across the bed, his feet hanging down, his eyes bloodshot, his face burning with fever. Natasha took off his shoes, made him comfortable on the bed, brought a basin of water and cooled his forehead. He moaned and whimpered, and threw himself about feverishly. His moans began to sound like words.

"My hands," he muttered deliriously and thrust his hot hands at Natasha's face, "look at them, have a good look at them, they killed people . . . many people . . . they killed, killed, killed . . . they were covered with blood, with red blood, with human blood. They shot, they knifed, they ripped, they choked. Look at them . . . look at them . . . at my red . . . bloody hands . . ."

Gromov had not been in the house long, but every time he had one of his attacks thereafter Natasha sat with him, soothing him, bathing his forehead and his hands, and helping him fight down his nightmarish visions.

CHAPTER 19
## Natasha and Peter

NATASHA also became friends with a newcomer in the house, black-eyed, dark-skinned Peter Kozlov, who was studying architecture. She fingered his books and drawings, and wanted to know all about them. Peter could not resist her endless "What does this mean? What is this for? This? And this?"

Still less could he resist her big eyes, full of curiosity. Natasha's curiosity knew no end, and one day he got out his most secret treasures and shared with her the dreams that had brought him to architecture. He showed her his drawings of the homes and cities he hoped to build and described his vision of the future.

"People would work a few, very few hours in shining clean plants or offices or laboratories full of air and sun. And the rest of the day—sun and water and grass; theaters, games, concerts, sports, museums, circuses, free to all, at any time. Children growing up amidst laughter and sun and trees." He had no definite ideas how to go about kitchens and laundries but he wanted to do something new and beautiful about them too, and he was working on it.

Natasha listened with an interest that was due not only to his architectural dreams. The inscriptions on Peter's drawings were in a girl's handwriting. Natasha would have given a great deal to know whether the handwriting had anything to do with the framed snapshot of a girl, the only picture in Peter's room.

One evening Peter, who until then had talked only about the future, said: "Natasha, I feel like talking about the past. Let me talk, will you? If it bores you, say so, yes?"

"Yes," she said softly.

She was sitting on a pillow on the floor, her arms around her knees; Peter was sitting across his bed, leaning against the wall.

"My father was a small clerk in the city of Tver. I was seventeen, like you, when the revolution came, and my sister Varya was sixteen. We both quit school. We wanted to serve the revolution. There were lots of jobs for us. We swept the streets, guarded the prison, searched the countryside for food, taught the alphabet to soldiers. And then—you remember how it was—the only way to serve the revolution was to take a gun and go out and fight. That's what we did. Varya and a few other girls went with us as nurses but they did more fighting than nursing. Anatol, a friend of mine, Varya, and I never separated. For two years we moved from one front to another. We slept on filthy floors and frozen ground. We marched knee deep in snow or in heavy mud. We moved through villages leveled to the ground. We saw what looked like human beings digging in manure for scraps of food. We were taken prisoner by the Whites and escaped after seeing our comrades skinned alive. We would lie in swamps, soaked to the waist, and dream of a clean room, of a bed with sheets on it, of soap, of hot food, of a toilet, of a bathtub; of a life without fleas or lice or stench. It was then that I started to picture the bright homes and the bright life of the future. And I said that if I lived through it I'd devote my life to building. Every scrap of paper we got hold of I covered with my drawings. Varya helped me.

"Then we were demobilized. The three of us arrived in Moscow about two years ago around the time NEP started. We were completely bewildered. Those unbelievable new words about free trade and capitalism. That wasn't what we had fought and risked our lives for! Anatol was the first to understand what was going on. For him it meant that once more he was called to defend the revolution. He offered his services and was sent to the Concessions Committee. His job was to deal with foreigners, and he hated it. But he was a soldier of the revolution and he said that he had to fight with whatever weapon he was told to fight with.

"It took me longer than Anatol. The new tasks seemed gray and dull compared to the heroics of the civil war. But then I too understood that the revolution wanted us now to fight with different arms, that it wanted us to become its engineers, builders, doctors, teachers, scientists. I got hold of the new arms, as Anatol did, and I began to study. It was hard in the beginning, Natasha. We were hungry, cold, dirty, tired from too much studying, too many words at meetings, and too little sleep in the partitionless noisy barracks. At meetings they praised us in rich oratory as the 'Red Specialists' and 'Men of the Future'—us, anemic, exhausted creatures! But I soon rediscovered my old fire and devotion, and I am ready to go ahead, whatever the difficulties may be."

They sat silent for several minutes, then Natasha asked hesitantly, "What happened to Varya, Peter?"

"Varya was the one who remained utterly lost," Peter said. "All she thought she had to offer to the revolution was bravery and physical endurance, which were not needed now. She finally took a job in Anatol's office in the Concessions Committee, filing papers, which she hated. She was full of contempt for the secretaries and interpreters with fluffy curls, silk stockings, high heels and silly giggles—the kind of girls who were being chosen for the jobs with foreigners. But they had what our girls didn't have—education, foreign languages, well-kept appearance, and graceful manners to please the foreigners. Varya, with her drab mannish clothes and manners roughened by war, felt like an outcast. And one day she felt she couldn't stand life any longer. She shot herself. The world seemed empty to me without my little sister. And I still don't think she was right. Death is no way out. Death is desertion."

Natasha cried. Peter walked over to her and kissed her hand.

"I have never kissed a woman's hand before."

They were both embarrassed, and she left his room quickly. Despite her tears, she was happy: the girl on the picture was Peter's sister.

The next evening Natasha had hardly closed Peter's door behind her when his arms were around her. Her knees grew weak. Their lips met first in a shy short kiss, then they were drawn together again and again till time disappeared. Their kisses left them in a state of longing, enchantment, and embarrassment. They did not know what to say. They did not say anything, and suddenly Natasha pulled herself free and ran out of the room.

She lay awake for a long time. Kseniya heard her sighs and wondered what was the matter with the girl. Was she in love? How was one to know about girls today? They walked in and out of young men's rooms, they mingled with them all day long, they were among men till late at night in clubs and at meetings. Kseniya listened to Natasha and prayed for her. Even God Almighty could not help the girl to an upright respectable husband, the kind they would have found for her had not the world turned upside down, but Kseniya prayed that Natasha's future husband would treat her with kindness and not run away from her.

Two nights later Kseniya woke up in the middle of the night and found Natasha's bed untouched. The night before she had again heard her sighing deeply and often, after she went to bed. Could it be? Her pure innocent Natasha, could she have thrown herself at a man?

"Peter, Peter, I must go now . . . I must. Grandmother will worry herself to death." Peter made it hard for Natasha. She tried, but she couldn't find the strength to struggle out of his arms. She could stay in his arms forever. Let Grandmother worry . . . let everybody worry . . . she couldn't . . . she wouldn't leave Peter's arms . . .

It was early morning when Natasha quietly slipped into her room. Kseniya's face looked haggard, her eyes miserable and anxious.

Gently Natasha took Kseniya's hands in her own. "Grandmother, don't cry over me!"

"Who . . ."

Kseniya's voice was very low, and Natasha guessed rather than heard the question.

"Peter."

For a second, Natasha buried her face in Kseniya's pillow; then she raised her head and looked at her with radiant eyes:

"Grandmother . . . grandmother . . . I am the happiest person in the world. No one could be as happy as I am. And this is how it is going to be for the rest of our lives. We will always be as happy . . . the two of us together. Oh, grandmother, grandmother . . ." Crying and laughing Natasha kissed Kseniya's face and hands.

Kseniya lay still, too dazed to say anything. A girl, an unmarried girl, her own granddaughter, spent a night with a man in his room, and came straight to her grandmother and told her that. Told her with pride and with joy, and with eyes as clear as before. Not a shadow of shame or remorse! It had taken Kseniya many years to learn, through the marriages of her daughters, that a woman's body could give her joy in married life, not only agony. Now Natasha was telling her that to give oneself freely and willingly to a man outside of marriage also meant joy and no shame at all. It was hard to learn at seventy-two.

Natasha's warmth and closeness made her feel uncomfortable. Natasha's lips and hands were feverish and her body—well, her body was sinful. If at least they would get married! Yes, that was it. They must quickly get married. But would a man want to marry a girl he could have without marrying?

"Will he marry you?"

Natasha's excitement found release in laughter. "Grandmother, dear, what are you talking about? What a funny thing to ask? Of course, he will marry me if I will marry him."

Kseniya almost gasped when Natasha went on:

"We haven't even mentioned it. Grandmother dear, we've hardly talked about anything. The happiness of having found each other, oh, darling, what happiness!"

Again Natasha hid her flushed face in the pillow.

Kseniya persisted: "Then why don't you . . . ? Why don't you get married immediately?"

"Of course, we could get married, why not? It doesn't make any difference, really. I am going to move into his room anyway, grandmother. We don't want to be without each other any more, never, never."

Two days later Natasha walked into Kseniya's room hand in hand with Peter, and triumphantly showed Kseniya a yellowish typewritten slip of paper with some words written on it in a pale watery ink.

"We are married, grandmother! Here it is, our marriage license! We just got it!"

Kseniya looked at Natasha, at her old patched dress with the turned collar, at Peter's shirt and trousers—the only ones he possessed, at his unshined boots, at his hair which badly needed cutting, at the sorry-looking little paper, and she turned away, not able to hold back her tears.

"Grandmother, why cry? Aren't you happy for us? Look at us! You can't cry looking at us."

Kseniya couldn't tell Natasha why she cried. She cried for the bridal gown and the white veil with the orange blossoms, for the church smelling of flowers and incense; the presents of silver and gold; the festive wedding dinner.

Peter continued his studies, and several evenings a week worked with a fellow student on his plans for new cities. Natasha's numerous activities did not leave her much leisure either. Out of the little time they had for themselves they drew every drop of happiness. There was always an endless number of things to talk about. Not one event was kept back, not one thought, or one moment of longing. And always there was the joy of being physically together. This was the one corner in their lives which excluded the Comsomol rules.

These rules spelled austerity and moderation. Pamphlets on behavior for Comsomol members recommended total sexual abstention for those who had no partners in life, and moderation for the others. Doctors were quoted as saying that indulgence in sex was harmful, and that once a week should be the limit for marital relations.

In everything else Natasha and Peter were model Comsomols. Peter gave up smoking and joined the Bukharin Club, which followed Bukharin's appeal to youth not to smoke. They had a box for fines for swearing in the room. Every Sunday they wrote out a detailed schedule for each day of the week. A typewritten "Personal Rules" hung on the wall: rules about keeping the room and their belongings in order; about Peter's helping Natasha scrub the floor; about being helpful to neighbors; subscribing to the Comsomol press and regularly reading it; never failing in their duties as Comsomols.

Their friends were drawn by the coziness of their room and by Natasha's cheerful friendliness. They had to comply with the strict schedule of the week; if they arrived at the wrong time, when conversations were excluded, they were handed a book and told to keep quiet. At hours given to talking, the room rang with young voices.

The regimented life of the young couple, the starched curtains, the insistence on decent manners, the white bedspread on which Natasha would not permit anyone's feet, aroused a great deal of argument.

Wasn't it a betrayal of revolutionary ideas? Wasn't it a return to the old ways of bourgeois life?

"Next thing you know, you'll get a canary and hang it at your window."

"I don't see," argued Natasha, "what is wrong with being clean, with keeping regular hours, knocking before entering a room, wiping one's feet, and even wearing a tie, yes, yes, a tie!"

"There you go again with your tie! Don't you realize that we are proletarians, that we have nothing to do with bourgeois traditions. A tie is a bourgeois tradition; it is a symbol of the bourgeoisie, and it is degrading for a proletarian to wear a tie!"

"Then why does Lenin wear a tie?"

"When he was in exile abroad he lived with the bourgeoise and was forced to wear a tie. But we are not! We fought so that the world should be free from bourgeois slavely."

"For the love of me I don't see why a tie or a toothbrush or an ash tray—yes, an ash tray, and I mean you—" Natasha pointed to a smoker who persistently ignored the ash tray—"should interfere with the world revolution!"

"Bourgeois! Bourgeois! They keep calling you that," complained a girl student, "till you get so tired of it that you stop cleaning your nails, and don't mind a soiled blouse or a foul word."

Kseniya had taken complete charge of their household. Natasha gratefully handed over to her all their money and ration cards. But soon the high quality of their meals aroused Natasha's suspicions. Meat, butter, eggs, fruit, cake began to appear regularly on their table. But their income hadn't increased. She was making a modest salary, and her and Peter's university stipend could cover the cost of only the simplest food. The low-priced government stores did not contain any luxuries. How could Grandmother afford food which could only be bought at exorbitant prices in the Nepmen stores? Natasha asked her. Grandmother looked confused and it was obvious that she lied when she said that she had been saving out of the money Natasha gave her. As if anyone could save a penny out of what they had! Natasha was disturbed. Where did Grandmother get the extra money? She had to find out. Natasha listened and looked around. The others in the kitchen were cooking meat too, and baking cake. Natasha went with her question to Manilov. "Where did they all get the extra money?"

"Don't you understand?" he asked. "What a child you are!" He chuckled at her naïveté but he loved her for it. "What do you think the NEP is? The NEP permits the exchange of goods for money in stores and among private citizens. Who of us didn't possess a ring or an old fur piece or a valuable book? Why not sell it and have some food for it? Everybody can well stand a little extra food. That's what we are all doing. No, no, my dear, there is nothing wrong about that."

Natasha ran back to her room, squeezed her grandmother in her arms, and kissed her. "You liar, you liar, you liar! So that's what you were doing behind my back! Tell me all about it."

Inexpressibly relieved, Kseniya confessed that after she had sold an old dress to a neighbor, others had come to her and sent their friends. Fur boots, jewels, old finery—she wasn't sorry to part with anything as long as Natasha and Peter could have proper food. And proper food these days was worth its weight in gold.

". . . and, thank God, people came to me. I didn't have to leave my room. I don't think I could have gone out into the street to sell things the way others have to do."

Her heart full of love for her grandmother, Natasha impulsively embraced her again and held her close.

Natasha had often watched men and women standing at a curb, selling mementoes of happier days: Wedgwood vases, silver spoons, baby shoes, binoculars, lace jabots, leather goods, snuff boxes, picture frames, skates, lorgnons—the most incredible assortment of articles. And the people who sold them also were relics of the past. Some women wore a veil over their faces, obviously ashamed to be recognized by old friends; they accepted the first offer, quickly took the money, and disappeared. Others argued and bargained, throwing into the bargaining a tale of woe, and, if the customer was a foreigner hunting for antiques, adding a few curses for the Bolsheviks. Others were too full of contempt for the buyers to say anything. They silently listened to prices offered, and, if they were acceptable, stretched out a hand for the money.

CHAPTER 20

## Katya

NATASHA had never happened to see her there, but her aunt Vera, the former belle of Moscow society, was a frequent visitor to the most popular street market on Petrovka. She was one of those who would not deign to show a sign of life to a prospective customer. Her stony face made even the unsympathetic unsentimental nouveaux-riches feel uneasy. Vera's coat, a Paris creation ten years before, hung loose on her emaciated figure. A shawl, tied around her head, hid part of her face. Her hands were always covered with gloves, even on the hottest summer days. She couldn't stand the touch of anyone's fingers, even for the short instant they were handing her money.

Vera's cook had finally left them for good. She had had the impudence to tell Vera before she left that no living creature could stand as much degradation and abuse as she had to put up with from her mistress. With cook gone, Vera would have had to stand in line in the government stores with people whose very presence made her flesh creep with repugnance. The money she got for her street sales saved her from this ordeal. In the Nepmen stores one did not have to wait, but Vera recoiled from any contact with their customers—shady creatures, void of any sense of propriety and refinement—with no less aversion.

But, contemptible as the Nepmen seemed to her, Vera, not unlike Kseniya and many other mothers and grandmothers, would have had no objection to her daughters' marrying them. There was never any doubt in her mind that the days of the Bolsheviks could not last, that their end was close. But how close? How long could the girls wait? Kira was twenty-two, Katya twenty. Besides, Katya liked men much too well. With that flash in her eyes when she talked to a man, Katya would be better off married. Every girl needed a man with money, and particularly Katya. Her beauty needed a very special expensive frame which nowadays no one but a Nepman could provide.

Vera was not concerned about Kira. Kira got along very well with the Bolsheviks. Let her find her happiness among them. But Katya needed luxury, she needed to be served and adored. Katya had to eat good food, so that her eyes would sparkle and her skin remain clear and soft. A former perfume salesman was selling creams, lotions, and perfumes. What Vera could spare from food she spent for his products. Katya's hair and skin had to be kept lovely. Now that a girl was not stoned and called names when decently dressed, Vera spent long hours over the fine woolens, silks, and laces she had hidden. Who knew but that Katya might someday get an invitation to a foreign embassy? They were on the lookout for well-dressed pretty Russian girls of good families, and some girls had already made their fortunes.

If only Katya weren't so crazy about men. Even at Katya's first children's parties, Vera had had to watch her carefully. She was not more than twelve when Vera found her on a balcony with a boy, her face flushed. She told her that it was indecent to be alone with a boy, that it was indecent to close her eyes when dancing. It made no difference. When a boy's hand slipped around Katya's waist, her nostrils quivered and she closed her eyes. It was in her blood, the blood that was her father's blood. Well, a good marriage would take care of that.

Katya liked the clothes and the perfumes that Vera provided. They made her even more desirable and irresistible to men, and that was all that mattered to her. She didn't think of marriage. Restless, always on the lookout for new admirers and new excitement, she enjoyed the game of playing with men and had learned early what they wanted of her.

One day, passing a boarded-up shack on a deserted lot, she heard voices inside. Looking through a crack, she saw a group of ragged youngsters crouched on the floor, playing cards. Piles of money were stacked in front of them, real money, gold coins and large paper bills. One of them wore what looked to her like a valuable ring.

"Interesting, young lady, isn't it? Wouldn't you join us?" A boy, pressing both her arms, pushed her to the back of the shack where, by loosening a board, he opened a door.

"Look what I found!" he called to the others.

Hands reached out and dragged her inside. Inquisitive eyes appraised her. She felt hot under their looks, which seemed to undress her. One boy covered her breasts with his hands, another slid his hand down her back under her blouse. She was torn between disgust at the touch of their dirty hands and disgust at herself for not minding their touch.

"What's going on here? Who is the girl?"

A young man had entered the shack. At the sound of his voice the boys jumped up in obvious fear.

"We don't know who she is . . . we found her spying on us. Don't scold, Nikolka, we did nothing . . . truly, we did nothing."

Katya stood in the middle of the room. The young man approached her. He had soft wavy hair, dark blue eyes, full lips, a clear bronzed skin. He was handsome and despite the softness of his hair and skin looked tough and strong. His wide-open shirt showed a hairy chest. His fingers had a strong grip when they touched Katya. He lifted her chin. She did not draw back. Her eyes looked straight into his. No, he must be wrong! Not a girl like that! He brought his face closer to her. Still she didn't move. It was probably fear, not willingness— but what was the difference? Who cared?

"Get out, you tramps, get out, every one of you," he shouted at the boys, "and don't dare show your faces . . ."

He didn't want them too close. A fancy doll like this one might be a nuisance and scream. But she was not a nuisance and she did not scream. The fumbling of the boys had excited her and she readily submitted to him. Minutes drew out into hours. She clung to him. She wouldn't let him go. In his arms she found what she had been so restlessly longing for. And he, Nikolka Heartbreak, forgot his usual tricks with women. In his most intimate moments he never gave up his pose of indifference, lest they should think they were important to him. He forgot about that now. This girl was different from the others. He could well let this girl know what pleasure she gave him.

Katya came home next evening her lips swollen and her eyes feverish. She came to get her things. She had found a mate, she told her mother, and had moved into his room. Vera, weak with worry over Katya's disappearance, was stunned. The word she used! "Mate!" And the way she said it! The wide naked smile. Vera had not recovered from the shock when Katya pressed a quick kiss on her cheek and flew out the door. Nikolka Heartbreak was waiting downstairs. His arms pressed tight around her waist, they walked away.

His room was untidy and unfriendly at first, but Katya did not notice it. A touch of his finger tips made the world disappear for her. He did not let her out of his sight. He had never cared before but Katya had to be his alone. The two were wild and happy together. There were no days, no nights, no work, no duties, no worries. His army of young gangsters provided all he wanted. They got him furniture and rugs for his room. He wanted to cover Katya's body with silks and furs, her ear lobes with pearls, her fingers and neck with diamonds. He got them all. It was too rich for the Moscow street. She wore them in the room for him.

Vera's hopes for a decent marriage for Katya were dead. Even in that immoral world no one would want to marry a girl who lived openly with a thief. But at least Katya was provided with all the luxuries her heart desired. And she did not forget her mother. Vera no longer had to sell her belongings in the street, like a marketwoman. She spoke to no one, spent her days alone in her room, cooked her food on a kerosene burner she kept in the room. Kira was seldom at home. When she was, they had little to say to each other. Vera hated Kira's work for the Bolsheviks, and Kira knew it and never talked about her job.

## CHAPTER 21
### Maxim and Kira

KSENIYA had long ago given up expecting to see Maxim more than once or twice a year. He was much too busy to have time for the family. During the six years since the revolution, he had held many jobs. He spoke well, he wrote well, he was an excellent administrator, and an untiring enthusiastic party worker. If a new organization had to be built, or an old one liquidated, if discipline had to be tightened in one place or relaxed in another, Maxim could always be depended upon to do the job properly. His task finished, he was sent to another strategic point.

Finally, in 1923, he was given a job in the Central Planning Commission, where the rebuilding of the country's economy was being planned. It looked to Maxim like a permanent job—certainly, it would take more than his lifetime to accomplish that task. Undismayed, he attacked the work with single-minded devotion. But if only, he sometimes thought wearily, there weren't so many papers to handle. All day long, without ever a letup, papers were brought to his desk. Half the secretaries' time was spent looking for an urgently needed paper buried under the steadily growing mountain. Girls kept coming and going with papers in their hands. He had no time to look at them, he didn't know their faces and didn't know their names. He saw nothing but hands, taking papers, sorting papers, arranging papers, filing papers, but mostly bringing papers. Slow hands, clumsy hands, efficient hands, rough hands, manicured hands, plain hands, expressive hands.

Late one evening when everybody in the office had gone and Maxim had settled down to his only undisturbed hours of work, two hands caught his attention. They did not throw papers into the incoming basket, snatch others from the outgoing basket, and disappear, as most of the hands did. They stayed, they arranged the papers neatly. They brushed the ashes off the desk, they put the blotter where it was handier for him to reach. They were large brown hands. They looked competent and comfortable. So did the girl to whom they belonged. She was tall and strongly built. The dark braids were wound around her head. Her face was not beautiful but could easily attract attention. It was oval, wide at the temples, and her eyes were gray, large and almond shaped and set wide apart.

If this girl ever has to wear glasses, she'll have to order them specially made for her; the regular sizes would never fit her eyes—that was his first thought when he looked at her face.

"I'll get you some hot tea; yours is cold," she said and left the room. Maxim returned to his papers. How did she know he was craving for a glass of hot tea? He asked her her name when she brought him the tea. She laughed. Her teeth were almost square, and very white, and when she laughed she opened her mouth wide. She seemed familiar; he must have seen her before.

"Don't you know me? You really don't know me?" She laughed again. "I am your niece Kira, the daughter of your sister Vera."

His face, friendly and interested a moment ago, grew annoyed. Her smile disappeared and she turned around to leave the room.

"I am on duty tonight in the Secretariat. Call me if you need something."

Maxim was alone again. What was that girl doing there? Spying for the Whites? How had she got in there? Should he report her? No, that would be hardly necessary. The Cheka under its new name, GPU, worked well. It checked and rechecked people before they were permitted to work in a place as strategic as the Planning Commission. If she was there, they must have made sure she was all right. But how could that be? Vera's daughter all right? Vera—that false, affected doll, that enemy of the people. Hard to believe that Kira was her daughter. A pity. She seemed to be straightforward and natural. Everything about her seemed so quiet and comfortable, especially her voice. She must be good to talk to. Quiet and comfortable. That's what he was longing for . . . he was so tired, so tired . . .

He jumped up, his hand clutching the revolver at his hip: "Who is it? Who is there?"

He had distinctly heard steps and the lock of a door click. No one was in the room. His coat had been spread over his knees. A slice of bread was covering a glass of tea. He touched the glass; it was hot. Kira must have poured it just before she left. He looked at his watch. It was 3:30. It was 11:30 when he had closed his eyes to relax them for a few minutes.

For two days Maxim watched the hands putting papers on his desk. Late in the evening of the second day Kira's hands were there again. She quickly put some papers down and left the room before he raised his head. It was all right with him; talking with her would only interfere with his work. But he must have been looking for her, because he soon knew that she was on duty only in the evenings, and only three evenings a week. About two weeks later he asked her, before she had time to disappear:

"How do you happen to be working here?"

He was glad to hear again her open pleasant laughter. He had been uneasy at the thought that his brusque behavior on that first evening might have hurt her.

"Don't you remember anything at all? I needed a recommendation from a party member working here. And you signed it. You didn't want to but Natasha asked you to do it and you finally gave in. Natasha knew I was all right. Don't you remember?"

His face was a blank.

"Don't you remember how you helped us keep our rooms? We were told to vacate them in twenty-four hours, with no place to go. That time Grandmother Kseniya asked for us. You didn't want to do that either. And you said about Mother, 'Vera is not my sister, she is nothing to me; no, that isn't true, she is my enemy,' you said, 'why should I worry about her?' But Grandmother begged and begged till you signed our appeal. Remember now?"

Slowly some of it came back to him. How he had resented doing it for Vera! And all the time this big gray-eyed dark girl was there knowing how he hated to do anything for them.

After a few more talks, Maxim did not worry about that. Kira had no tender feelings for her mother and never reproached him for his attitude. Had she been in his place, she said, she would have acted exactly the same way. She too considered her mother an enemy. What she did for Vera she did only out of duty and pity.

"I don't fool myself; I haven't a bit of love for her . . . nor for Katya either, now, though I used to love Katya very much. I am not ashamed to admit it. I think it is worse to pretend to have feelings we don't have."

The directness of Kira's thinking warmed Maxim. It was easy to understand, he thought, why as a child she had felt a stranger in her own home, and why she had turned away from her parents' world when she grew up. It was many years since Maxim had indulged in the luxury of a friendly chat. There had never been the time or mood for that. Neither had there been a companion as comfortable and soothing as Kira.

It was a pity she came only the three evenings a week. Couldn't she come more often? he suggested tentatively. No, it seemed she had taken this job only as an addition to her regular work in the library, which did not pay enough, and also because she did not like to be at home in the evenings. So she spent three evenings there in the Planning Commission, two in evening courses, and two at theaters or visiting friends. Then . . . why not spend one of those two evenings together sometimes?

Kira called for him on her first free evening. He had no idea where to go. He had heard that there were places now where people went to eat, to listen to music, to be gay, but he had never been to one. Kira took it into her hands. She was good at deciding things and solving problems. She would knit her brow, then smile and say "Very simple," and the problem was solved for her. That evening too, when he asked helplessly, "What do we do, where do we go?" she said, "Very simple," and took him to a gaudy gypsy restaurant. It was the first time either of them had seen the lavish money spending of the Nepmen, and the vulgarity and noise of the smoke-filled room disgusted and silenced them. They left the restaurant and walked through the snowy boulevards, finding again the pleasant easiness which had made them seek the other's company. Soon all Kira's free evenings belonged to Maxim whenever he could get free himself. They would go to a theater or walk for hours through Moscow's evening streets, deep in animated talk.

Once, when it was too cold to walk, they went to a workers' tea-room. It too was noisy and smoky, and they found it impossible to talk.

"How about my room?" suggested Maxim. "I haven't much to offer but we can make tea and there might be a few crackers left."

His room was almost bare. Maxim was indifferent to earthly goods; his salary as a party member was low, and he would not have thought of asking for any special privileges. Books and magazines were lying everywhere, on the floor, on the table, on the window sill, on the only chair. Maxim cleared the chair for Kira. A restraint fell on them. Kira spoke in a halting forced way in a timid voice which wasn't her voice at all, and her eyes avoided his.

He looked at her, waiting, and wondered what he was waiting for. During the weeks of their companionship she had been the one who always knew where to go and what to do and what to talk about. But this was different. She, with her twenty-two years, was a child compared to him, an old man of thirty-six. He couldn't expect her to take the first step. He checked himself, a little startled at the trend of his thoughts. Step to what? How did he know she wanted him? Old as he was, he had had no experience with women. Dunya—long, long ago; then many years of burning up all passions, all fires in the revolution, with little left for personal emotions. Until this big dark girl with her warm voice and warm ways got hold of his heart.

He cleared his throat.

"Kira . . . ?"

"Yes, Maxim?" She waited. Nothing more came. She looked at him. O God, his eyes! Those miserably hesitant eyes! Who said that a girl had to wait for a man to declare his love?

"Yes, yes, yes, Maxim!" Kira covered the distance between them swiftly and put her arms around him.

"Very simple, Maxim, it really is very simple!" she was saying a little later. "See, all you have to do is to push the bed to this wall and get a bookcase here where the bed is now, and put the table closer to the window, and a shelf here . . . That's all we shall need."

Yes, it was very simple. The big girl had walked into his life, and she was going to stay there. She was already part of him; she was in every corner of him. She talked and she laughed and she kissed him as if she had always belonged in his life.

When Kira told her mother that she was going to marry Maxim, Vera couldn't speak; her anger choked her. Then she spat out words in a fury:

"You shameless creature . . . That's what you have been waiting for . . . your own uncle . . . a jailbird . . . a criminal . . . a man to whom nothing is sacred . . . a man whose friends killed your brother and your father! Don't expect to live with him here! Don't expect to bring him here! He's not going to put foot over my threshold!"

"Don't worry about that, mother, even if it is a threshold he saved for you. We wouldn't think of coming here. His room is big enough for the two of us, his bed is big enough for the two of us, and if we can squeeze in another chair, it's all right; if not—who cares? We have each other."

That happy laughter! What was there to be so happy about? Vera wondered wildly. One would think she had got a corner in paradise instead of a garret room in the slums.

Later, her eyes closed tight and her hands pressing hard at her temples, Vera burrowed her face into the pillow. Her past was with her again. She was a young bride. Her Michel, her young handsome husband, leaned over her, calling her with his eyes, his hands, his lips, his body. Would she then have minded a narrow bed, a garret room? Michel, Michel . . . She couldn't stand the thought of the grime and darkness of her life. But why live? Why not put an end to it? What made her go on? Was it the hope that Michel was not dead? Was it the fear of going against God's will? She did not know. All she knew was that there was nothing for her to live for, nothing to get up in the morning for and to perform the ugly daily tasks for.

It seemed like a dream to Maxim that when he reached the top of the dark time-worn staircase, a door would open and behind it would be light, laughter, warm arms, warm lips. He had had to learn to be happy but Kira was a good teacher. She made him take off whole Sundays, which he had never done before; she made him go to theaters with her, took him off on long walks, urged him to visit people, persuaded him to take up skating again. It was not an easy task to teach Maxim that one could at times be lazy, do nothing, think nothing, and enjoy it without a guilty conscience. Maxim was a puritan at heart and had been strengthened in his puritanism by the party's propaganda on abstinence and proper revolutionary behavior. The one woman he had known had been a puritan too. Dunya would never have kissed him first or shown her desire for him in any way; she wouldn't have thought of having him make love to her with the lights on, and she would never have dressed or undressed while he was looking at her. He had hardly known how Dunya's body looked. Kira loved lights. And if he had let her, she would not have minded getting dressed and undressed with all the neighbors as an audience.

"God or whoever it was that created us," she protested, "created us naked. We were meant not to be ashamed of our bodies. We have invented this being ashamed. Why should we? Now look, Maxim, look at me. Is there anything to be ashamed of? Look, why don't you look? Don't turn your head away . . . look."

She laughed and teased him until he became fully conscious of her body.

Kira had a loud voice. It was not unpleasantly loud, but it rang with exuberance and zest. She embarrassed Maxim by talking too loudly in public or by impulsively kissing him on a park bench, in the streetcar, or in the kitchen. She laughed at his embarrassed "Kira, people are looking at us, come to your senses."

"I don't want to come to my senses," she once said, "I never want to come to my senses again. Throughout my whole childhood I always had to do things I was told to do, things I hated to do. I always had to be sweet and charming even when I felt the devil in me. And then the revolution came, and on that day I went out into the street alone for the first time with no one chaperoning me, and joined a demonstration. I yelled at the top of my voice, I laughed and I sang. Everybody else was doing it too, but I am sure no one felt the way I did. I celebrated my own, my very own private revolution. I became free that day, free inside! I decided on that day, Maxim, never again to say a word I didn't mean, or to pretend to feel what I didn't feel. You call me a pagan. If being a pagan is to follow impulses which don't harm a soul and make me feel good, then I am a pagan and I insist on my right to be one. And, for instance, if I suddenly want to know again, as I do right now, at this very minute, how you taste, I must kiss you, this very minute I must kiss you. You taste good, darling, very very good."

Maxim had never noticed before how miserably poor his living quarters were. The walls of his room were damp and so thin that the room was always filled with outside noises. The kitchen, converted from a former bedroom, had no water or stove and was shared by three other families. The neighborhood was one of the poorest in Moscow. Maxim wondered if he shouldn't try to make it a little easier for Kira. Ludmilla, for instance, and some other women he knew, didn't go to work and had only their housework to do. Kira had both. It was true. Communists earned very little, and their wives had to work, but perhaps he should try at least to get a better room. Some of his colleagues, he knew, lived much more comfortably than he did. It shouldn't be hard; he had never asked for any personal favors. This would be the first time he had ever asked for anything and the authorities couldn't well refuse him. Nevertheless, he disliked the idea of accepting special favors and was relieved when Kira wouldn't hear of it.

"What's wrong with this room? Millions of people live in rooms like this."

"It's you I am worrying about."

"Me?" For the first time Maxim heard anger in Kira's voice. "Who do you think I am? Are you still thinking of the spoiled brat I once was? Remember you said this room was a palace for you? Don't you think it's also a palace for me as long as we are in it together, the two of us?"

Kira continued to work in the library; she enjoyed working among books. Her evening job with the Planning Commission she had to give up, for according to law a wife couldn't work in her husband's department. In any case, she preferred to stay home in the evening, so that she would always be there to greet Maxim.

As a child, Kira had admired and envied Natasha, whose life had seemed almost fabulously exciting and interesting compared to her own, and she would have given anything to have had Natasha consider her an equal. Early enough, however, she had recognized the barrier that being Vera's daughter raised between them. When she discovered that Natasha thought well enough of her to make Maxim give her a recommendation for a job with the Planning Commission, she felt that she had advanced far in her life. Now, as Maxim's wife, she hoped desperately that she had really become one of them; that now, perhaps, Natasha would accept her fully, as an equal.

She was feeling more than a little nervous, therefore, the evening Maxim took her, as his wife, to see Kseniya and Natasha. Kseniya and Natasha were totally unprepared, and they could not conceal their shock. Kseniya kissed Kira with an anxious look in her eyes. While Maxim and Kseniya were talking, Natasha called her cousin out into the hall.

"Kira," Natasha said, "even if I hurt you, I have to say it. If you married Maxim because you love him, you will be my beloved sister and friend. But if you have betrayed my trust in you and have done what others of your kind have done—married a Communist for protection and to hide your family past, I won't rest till he finds out the truth. Maxim is too dear to us, he is too good to be used as a screen. Now, which is it?"

The two girls stood facing each other. Her figure tense and eyes stern, Natasha, smaller and slighter than Kira, seemed to dominate her. Kira was heartbroken. Her cheeks paled and she trembled under Natasha's insult. How could Natasha, the kindhearted Natasha, misjudge her so greatly? Would she forever have to go on paying for being her parents' daughter? Natasha couldn't have meant to hurt her so cruelly. It was her devotion to Maxim and her fear for him that made her . . . She must, she had to make Natasha believe her.

"Natasha, I swear," said Kira desperately, "I love Maxim . . . I love him . . . I love him dearly. I would die for him."

It was not so much her words that convinced Natasha, as the naked, unmistakable sincerity in her voice and eyes that could not be pretended! Natasha hurried to apologize.

"Kira, you understood me, didn't you? You will forgive me and forget? Will you? If we didn't love Maxim as we do, I wouldn't care. But, you see, he doesn't know much about life. He doesn't know what goes on around him. A girl could easily trick him. I know now that you didn't, Kira. But I was so afraid. Let us be friends, Kira, real friends. Forgive me."

Kira's eyes laughed again. Arm in arm the girls returned to the room. Kseniya sighed with relief. She had been worried about the way Natasha had looked at Kira earlier. Now everything seemed to be all right. And Maxim! She couldn't remember having seen Maxim so happy since his very young days. Imagine having waited all these years to marry and then marrying Kira, the little niece whom he used to call a pest. Vera's daughter! Kseniya sat still holding Maxim's hand. Maxim, her son, whom she had seen so seldom since he had grown up. He had gray hair around his temples. Wasn't Kira too young for him? Kira didn't seem to think so, not the way she looked at him. Kseniya stroked her hair.

Later in the evening, Kira slipped out and went over to Vera's house. Vera was having supper. The room looked tidy and the food on the table plentiful. In her great happiness, Kira had wanted to see her mother. But it didn't look as if Vera wanted to see her. The stony expression on her face did not soften when Kira came in. She didn't ask any questions, was close tongued and sharp when answering Kira's questions: Yes, Katya took care of the food; a cleaning woman came regularly, Katya paid for it; yes, Katya took care of everything, she had the means and she remembered she had a mother. . . . Laid out on the table was a card game, obviously interrupted by the meal.

Once again Kira went to see her mother. That time, Vera was playing cards with another woman, a woman who had the same stony face, and was dressed with the same faded shabby elegance. The two women hardly exchanged a word. They sat in dead silence playing cards. Kira felt like an intruder and left shortly, determined, if her mother didn't want her as a friend, not to force herself on her.

The next time Kira saw her mother was a few weeks later, in January, 1924, through eyes blinded with tears. It was the day of

Lenin's funeral. In deep snow, Natasha and Kira had stood many hours during the night waiting to be admitted into the hall where Lenin's body lay in state. Tears froze on people's cheeks; feet and hands were numb from the biting cold, the like of which Moscow hadn't seen in many years. Few Muscovites had gone to bed that night. Millions wanted to see the beloved leader for the last time. Soldiers steeled in many battles, old peasants, workers, school children, housewives—none held their tears back. Hungry and half frozen, again and again they stood in the long line to see him once more. When the hall closed, the millions slowly dispersed only to assemble again a few hours later for the funeral.

Kira was returning with Natasha from the night vigil to warm themselves before starting out for the funeral. Their faces were swollen from weeping and blue with cold. As they passed Vera's house, Kira cast a glance at her mother's window. The curtain was slightly pushed aside and behind it was Vera's face with a terrible triumphant smile on it. In horror Kira stopped. There was no mistake: Her mother was looking at her with a smile more terrible than anything Kira had ever seen on a human face. There was glee in it over Lenin's death, over her daughter's grief, a glee mixed with an almost insane look of hatred. Never would Kira forget that look and never again did she want to see her mother.

## CHAPTER 22
### Maxim and Kira

FOR a short moment five years later warmth for her mother welled up in Kira. Kseniya was lying on her deathbed. As gently and quietly as she had lived she was dying. She murmured prayers for her children and grandchildren. The last hour came. Her mind wandered between past and present, no longer able to keep them distinct.

"Don't cry, Olga, don't cry." With weak fingers she tried to stroke Natasha's hair. "Don't cry. Igor isn't hurt. He only fell. Vera, put your hat on . . . don't let father wait . . . the dress is pretty. Zena's too . . . very pretty . . . Little children . . . where are all the little children? Anton likes little children. Maxim . . . Igor . . . little children . . . God bless you all."

Grief held back while Kseniya breathed was released now. Vera remained on her knees at the foot of the bed. She had not moved for hours, her eyes on Kseniya's face, seeing no one around her. Kira's heart went out to her. She had never seen her mother so forlorn. She knelt at her side and took her in her arms. With a heartbreaking sigh, Vera put her head on Kira's shoulder. Kira had seen her lips move during Kseniya's last minutes. Now her lips moved again:

"Mother . . . mother . . . hold me . . . don't leave me . . . don't leave me alone here."

"Please, mother, don't feel this way . . . you are not alone. You have me, you have Katya."

As if awakened from a trance, Vera pushed Kira aside and got up. The hardness came back into her face at the sight of Maxim and Natasha. She wouldn't let Kira take her home. She opened the door and rudely pushed aside the neighbors who were waiting to say their good-bys to Kseniya.

"Maxim, believe me, she was another woman for that one moment," Kira said later. "She was soft and human. What can I do to make her be that way again?"

At the funeral Vera showed clearly that she did not want Kira to do anything about it. She stood alone, her eyes dry, and left the cemetery before anyone else.

Why was Vera alone? Kira wondered. Where was Katya? Why hadn't she come to have a last look at Grandmother? When Kira asked her mother about it, Vera did not answer.

Soon Kira found out the reason. Katya was in prison, as the "accomplice of a notorious thief." The authorities had known all along of the activities of the notorious thief, Nikolka Heartbreak, but they had not bothered about him until now. He was one of the many shady figures who thrived in the mire of the NEP. Now the NEP was finished. It was 1929; a new era had begun and a monumental house cleaning was going on.

The new era marked the death of the NEP and of the detour that Lenin had taken in 1921 amidst fears that it meant the end of the revolution. Now the Bolsheviks had returned to their original road, a road with no signs marked "private trade" and "foreign capital," the road that was to lead them to the final victory of communism. The First Five-Year Plan had been announced. Few could at first find their way through the maze of the plan's figures and statistics. It was the task of party propagandists, of newspaper editors, of teachers to bring the figures to the people in the understandable terms of daily life.

"It is like this," the official instructors were telling the people. "A few years ago we were so weak that we couldn't go ahead unless we stopped to catch our breath. Now we have regained our strength and can go ahead again. Our goal is a good home for everyone, plenty of food for everyone, warm clothes, good schools, well-equipped hospitals, art, sports, for everyone, not only for the chosen few who enjoyed these things before the revolution. But all this doesn't grow out of the soil just because we want it. We need building material, we need metals, oil, cotton, chemicals, and many other things. And most, and first of all, we need machinery to build plants in which we can produce what we need. We are industrially a backward country—the czars were never interested in developing Russia—so we have to get the machinery to build up our industry from abroad from the capitalist world, and this capitalist world hopes to choke us by forcing us to pay immediate cash for everything we buy. There might have been some other way out if there had been a world revolution. Unfortunately that hasn't happened, and it doesn't look as if it would at the present moment. So our only way out now is to use everything we produce, everything we possess to pay for the machines we buy abroad. The few years ahead will be hard years. We will have to tighten our belts more than ever, but we have no choice. Now, with this in your mind, have a good look at the plan. Our best minds have worked on it and they have figured out what each of us can do during the next five years to achieve our goal in the best and quickest way. Every little nook in our lives has been covered by the plan. Look at it; each of you can find his own place in it . . ."

In every factory, office, and school the figures concerning them personally were explained to the workers at meetings, in pamphlets, and in study groups. Great enthusiasm was whipped up. As in the early days of the revolution, the spirit rose high. Visions of a future filled with unheard-of plenty within only a few years beckoned to the people. The revolution had not been betrayed! The ugly NEP with its fat speculators and unclean profits was gone. The revolution was alive again.

Maxim was one of those who helped prepare the plan. The Planning Commission, limited in resources and possibilities during the NEP years, had now become the seat of bustling seething activity. On it depended each breath the country drew.

Maxim again forgot how to relax. There were many nights when he didn't go home at all, when tired men interrupted their never-ending conferences to catch a few hours' sleep in an office chair or on a pile of newspapers on the floor. They were always conscious of the admonishments of their Leader:

"Go on, on, on . . . move quicker, quicker . . . there is no time . . . the world is arming, the world is ganging up against us . . . our life depends on speed . . . quick . . . quick . . . quick . . . every minute counts!"

Quicker . . . quicker . . . The words pursued Maxim day and night. More machinery to be got from abroad. More gold, more foreign currency to send abroad for it. But where get so much currency? By sending out of the country more textiles, more raw materials, more food, more food. But how much more could they send? How much longer could they starve, despoil the country? There was one answer to it: Quicker! Don't lose a moment! Get the food, send it out! Get the leather, send it out! Get everything, send out everything! Hungry children! Barefoot children! They must hold out, they must! There was no other way out. The world was ganging up against them; they were racing against time! It lay in their hands, in the hands of the Soviet planners, to get ready for the assault, to save the Soviet Union, to save the revolution!

Absorbed and worried, Maxim smoked cigarette after cigarette brooding over charts and plans, working at home in the evening. From time to time a glass of tea appeared before him, the sugar stirred into it. A hand touched his forehead, a cheek touched his cheek, a voice whispered:

"Darling . . . you will kill yourself . . . go to bed."

Oh, yes, Kira. Sometimes he tore himself away from the papers and, dizzy with fatigue, let her put him to bed. She too was tired. The figures on his plans, which meant to him butter and meat and fish and canned food and eggs to be sent abroad, meant for her hopeless hours spent standing in front of almost-empty stores. Then, sometimes almost stumbling from exhaustion, she would hurry home to wait for Maxim. When Maxim did come home he was usually so exhausted that he hardly noticed her presence. He ate in silence. Silently he spread his papers before him and lost himself in them. She too sat in silence, looking at him, loving him, longing for him. She did not have her husband any more, but she was not the only one. Other women had lost their husbands to the plan too. They breathed, they slept, they lived the plan.

Kira forgot her waiting and her longing when they went to bed. She pressed close to him with his arm around her. His face would relax, he would smile and kiss her, and for her the whole world would disappear. He seldom was the lover now, for there was little vitality in him, but simply to lie close to him gave her the same blissful feeling of belonging together that their most passionate lovemaking did. Maxim fell asleep quickly. Kira fought her sleep; she wanted to prolong the happiness his closeness gave her, she wanted to look at him, touch him. If she fell asleep she wouldn't feel him any more.

In the rare moments when he relaxed enough to talk, their conversation invariably revolved about the plan.

The plan aimed to destroy utterly all remnants of capitalism and the bourgeoisie. Sons and daughters of workers and peasants were to come up from the bottom and take their places, not only at the lathes and behind the plows. Theirs was to be every job the country had to offer. They had to be trained now. The plan demanded superhuman efforts, miraculous feats of speed and efficiency. At the same time, posts requiring the performance of these feats were being filled on the government's orders by men and women whose only qualification for occupying them was a birth certificate proving their humble origin. Those who complained that the newcomers interfered with the work not only because of their inexperience but because they took the valuable time of the people who had to train them were accused of antiproletarianism and counterrevolution.

After getting a reprimand from the party for having said that now was not the time to initiate people who had to start from scratch, Maxim had given up his useless struggle to get rid of the unwelcome helpers being thrust upon him. He found in Kira understanding sympathy for his troubles. She had the same troubles.

". . . if I should say anything," she unburdened herself, "they will call me a bourgeois. It doesn't make the slightest difference to me who one's parents are, it's the person who counts. Now they've sent me two girls, both peasants. One is so stupid she will never learn to distinguish a book from a magazine. She had never heard of Pushkin or Tolstoi; she still believes that proofreading means reading every copy of a newspaper or of a book. Why on earth did they have to pick a library job for her? She sweats and moans, and is thoroughly unhappy. She won't be the first one to crack under an effort much too big for her brain. The other girl is quick and eager, and in a few months I could make a good librarian out of her. No, they told me, not in a few months, right now, immediately, and not a plain librarian, but the chief librarian assistant. She isn't ready for it, she knows it and we all know it. Can I protest? I, one of the small fry, not a party member, the daughter of the enemy, Michel Dolinin? The hunt for 'bourgeois relics' is on again. Hadn't I better keep quiet before I get you into trouble?"

The hunt was on indeed. Maxim did not have the heart to tell Kira that she had already added to the trouble this hunt brought him. In the midst of the almost unbearable press of his work he was constantly being called in for questioning by the new personnel head, named Smirnov, a twenty-two-year-old redhead, whose eyes popped out when, as a preliminary to the current party purge, Maxim answered the routine questions. Anton Nazarov's son? Married to Michel Dolinin's daughter? Wasn't he lucky to have caught such a big fish? Smirnov was hurt when his superior, instead of congratulating him on the catch, glanced indifferently at the thick red pencil marks on Maxim's questionnaire:

"Don't bother about him, Smirnov, we know him well. He is an old party member . . . he is all right."

Was he really? How could one be so sure? What about Trotsky? What about Trotsky's friends? Weren't many of them old party members too? That didn't prevent them from going against the party. No, he, Smirnov wouldn't trust anyone. This Maxim Nazarov needed watching. Smirnov found excuses to call Maxim into his office almost daily. It made him feel good. He, the homeless waif, whom they used to call the Red Scamp, who if not for the Bolsheviks, would have remained forever a worm crawling in dirt, he had the power to push a button and tell one of the top men in this most important institution to drop everything and come to him immediately. It didn't matter whether Maxim had an important job to finish, whether he had to interrupt a conference and leave unsettled most urgent matters. Maxim had to obey. "Quicker . . . quicker . . ." lost its magic when the GPU man with the reassuring title of Personnel Head called.

Smirnov leisurely fingered Maxim's fat dossier. He tried to make his youngish voice sound manly and important: "Don't you think, comrade Nazarov, it would have been more proper for a man like you to have married a party member?"

Maxim's palms could hardly stand the pain of the nails pressing into them. He must get hold of himself. What would be the sense of knocking the windbag down? Two years ago he would have lashed out quickly, but since then much had happened. The unprecedented liquidation of Trotsky and his followers, the trial of engineers in which men Maxim had known and trusted were sentenced for sabotage, the witch hunting of the GPU and the ever-present sword of Damocles it suspended over their heads had taught him to control his tongue and his temper. He even succeeded in forcing something resembling a smile when he said:

"Well, you know how it is, comrade . . . love . . ."

Smirnov called him in again the day after Maxim had permitted Fedor to use his name in defending himself against a wrong accusation. With that revolting gesture of his, Smirnov was teasingly fingering a paper which he must have just received. His eyes were still on the last lines of it.

"Well, comrade Nazarov . . ." Smirnov's snickering tone exasperated Maxim. "If I were you, comrade Nazarov, I wouldn't be so interested in . . . he-he-he . . . former capitalists. I wouldn't, not if my record were as open to, let us say, to question as yours."

Maxim waited a moment till he was sure he could give his tone the lightness he intended.

"Now, now, who will take so seriously a word said for Fedor Gavrilov, an old friend . . . rather an old family connection."

The correction came too late.

"Old friend . . . well, well." The snickering sounded triumphant now, and Smirnov's pen slowly—for Maxim's benefit—wrote out the two words on the paper he had in front of him.

Maxim kept silent until Smirnov let him go. What could he say? One did not fight the GPU, even if the GPU in this case was represented by a despicable little scoundrel. Smirnov had graduated with high honors from petty spying and the denouncing of former bourgeois families. He was now told to brandish his GPU stick in the faces of party members, some of them in high places. It went to his head like strong wine. Maxim was helpless against him. The GPU had shown that it was stronger than any of them. It had broken better men than he because a puppy like that Smirnov reported that the man had once sat next to Trotsky at a meeting. What Bolshevik had not considered that a high honor then? No, he'd better keep still and go quietly back to work as soon as Smirnov let him.

Maxim wished he dared complain that this kind of questioning and investigation took his time and distracted him from his work on the plan. But others had tried to complain and had paid for it with their jobs and even their freedom. Some had complained to the very top, to the Leader, to the boss. It had helped them little. Wasn't Stalin the one who had turned the GPU from what had been the secret police's job in the past—fighting the enemies of the revolution—and given it the green light and the power to fight instead those who had made the revolution? Could that have happened if Lenin had lived? It was better not to think about it. Better to think of nothing but the plan. The plan was above everything, above party struggles, above petty denunciations and the elimination of some men, even if he himself should be one of those eliminated. They didn't belong to themselves. They belonged to the party, to the plan, to the Soviet Union.

But not always could Maxim force himself not to think. What had happened in the past two years? There had been discussions and quarrels in the party years ago too, and there were often attacks on those who rebelled against its judgment. The party had never encouraged disagreement with its decisions. Lenin used to give the dissenters a good sermon, and more often than not convinced his opponents with his arguments. But if he didn't, it never made the other fellow his enemy. Lenin used to thunder at Bukharin and then sit quiet and even enjoy listening to Bukharin hit back at him. It had been a delight to watch these two sharp clever minds clashing with each other. And afterwards they would joke together. Lenin had treated Bukharin as a father treats a beloved spoiled son. It made Maxim sick with nostalgia to think of those old days. Now when one disagreed with the party it wasn't safe to say so even in private. Too many eager spying ears around. Until two years ago the press and meetings had been open to party oppositionists. Now the press was closed to them, meetings were handled in such a way that no dissenter ever got a chance to open his mouth, even if he was ready to risk his neck.

What had happened? Trotsky, the creator and the idol of the Red Army, exiled, declared an enemy of the people, because he refused to accept Stalin's word as the only law. Trotsky's friends arrested, thrown out of jobs, sent to places where the czar used to send those same people before the revolution. One had never been afraid to contradict Lenin, but few today dared to say aloud what they thought. Some, for instance, thought that they would never succeed in building socialism in the Soviet Union if they betrayed and turned their backs on the world revolution and concentrated only on themselves. Others thought that Stalin had overestimated the strength of their backward country; that only with superhuman sacrifices would their people be able to create the industrial giant the plan called for. The few who had dared to say this were branded as cowards, as demagogues, obstructionists, extremists, right deviationists, left deviationists, and were finally silenced by threat of exile.

Maxim did not talk about this to Kira but she guessed that something worried him. One evening she determined to find out what it was. She wouldn't ask him questions while he worked—nothing was allowed to disturb him while he worked at home. She had hung blankets on the door and the walls to deaden the noises from outside. His pencils were always sharpened, his cigarettes, matches, and ash tray handy, the teakettle always hot. But that evening, the moment he put the papers back into the folders and pushed his chair away, she was at his side.

"Anything wrong, Maxim?"

"No, darling, nothing at all. Why?"

"I thought something was wrong."

"No, no, everything is all right."

She didn't give up. Her "Anything wrong, Maxim?" became more persistent. Finally she won. He told her about Smirnov and the nerve-racking questioning; about the persecution of Communists by the GPU; about the whip wielded from above, which grew heavier every day; about the fear of talking out of turn. So Maxim too saw shadows cast by the plan. Until now he had refused to admit it and had chided her for taking the difficulties so seriously.

"Oh, you women!" he had exclaimed only a few evenings earlier. "Can't you ever rise above these things? I agree with you that all is not as I would want it to be, but must you always put the petty things of life above the greater?"

"Petty things of life?"

They were having supper. Full of indignation, Kira pointed her hand to the food on the table.

"You call getting this and cooking this in our kitchen petty things of life?"

She pulled at his shirt:

"You call laundering this without soap petty? And having your shoes repaired when there is no leather? And supplying you with cigarettes? There isn't a tobacco store in Moscow I didn't go into today to get you enough cigarettes for one evening. Oh, you men, when will you stop living in the skies and come down to earth?"

Kira laughed, but she was a little hurt nevertheless. It was true, however, that she now had all day in which to stand in line and to see that things at home were comfortable for Maxim, for she had quit her library job. Let this "birth certificate orgy," as she called the current investigation of people's social origin, blow over and she would go back to work. But not to the library, not unless that other orgy, the orgy of idolization of materialism, blew over too.

What Kira called the orgy of materialism had at first seemed to her nothing more than a whim of somebody in the Commissariat of Education. A decree was issued against fairy tales. Fairy tales were harmful, it said. A child shouldn't be permitted to read about animals or flowers talking, about ugly ducklings changing into beautiful swans, about a noble knight, a champion of the poor, destroying his enemies with one stroke. Why? How could anyone who knew anything about children object to that? She couldn't take it seriously at first, not even when the press came out with ranting attacks against fairy tales and anything based on imagination instead of on a scientific explanation of life. But soon she had to take it seriously. Fairy tales and those illustrated books which were not realistic were eliminated from the library and crossed out in the catalogue. New books took their place, modern fairy tales. Kira liked the vivid coloring of some of the illustrations, the musical rhythm of some of the verses. But could any child get excited over the evolution of a cotton plant into a shirt or over the workings of a tractor or the milking of a cow told with minute technical details? A few of the writers could make interesting the subjects they were ordered to write about. But they were apt to cheat: One made a plant walk, another had his screwdriver cry. When the cheating was discovered, these books too were removed, and their authors rebuked.

With many of her favorite books gone and the librarians under a vigilant watch, Kira lost interest in the library. She started to reread old classics, for the new books seemed dull. And no wonder. The writers had burned their fingers. One of them had in all innocence made his hero, a Communist, jealous of his wife who preferred another man. Slanderer, calumniator, reviler, the critics called the amazed author. A Communist jealous! What an absurd idea! No real Communist would ever succumb to such petty bourgeois notions! And the wife of a Communist, a Communist herself, would never think of behaving the way the author made her behave; she had other things to do now, far more important things than indulging in love affairs. Wasn't she working for the plan? Wasn't she building socialism? Only an enemy of the people could so vilify the new Soviet womanhood!

Another writer had the misfortune, in mentioning a former White officer, to use slightly fewer than the exact number of abusive epithets prescribed for the purpose. He became a lover of counterrevolutionists, a hidden enemy of the proletariat, a serpent's tooth. No, one could certainly not blame the authors for writing lifeless books. But no one could force Kira to read them. She preferred to reread, perhaps for the fifth time, books which she knew by heart. The people moving through the pages of these books were alive and their creators, even though writing in czarist days, did not have their ears to the ground in order not to miss a warning signal from above.

Soon Kira found herself with more time on her hands, for the Kremlin restaurant for top members of the government began to serve a few selected responsible workers. To be admitted to it meant that one had reached the higher ranks. When Maxim was admitted, he was conscious of a great feeling of relief: it meant that Smirnov had been unsuccessful in his machinations, and that he was clear of GPU suspicion. Kira let out a shout when she heard the news, and whirled Maxim around the room.

"Kira, Kira, have mercy on an old man! You seem to be quite happy not to have me around at mealtime."

Oh, that was true! She hadn't thought of that; it meant Maxim would be at home even less than before. But she was so fed up with running uselessly in circles, afraid to miss a drop of milk here or an ounce of fat there, that she couldn't help feeling relieved. There was little she needed for herself.

Rationing was introduced, a few items at first, gradually everything. It was a complicated, painful procedure, involving many colored booklets for products which the stores didn't have to sell anyway. But at least the eternal search for food was at an end. Every woman was assigned to one store and one store only; no other store would sell her anything. About once an hour Kira looked through the window from which she could see her co-operative. If there was a line, she joined it quickly with an old newspaper, a jar, or a string bag in her hands. There was no way of knowing what the store was selling that day, and they wouldn't give you the food unless you had the proper container to put it in. If there was no line, there was no use going down; the store was empty. Kira did not complain as long as Maxim was well taken care of. Lately through his office he was even supplied with all the cigarettes he needed.

One day Maxim brought home more big news. The department heads of the Planning Commission had been given ration books for the Government Apartment House store. A great many rumors were going around town about this store. It had all the food and clothes and shoes and furniture imaginable; there were never any lines; service was quick and polite; purchases were wrapped in paper. Now she, Kira, could go in there to buy what she wanted! No more salesmen who treated the customers as if they were obnoxious intruders, no more hours of waiting, only to get a carrot or a handful of sunflower seeds. No more whispering stony-faced women who reminded Kira of her mother:

"Did you hear . . . there are signs enough . . . a little more patience, they say. Russia will belong to the Russians again. God will forgive us our sins and return to us. Did you hear? . . . The peasants revolt, they say. Did you hear? . . . they say . . ."

Kira was relieved to be through with all that, of course, but in the midst of her excited exclamations and laughter, suddenly whirled on Maxim:

"Maxim, quick, tell me honestly, without thinking, from the bottom of your heart—are you really, completely glad?"

Maxim drew her onto his lap. "Are you, my dear?"

That was all he said, but they knew that they felt the same way. It would be pleasant to be relieved of the daily drudgery and Maxim was glad that could be. But during the NEP years, when comforts and good food could be got for money, they had never let themselves be tempted by it. They could have had extra money without doing anything wrong. A Communist was paid only a low salary, but he could write articles, for instance, and get paid for it. Some Communists did so. Kira might have asked Vera for one or two of the jewels she had hidden, and could have sold them. They had never even wanted to do it.

"When everybody has everything, we shall also have it, not before" was their rule.

The Kremlin restaurant—well, that was done so that men with important jobs wouldn't have to waste time going home to eat. Cigarettes—they needed plenty of cigarettes to stand the strain of their work and the late hours. But this was different. Maxim and Kira were being lifted out of the ranks of the common people and set high above, among a chosen few. This couldn't be explained away on the grounds of its usefulness to his work. It relieved Kira, but she wasn't working now. Even if shopping was an unpleasant task, millions were doing it, women with large families, whose husbands didn't enjoy the services of the Kremlin restaurant. After her first outburst of excitement, Kira was troubled.

"Must we accept it, Maxim? Can't you say, 'No, we don't want it'?"

"No, dearest, that can't be done. Nobody would understand us. With all the suspicion and distrust that's around, they might suspect something sinister behind it. You and I, we are trailing behind anyway. Many had this privilege long ago; they asked for it when things started to get difficult. I was given this privilege as a routine matter, through a circular letter, sent probably to many others. No, it wouldn't do to refuse."

"The more I think of it, Maxim, the more I hate the idea. I will be ashamed to look at my neighbors. I will be ashamed to pass the line at the store. I will be ashamed to walk into the house with packages or to go into the kitchen to cook food they can't get."

It was several days before Kira made up her mind to go to the Government House store. There was a line at the corner co-operative and she made a detour to avoid the questions of her neighbors. She took a streetcar. The store was on the other side of the Moscow River, not far from Natasha's. She never visited that neighborhood without dropping in, but she couldn't face Natasha today; she couldn't face anyone today. She walked into the store feeling extremely uncomfortable. She headed immediately for a corner and stood there for a long time, taking everything in. Meat, butter, sugar, fresh fruit and fresh vegetables, white bread, cheese, sweets, canned fish! The rickety children of their handyman at their house came to her mind. She would have loved to fill a basket and take it home to them, but she knew she couldn't. She had read the strict rules of her new ration book. It was a liberal ration, much too liberal for their small family, but to use it for someone not entitled to it was a severely punishable offense.

Some of the women in the store were well dressed, young and good-looking, with fancy hair-dos and manicured nails. And they chattered. It was long since Kira had heard women's chatter. The voices of the only women she had known for years were worried or eager or angry or passionate voices but not chattery voices. A few of the women had maids or chauffeurs walking behind them to carry their packages. Most of the other women in the store were the kind one saw everywhere, only slightly less harassed looking, and better dressed. They took their time making their selections and the salesmen helped them and joked with them. One didn't hear the mocking:

"Well, citizeness, if you don't like it, why don't you go look somewhere else? . . . Next!"

Timidly Kira made her modest purchases: a loaf of white bread, a pound of apples, and a bag of candies. She would find a way to give the children the candy without breaking the law too much. She was not prepared for the buzz of excitement the candies started in the house. Where had she got them? Kira felt like a criminal as, flushed and unhappy, she told the neighbors of her new store. Cold unfriendly looks were her answer.

Maxim found her in tears.

"Maxim, Maxim, I can't . . . I don't belong there . . . I belong here. What shall I do?"

There was nothing she could do. She broke the law constantly; she bought for her neighbors more than she did for herself. She deprived herself of much she could now afford so that her condition would not seem too different from theirs. It didn't help. No bribes or gifts could change the fact that she had moved on to a different, higher level.

The Planning Commission received new cars and Maxim was assigned a car with a chauffeur. He had no qualms about that. Too much of his time had been wasted on the long crowded streetcar rides. The car saved two hours a day at least, and he went to work and came home unbruised, his coat buttons intact, and himself refreshed by the drive. The chauffeur, a middle-aged man who had once been a cab driver, turned up his nose when he called for Maxim for the first time.

"What do you live here for? I've driven a lot of you people and no one in this kind of hole. Why don't you get yourself something better?"

"And where do you live, comrade?" Maxim asked.

"Ah, me, that's different. But you people, you don't have to."

Another time he pointed at Maxim's coat:

"Why don't you get yourself a decent coat? They have them in your store. By the way, I saw your wife in the store the other day. Why doesn't your wife call me to drive her?"

Maxim would not have considered having Kira use an official car for her personal affairs. But the chauffeur came back to it again. It was as if he, wiser in the ways of the mighty than this obvious innocent, considered it his duty to instruct him in what was due him. One morning when Kira came out to tell the chauffeur that Maxim was not yet ready, he tackled her about the matter:

"You listen to me, comrade. That husband of yours doesn't know how to take care of a young wife. Did he tell you about the beauty parlor they've opened for you women? And why don't you both get new coats? The other comrades all got coats for themselves and their wives. Tomorrow the store gets a shipment of berries, for canning. Sugar too. You can't carry it home in the streetcar. Why don't you go with me tomorrow and get the berries, and I will take you to the beauty parlor, and afterwards you could have a look at the coats?"

No. She didn't need a beauty parlor, and their coats were good enough for them. As to canning, where would she can? In their pigeonhole of a kitchen with everybody watching her waste the beautiful sugar their children were vainly crying for? The funny man! She didn't say anything, just shook her head and flashed him a smile before she disappeared into the house.

Kira knew she would never have the heart to tease her neighbors with jam making. They couldn't get any fresh berries, although it was the berry season, when Moscow was usually flooded with them. But this year the peasants hadn't brought their berries and vegetables into the city. There was nothing in the stores for them to spend their money on, so why bother? They ate their produce themselves, they pickled and preserved it and stored it in their cellars. Why should they worry that the city people didn't have enough to eat? Did the city people care about them?

It was unpleasant enough for Kira without any jam making and canning. Much as she tried to limit her own purchases, every morsel of sausage, every slice of cheese aroused envy. She met a hostile silence when she walked into the kitchen. For the first time, she wanted to get out of the house.

Her wish was answered sooner than she expected. The Moscow Soviet had assigned additional apartments to the Planning Commission for its employees. Maxim, feeling that larger families had the first right to better apartments, had not put his name on the list of applicants. He was astonished therefore when two rooms were assigned to him in a building which had recently been repaired and modernized. It was near the pond where he used to go skating as a boy, in a quiet pleasant tree-lined street. Why had he got the rooms? Some of his assistants, who lived with large families in one room, had begged for better living quarters and had been refused. Why he? Because he was the department head? If so, it wasn't right.

Maxim well remembered Lenin's warnings that Communists should never be carried away by the power they possessed and that they should never accept the material advantages that their positions might give them. The only people who got material advantages for their work in Lenin's time were the bourgeois experts without whose services the country couldn't have got along. Why did he, Maxim, have to live better than others? He had always considered it a great privilege to work for the party and the Soviet Union. He had never needed any other incentive. It had never occurred to him that he should be recompensed with special material benefits for his work and that others must be made to feel that he was more important than they were. But now, invisible dividing lines were being drawn between him and those who were not in the top ranks. The Kremlin food, his car, his special ration card—and with the new apartment his last tie with those among whom he had lived since he left his father's house would be gone. What he had fought for and won then—his right not to live differently from people less privileged—was being forcibly taken away from him now. Yes, forcibly. As he had told Kira, he couldn't refuse what the government gave him. If only he could explain openly why he didn't want any favors. But that would mean saying that he didn't want to get away from Lenin's road, that he still believed that a Communist should not strive for privileges and advantages, that a Communist did not need any special recompense for serving the party. And that would be considered criticism of the government. One could no longer criticize the government without being punished for it.

When Maxim got home with his news, as had often happened lately, he found Kira with traces of tears in her eyes.

"What is it, Kira, my dear?"

She looked at him desolately, and the tears welled up again.

"Nothing new, Maxim, the old story, they all envy me so much that they hate me . . . even the children. I wish we could get away."

Maxim felt suddenly younger.

"When do you want to get away, Kira? Today? Tomorrow?"

"Don't joke, Maxim. I meant it, I truly meant it."

"I meant it too. Come, let me dry your tears, so you can see this."

He kissed her eyes and pulled out of his pocket the paper with the momentous words on it.

Kira read them quickly, her face lighting with joy. Then a new torrent of tears threatened.

"What now, Kira? I thought you were glad. What is it, my darling? Don't cry so."

"Don't you see, Maxim, it's being so glad that makes me so sad," she sobbed. "I don't want to be glad. I think it's terrible to be glad to get away from here. I don't want any of the things. I don't want the store, I don't want the apartment. Maxim, let's do something . . . please, Maxim, can't we do something?"

"No, dearest, we can't. I'm unhappy about it too; I wish it weren't so; I wish things were as they used to be. I wish people's enthusiasm didn't have to be fed with extra rations and extra rooms. Oh, Kira, how I wish it weren't so."

Suddenly Kira's laughter, her loud hearty laughter, which Maxim hadn't often heard lately, brought him to his feet.

"Kira, Kira," he shook her with both hands, "stop it, don't be hysterical, Kira. Kira, calm yourself."

"I'm not hysterical," Kira gasped. "It just struck me so funny that here we sit as if the greatest calamity had befallen us. Millions of people would give their right eye for this slip of paper, and we two big fools lament over it and break our hearts."

In a few days they were ready to move to the new apartment. Bare now of their few belongings, the old room looked even to them on that last day what it really was—a dark dilapidated attic. They stood for a long time at the window in the empty room, their arms around each other.

"Can we ever be as happy anywhere as we were here, Maxim?" Kira was subdued, afraid to step into an uncertain future. "Remember our first days here? Remember the horrible holes in the walls? I covered them up with colored crepe paper and it looked like ballet scenery. Remember when I cooked our first meal?"

Maxim laughed. "How could I forget? You had three chops in the pan, and you left the kitchen for a moment. When you returned, all we had left for our dinner was one, the smallest chop. And I remember how they poured out your coffee and filled the pot with water . . . how they stole our only sharp knife . . . how the roof leaked and we moved the bed around when it rained . . ."

Their new rooms were freshly painted, the floors were waxed, and the spotless windows looked out on the branches of elm trees. But the rooms looked bare, for their meager furniture hardly filled one of them. Maxim asked the head of their Economic Division, which took care of the needs of the staff, for a few chairs and a desk.

"Oh, certainly, comrade Nazarov, most certainly. But are you sure that is really all you want? Here, you'd better take this slip and have a look at the Foreign Office storehouse. They have a big choice of furniture, curtains, lamps, kitchen equipment. Send the chauffeur for your wife. You know, women don't trust us men with such a job."

It was unbelievable. Maxim and Kira walked through rooms packed with everything a well-equipped apartment required, and it was theirs for the asking. Maxim's small voice reminded him of the empty furniture stores, of the hardware stores, completely bare of paint, nails, wire, wallpaper, electric bulbs, of everything people needed to make their rooms livable. And here these riches! For foreign diplomats, foreign correspondents—and Responsible Soviet Workers! Kira did not believe in small inside voices. What she felt had to come out loudly.

"I think it's outrageous, with people sleeping on floors and using boxes for tables and chairs! I can't believe the authorities know what goes on here."

"They do, Kira, I am sure they do. But don't you see, even if everything here were put into the stores today, it would be only a drop in the bucket. It would help only a handful of people. The rest will have to wait anyway till the plan is finished and we can start producing at full blast. The foreigners have to get decent things, you know how they are. And what remains, since there isn't enough to go around, well, it goes to the people who bear the responsibility."

His voice did not sound too convincing. He didn't believe in what he was saying. Neither did Kira.

"And that's exactly what I find so outrageous! If there isn't enough for all, give it to those who need it most. Wouldn't that be the fairest thing to do? There are enough families with lots of children, old people, sick people, who need it more than we do. While we . . . I really don't know why we deserve it all."

Again they finished by laughing at themselves. When they had picked out the few pieces they wanted, the official in charge said he was sure that they hadn't looked into all the rooms, that there was certainly much more they could use. He took them around himself, urged them to take this and that, and by the time they had finished, a truck was filled with furniture.

Kira lived quietly in the new apartment. Her shopping and house-keeping work in those clean comfortable rooms with running water and a gas stove did not take much time. Sometimes she visited Natasha and other friends, but they were all always busy, working and struggling to keep their families fed, clothed and clean, which made Kira feel ashamed of her own easy life. She lived for the moment Maxim came home. And then—then she blessed their new rooms. She had made them attractive and pleasant. When he worked in the evenings, it was quiet, nothing disturbed him; the lights were soft; the chair in which she sat looking at him was deep and comfortable. And when finished he stretched out on the couch, his head in her lap.

"You know, Kira," he once said, lying on the couch peaceful and relaxed, "there is something in it, having it easy and comfortable. After all, I work all day long with every nerve strained, with my brain working at full speed, with decisions to be taken on which millions of rubles depend. One wrong calculation—and it may take years to straighten it out, and be the end of me, by the way. If I spend the few hours I have to rest in comfort and peace, it gives me the strength to go on."

She enveloped him with her hands, warm and soft, and with her love, as warm and soft. Weren't these moments what she lived for? Suppose she were working, as she often thought she ought to be when she read the government's appeals to women to get out of their homes and help the plan. She would have meetings in the evening, and working at the speed demanded now she would come home after work as exhausted as Maxim was. It might be contrary to the ideals of the new woman, she might be laughed at and despised for doing nothing, but she was what she most wanted to be in life—the woman to whom Maxim came to rest his tired head, to open his heart, and to satisfy his senses. If in addition to that she could be the mother of his children, there would be nothing more she could ask. But something was wrong with her. Recently, a doctor had told her it might be corrected.

After all the privileges they had got, what harm in getting one more? Sanatoriums and rest homes were equipped specially for Responsible Workers, and several Kremlin doctors spent the vacation seasons there as attendants. Maxim had never taken a vacation, and never would until he thought his work could permit it. There was no point in even suggesting it. But perhaps she could be helped. There was a place in the Caucasus, Matzesta, near Sochi, where the waters were famous for restoring virility and fecundity. Middle-aged women, she had heard, had borne children for the first time after a cure in those waters. She was only twenty-nine; certainly she could hope.

She talked to Maxim about it. A few telephone conversations with the right people provided her with a sanatorium bed, with a berth on the train, and with a letter To Whom It May Concern bespeaking attention for her. These letters had subtle differences in wording, indicating to the authorities concerned the importance of the bearer. Kira's was apparently a very good letter. She got a room for herself, which was a sign of great distinction, and she was assigned to the outstanding woman doctor, to the envy of those who had to be satisfied with less prominent physicians.

If not for the daily letter he found there, Maxim would not have wanted to go home at all. For the first time in their seven years, Kira was not there to greet him, and the place seemed unbearably empty without her.

"It is the same here as in Moscow," Kira wrote, "not enough doctors, not enough medical equipment, beds, sheets, table silver. So we, the chosen few, get the little there is, we, the lucky wives of Responsible Workers . . . As if being your wife wasn't enough of a reward! Do I have to be paid constantly for being your wife?

". . . It's lots of fun to watch the women. They have worked out a kind of hierarchy according to their husbands' positions. It seems that I am quite advanced in it. Never knew what an important man I was married to. Did you? I disturb them, I keep upsetting the ranks. I'd much rather play a game of croquet with the nurses than with any of them. . . .

"I am one of the privileged who are given the spray that is supposed to perform miracles. . . . My doctor is besieged by the women. They all beg for the spray. They promise her soap, stockings, sugar, the address of a dream of a dressmaker. . . . The doctor told me she would gladly spray all of them without taking sugar or soap for it, but she has a busy schedule of nearly fourteen hours a day and besides, she is being watched all the time. Those precious souls, her patients, are so jealous of one another that they would be sure to denounce her if she gave anyone even one little spray without the sacred stamped slip of paper from the Health Board authorizing it.

"The waters here work. . . . Everybody runs around with their tongues out, flirting, looking for romance and finding it easily. . . . I dream of you every night. . . . And the hungry looks in the men's eyes are beginning to disturb me. I wish I were home with you. . . . I catch myself looking at a man's lips wondering how his kisses would feel. . . . You can't blame me for feeling this way. Why are we made this way? It is very cruel to have created us with thirsts and hungers which must always be satisfied . . ."

After this letter Maxim wished more than ever that she was back. If her thirst and hunger got strong enough, she would satisfy them, he knew, and feel very natural about it. She had done that before she married him. And even though Maxim told himself that a woman had the same right as a man to enjoy her own body and that jealousy was a bourgeois tradition unworthy of a Communist, the image of Kira in another man's arms came back to torture him in the midst of a conference or in a nightmare of a dream.

Kira returned strong and bronzed, full of radiant warmth and tenderness, her body vibrant with longing for him. She came back on a Sunday morning and for twenty-four hours they did not leave the house.

"Never, never again shall I go away from you. Never must we be separated again. Never . . ." Kira repeated over and over.

Their short separation drew them still closer together but it did not accomplish its real aim. Kira bore no child for Maxim.

## CHAPTER 23
## *Natasha and Peter*

AT the time of Kseniya's death in 1929 Natasha had two children, Volik and Maya, five and three years old. They still lived in Peter's old room to which, after Volik's birth, they had been permitted to add the small adjoining room which in the old days had been the sewing room. They might have been able to get Kseniya's room when she died, but they did not apply for it. An application for extra living space entailed a thorough investigation, and in the midst of a campaign against all Trotskyite sympathizers, Peter preferred not to remind the authorities of his existence. During Peter's Red Army and student days, Trotsky was his great hero, second only to Lenin. When Trotsky became the target of violent attacks for his disagreements with Stalin, Peter remained on the side of his idol. With many of his friends, as devoted to Trotsky as he was, he devoured the pages in *Pravda* given to Trotsky for his replies to the official attacks. With these same friends he paraded on the Red Square on November 7, 1927, the tenth anniversary of the revolution, and they expressed their feelings by adding to the official slogans of the day their own slogan: "Long Live Trotsky!"

When Trotsky was expelled from the party and forbidden to express his views in writing or in speaking, his followers hoped that it was only a temporary setback, and that he, the only one worthy in their eyes to be Lenin's successor, would ultimately take over the leadership. They continued to agitate for him among students and young workers. When it became dangerous to do it openly, they resorted to methods used in the czarist days: they worked under cover. But soon their wings were completely clipped. Trotsky was exiled to Alma-Ata in Central Asia; so were many of his followers. All those friendly to Trotsky's views were declared enemies of the Soviet Union. The jails were full of young people but Peter miraculously escaped the fate of his friends, most of whom were arrested. The few who remained, like Peter, retreated into political inactivity and avoided former associates. Trotsky was hopelessly beaten, there could no longer be any doubt about that. Stalin sat securely in the saddle. What was the use of fighting any longer, of endangering his own and his family's existence? Perhaps Natasha was right when she said, "Where do you get the wisdom to judge the party?"

After all, Peter argued with himself, Stalin was not a counterrevolutionary; he must have the interests of the Soviet Union at heart. Suppose Trotsky was wrong and Stalin was right? Suppose it was true that the rest of the world was not yet ready for a revolution and that the Soviet Union could wait no longer; that the only thing to do now was to build socialism in their own country?

Whatever doubts still troubled him at times, Peter was inspired by the tremendous scope of his present work. The Five-Year Plan made ample provisions for the building of homes and cities, and attached great importance to the study of new building materials. Foreigners were invited to help. Some of the German architects' plans called for cities like the ones Peter had always dreamed about, cities surrounded by green belts, with huge playgrounds for children and for adults, with public buildings spelling a friendly welcome to the people they served, with homes full of sun and light, straight and plain without any ornamentation to detract from the beauty of their lines and materials. It was exciting for Peter to have a part in this work.

When a year later, in 1930, there came one of the party purges which occurred at frequent intervals, Peter passed it easily. The young quiet architect, so thoroughly engrossed in the planning of the wonderful Soviet cities of the future, seemed all right to the members of the Purge Commission who sat in judgment. Neither they nor anyone in the audience knew of his past sympathies for Trotsky. Peter thought it would hardly hurt them to continue not to know. Why play Don Quixote and go to jail instead of working for socialism? His party membership card secure in his pocket, he could now forget completely the past political storms and devote himself entirely to his work. He might even risk applying for better living quarters.

Natasha had never been involved in any party discussions and had never seriously questioned any of the leaders' decisions. When her turn came, she appeared before the Purge Commission with the tranquillity of an unquestionably clear conscience. She stood before them, showing in her pale tired face the load she was carrying. The members of the commission were full of sympathy for her: A new Soviet woman thirty years old with two small children, who had answered the party's call for a Thousand Party Members to study engineering at the universities. She continued to teach adult evening groups and to lead the two Pioneer groups in her district; she carried out scrupulously her party duties, had her family to take care of, and had just passed her university mid-term tests with flying colors. Their questioning was light, and was quickly finished.

The Purge Commission sat in open sessions. Anybody had the right to be present, to ask questions, and to accuse or praise the person who was being investigated. Before dismissing Natasha, the commission chairman asked the routine question, "Has anyone anything to say?" not expecting any response from the audience in such an obvious case.

"Yes!" Quick as lightning came the reply; the man could hardly wait to be heard.

The case, which had been almost boring, became interesting, after all! Eyes turned to the man as he approached the commission's table.

"May I ask the citizeness a few questions?"

Natasha's heart began to flutter. This was a bad beginning! A party member was usually called comrade. Why didn't he call her comrade? Natasha knew the man—he had lived in their house until recently when, after many drunken scandals, his wife had left him. Following an especially noisy scene, the tenants had asked Natasha to send a complaint about him to the Moscow Soviet, which she had done, and the Soviet had ordered him to give up his large room for a smaller one in another house. Was he going to give her trouble?

"Now, you said before that you agreed with all the principles of the Communist party. Do you also agree with the principles of the Pioneer organization? You are working with Pioneers, aren't you?"

"Yes, I am, and I certainly agree with the principles of the Pioneer organization," Natasha said promptly.

"In that case, how could you have said—" the man spread out a paper before him, and read slowly— "How funny the Pioneer oath sounds when you hear those tiny voices say, 'We pledge to help the World Proletariat . . . break their chains.' You laughed when you said it. True?"

Natasha recalled the day she had said that. It must have been three years ago, she thought. She had been in the kitchen washing diapers. Another woman had been with her, a woman who also worked with Pioneers. They both loved their work with the children, and the remark had reflected only Natasha's affection and pride in the little Soviet citizens who, hardly out of their babyhood, felt themselves a part of the world's class struggle. How could anyone have taken it differently? Natasha tried to explain what she had meant, but the changed expression on the commission members' faces and the tense curiosity of the audience made her forget the clear simple words she wanted to say. Instead she murmured something which sounded like an apology. Before she had finished, the man interrupted rudely:

"Do you agree that the party was right in putting an end to the NEP, in getting rid of Nepmen, and engaging again in building socialism?"

"Most certainly, yes!" Natasha's voice was emphatic. "How could I ever disagree with that?"

"Fine sentiments, very fine sentiments indeed. But then, how could you have said—" he read from another paper now— " 'I think it is unfair, I think it is terrible. Nepmen engaged in trade because they were permitted to do so. How can they be punished now for something which was not a crime then? I think it's terrible,' you repeated . . ."

Natasha grew cold. Could he have heard the rest of her words too? But how could he have heard her at all? He didn't live in the house any more and it was very recently that she had had this conversation with Peter. They'd spoken quietly, the door had been closed; nobody could have heard them. Then she remembered. The maid had come in to get something. The maid was the only one who could have heard her. That man must have got her to spy on them. She was such an innocent little girl, who couldn't have known what she was doing.

Word by word, Natasha remembered what she and Peter had been talking about that day. She had just come home after a heartbreaking scene in the adult school. They had had to dismiss one of their pupils, a middle-aged woman, because her husband was a Nepman, not one of the rich speculators but one of the thousands who had engaged in petty trading which barely provided them with a living. Now they were disfranchised, their food cards were taken away from them, they had to vacate their room with no other place to go; their two children had been expelled from high school—and now she, too, was expelled. The woman had stood still, her face gray with despair. Then she had slowly walked out, and a minute later they had heard screams in the street. She had thrown herself under a truck.

"Try to understand, dear," Peter had attempted to calm Natasha, who cried hysterically. "Think of—"

"I know, I know everything you are going to say. You don't make revolutions in kid gloves; when you cut wood, chips fly, and all the rest. Everything is justified so long as we win."

"I know it all, Peter," her voice had dropped wearily, "there isn't a thing I don't know. I have heard it often enough and have said it often enough myself. But innocent women, children," her voice had started to rise again, "indiscriminately . . . because their fathers, their husbands did something the government permitted them to do. How cruel, how inhuman! Isn't there another way, a gentler way, without hurting people so much? There must be another way . . . it can't be right this way. You can't build happiness and kindness on injustice and tears."

It had been a momentary outburst, the only time Natasha had questioned the necessity of wiping out all traces of the NEP.

Now she stood silent before the commission, her head down. She was unable to say anything to defend herself.

Her tormentor went on:

"Didn't your parents belong to the Social Revolutionary party?"

"Yes."

"You know that party turned against the people and fought us?"

What could she say? That at the time her parents had belonged to the Social Revolutionary party, that party had fought czarism as fiercely as the Bolsheviks had? That the only difference was that they believed in the peasants rather than in the city workers? That her parents have devoted their lives to the people? She said nothing, her head still lower.

"Aren't you the granddaughter of Anton Nazarov? Weren't you his favorite granddaughter? Aren't you the niece of the White general, Michel Dolinin? Wasn't your cousin, the young Dolinin, killed while fighting the revolution? Isn't another cousin of yours in jail as a member of the criminal underworld?"

Only a short while ago presented to the audience as a proud example of Soviet womanhood, Natasha now stood shrinking under the vicious assault. Nothing she could say would make people forget those incriminating slurs. And there was nothing the commission members could do. Could they afford to ignore the accusations of a representative of the proletariat against a member of the former bourgeoisie? If they did, their own party loyalty would be under question. Natasha's fate was sealed.

The short distance home seemed like miles. Heavy loads weighed down Natasha's feet, her head swam dizzily. She bumped into people, almost fell into a store window. "Midday, and dead drunk already . . ." somebody laughed at her. She never knew how she got home. There she was, in the room, the beds unmade, the breakfast dishes still on the table. Messy, crowded, dusty. The maid probably went shopping after taking the children to the kindergarten, and wasn't back yet. Oh, yes, she was back. Natasha heard her voice in the kitchen, talking very fast and laughing. Was she still being used by that terrible man to spy on her? Natasha thought of it without bitterness. Hadn't the government trained people to consider it the duty of every loyal Soviet citizen to report counterrevolutionary talk?

Natasha threw herself on the bed and gave free rein to her grief. How could they have done this to her? To her, who had given herself to the Cause from the moment she could think and feel? To her, to whom the party was the Holiest of Holies? How could she, the outcast, discarded by the party as unworthy, face people now? But worst of all, how could she face life outside the party? The roots of her entire being were in the party. And soon the children would be big enough to know the disgrace their mother had brought upon them. What would she tell them? And Peter? Not more than four hours ago he had kissed her good-by, completely unconcerned about the outcome of her appearance before the Purge Commission. If he, with his heretical past, had had no trouble, how could Natasha, whose loyalty to the party approached saintliness, expect any? Peter had only warned her not to answer any questions about him.

"Say you don't know, and that I have gone through the purge already ... If what you say should by even half a word differ from what I said—my God, I shudder at the very thought of it!"

Natasha did not like Peter's light touch upon matters that were sacred to her. She was going before the Purge Commission as her grandmother used to go to the confessional, and Peter was treating it as if it were an ordinary occurrence. What would he say now? How would he take it?

Hearing the maid's voice in the hall, Natasha jumped up and plunged her face into a basin of water. The water was soapy, the children had washed in it. It stung her burning eyes and made them still redder. The maid mustn't see her; she'd find a refuge in Manilov's room.

"Natasha, my little Natasha, what have they done to you?" Full of anxiety, he stretched out his arms to her. "No, no, no . . . this isn't possible. Don't tell me they—"

"Yes, grandpa Manilov . . ." That was all she was able to say. She crouched at his feet, her arms in a gesture of hopeless despair folded on his knees. He bent down and his white beard touched her dark hair. He let her cry. Manilov never ceased to seek honestly a justification for the suffering he saw around him, but it was getting harder and harder always to find one. Could there be any justification for Natasha's suffering?

Natasha grew quieter, and soon the whole story came out. He had lately heard several such stories, of a life broken because a word dropped long ago was later willfully distorted by an evil-wisher, or because children had to pay for their parents and grandparents.

He listened to Natasha, remembering her as she had been when he first saw her over ten years before—almost a child, sweet and eager to help the whole world. She'd never stopped asking questions, she'd wanted to understand everything, and she had been full of faith which nothing could shake. What life had done to her! She could hardly be over thirty, he thought, but her eyes were sunken, she was skinny, beginning to dry out. She neglected herself; she ought to remember she was a woman, a young woman. But, then, where could she find the time to take care of herself? Where did she find the time and the strength to go along as she did? Manilov hoped that Peter would never stop looking at her with eyes of love.

". . . if he weren't a worker, grandpa Manilov, they might have demanded proof of his accusations, they might at least have let me defend myself. But a proletarian can't be doubted . . . even if he is as mean as this one was."

Manilov had never before heard such a bitter note in Natasha's voice. They had hurt her, and he was helpless to do her any good. What had been the guiding principle of his life was of no use today. He had believed that, armed with principles and faith, one should go straight ahead, fighting obstacles and never weakening or compromising. That was the way he and his comrades had lived, that was the way the younger generation, Natasha's generation, had started out. Of what importance to them what a person had said many years before, or whether his grandfather had owned a piece of land? The only thing that had counted then had been what a person believed in. How else could it have been? Where would they have found the leaders who prepared and made the revolution if they had engaged in the kind of man hunting the party engaged in now? They were educated people, those old Bolsheviks, some from rich families. And a few came to the revolution from the nobility . . . Ah, that's what Natasha was saying now.

"I can't glorify workers just because they're workers. If a worker is mean, he's mean; if he is good, he's good. To tell you the truth, grandpa Manilov, to me people who came to the revolution from other classes have even more value. They came to it the hard way, after their convictions grew so deep that they broke with their families and with their past. It was much simpler for a worker. For him, that was the only thing in the world to do. Life pushed him into it without any effort on his part. But people like you, not to speak of Lenin, like Maxim, like so many others, they gave their heartblood to the revolution when they could have chosen an easier life. Remember, grandpa Manilov, our old talks about morals? Why don't we ever talk about it now? Maybe if we did we'd understand better how this could have happened to me."

The anger in Natasha's voice made Manilov wince with pain and pity.

"It's true, Natasha, there is little talk about morals these days. All one hears is figures and economics. It's a good thing we are building up our country, making ourselves strong; that is good. But somehow, in getting strong, we are losing sight of the human being, forgetting his soul. There's too much worship of machines and statistics. The human being should not have been forgotten. For whom is all this being done if not for him? We do a lot for children; no one can say that we don't; but if we don't teach them the importance of the human being and his soul, and if we teach them to worship only machines and statistics, what good is our care of them? I may be all wrong, Natasha. Maybe it is better for children today not to worry too much about their hearts and their souls. Hearts and souls are old-fashioned." Manilov stopped, reminding himself that Natasha had come to him for help. He patted her arm.

"But, Natasha, my darling, there is something else we must decide now. What should you do now? Eating your heart out till you become a wreck and a burden to your family—that you can't afford. Going around as if nothing has happened, with your head up—you won't do that. But you do think it shouldn't have happened, that it was unjust and wrong? You do, don't you?"

"Of course I do. It was wrong and mean and—"

"Sh-sh . . . no anger, Natasha . . . Indignation over a wrong, yes. Determination to fight against it, yes. But anger, no. Anger is bad for a person. What you must do is say to yourself that you are right, that you haven't done anything wrong. And go wherever you have to go to say that; go without fear, because you know that you are right. And if you lose, don't let that embitter you; don't hate the whole world for the wrong done to you by a few individuals. 'When you cut wood, chips fly,' you used to say, and you believed that it was unavoidable in a revolution for innocent people not to be hurt too. Now, my dear girl, it may be that you will be the chips. The revolution is still on and plenty of chips keep flying."

Natasha heard Volik and Maya at the front door, and got up to go. She leaned over and kissed the old man.

"You have never failed me yet, grandpa Manilov, and you haven't failed me today."

Manilov wondered if Natasha would have the strength to fight. He wasn't sure she would fight, even if she had the strength. The young people today didn't hit back; they said they couldn't hit back at their own government. Ridiculous! Manilov could never agree with that—as if their own government couldn't make mistakes. What were they— peerless saints sent down from heaven or human beings like everyone else? And that scoundrel who broke Natasha's heart, was he a saint too? Why couldn't he be hit back at and hit back at hard, so that he would never again dare open his foul mouth?

Volik and Maya let out a delighted yell over the surprise: Mother was home! They never saw Natasha during the day, and sometimes she was not at home to say good night to them for several evenings in succession. The neighbors complained that they were noisy when they were alone in the evenings; their kindergarten teachers complained about them, and Masha, the maid, called them "bad." Even now they were fighting.

"Maya sits all over your lap, mother, she is littler, she is only four years old, she should have less lap."

"Volik pushes me, mother . . . he hurts me . . . ah-h-h . . ."

Feeling sorry for herself and crying, Maya succeeded in pushing Volik completely off Natasha's lap. Volik began to howl loudly.

"See now what I mean? That's the way they always behave!" Masha was triumphant over such an undeniable proof that she was right. "What gets into these kids is more than I can understand. What more could they want? Go to a fine school, eat well, are warm, have a father and mother to take care of them . . ."

Did they really have a mother to take care of them? Natasha wondered. They ate enough, and kept warm, their kindergarten was fine, and Masha was not a bad girl. But what did a little uneducated village girl know about bringing up children?

Finally the children were quiet and happy in Natasha's arms. How seldom the three had a peaceful moment together, Natasha thought. Wouldn't the children be much quieter, not so restless, if they had such moments more often? There was always such a rush, to eat, to sleep, to go to school, to go to work, to go to a meeting, to get dressed, not to be late, not to forget anything . . . If she were home more and could give the children the feeling that they had a real mother, it would do them a lot of good. Should she stay home and take care of the household? And see to it that Peter came home to a pleasantly set table, to a clean room, to happy children? Maybe being expelled from the party was a sign that she belonged here, that she should devote her life to this neglected little world of hers—the messy room, the children starved for their mother, the husband for whom she had as little time as for them.

But what about the new Soviet woman, who served society, had her profession, her independence, her equality with man? Had the morning's shock unhinged her mind? Give up her work, her duties, and the ideals she had believed in since she was a little girl? No, she would keep on going; she must, even though her family and her personal life were neglected. Weren't they all chips of the revolution? Their generation and the children of their generation?

It was all very well to decide she would keep on going, but how was she to do it, now that she was an outcast? She would be dismissed from the university. She had been one of the Thousand, one of the future "Red Engineers," but they had to be party members. She was not one any more. She couldn't let go at that. Manilov was right. No, she couldn't submit to that. She must fight. Life would not be worth anything outside the party. She couldn't live that way.

Natasha turned the pages of the book she was reading to the children, but the words made little sense to her. She was dreading the moment of Peter's return. He had become so cautious lately, wary of anything that could throw a threatening shadow over the straight road he was now on; keeping away from anyone who was under the slightest suspicion of the party. And now his own wife was under the suspicion of the party. When Natasha heard his step, her heart shrank to a tiny lump. She needed his sympathy more than anything else, and it gave her a sick feeling to realize that she wasn't certain she would have it.

Peter stopped at the door, taking in the peaceful sight of Natasha sitting with both children on her lap, picture books, beads, crayons in front of them. The table was set and the room was clean. The children called out happily:

"Mother is home, Mother is home with us!"

O God, what was the matter with Natasha? Peter had never seen such agony in her eyes! He followed her into the other room, and there he heard the unbelievable words whispered in the ghost of a voice:

"I was expelled from the party."

"No, no! This can't be, Natasha, it can't be."

All she wanted now was to be taken in his arms, to be comforted like a child, and made to feel that it really wasn't as dreadful as she thought it was. But Peter didn't take her into his arms, and his horrified eyes told her that what had happened was quite dreadful, as she had thought.

"How could that happen? It's a nightmare. What was it? Why?"

In a voice faint with misery she told him the story.

"That's all," she finished, and unable to suppress her longing for his sympathy any more, she threw her arms around his neck.

Peter was swept with a sense of guilt. This damned overpowering fear! He'd let himself be carried away by it and had forgotten Natasha. She must be going through hell!

Natasha finally found on Peter's shoulder the support and sympathy she had been longing for.

"Mother, mother . . . don't cry . . . I'll cry too . . ." Maya was tearing at Natasha's skirt and her eyes started to fill with big tears. Volik looked at his mother with frightened eyes. He had never seen her cry. There could be only one reason for her crying: something hurt her.

"Where does it hurt, mother? Let me rub it. Maybe if I kiss it . . ."
Natasha dried her tears and embraced the children.

"It's all right now. It doesn't hurt any more. Let's go and eat."
They had a pleasant dinner, more pleasant than any they had had
for a long time. Even Natasha enjoyed it. It was not the food, the
familiar cabbage soup and macaroni. But nobody was in a hurry, nobody rushed to get away. To distract Natasha, Peter made faces and
told funny stories. Natasha forced a smile to her face, but the children
laughed and screeched happily. When they went to sleep, both parents
sat on their beds and did not hurry away. The children were quiet,
and showed none of the crankiness that exasperated Masha on the
nights when she, scolding and rushing them, had to put them to bed.
Kissing them good night Natasha was again disturbed by the thought
that maybe she should devote herself entirely to the happiness of the
family. She told Peter about it when they were getting ready for bed.

"I thought of it myself tonight, Natasha. It has been long since I
felt so good at home, with you, with the children. And this despite
what happened. It must be good to have a wife who always has time
for her husband." He smiled and drew her to him. "Please, darling,
you so seldom let me love you. You are either tired or not well, or—I
know, darling—you are afraid. Let me love you tonight. Let me . . .
please . . . Natasha . . ."

She wanted to lie still in his arms and talk with him about what she
was to do now; she wanted to feel the warmth of his body close to
her while she spoke. But she did not want him as a lover. She was
afraid of his passion. She had been afraid of it since Maya's birth. They
had not wanted a second child, but nothing they had done helped and
Maya was born. And nothing they did after Maya was born helped.
She had had three abortions during the past four years, and her body
was exhausted; she didn't want any more babies or any more abortions. She was afraid, and this fear had drained her own passion out
of her. But he wanted her badly tonight, and she couldn't always say
no to him.

Afterwards, he teased her:

"It was very good, darling, as good as always. I am afraid that I
shall enjoy sleeping with a nonparty member just as much."

He soon fell asleep, relaxed and smiling.

Natasha cried silently into her pillow. No, Peter didn't understand
her any more. He wouldn't have joked about sleeping with a nonparty
member if he did. The only thing she had needed from him tonight
was understanding, and that he didn't have for her. What he gave her
—jokes and passion—she didn't want at all. "Somewhere on the way
. . . the human being is being lost, his soul forgotten." Manilov had

said that today. That was true of her and Peter too. There had been such a human closeness between them in the beginning. Neither had a thought the other didn't share.

But ever since the Trotsky days Peter had been all closed up. Did he want to forget his political mistakes? Was he afraid of bringing back the past? Natasha did not know; he wouldn't talk about it. The only subject he would talk about was his work, and on that he was open and eloquent. But he brushed everything else aside. Natasha didn't know what was going on in Peter, and he didn't know what was going on in her. He showed that tonight.

Had it happened then, during the Trotsky days when Peter was all out for Trotsky and she took Stalin's side because Stalin, as general secretary of the party, was for her the highest authority? They used to talk about it for hours, trying to convince each other. Then Trotsky was exiled and Trotskyites declared enemies of the people. How had she behaved then? Well, how could a loyal party member behave? She could not be influenced by the fact that her own husband was in sympathy with the Trotsky opposition. Of course she had condemned the opposition; of course, she had voted for every resolution against them; signed every appeal against them. It was then that Peter had stopped confiding in her. She had felt very bad about it for a while but soon he became absorbed in his work, she in her studies, and both found common joy in the children. They were so busy that they hardly realized that their talks no longer reached below the surface.

Tonight, she had desperately missed the give-and-take of their old discussions, when they had got rid of their doubts and troubles by sharing them. But back in the Trotsky days when Peter had doubled and fought within himself, hadn't he needed her as much as she needed him tonight? And had she given him understanding and comfort? No, she had not. She was the obedient party member who was told that opposition to the party line was a mortal sin, and she had behaved accordingly. Instead of being friendly and warm, she had been rigid and stern. But how could she have behaved in any other way? Wasn't the party above love, husband, family, above everything on earth?

And how about her willing body, which he wanted and which she didn't give him? She could do without sleeping with him; she never wanted to now. But not so long ago it had been different. The moments in his arms had been heaven and had brought them still closer together. Then a new thought struck her, and she sat up in bed in terror. If Peter had to fight every time for her love, wouldn't he tire of it and look for a woman who would give herself to him willingly and happily as she herself used to do? It wasn't his fault that a woman's body broke down under the strain and fear of childbearing and abortions. His body, so young and so virile, should not have to do without love because she couldn't stand the burden of her body.

They, the young Soviet generation, had rejected the old conventional traditions of enforced faithfulness, Natasha reminded herself; they were free to change partners; they did not have to be faithful when they did not want to. Why, then, did her heart almost stop at the thought of Peter's turning to another woman? What could she do? She couldn't deprive him of love and then object if he looked for it elsewhere. Why, why did the fire in her body have to go out? What went on in other women's lives?

Bits of overheard conversations, overheard and forgotten, came back to Natasha's mind. In the kitchen, in the evening schools, in the university, everywhere, women talked about their husbands and lovers and abortions and children. No, she was not the only one. Other women were faced with the same fears. Some of them believed in violating their bodies to keep the husbands; others preferred to stop torturing their exhausted frightened bodies and lose their men. And some were ready to share their husbands with other women. Once a woman doctor, during such a talk, said:

"Women, women, come to your senses! Stop killing your bodies with abortions and stop killing your nerves by sleeping with your men in an eternal dread of pregnancy. Birth control, birth control is the cure for you! Only birth control will rid you of your fears. And only when you get rid of your fears will you regain the joy of your body . . ."

Oh, yes, birth control; the women agreed about that. The only fault they had to find with it was that it didn't work. With everything going to build up industry, with no rubber, no chemicals available for the population, what they got as preventives could fool them once but no more. Natasha knew that too well; her abortions were witness to that. What to do? What to do?

The future rose like a nightmare. She would never be able to face it, still less manage it. Thrown out of the party, out of the university, found unsuitable to be a youth leader, maybe not even permitted to teach, suspected by everybody . . . Peter unhappy, the children neglected, their life rushed, messy, without warmth and relaxation . . . Natasha looked miserably at Peter's bed. His head was half covered by the blanket; she couldn't see his face but he was breathing quietly. How much easier it was for men! They satisfied their senses and all was forgotten.

Natasha was mistaken. The relaxation which the satisfaction of his senses gave Peter did not last long, and nothing was forgoten. He heard Natasha turn and toss in her bed, he heard her cry, and he wanted to take her in his arms and comfort her. But he did not trust himself. He had been starved for her so long that his senses were alert again. Even if he controlled himself, as he had so often done, she would feel it and get scared and all cramped up, and he wouldn't be of any help to her then. Better leave her alone. He felt a great pity for her and at the same time he couldn't free himself of the irritation he felt mingled with the pity. He knew very well that Natasha was not at fault, that she had been meanly and unjustly accused; still he couldn't help feeling irritated. The whole thing came at such a bad time; it would upset everything he had planned. After he had passed his purge so successfully, he had been advanced in his job and had moved closer to the category of Responsible Workers. He had begun to breathe freely and, sure that now he could face any investigation, he had filed an application for better rooms, and also for the privilege of using one of the special stores which served employees in the ranks. But now he wondered whether he dared expose himself to the investigation that the applications entailed. In them he had proudly stated that his wife was a member of the party of long standing. The punishment for a false statement in a questionnaire was severe. First thing in the morning he would have to report to the party secretary in the office and have the statement changed—an unpleasant prospect. As if life wasn't full enough of petty irritations and humiliating fears of the party secretary, of the GPU, of a denunciation, of a careless word. Lucky for him that he had his work. That was something worth all the troubles. They were working now on tremendous housing projects. Workers in Dnieperges, Magnitogorsk, in Kuznetsk, in Stalingrad, wherever the new giant plants and power stations were being erected, would be the first ones to live in the exciting new homes he was designing. The previous job had been satisfying too—designing school buildings. With a comfortable glow, Peter thought of the photographs of the buildings under construction which one of their men had just brought back from a long inspection trip. In the Ural steppes and the Caucasian mountains, where people had never had any schools at all, the beautiful modern schools would be a symbol of a new life and a happy future. And Peter had had a hand in it! His mind on his work, he forgot Natasha's misery and his dread of facing the party secretary in the morning.

Natasha dozed off, but kept waking up to look anxiously at the watch. After her restless night, she was afraid of oversleeping. It was dark, the stars were still in the sky when she got up. It was twenty to six. At six the line for milk formed; before that she had to get her number for the bread line. This was something she had to do every morning. The maid slept with the children and if she got up they would wake up. Besides, no maid would stay with them if she had to get up at that hour in the wintertime.

Maids were a sore spot in Natasha's life. She had never wanted a maid in the first place, even though they were now called by the more respectful name of houseworker, and for a long time she had fought against hiring one. She finally succumbed like so many other women who did not want to give up their party work, their studies, their jobs, and who did not have a mother, a grandmother, or an aunt to take care of the household and the children. Even if a child was in a nursery or a kindergarten, it did not help. Standing in line for hours, cooking and washing in a kitchen shared with ten other women was a full-time job.

With the many duties the maid had, it was no wonder the children were neglected at home. They were left to themselves with no place to play; everyone scolded them for being in the way, and no one had the leisure and the peace of mind to be patient and kind to them. If there was sickness in the kindergarten, which happened frequently, owing to the overcrowded houses—the children had to stay home. And if the children were sick themselves, they did not have the proper care, for, unless the illness was serious, their mothers were not excused from work.

Natasha lived in eternal fear that Masha would leave them, and every day it became harder to find a maid. By the thousands girls flocked into town from their villages; but for the most part they got jobs in factories. Only girls who found no place to live did housework for a while, and those who did were constantly encouraged by their unions to go to evening schools to learn trades. Obviously, rather than interfere with that, any decent employer gave her maid several free evenings a week. Natasha had wrestled with this problem for years and found no other way out than to spend most of her own free time doing part of the maid's work.

Natasha did not spend much time getting ready. Without looking into the mirror, she combed her hair hurriedly and dressed. She had never paid much attention to her looks, a disposition that the party propaganda in favor of austerity and against frivolity of appearance had encouraged. But she had inherited from her mother some of her loveliness; she had Olga's white skin, her big dark eyes and quiet grace of movement. Little of it was obvious, however, in the thin drab figure, bundled up in a big shawl over her coat, clumsy in Peter's galoshes over her houseshoes, who rushed out of the house into the cold unfriendly morning, tired, sleepy, miserable.

From all over, women were moving in the direction of the milk store. They were carrying cans, pots, bottles, kettles, tureens, anything suitable into which milk could be poured—if the store had any milk. There was a sprinkling of men among them, but mostly they were women, women tired after too few hours of sleep, and worried, worried, worried. Would the store have any food today? Would the children be safe while they were away? Would they return on time to get the family off to school and to work? Would they be on time for work themselves?

They met every morning at the same time. They called greetings to one another, but there wasn't much loud talking, not at that hour of the morning, only the usual complaints exchanged in low resigned voices, complaints about the wet wood, which was so hard to get and wouldn't burn, about the rotten potatoes, which the store wouldn't take back, about the oil that was promised them months ago and never came, about the needles they couldn't find anywhere, about the stockings they couldn't find, the towels, the diapers, the galoshes, teacups, pencils, combs . . .

"But you find bathing suits now; the stores are full of them."

"That's true, you see them displayed all over. And in the summer when we wanted them, they offered us woolen mittens . . . I wish they would offer them now."

"Those who had the money bought them in the summer. But how do you expect me to buy mittens in the summer or a bathing suit now when I can't manage to get together enough for the little I can buy right now?"

The stillness of the early morning was broken by loud lively voices and laughter. A group of young men and girls were going to work. The women in the line looked at them with envy. Ah, they had it easy. Someone was standing in line for them. No children to worry about. They were young and could enjoy so many things—theaters, lectures, movies, sports, museums. It was good for them now and it was going to be still better for them in the future.

"They were born in time," said one woman, with a sigh. "We were in too much of a hurry to come into the world."

"Well, it will be even better for our small children. By the time they grow up, they won't know that there ever were any hardships at all."

It was that thought which kept up the spirits of the women. It helped them rise morning after morning in darkness and cold; it helped them spend their lives in an endless rush of work, worry, quest for food and clothing and fuel.

Natasha knew most women in the neighborhood, through either the adult school or the children Pioneer groups, and usually talked with them while they waited in line together. But today, from the way some of the women looked at her with a mixture of curiosity, embarrassment, and pity, she knew that the news of her expulsion had spread through the neighborhood. She stood with her eyes lowered, every nerve trembling with impatience to be through with the ordeal. Her turn came; she got her milk, then her bread, and reached home by eight o'clock. The house was as busy and noisy as a beehive. Apparently everybody had had to go to the toilet or to the bathroom or to the kitchen at exactly the same minute. Anyhow, they were all busy and nobody bothered to look at her. Natasha opened the door of her room.

Peter was shaving, nervous and irritated as he always was at that time. The razor was dull, the mirror too far from the light, and the soap didn't lather. He cut himself, swore under his breath, and kicked Maya's favorite doll from under his foot. Maya, who had just been scolded by Masha for fidgeting while her hair was being combed, cried out and rushed to the doll's rescue. Masha pulled her back roughly, whereupon Maya cried louder, and Volik let go with his fists in defense of his sister. To mistreat Maya was his personal prerogative. Peter's face twitched with nervousness.

Natasha closed her eyes, dizzy after her night of tears and agony. If only she could help them; could ease the tenseness, the anger, the nervousness out of them; if only she could find something Peter could sharpen his razor with, if she could buy a larger bulb for the lamp or get an extra lamp, if she could get real shaving soap instead of that gray hard mess the store sold her—but those were vain dreams. She couldn't get any of those things any more than she could have room enough for the children so that they wouldn't be constantly under someone's feet.

The family noticed Natasha's presence. The children clung to her hands and wouldn't let her go till she had heard the full story of their woes. Masha went to the kitchen, slamming the door behind her angrily. "Whoever expects me to stay one more hour with these brats is thoroughly, but thoroughly mistaken."

Peter had finished shaving.

"I thought you were never coming back. It's a madhouse when you're not around."

His normal manner shocked her: had he forgotten what had happened? He had not forgotten. He remembered it well and, remembering it, his inability to help increased his usual morning irritation. The unaired crowded room, the sound of angry voices and doors being slammed all over the house, the loud quarrels in the hall over the bathroom and toilet and kitchen—every morning this was a source of agony to him. And Natasha's face! It was bloodless and drawn, with deep dark rings under eyes filled with unspeakable misery. Her lips were white, dry, quivering. Peter's irritation gave way to a pity for her which he could hardly bear. But how was he to express it with the children fighting and screaming, with Masha coming in and out of the kitchen, angrily slamming the door every time?

They finally sat down to breakfast. Peter poured the tea for Natasha. He spread the jam on her bread, and smiled when she raised a surprised face to him. Tears filled her eyes: Peter hadn't forgotten! It was only that this accursed business of living practically on top of each other made it impossible for him to say anything in any other way.

The children noisily demanded their attention. These were the last moments with their parents for the day, perhaps for several days. It wasn't often that Mother was at home with them as she had been yesterday. They asked questions and demanded answers; they pressed against their parents and climbed on them, reassuring themselves that father and mother really belonged to them. By the time Masha took them off to the kindergarten, Peter had only a few moments left.

"Whatever you decide to do, first of all go see your party secretary. I know he won't do a thing for you but he will never forgive you if you don't see him first. Pull yourself together, darling, it may still work out."

"I'll be all right, Peter, don't worry. Yes, I'll see the secretary first. Yes, it may still work out."

Maybe it will work out. Maybe the nightmare will pass . . . Natasha sat down, limp and motionless. If she could stay like this, without moving, without doing anything, maybe even falling asleep, with someone meanwhile doing everything for her . . . How did that verse go?

> I don't want to be strong . . .
> Let someone take my hand
> And lead me on the road of life.

Natasha used to scoff at the poem, at the weakness of the old-fashioned woman who wanted to be led. She didn't scoff now. That was the one thing in the world she wanted—to have someone take her hand and lead her, and take the burden off her shoulders.

Her head drooped lower and lower, her eyes began to close. Oh, no! She couldn't fall asleep. There was no one to take her hand and lead. Whatever was done, she was the one who would have to do it.

CHAPTER 24
*Natasha*

THE district party secretary was glad to see Natasha. When he had been new on the job, she was the one who stood at his side and guided his first steps in the unfamiliar neighborhood. Since then, whenever he had called on her she had always been ready to help him. Few knew the district as well as she did and she had twelve years of party membership behind her. The young party secretary had only seven. His respect for Natasha was great and his pleasure at seeing her was sincere.

But his smile quickly disappeared after her first words. He fidgeted on his chair in a most undignified way. What a predicament, what a predicament! His first impulse was to comfort Natasha, to tell her that she could be almost sure of reinstatement, that many who had been expelled had been reinstated lately. But suppose there was truth in the accusations? Suppose it was more than the revenge of a crank? Suppose she had really remained true to her class and had wormed her way into the party in order to destroy the revolution from within? Cold sweat covered the young secretary's brow. What a predicament!

Many men and women who had been expelled from the party had sat in the chair where Natasha sat now. They all had had the same look of utter despair in their eyes. He had always found the right tone with them, in keeping with his position as representative of the party. A light sermon, not too severe—one never knew whether the miserable wretch of today wouldn't swing a stick over his head in the future—a few words on the infallibility of the party leadership and the unquestionable wisdom of the Great Leader and Teacher; finally, the customary advice on which to do: how to address the appeal, whom to see, what rights the expelled was deprived of immediately and what he was entitled to until his case was reviewed. It had not always been easy, especially when old party members came trembling to him for advice. But it never was so hard as in this case. Natasha! The most selfless, the most devoted party member of them all!

"That is all. What shall I do now?" Natasha asked.

She hung on his answer as if her life were in his hands. He had to say something, but he couldn't force himself to give her the usual sermon and the official spiel. All he could do would be to tell her what she was to do about her appeal.

"Yes . . . kh-kh . . ." he cleared his throat. He had almost said, "I am sorry, Natasha . . ." but fortunately had caught himself in time. He must be very careful. He had been until now. Other secretaries were not and they had had to pay a hard price for misplaced softness or severity, for not having guessed whose expulsion was a mistake and whose was permanent.

"The thing for you to do now is to go to the Central Committee; there ask for . . ."

It couldn't possibly be regarded as misplaced softness if he wrote it down for her. She would never be able to put anything down on paper with those shaking fingers of hers.

"Then report to the university secretary . . . most likely he will let you continue till your case has been reviewed. Continue your teaching . . . but—" he felt most uncomfortable about what he had to say now; his younger brother was in Natasha's Pioneer outfit—"you better stop working with the youth group."

The secretary had to catch back a friendly word. Uncomfortably he watched Natasha leave his room without a single gesture of friendliness or of encouragement. Why didn't he run after her to tell her what he really wanted to tell her? Why? He sank back in his chair. Had he talked to Natasha the way he wanted to, it would have made it easier for her but it would have endangered his safety. He hated himself but he chose safety.

Natasha was already too wounded to feel the additional sting of the secretary's behavior. She had to wait for a long time in the Central Committee. Many comrades in misery were sitting drearily in the waiting room of the man who was in charge of reviewing expulsions. Every one of them presented a picture of wretchedness. There was complete silence in the room; their ordeal was not the kind people exchanged confidences about. They avoided looking one at another, and tried to conceal their faces under shawls and caps.

When the Central Committee man spoke to Natasha, she summoned all her strength to hear and understand what he was saying. Every one of her statements refuting the accusations against her, he said, had to be proved on paper with the customary signatures and stamps: that she never possessed any of her grandfather's money . . . that her parents had never engaged in counterrevolutionary activities . . . that she had never harbored any anti-Soviet thoughts . . . Did that mean that she had to get testimony from people who knew the family before the revolution? Certainly, he said, and reliable people they had to be, people whom the party could trust. Did that mean she had to go to her parents' village and get testimony from people there? Her father was dead and her mother lived far away now with her brother.

Yes, the testimony must come from the village, and, of course, in that case, too, the party would accept the word only of people it considered reliable. And it went without saying that she had to bring proofs of her party loyalty from people she was associated with through work, study, and party duties. And a few personal recommendations from old dependable party members could only help . . . That would be all.

The man had hardly once glanced at her face. He was scrutinizing papers concerning her; she, as a living person, with heart and soul and mind and body, did not exist for him. For a moment, while sitting in that awful waiting room of his, she had had the wild idea that if he would let her talk, she would tell him all about herself, how she came to Moscow, about her high school days, how she became a Bolshevik, about her parents and about Maxim, how the party to her was home, roots, the very foundation of her whole existence, even more than her family. He would then understand that it all had been nothing but a ridiculous misunderstanding. He would be indignant about it and would promise to bring to justice the man who had maligned her. And he would give her a paper saying that it was all a misunderstanding and that she was above reproach.

But how could she talk to a man who had no eyes and ears for her but only for the dead words on the papers before him? For whom she was a case number and nothing else. He chilled her with fear. And he made her say yes and no, and made it impossible for her to say anything else.

"That will be all," he said again, and impatiently pushed back his chair, to show that she was to go.

"Good-by, comrade," she almost whispered getting up.

"Good-by," he answered, his eyes on the files of the next case.

Not to be called comrade any more! That was almost worse than anything else.

She telephoned Peter. He knew that the operator was listening and cut Natasha short.

"All right, dear . . . all right, dear . . . Let's talk about it at home . . . I'll try to be home early . . . Oh, you will have your classes? . . . Does that mean . . ." He quickly interrupted himself. "All right, all right, you will tell me about it later."

Natasha felt that she had to talk to somebody and her mind turned to Manilov. He at least was always ready to listen to her. She went straight to him, her feet wet and numb with cold, her head swimming, black spots circling before her eyes. What a relief it was to sink into the big soft chair, to put slippers on her frozen feet, to drink a cup of hot tea. And now, now she was going to talk to him, to slip off the heavy load that was weighing her down, down, down . . .

Manilov gently moved her head so that it rested against the back of the chair; he put his coat over her knees and a warm shawl around her shoulders. His inability to help her made him miserable. It would have been so easy a few years ago. Just a telephone call or a visit to an old comrade, and any injustice would have been quickly righted. But what could he do now? Rykov, Bukharin, Tomski, Kamenev, and his many other old friends—how could they listen to him now? They were too busy defending themselves against the attacks and accusations leveled at them by Stalin and by those who had taken their places in the old party hierarchy. Besides, Manilov thought unhappily, old comrades had become suspicious of one another, and instead of rushing to help a comrade who was in trouble, as they had in the old days, they avoided him.

All his life Manilov had been quick to forgive. Now, however, he found no readiness in himself to forgive those responsible for the lost, drawn look on Natasha's face. He was conscious only of a great bitterness and indignation. All the new factories and bridges and roads they were building and getting people excited about were worth nothing if injustice and suffering were inflicted on innocent human beings like Natasha. Was this hunting of people never going to stop? First they'd hunted counterrevolutionaries, then people with the wrong parents, then Nepmen. Now the big enemies were the party oppositionists, on the left and on the right. Half a step off the party line, and the chase was on.

How could anyone be so sure of his rightness? Didn't Stalin ever have any doubts about the party line, which he dictated? What made him so sure of his infallibility? Lenin never had that sureness; Lenin was not ashamed of being human, of listening to other people's opinions, of admitting he was wrong. And now? What Stalin declared right yesterday, he declared wrong today—and woe to anyone who was half a minute late to catch on. If Stalin was so infallible, why did he keep changing the party line? It would be easier to take it if just once he would have the decency and courage to admit that it was he himself who was wrong, and not always fasten the responsibility for his mistakes on other people. But hardest to forgive, for Manilov, was the unnecessary suffering, the confusion and fear and uncertainty that the unjust persecutions caused people.

Natasha slept for several hours. When she at length woke up, Manilov thought the dark rings under her eyes were less noticeable and her face less drawn. Her eyes fell on Manilov and she sat upright in the chair.

"What is it? Why am I here?"

Manilov smiled his kind smile, which made his still young blue eyes almost disappear amidst a thousand crow's-feet.

"Nothing child, nothing at all. You came to tell me something, and instead you preferred to sleep. That's all. Now, what was it you came to tell me?"

With a rush it all came back to her with the force of a blow. She moaned and covered her face.

"Now, now, now, Natasha, where is my strong new Soviet woman?"

Natasha didn't want to be strong. She wanted to hide and feel safe and guarded. At the moment Manilov was her refuge. And when the warmth of his presence and his comforting words reached deep enough, she talked to him. But as she recounted the tasks lying ahead of her, the thought of their difficulty and immensity brought terror into her voice.

"Never, never shall I be able to do it. Better let it go at that. Come what may, I haven't the strength, I haven't, grandpa Manilov, I haven't."

It was true, she probably hadn't. But she must believe that she had.

"Oh, yes, you have, Natasha. Of course, you have. Now let's take one thing after another and let's put it all down on paper. You see, Natasha, I am getting real old, don't mind me, but my head doesn't keep more than one thought at a time. And let's number everything . . . it will be easier for me that way."

On a sheet of paper he started to write out the names of the people she had to see and the order in which she had to see them and what she was to tell them.

"Not so quick, Natasha. I can't follow you. Say it again."

Pretending that he couldn't grasp things quickly, he made her repeat everything several times. From sheer repetition it began to sound less formidable, almost familiar like something she might really be able to do. Soon the sheet of paper was covered with a neat outline of her actions for the next few days.

"And don't lose any time, Natasha; start right away. Take two weeks off; you will get them, and you will need them. The trip to the village will take you at least a week."

His voice was natural as if there was nothing extraordinary in what she was going to do, and the conversation took a businesslike turn. On a map of Moscow he outlined the best way to combine the many trips she would have to make. She must ask someone to get her train ticket to the village—she herself would never have time to stand that many hours in line. The neighbors would keep an eye on the children while she was away; there'd be nothing to worry about on that score. And she must be sure to keep warm and dry, no use getting sick.

When Peter came home, he was relieved to find Natasha looking composed, with a plan all worked out and ready to act. Her few words over the phone earlier in the day had sounded like a cry for help. He needed help himself; his conversation with his party secretary in the morning had been even more unpleasant than he had expected.

"It's too bad, it's too bad, Peter," the secretary had said. "We had great plans for you. What a pity . . . I am sure you would have been pleased. Too bad it had to happen now."

The secretary had paged through Peter's file, making notes. Then he had closed the file, leaned back in his chair, and taken out a cigarette without offering one to Peter. The significance of this had not been lost on Peter. A party secretary's manner was the surest barometer of one's party standing.

"Let's hope it won't interfere too much with your work, Peter. The past has a funny way of suddenly popping up where you least expect it."

Peter's skin had prickled. Did the secretary know about his past? When Natasha telephoned, his fear of being overheard and an uncontrollable inner resistance against being reminded of his troubles had made him rude to her. He had dreaded the return home, the necessity of making decisions, of advising, of consoling.

Peter was not proud of himself. Natasha should have found in him a strong support. Instead he was irritable and weak. He had faced bullets in the Civil War, he had suffered hunger and privation and years full of hard work and hard study, and had never felt weak or discouraged. But he was now. And he was not the only one. The exaltation of building, of reaching for heights never dreamed of before, of seeing those heights come closer and closer should make men feel adventurous and indomitable. Why, then, were they made to feel afraid, afraid even to make a decision, to sign a name, to speak out? Why, then, were they made to feel like criminals when they made even a slight error or when something happened for which they were not responsible? Why were they made to act like small, cowardly men? Why make a man so unsure of himself that he is afraid to stand by his wife, afraid to do anything to help her?

And here was Natasha, whom he had dreaded facing, brave wonderful Natasha, still white and shaky, but with decisions made and mind all set to rush into the fight. And with no resentment at all against him for having let her down. Throughout the evening he was considerate and affectionate, and when they went to bed he took her in his arms, tenderly and carefully so as not to scare her. With a deep sigh Natasha lay against his chest. She finally had what she needed so—Peter's arms around her in sheer sweetness. They did not talk. They lay still, relaxing from the harsh tensions of the day. Soon they were asleep. In her sleep Natasha felt the close grasp of Peter's arm, as if he was afraid to let her go. It was very hard in the morning to leave Peter's warm closeness for the unfriendly reality of the day. She thought of the mornings she used to jump hurriedly out of bed with a fear of having missed something while she was asleep and with the excited anticipation of a new wonderful day. She forced away the sting that the image of the young Natasha bristling with life gave her. What a time to think of that!

The morning hour with its rush, disorder, and noise was over. With a kiss from the children and an embrace from Peter, with a warm wish for success, Natasha went off on her unpleasant errands. First of all, she had to get permission from the adult school to be away for a while. That did not take long, for she was not the first to ask for it since the purge began. The party had shown itself magnanimous in at least one respect: when the expelled was ready to go through the torturous task of trying to rehabilitate himself, the party secretaries had been told to be lenient in granting time for it. With the papers releasing her from work for two weeks "for personal reasons" secure in her pocket, Natasha faced the ordeal of procuring a dozen or so signed and duly stamped testimonies from "reliable" people.

First on her list were those who had known her well for many years. Her thoughts had gone at once to Maxim and Dasha. But Dasha had her own troubles. She had the purge ahead of her and was worried, for people whom she had offended in the past with her unrestrained tongue were out to settle old accounts. She had to be careful, and vouching for a person the party had rejected would be an additional charge against her. So Dasha was out. There remained Maxim. She went to see him at his office, afraid she might weaken in the friendly atmosphere of Kira's home, which had a way of inducing in her a sentimental reminiscent mood.

Maxim's waiting room was full of people but when his secretary told him that his niece Natasha wanted to see him, he called her in immediately. His hands outstretched, he greeted her with boisterous warmth.

"Well, well, well, it has been ages, literally ages since I saw you, Natasha darling. Remember how I used to make you angry by greeting you with 'My, how you have grown!'"

Maxim laughed, his young laughter of years ago. It was good to see Natasha. It made him feel young. She was part of his youth, part of his adored mother, part of a past rich in adventure and idealism. To Natasha too Maxim was the living reminder of a happy childhood and youth, and it made her feel equally good to see him, the same old Maxim, his hair tousled, his shirt collar wide open, his cheeks in need of a shave.

He made Natasha sit down at his desk which was, as usual, piled high with folders, papers, and books. Now her face was in the light, and his exuberance subsided. Troubles! Natasha had not looked well for a long time, but her eyes had never before lost their serenity and that straight look which Olga had, the look of people who, as his father used to say, didn't believe in evil. Her eyes frightened Maxim now.

Her news gave him a shock. It was the last thing he would have expected. He had imagined her troubles were purely personal, probably something to do with Peter.

But this was serious! For Natasha this was probably more serious even than losing Peter. Even as a very young girl she would rather have done something for the party than eat or sleep. And since she had belonged to the party nothing on earth had been more important to her. By all means, Natasha must be reinstated! Of course, he would give her a testimonial and a first-rate one it would be. But, then, it might not be the cleverest thing for him to go all out in that testimonial. He had to be very careful himself, with suspicions lurking constantly in every corner. No! He hadn't sunk that far yet! Natasha was innocent, he was sure of that. He could vouch for her by everything he cherished on earth, and he would. It was good once again to let his heart speak louder than his reason. It was so good that he grew exuberant again, and Natasha thought, If Maxim can take it this way, then maybe everything will be all right. He wrote out the testimonial himself, he signed it with an impressive signature, and pressed the stamp on the prescribed spot.

"Here you are, my dear, and let it bring you luck. Keep me informed, will you? And chin up, dear, chin up . . . the way we used to."

He kissed her and took her to the door. "Chin up"—it was easy to keep chins up "in the old days." But when someone like Natasha had to fight with the party for reinstatement, small wonder that her chin and his chin and so many other chins were down. Throughout the day, in the midst of conferences and dictation, Natasha's eyes confronted him and he saw her knocking at doors and at hearts which he knew wouldn't open to her.

Maxim was not mistaken. Many doors didn't open to Natasha at all, and when some did, the hearts behind them didn't. Her old high school made it very hard for her. There was evidence on record that even as a high school student she had been engaged in revolutionary activities on the side of the Bolsheviks. But the school itself had been in trouble recently, when some of its teachers were accused of opposing the new group methods of teaching and the party's latest approach to science and pedagogy. Several had been exiled to Siberia; others were still going through an investigation. No one in charge was inclined to get into more trouble by signing testimonials for former pupils. All they were willing to do for her was to certify the dates when she attended school. That wasn't at all what Natasha needed but the frightened principal refused to add a single word.

With great difficulty, Natasha succeeded in tracing the addresses of the two teachers who besides her mother's old friend, who had been dead for years, had looked with favor upon the activities of Natasha and her group. One, the history teacher, had been exiled to Siberia two years before as a follower of Trotsky, his family told her. She found the other, her old literature teacher. He had known how, under the noses of czarist authorities, to teach classical literature in a way that instilled in his pupils love for freedom and a desire to fight for it. He was worshiped by the students, who had covered up for him when government inspectors visited his classes to make sure that young minds were not being contaminated by anything liberal. Natasha found him in the public library, where he was compiling a literary anthology for senior high schools.

Natasha had been one of his favorite pupils and the old man remembered her well, though he had difficulty recognizing in this slightly faded young woman the buoyant girl who had such an insatiable love of life. Natasha went straight to the point. Would he testify that he knew of her revolutionary sympathies and activities during her high school years? She told him why she needed it. Natasha was used now to the quick change in people's faces: first, pleasure at seeing her, then, in the face of her obvious distress, a slight look of worry, followed upon receipt of her news by an undisguised look of worry and, in some cases, embarrassment over that worry. The old teacher seemed no different. He suddenly looked so miserable that Natasha got up to leave immediately.

"No, no, don't go, my child, you misunderstood me." The old man was distressed. "I shall write it for you, of course, I shall. How could I refuse to say something that I know is true. It wasn't that at all, my little friend. What troubled me so when you were talking was that other old pupils, good ones like you, have come to me with the same request. Why, my dear, why is it so? I don't seem to understand anything any more. Here, look, I have been working over this anthology for two years now. It should not have taken me more than two months to collect samples of Russian literature. But I keep getting instruction after instruction, one changing the other. Throw this out and put this in, they tell me, and then again throw it out and put something else in. Pushkin out, Turgenev out, Lermontov out, Tiutchev out, but Mayakovski in, Demyan Bedny in. Now, Mayakovski has a few powerful poems; the man has great talent; though when I saw him first many years ago he, for some reason, which completely escaped me, wore a carrot in one lapel, a weed in the other. Demyan Bedny can be studied as a new kind of folklore but no more than that. But substitute them for Pushkin! This is the end of everything. Help me to understand it, Natasha! You are young; you may know the reason for it. Can you tell me, Natasha, what it is? What can be harmful for young pupils in Lermontov or Turgenev? Take, for instance . . ."

He was far away from Natasha and her troubles. His world was crumbling: Pushkin had been taken down from his pedestal. It had disturbed Natasha too when her favorite poets, when music by Tchaikovsky, when old paintings she admired were declared harmful for the people, and it was forbidden to print, play, or exhibit them. But just now she had only one thing on her mind—to get the testimonials she needed. Nothing else mattered, not even the troubled old man. With a rudeness she would not have thought herself capable of, she interrupted him:

"Will you give me the paper you promised? I must hurry."

The old man stopped in the middle of a word, his hands trembling as he reached for paper and pen.

"Oh, yes, yes, I am sorry. But, you see, I have no one to talk to, I am a very lonely old man, and it all pains me so. I am sorry. Now, what shall we say?"

He was not conscious of Natasha's rudeness and with great pleasure he wrote a eulogy of her in old-fashioned flowery language. Natasha was deeply moved, but she did not show it. Her nerves were too taut; any show of feeling would have made her break down.

Among the things Natasha looked back to in later years with a burning regret, nothing gave her greater pain than this moment when she took the paper and, without more than a formal word of thanks, quickly left the old man. When on an errand in the library a year later, she went to look for him. She wanted to explain to him her state of mind during her visit and apologize for her rudeness, but he was not there. Two months after her visit, library workers heard the old man scream. They found him clutching a paper in his hands, kicking at the books, and yelling:

"Take them away, take them all away, books are prohibited, books are poison. Away, away with books!"

He was taken to an insane asylum. Strong hands were needed to get the paper he clutched to his breast. It was a letter from the Commissariat of Education, informing him that they were not going to publish the anthology he had prepared. They could not permit it to be used in schools; it would poison the minds of Soviet youth; it would make them unfit for the tasks ahead of them; it would make them tools in the hands of enemies of the Soviet Union. Natasha received permission to visit him. She found a quiet old man with snow-white hair, docile and contented, who did not recognize her but who smiled at her with a new empty smile. When an attendant passed by with a newspaper, the old man ran over to him and threw the paper on the floor.

"Don't you know"—he spoke fast in a high-pitched voice—"don't you know this is poison? Don't touch it, don't touch it, burn it."

No one except Maxim and the old teacher gave Natasha more than bare dates and facts testifying to work she had done or classes she had attended. The hardest task of all still lay ahead of her—the trip to the village. She hadn't been there for seven years, not since her father had died, as Mother said, from a broken heart, and she doubted if anyone would be willing to put in a good word for her.

As members of the Social Revolutionary party, Olga and Gregor had not agreed with the way the Bolsheviks relied solely on the city workers and neglected the peasant; and they said so openly. In retaliation, the government had forbidden them to teach and had closed the school that was their life. The villagers had been hostile to them too. While everywhere else peasants were burning and plundering estates, killing the owners, cutting up priceless paintings, smashing pianos and rare china, Olga and Gregor, at the risk of their lives, had kept their own villagers from doing so, and the villagers never forgave them. It mattered little to them that the government wanted the estates for museums, children's homes, and sanatoriums. What mattered was that in other villages there was hardly a house that didn't have a musical instrument, fine linen, fur coats, or furniture from plundered estates. And the luckier ones got themselves machinery or a cow or a horse. Consequently, when the Soviet authorities started to make trouble for Gregor and Olga, the villagers were pleased. Gregor could not stand the double blow—the loss of the school and the animosity of the people to whom they had given almost twenty years of their lives. When he died, Olga left the village.

Natasha boarded the train with little hope in her heart. Peter helped her fight her way through the crowd surging to the train when the gates opened.

"Keep your food basket right under your feet," he said softly into her ear, "so you can feel if someone tries to pull it out. And the suitcase, never let it out of your sight for a moment. If you think you might fall asleep, sit on it or lie on it. And the little bag, keep touching it with your hands . . ."

When the station bell rang twice, Peter wormed his way through the aisles packed with people and baskets and bags, and stood under the window looking at Natasha, forming words with his lips. As the train moved off, Peter ran along the platform for a last glimpse of Natasha's white face, which looked so pitifully small and frightened.

Thirty-six hours later, Natasha stepped from the friendly refuge of the train into the dark night at the little station that was nearest to her village of Bronovo.

She remembered the old routine—to ask the stationmaster whether there was anyone around from her village. The stationmaster looked at her with suspicion. "Why should there be anyone here from Bronovo? What would they be doing here?"

Could she stay overnight in the station?

"Why not?"

The waiting room was dismal and dark. A few sleeping figures were sprawled on the benches and on the floor. Natasha found an old box in a corner and, keeping her belongings within sight and touch, she settled for the night. It was a long night for her, a hungry and cold night. When the gray day began to worm its way into the room through windows thick with dirt and last summer's cobwebs, life came into the station. A few peasant carts appeared, but none of them were from Bronovo. Natasha was desperate; she couldn't walk the fifteen miles with her luggage. An old peasant took pity on her.

"Eh, eh, listen," he called to her when she turned back to the waiting room, her bundles weighing down her tired arms. "I'll take you. It's out of my way though but I don't care. No hurry to go anywhere. You wait for me here, I won't be long. Not much to do in town now. You wait, I'll be back for you."

He was back soon and fixed a board for Natasha across the cart. Holding on to it with both hands she looked around for familiar landmarks. Yes, the old church was there, but its bell was gone and the big new sign said "Club." The saloon where on fair days the peasants left their last shirt and boots, and dead drunk were dragged away by their wives, showed no trace of its former character. It was a library now. The one-story building had been repaired and freshly painted, with paper flowers in the windows and a friendly welcome to all written out in large letters over the entrance.

They left town and soon the eye saw nothing but a virgin blanket of snow. The old peasant was talking, murmuring to himself in a weary monotonous voice. At first Natasha listened with interest and then, as the same words recurred again and again, his voice began to sound like a lullaby. Natasha dozed off. The barking of dogs announced the nearness of a village. A thin tongue of smoke rose from the schoolhouse toward the heavy low sky. A Reading Hut stood next to the school, and beyond it lay a playground. Poles and bars were sticking out of the snow, and a swing was half buried under it. They never had a playground before. In this village too the saloon was gone, and a Club for Former Red Army Men took its place. They passed the co-operative store, which seemed to be empty of goods and of people. Not one peasant cart stood in front of it. The horse slowed down as they approached the store.

The old peasant changed from his monotonous singsong into an angry outburst at his horse!

"Go on, go on, don't stop, you fool. Nothing for you to stop here for . . . Go on, go on, I am as hungry as you are."

Out of the village, he settled back to his old tune:

". . . has the world ever heard of a peasant going in to town to buy bread for himself and oats for his horse and if he finds an extra slice of bread he feeds his horse because there is even less oats than bread not that there is enough bread. . . . Yes, that's what we have come to now and it's a sin against God to feed a horse bread but a horse has to eat something. . . . And look at the fields last year's wheat rotting it's our fault they say and I say it isn't our fault why should a peasant work his field if he doesn't get the harvest. . . . Land they gave us they say what do we want land for if we can't get out of it what we need. . . . Land is no good if it doesn't feed you it's only good if it feeds you. . . . We'll starve to death all of us will starve to death we are starving already and they tell us work your fields work your fields work your fields how are we to work the fields when we have eaten the seeds and when we go in to town to beg for a piece of bread. . . . Yes beg we do because they wouldn't sell it to us cards they want from us they say no bread without cards. . . . Has the world ever heard of a peasant having to beg the city people for a piece of bread. . . ."

They passed three more villages and everywhere it was the same. Few houses had smoke coming out of the chimneys; the few lonely figures in the street looked thin and miserable, but every village had a school, a reading hut, a club, a co-operative store, a medical center; two had nurseries. The old peasant's lamentations, the obvious misery in the villages—and the fresh gay signs heralding their new life; back and forth Natasha's feelings went from one to the other, from one to the other.

Her body numb with cold and aching from the jolting ride on the shaky board, Natasha got out at the office of the village Soviet. This was where she was to report. If the chairman was one of those who had borne a grudge against her parents, she would be lost. Her knees shaking, dragging her belongings in half-frozen hands, she pushed open the door. A stench of cheap tobacco met her and made her almost sick. Peasants were talking to a man who was sitting at a table. They turned around and stared at the stranger in city clothes.

"Yes?" It was the voice of the man at the table. That must the chairman.

Natasha wanted to go over to the table and tell him her name. Her feet wouldn't carry her, and her voice stuck in her throat. I can't help it, she thought dismally, I can't go on any more.

Then the man at the table got up and walked over to her. "Who are you? What is it you want?" There was something familiar in her face. Oh, no, that couldn't be. What would she be doing here, the girl who was a big shot in Moscow? But those dark eyes, the white face . . .

She was the first to recognize him.

"Ivan . . . ?"

"Sure, I'm Ivan, who else would I be?"

The thin weak voice which so hesitatingly spoke his name sounded very different from the one he expected if the girl was Natasha.

"Ivan, don't you know me?" Now it sounded fuller and had a trace of the spark that had brought the village youth to life when Natasha came home on a visit.

"Natasha . . . ?"

She nodded.

"Natasha, Natasha, Natasha . . ." Beside himself with joy, he repeated her name while he shook her hands.

Natasha could hardly believe her luck. Ivan—her parent's favorite pupil, the pride of their school, the Partisan leader, the first Communist in the village—Ivan was the chairman of the Soviet; on Ivan, the best friend she had here, depended her fate!

Ivan quickly ended his business with the peasants, loaded her luggage on his shoulders and, taking her hand as if she were a child, led her through the snowdrifts to his house.

"Grusha, Grusha," his booming voice brought his wife out on the porch. "Look whom I brought! What a surprise, eh? Don't you know her? Look well at her! You know now, don't you?"

Grusha threw her arms around Natasha.

"What good wind blew you here? Come in, Natasha, come in, get warm . . . get rested, you look as if you needed it. And you, big loafer, don't stand there grinning as if there was nothing else for a man to do around the house . . ."

Grusha began to whisper fiercely into Ivan's ear. Ivan spread out his hands in a hopeless gesture. Grusha wouldn't take it for an answer and continued her whispering, which was getting louder and angrier. If Natasha had not been so desperately exhausted she would have heard:

". . . you must, you must, you must. She is frozen, don't you see? Have you no heart? Say it's a loan, say he'll get it back tomorrow, say anything, but for Christ's sake get a piece of real wood. I'll put in ours meanwhile but you know that won't last half an hour."

In the kitchen, on boards above the stove which gave out no warmth, three children were lying under a pile of clothes. Three blond heads, their light-blue eyes tense with curiosity, were bent low over the boards so as not to miss a single movement and word of that unbelievably exciting event—a visitor from the city. Ivan disappeared; Grusha bustled around, pushing dry branches into the stove, filling the teakettle, throwing quick glances at Natasha, and out of sheer habit constantly hushing the children though not a sound came from them. Their fascinated eyes did not leave Natasha. Unlike Mother's usual visitors, whose mouths did not close for a moment, this one had not said a word yet. With slow movements, her eyes wandering around but obviously seeing nothing, she started to unbundle her shawl, pull off her galoshes, take off her coat. In the midst of it all, without having finished any of it, she let herself down on a chair, threw her arms on the table, and broke into tears.

"Natasha, dear dear Natasha, what is it? What is it? Tell me, honey, but don't cry so, please, don't cry so . . . I can't stand it." Grusha rushed over to her.

Truly, Grusha couldn't stand it. To have Natasha suddenly walk into their house was excitement enough, but to see her move around like a stone statue without uttering a word, and now to see her crying—that was decidedly too much for the tenderhearted Grusha, and she began to cry too. The children, whose eyes had begun to fill as soon as Natasha started to cry, now opened their mouths wide and howled heartily. At this moment Ivan walked in, dragging a few logs behind him. He dropped the logs and ran back and forth between the children and the women.

"What happened? Tell me, what happened? Shall I get a doctor? What happened?"

Again Grusha whispered fiercely into his ear.

So they were crying because Natasha was crying. But why was Natasha crying? There was no way of stopping her, and soon Ivan and Grusha gave up. Let her cry it out; she would stop by herself. They put wood into the stove, they set the table, they helped the children get dressed and come down now that the kitchen was getting warm. Natasha still cried. Her tears were long overdue. Held back by the pressure of things that she had to attend to, by the fact that she was never alone, that she did not want to be weak, they rushed out now and nothing could stop their flow. Gradually the tenseness that had felt like armor around her heart melted away, and she began to feel deliciously weak. She wiped her eyes and raised her head. Ivan was quickly at her side.

"Natasha, you must tell us, dear, what happened. Why the tears? Tell us . . ."

In a few words Natasha told them.

Ivan shouted with relief. "What? Is that all? And the thoughts we had! We were sure somebody had died and we wondered who? Well, if that is really all, that's easy, that's not worth crying about! And I thought at least . . ."

He sounded almost disappointed, and Natasha laughed. How good it was to laugh! How good it was to be among friends, and how good it was to be told "that's easy." All of a sudden it really sounded easy, and it was easy to tell the whole story, everything, the hurts, the disappointments, the doubts.

"Ah, the scoundrel. If only I'd been there, he wouldn't have got away with it. We've had the same kind around here too. Rascals who fish in muddy waters . . . they didn't get far with me. Now, don't you worry, Natasha . . . don't you worry about anything. In Moscow they may play a dirty trick on you, but we wouldn't. Oh, no, we wouldn't, don't you worry."

How warm and good it felt! Natasha laughed and her voice wasn't thin and weak any more. She talked to the children, and she helped Grusha around the kitchen while Ivan went back to the Soviet. In the evening, after the children went to sleep on their boards, they sat up till long after midnight talking.

It was obvious that the party members in Bronovo did not take the party purge as seriously as they did in Moscow, and were little impressed by accusations made at a purge. Ivan had spoken in the afternoon to some of Natasha's old friends and classmates. They all were ready to help her. A few of them had had the same kind of trouble because some jealous or vindictive person had dug up an uncle or grandfather who had owned four cows or a great-aunt who had sold hot buns at the county fair. They had learned to laugh about it. That settled Natasha's case.

But it was also obvious that they had troubles in the village which Moscow did not have. It was 1930 and collectivization was being forced on them. Ivan and his friends were in favor of it, and they were working toward it in their own way. They knew their villagers, they knew how to approach them. They were sure they could convert their village into a model collective farm, to the benefit of the peasants and to the benefit of the country.

". . . you would think they'd leave us alone . . ."

Ivan had made clear to Natasha that to him "they" meant bureaucrats, penpushers, chair warmers, red-tapists, and in general city people who had never walked behind a plow.

". . . you would think they would let us do it, that they would beg us to do it. Oh, no, not they. They send their own people to do our job. Dozens of them have been here already, people who get jittery when they see a cow and who even in their sleep will not part with their bulging briefcases filled with papers, with dozens, with hundreds, with thousands of papers. And it's we who have to read all those papers and sign them and remember them. And few are the days when we don't get at least one questionnaire. Believe me, they don't know a thing about peasants and villages. But try telling them they're wrong: I used to try it; now I keep my mouth shut. And just try not to do things their way! They don't care that it doesn't bring results. As long as you do things the way it's written in those damned papers of theirs . . . So they make us force our peasants into the collectives. The peasants don't want it. They kill the cattle, they break the machinery. Scores of them were sent to Siberia, families separated, children dragged away by force. They were kulaks, we were told. We don't have to be told who our kulaks are: We know them and we were ready to take care of them in our own way. But not by sending them away to Siberia, not by tearing children away from their parents. Oh, no, we'd have given their land, their machinery, their cows, and their horses to the collective, and we'd have made them work for the collective, made them work hard, made them useful to us. And their children would go to school right along with our own children and grow up in the right Soviet spirit—not like outcasts, their hearts full of hatred for our Soviet government. . . . So what do we have now? Our peasants are discontented. Every day new rules more stupid than the last! Can you imagine having all those woods around us and our being so afraid to break the ever-changing regulations about chopping down trees that we freeze? It's that way with everything. How on earth we are going to plant the fields come spring—don't ask me. I don't know. We are supposed to have old supplies, they tell us. Until we deliver them, we don't get seed. What do you want me to do? Dig up every cellar, every back yard in the village? I am sure we have squeezed out the last ounce of grain in the village. I don't know of anyone who could have any grain left. If he has, he is crazy not to give it up because he can't use it anyway. No one can bake a loaf of bread in the village without the rest of us knowing it. We are all in the same boat. The letters we have written, the appeals we have sent! And what do we get? Another city visitor with a fat briefcase, another form to fill out, another regulation the very opposite of the last one. Oh, Natasha, we are all mixed up."

Ivan spoke with vigor and heat. After he had finished expounding his troubles, he told Natasha with the same vigor and heat, pride added to his voice, what they had done in the village during the years she'd been away. They had built a nursery, the first in the entire region, they had a tractor repair shop, they had a medical center with a nurse always on duty and a regular visiting doctor; they had a reading hut with a special room for games; they had their own veterinary doctor; and many of their children went to the city to high school.

". . . let them get knowledge in all fields, no matter what it is—science or arts, crafts, soldiering, let them learn all there is to learn. They'll come back to their own village afterwards, and they'll raise the standard of living and culture in the entire village. Another ten years, maybe twenty years, and ours will be the first land on earth, a happy land for happy people . . ."

He had completely forgotten his recent exasperation, Natasha thought with amusement. But it was plain he felt the way she did. He too was swinging back and forth, from the light side to the dark, and back again. Throughout the three days Natasha spent in the village, she was constantly torn between the two feelings. Misery, poverty, starvation, but the school was enlarged and well taken care of. It had new maps, charts, games and sports, even a chemistry laboratory. Some of the children had nothing on their feet but old rags, and they sat barefoot in class while the rags dried on the stove, but their eyes were lively and bright. And though their stomachs were not too well filled now, they listened eagerly to their teacher, who assured them that with a little patience their stomachs were going to be well filled for the rest of their lives. The teacher had answers and explanations for everything.

She found them in the new textbooks, in the *Agitator's Companion*, in the *Educational Bulletins*, in the *Pravda* editorials. Her answers were filled with such a sincere unquestionable conviction that it would never have occurred to the children that anything she said was not gospel truth. Sometimes what their parents told them was different from what the teacher told them, but the teacher was well prepared for that; that was what her textbooks and notes were most concerned with. The young peasant generation must never take their elders' word about anything. There was One Word, One Truth, and that Word and that Truth were what they heard from their teacher.

Twice Natasha sat in a class listening to the young teacher. No doubt would ever enter her mind. She had been born at the right time, not too early, as Natasha's generation had been.

Natasha saw her parents standing where the young teacher stood now. Mother, tall, straight, beautiful, her big black eyes soft when looking at the children. And always a tiny white collar and white cuffs on her dress. Father was all movement; his eyes, his wavy hair, his hands, his whole slim figure slightly shorter than Mother's, all seemed to move when he was explaining something to the children. And whatever they were saying, Mother in a low voice that was almost a monotone in its quietness, Father with eloquence and fire, they, like the young teacher now, were full of the unshakable conviction of being right. But their conviction came from the very depths of their own hearts and minds. It was not checked up for them and given to them by somebody else with a strict order to follow it or be penalized. The sadness in Natasha's eyes came not only from the memory of her parents standing there but also from the pain of opening her eyes to something which it would have been better for her never to have seen.

During the entire thirty-six-hour trip back to Moscow, the struggle within Natasha went on. She had achieved what she went for. She got in the village excellent recommendations, better than she could ever have hoped for. Ivan wrote a personal letter in florid but most heartfelt terms. "Natasha's parents," he wrote, "brought the torch of knowledge into the darkness of our forgotten village. Their memory will always live in gratitude in the hearts of people like the signed for whom they were the first guiding light on the road to the revolution. . . . Natasha was another guiding light who taught us the ways of a true revolutionary in whose heart one fire burned—the fire of devotion to the revolution and to the party . . ."

With this, Natasha was more than satisfied. At the same time she was plagued by doubts. Why had it been necessary to go to the village at all? Why were thousands made to travel all over the country to get proof of what should never have been questioned? Until now joy to her had come only from real accomplishment. She couldn't accept a joy that came from something she found so wrong. The wall, the solid wall at which she had worshiped, had a crack. And into the crack were crawling the injustices visited on her and on others in the purge, the stories she heard in the village, the memory of the teacher repeating thoughtlessly words made up for her by others.

Back home things moved quickly. Only for a few hours during the first evening did she enjoy the pleasure of having her family with her again. Early next morning she was waiting in the reception room of the Central Committee. When her turn came, the secretary threw an indifferent glance at the papers she handed him. Natasha's heart was beating furiously. The secretary did not read any of the papers she had secured with so much pain. He pushed them aside with a careless:

"It looks all right, comrade."

Comrade!

"See your district secretary tomorrow. He may have good news for you."

As simple as that! Later Natasha learned that the Central Committee had been flooded with appeals for reinstatement, with indignant protests from old party members, with reports of numerous suicides among the expelled. But the purge was on by orders from higher quarters and there was no way of stopping it until these quarters reversed the orders. Then one day the Leader pushed a button marked Stop! and the Purge Commissions instantly slowed down and secretaries began to stamp their OKs on appeals for reinstatement.

Next day Natasha was reinstated in the party and in all her activities as if nothing had ever happened. When she was handed back her membership card, it was with the indifference of a streetcar conductor handing out a ticket. Not a single word or gesture of regret over the obvious mistake that had caused her unspeakable agony. It took half a minute, no words were exchanged. "Next!" someone called.

Natasha's busy life immediately took hold of her again. There wasn't any time left for thinking. The crack in her wall grew gradually smaller until amidst the great activities of reconstruction and the enthusiasm over them, it closed completely. With the closing of the crack, Natasha's mind also closed. After its short moment of thinking and questioning, it became again the docile submissive mind of the disciplined party member for whom only one Word and one Truth existed.

CHAPTER 25

*Fedor and Ludmilla*

AS in the case of everyone else who could not boast of proletarian parents, Fedor's past hung like a dark cloud over his life. It stole upon him whenever a new personnel official, studying his dossier, struck the words "former industrialist and houseowner." Before 1927, Lenin's letter thanking Fedor for his readiness to serve the revolution, and the good word of one of the Old Guard who knew of Fedor's past services to the young Soviet Republic quickly dampened the zeal of the most ardent headhunter. Lenin's name did not lose its old magic, but for young party members it became less effective as a signature on a paper than the name of the new Leader. And after 1927, when the might of the GPU turned mercilessly against party dissenters, no member of the Old Guard was willing to risk his neck for Fedor. Forgotten was Lenin's advice that, if a man could be of use to the revolution, his usefulness should be accepted whoever he was. Those were dangerous words to remember in 1929, when the latest party instructions proclaimed that "we are entering now the last phase of our struggle against the bourgeoisie." Fedor was a member of this bourgeoisie, of the capitalist class, and no good Bolshevik could be instrumental in relieving the last convulsions of that class by harboring one of its sons. The air was full of government appeals to strike the final mortal blow against the bourgeoisie, to destroy every vestige of capitalism in the Soviet Union, to get rid of the last remnants of old specialists and intellectuals, and to bring to the forefront their own, their young Soviet specialists and intellectuals. The appeals were imbued with distrust of anything that belonged to the past. How, then, could a Communist dare put in a good word for a former member of the class which his party and his government were out to destroy?

Fedor fought hard for his right to work for the Five-Year Plan. He had drafted the plan's section covering the textile industry, and he was ready to give every moment of his life to make it a success. He fought singlehanded, for no one had the courage to help him. He lost his fight, and he was told to leave the Textile Trust.

On the day he gave his job over to the man who was to take his place, Fedor came home with death in his looks. His eyes were the only color left in his face. His lips and his cheeks were as white as his hair.

Ludmilla took him in her arms and led him to the couch. He did not say a word. He shivered and almost bit his tongue between his loudly chattering teeth. She covered him with a blanket, she rocked him in her arms and sang a soft lullaby, and he quieted down under the warmth of her arms and voice. Then, without warning, he began to cry. Ludmilla had never in her life seen Fedor cry and he had once said that he had never cried since he was a boy of eight. But he was crying now. He cried like a man who did not know how to cry. Sobs seemed to tear his chest apart but almost no tears came from his eyes. There had been many dangerous and frightening moments in their life together but never had Ludmilla felt such a horror in her heart.

"Fedor, my beloved, please, don't. This is not the end, don't despair, we are still together. Fedor, please, please, for my sake, stop."

Later, his first outburst of despair over, his fingers intertwined with Ludmilla's, he talked. His voice was heavy with a hopeless tiredness.

". . . this is the end, Ludmilla, I know this is the end . . . I am nearly sixty, I have done all the fighting I can, I can do no more. This is the end of me. Oh, why, why didn't we go away, Ludmilla? Why?"

"Sh-sh-sh!" In panic she pressed her fingers on his lips. "Don't say it! The walls have ears. Don't ever say that."

All night long she held him in her arms and fought against his despair.

". . . don't you see, we can go away from here. We can go to a small town where nobody knows us. You can find work, any kind of work, and they will soon find out how gifted you are, how useful you are, and you will again do big work, real work. You will see, dearest, you will see. And it may even be good for us to live in a small town, it will be quiet and peaceful, the way we like it, oh, yes, it will be very good, I am sure."

She knew he couldn't get work in a small town or anywhere else. They could have done it a while ago—Ludmilla knew people who had stripped themselves of their skills and their identity, and had got lost somewhere in a sleepy small town to start life anew as an unskilled laborer or domestic servant—but this was no longer possible. In 1929 identification papers had become as much part of a man as his skin. Ludmilla knew that they were caught in the trap of Fedor's papers, which stated that he was too dangerous to be given work. But she had to talk, talk, talk, give him hope, talk him out of his despair.

This was a hard task during the black days that followed. It was not only Fedor's right to work that he was deprived of; they were ordered to leave their rooms immediately, and their food cards were taken away from them.

"Ludmilla, listen to me."

"No, no, and no! I won't listen to you! I refuse to listen."

She covered her ears with her hands. She knew what he was going to say; he had been saying it all day long. And he was saying it again.

". . . you must listen . . . there is no other way out . . . I am telling you this is the end . . . but I can't go alone and leave you here . . . we must go together. There are ways, quick ways, not painful at all. We must, Ludmilla . . . together it will not be hard."

And again Ludmilla found strength enough, and talked to him and caressed him and talked again. And while she talked a plan came to her mind and she did not stop talking to him about it until she made him agree to try it out.

". . . we never liked living in the city anyway. Remember you always said when we returned in the fall that you would prefer to stay there. Well, now is the time to do it. Oh, Fedor, it will be heaven to live the whole year round at Dubrovka. Aren't we lucky they didn't take it away from us? We won't have to garden the whole place—a small vegetable plot will be enough for us to live on. And we still have some things and I can always exchange clothes and furniture for flour, maybe even for sugar or meat. And we can have chickens, you always wanted to have our own chickens. That will give us meat. And we will have plenty of fruit. Nikon promised to spray the trees, and I am sure he did. And all the berries, and mushrooms. You see, dearest, we'll never have to worry about our food there. And the books we'll read— you always complained about how many books you wanted to read and never had time for. And we will chop our wood and be cozy and warm in the winter. And we will be together, we will have each other, Fedor. Think of it, no one can take that away from us."

Next morning Ludmilla boarded the slow cold train to Dubrovka. The bungalow was quite a distance from the station; the snow was high and there was no path. In her heavy felt boots, she fought her way through snow that reached above her knees. When she finally got to the bungalow, she could not suppress a loud groan. They would never be able to come out here. The bungalow was covered with snow almost to the roof; the windows were broken, and the snow was piled high in the rooms. This house could not be made livable in the winter. But she couldn't go home, look into Fedor's ghostly face, and tell him they couldn't come there. She couldn't destroy the flicker of hope she had given him. She would rather stay there, she thought, and slowly sink into the snow and freeze to death.

But there must be some way. Nikon! How could she have forgotten Nikon, the old man who was the local forester long before the revolution, who had known her since she first came to Dubrovka thirty years ago. He would know what to do. Nikon lived on the other side of the railroad tracks. Thank God, there was a path from the tracks to his house, a path which had been driven on and walked on. What a relief it was to walk without falling into the snow at each step. And it was sheer happiness to sit in Nikon's warm clean kitchen with its wonderful smell of burning pine and freshly baked bread, to be waited on and worried about.

"Ai, ai, ai, Ludmilla, how could you?" He was full of reproach. "As if old Nikon didn't exist, as if he had forgotten what you did for his old woman, as if he was too old to shovel away a little snow . . . ai, ai, ai . . ." Nikon kept shaking his head in disapproval.

Ludmilla would have liked to stay forever in that kitchen, warmed by the stove, by the hot tea, and by Nikon's fatherly concern over her. But she was worried about Fedor and did not want to leave him alone too long. She had arranged everything with Nikon. They were to come immediately and were to stay with him for a few days, till their house was cleared of snow, and the windows repaired. They would live in the kitchen and in the adjoining room which used to be the cook's room. It would be easy enough to keep that warm. Nikon had a little food stored up, they could have some of it. Fedor could go hunting with him. And they could always have fish. Only the other day Nikon had cut a new hole in the ice. Tomorrow his son-in-law would go into town and move out their belongings on the big sled, the one they used to log wood in. All she had to do, Nikon told her, was to pack her things and come out; he would see to the rest.

When they arrived late in the evening, the kitchen was even warmer and more inviting than it had been the day before. There was food on the table, and a bed was ready for them.

"Believe me, Nikon," Fedor felt it his duty to explain, "if not for these unfortunate circumstances . . ."

"Sh-sh, not a word," interrupted Nikon. He opened his shirt and pulled out a cross. "I may not be a churchgoer, never was one, but I believe in His teachings. I was not afraid of the czar, I am not afraid of the Bolsheviks. My conscience has to be clear not before them but before Him. You are in need, aren't you? Is it any business of mine why? No." He clasped Fedor's hand and held it. "When my poor wife needed her, did Ludmilla ask any questions? Like an angel she came and stretched out her hand to help us. Well, how about some food?"

Next morning Nikon, his son-in-law, and a villager to whom Ludmilla used to send cakes on his little girl's birthday went over to the bungalow with picks and shovels. Three days later Ludmilla and Fedor moved in. The wind was blowing through the house but Nikon had supplied them with enough wood to keep the kitchen and their tiny bedroom warm. Soon the snow began to soften and then to melt, and Ludmilla tramped in the slush planning the vegetable patch and her flowers, and with Nikon's help ministering to fruit trees and berry shrubs. When the soil was ready to be handled, Nikon gave Ludmilla every minute he could spare from his work on his own field and garden. Ludmilla's hands quickly became hard and calloused and rough. It was the roughness of her hands that more than anything else shook Fedor out of his deadly apathy and he took over the harder part of clearing away the ravages of the winter, the digging and spading.

In the summer, the predictions that Ludmilla had conjured up out of her imagination in a last desperate effort to take Fedor's mind away from death came true. They had their own chickens, their fruit and vegetables. And when, after their evening tea, they sat silent on the porch listening to the night sounds with a light breeze bringing them the smell of the flowers and the earth, they knew a long-unfamiliar peace and had no thought of the past. Once when Natasha and Kira came to visit them, and returned from their morning swim, wet hair flying in the wind, wet towels around their shoulders, the happy days of the past came back for a fleeting moment with poignant vividness.

Ludmilla had not lost her old skill with flowers and her roses attracted many summer visitors to her garden. She did not mind sharing the lovely blooms but some people refused to accept them as a gift and insisted on paying. Ludmilla would not permit it at first, but she and Fedor needed money. They had no ration cards, and they had to pay exorbitant prices for the food they did not grow themselves. Reluctantly, Ludmilla accepted money, first for the roses, and by and by for her other flowers, for berries, eggs, vegetables, for everything people were ready to buy from her. It was a summer of hard work but of great enjoyment in the results of the work and in the pride of Ludmilla's life—her garden.

The autumn brought a great deal of labor too. The garden had to be well prepared for winter when in the soil, covered with burlap and mulch, life would go on and fill the roots and bulbs with sap. The summer had dispelled Fedor's bitterness and he was looking forward to the winter evenings with Ludmilla, his pipes and books. Ludmilla could hardly wait for the winter. She wanted snow. The autumn storms and rains made her restless and nervous, and she began to feel the strain of the last months. And now that her garden was put to sleep she wanted to see it securely covered with a warm snow blanket.

It was a dark late October morning with skies hanging heavy and very low as if pregnant with the first snow. Out in the shed Fedor was chopping wood. Ludmilla was standing on the window sill, filling cracks in the window frames with cotton and rags, when she heard the dog bark and heard Fedor call him.

The barking continued. Ludmilla climbed down and went to the door. Fedor and three peasants were standing at the gate. Fedor led the men into the house, and Ludmilla asked them pleasantly to sit down and pulled out chairs for them.

The men sat down without saying a word, without taking their caps off. One of them took a paper from inside his sheepskin. He held it upside down and pushed it over to the youngest of the three.

"Read," the older man ordered.

The young man cleared his throat:

"On October twenty-fifth, nineteen hundred and twenty-nine, the Village Soviet of Dubrovka, having heard the report of the Moscow representative of the Central Soviet on the necessity of eternal vigilance against our external and internal enemies and the remnants of the despised bourgeoisie, have unanimously decided that Fedor Gavrilov and his wife, Ludmilla, members of the above-mentioned despised bourgeoisie, were guilty of employing hired labor as a result of which they were enriching themselves by living on an income not earned by the work of their hands. Furthermore, they engaged in private trade which has been denounced by our great leader Stalin as hostile to the teachings of the Marx-Lenin-Stalin ideology. Therefore, the aforesaid Fedor and Ludmilla Gavrilov are to be declared enemies of the working class and are immediately to leave the property acquired by them as members of the capitalist class. . . ."

It was Nikon who explained to them later what it was all about. Ludmilla and Fedor were too stunned to grasp what had happened. Nikon was the "hired labor" and the few kopecks they earned from their flowers and vegetables was the "private trade" they engaged in. Nikon did not tell them that he had stormed and fought for them in the Soviet. He could easily have changed the minds of the villagers, for they all liked Ludmilla, and would not have hurt her; but the Moscow representative had signed the paper and put the stamp on it, and nothing in the world could change anything after that. The local Soviet remembered too well the occasions on which they had gone against Moscow's decisions. It had ended disastrously for them in each case, and they could not afford to have that happen in these hungry times.

Nikon did succeed in getting permission for the Gavrilovs to stay in their house until they could dispose of their belongings and agreement that he himself would not be molested if he offered them hospitality in his own house.

"Well—" the Soviet chairman had thoughtfully scratched his head—

"you understand, old friend Nikon, you can do as you please—what do I care whom you have in your house? But suppose in Moscow they think it's wrong? What then? There will be nothing I can do then, you know that . . . Meanwhile do what you think is right. After all, someday we shall die and have to answer for our sins to a higher judge, not to Moscow."

Ludmilla suddenly walked like an old woman, stooped and weak. She and Fedor wandered about the house going through the motions of sorting things, packing them, following Nikon's instructions like children. Treating their departure as the most natural thing in the world, Nikon kept them busy in order not to leave them any time to think. He didn't like the look in Ludmilla's eyes. Fedor's eyes were like those of a dead man, he might be suffering, but people with such eyes didn't act. But something prickly appeared in Ludmilla's eyes. She didn't say a word but suddenly that prickly flash would be there in eyes which had always been soft and tender. Once, many years ago, Nikon had seen such a flash in the eyes of a woman who had lost her children in a fire. The woman drowned herself. Not for a moment did he let Ludmilla out of his sight. On the last morning the boxes were ready, the bedding tied in bundles, the furniture which had been sold was taken away, the rest ready to be stored in Nikon's barn. The men had started to load the carts when Nikon missed Ludmilla. He jumped down from the cart on which he was fastening a table and slowly at first, in order not to worry Fedor, then running, he returned to the house. Ludmilla was not there. He found her in the rose garden. She was kneeling on the wet ground, her hands gently touching the boughs that covered the rose beds.

Hidden behind trees Nikon watched her, saw her kneel at the other flower beds, saw her touch them with lingering fingers. Then she knelt by the bench on which she and Fedor often sat listening to the nightingales. Her head pressed against it, she prayed:

"O, my Lord, give me strength. You know I have sinned, You know the thoughts I had . . . I didn't want to live. I put myself now in Your merciful hands. I don't ask for anything else, only give me strength to help Fedor, Lord."

She rose painfully. Slowly her eyes wandered over the garden. The sadness in her eyes made Nikon's own eyes smart. He waited for a while, then came out from behind the trees lugging a bench as if that was what he had come for.

"Ah, there you are, Ludmilla. That's fine, you could help me with this. And while you are here let's make sure we forgot nothing . . ."

Talking in a matter-of-fact voice about the luck they had with the weather today, he led the way toward the house through the rose garden.

"By the way, you know what I think? We could dig up your roses and anything else you want to. I wouldn't touch them now—it's too late to disturb them—but at the right time it will be an easy thing to do. And we could dig up some of the berries and the younger fruit trees . . ."

Ludmilla pressed his arm and he quickly went on:

"See, I was sure we had forgotten something. No use leaving the flowerpots here, we can start cuttings in them. And look at this perfectly good string, and the broom, and the plate . . . Come, Ludmilla, help me. There, we can put it all into this cardboard box. Hold on to it, that's the girl. Now, give me a push . . ."

The box on his shoulders, odds and ends in his hands, he talked till they reached the carts: how Fedor could do this, and how she could do that, and how it would give him time for other things.

From the moment they entered his house, the household was in Ludmilla's hands, and Nikon saw to it that it didn't give her many free moments. He kept Fedor constantly at his side, hunting, fishing, fetching wood, building shelves for the cellar, repairing broken steps on the porch, fastening window shutters, always wondering out loud how he could ever have managed all this without Fedor's help.

Soon the first snow fell and was followed by the first frost. The monotonous but busy rhythm of their days left little time for despair. While Fedor helped Nikon, Ludmilla cleaned and cooked and washed. But the evenings were hard. There was little to do, and it was then that the sense of catastrophe, of futility, became oppressive, drained them of all power to make decisions, of all desire to do anything but sit close together, brooding, too desolate to talk.

Toward the end of the winter, Ludmilla began to watch the melting snow eagerly. How soon would Nikon be able to dig up her garden? Her hands itched when she thought of it, and her fingers made the gestures of lifting up plants. To get her hands in dirt again! Nikon had given her for her new garden a plot of ground on which an old arbor stood. She saw her yellow climbing roses covering it, she saw their old bench beneath it. And here she would plant the red roses, and here the white . . . and here the peonies, and here the irises . . . and here the chrysanthemums, and here the lilies . . . and here . . . and here . . . and here . . .

Every day Ludmilla walked over to her old garden. It had been a good winter for the plants. From the first snowfall on, the ground had stayed under snow—no thawing and refreezing, not even once. One morning when she woke up, the snow was completely gone. The ground was soft, and Ludmilla sank deep into the mud on her walk to the bungalow. There had never been any but her own footprints between the railroad tracks and the house, but that day she found many new ones and the deep marks of wheels. From a distance she heard voices coming from the house. Men were building a fence around the grounds; the window sills were covered with jars of paints and brushes, carts were being unloaded. Beds, tables, chairs, washstands. It couldn't be for one family. There were too many of them. And they were all small. As she watched from behind a tree, a man came out of the house and hung over the gate a large sign with the paint wet and shining: TEXTILE WORKERS' UNION. KINDERGARTEN NUMBER FIFTY. ENTRANCE FORBIDDEN. TRESPASSERS WILL BE SEVERELY PUNISHED BY LAW.

Too late! It was too late to get the plants! They would never be hers again. And they would never be anybody else's, judging by the way the men were trampling over the beds and letting their horses roam through the garden. Standing there behind the tree, Ludmilla felt as if she were watching a murder.

"Ah, Ludmilla, don't take on so." Nikon tried to make light of it when she told him the news. "I'll get you plenty of other flowers. I know people around here who have roses and peonies and lilies-of-the-valley, and anything you want, and we will plant them exactly where you wanted your own flowers. What difference does it make as long as you have your garden to take care of? That's nothing to cry about."

The loss of her plants grieved her; but a deeper pain came from again having something taken from them which had been part of their lives, something it would have hurt no one to let them keep. It was the pain of the never-ending blows of hope repeatedly killed. What was the use of reaching into herself for fresh strength, of believing again, of hoping again?

Ludmilla's mind was enveloped in a dark cloud, and the shadow of it fell on Fedor. Nikon kept them constantly busy, and they did what he told them to do, but their eyes were lifeless and they moved like automatons. Ludmilla tortured herself by walking over to the bungalow and watching from behind the trees. The plants did not die and the garden was in flower when the children came, forty-five of them. A few days later almost no blooms remained. Ludmilla had heard a teacher telling the children to take care of the flowers. But the children were small and they were city children. They did not know what it meant to take care of flowers. With an aching heart, Ludmilla watched the children playing games among the beds, pushing aside the flowers and shrubs in their way, plucking them curiously or carelessly, and sometimes lovingly. Nikon found her leaning against a tree, tears running down her cheeks.

". . . it isn't that I don't want the children to have our house and our garden," Ludmilla said pitifully. "That isn't why I am crying. I want the children to have the best in life and I am glad to see them so happy. But why ruin something created with so much love and labor? To see it uselessly destroyed, that is what hurts, Nikon."

Every day it became harder for Nikon to draw any spark from Ludmilla. She worried him. If some new blow fell he was sure she couldn't stand it. So when a messenger from the local Soviet brought a special-delivery letter for Fedor, Nikon stayed in their room while Fedor read it.

On the stationery of the Textile Trust was written:

> To the Chairman of the Dubrovka Soviet:
> The enclosed letter is to be delivered under receipt to Fedor Gavrilov residing in Dubrovka whose address is unknown to us. The signed receipt is to be returned to us immediately.

Fedor opened the enclosure with shaking hands.

"Dear Comrade Gavrilov," it began. The "comrade" startled them, and Ludmilla sank abruptly into a chair, her face white.

> We have in mind a new project which we are sure will be of interest to you. We could start working on it as soon as you are ready for it. You will oblige us by coming to see us as soon as you receive this. It also might interest you that the new building for our employees has just been completed and that a four-room fully furnished apartment has been reserved in it for you.
>
> With friendly greetings . . .

The letter was signed by the vice-chairman of the Textile Trust. Fedor leaned over Ludmilla's shoulder, put the letter in her hands, and they read and reread it. Suddenly it fell out of Ludmilla's hand. She had fainted. Fedor and Nikon rushed for smelling salts and cold water. In a few minutes her eyelids fluttered slightly, and her lips moved.

"Was there a letter?" she asked. "Did I dream about a letter?"

"You didn't, you didn't dream, my darling. Here it is, Ludmilla, here, look at it. Everything is all right again. We are going back, I will work again, we will live in a wonderful new house. It is not a dream, dearest."

Fedor held the letter before Ludmilla's eyes. She read it again, she took it into her hands to make sure it was real.

"I will work again, can you imagine that? I will work again. Why don't you smile? Aren't you glad?"

"Yes, Fedor, I am glad, of course, I am glad. But why? Why all our unhappiness and then suddenly this? Why?"

They had read the speech Stalin had made a few days before. They had even commented on what he had said about nonparty members being as good as party members in their usefulness to the country, but they had never thought it could have any bearing on their lives. They did not know that immediately after his speech thousands of scientists, engineers, and teachers were recalled to work from exile and retirement, given an extra food ration, an apartment, and every available comfort.

Fedor was suddenly a changed man. He was ready to go to Moscow immediately. He wouldn't waste a minute. Before rushing off to the train he tried to cheer Ludmilla.

"Why don't you smile, dearest? Aren't you happy? Life is good to us again. Smile."

She couldn't smile. She couldn't rejoice. Why, she asked almost fiercely, had they had to go through all that? Why should they be played with like wooden soldiers? Up, down! Up, down! She couldn't stand those ups and downs anymore. She was afraid of this new up: wouldn't another terrible down follow it?

"Don't, please, Ludmilla, don't. Let us simply accept our luck and be glad. And don't say anything, don't even think anything, don't think at all, Ludmilla, please." His voice dropped almost to a whisper and there was great anguish in it. "Darling, believe me, it tortures me too—why, why, why? But asking this can only bring ruin again. Forget questions. Let's take what comes and not think about it. Believe me, darling, this is the only way. Please, smile, please."

He returned late at night, hardly able to stand on his feet from exhaustion but tense with excitement:

"What a job, what a job, Ludmilla! And all on my own, no one to interfere with me, and I am to pick my staff myself—subject to confirmation, of course—but I can name anyone I want. Don't ask me what it is, because I can't say anything about it. They trust me, imagine, Ludmilla, me, with a confidential job, with work of highest secrecy . . . but you mustn't ask any questions about it."

Ludmilla had no intention of asking any questions about his work. Something else was on her mind.

"Fedor, did they . . . ?" she started hesitatingly. He looked so pleased and excited, it was hard to come out with her question. "Did they say anything else? Did they explain why we have been persecuted so? Did they?"

Fedor wiped his face with the back of his hand as if he wanted to rub off the cloud which Ludmilla's words had brought to it. His voice lost its excited pitch and dropped very low:

"No, they didn't, they didn't say one word about it, and I didn't either, and I am not going to. Please, Ludmilla, please, please, don't say anything more . . . and don't think. If you do, I shan't be able to help thinking too . . . and I don't want to think. Let us live without thinking. I am going to do a job, bigger and more important than any I ever did in my life. Don't let anything interfere with it, please!"

## CHAPTER 26
## *Katya and Gromov*

FEDOR'S job was the result of a daring new idea in modern warfare. Old-fashioned armies fighting face to face seemed obsolete in an age when man took to the air. The future war would be fought above the ground. What could be more effective than an army that descended on enemy territory from the skies? An army equipped with everything an army needed: men, ammunition, food, tents, field hospitals. Good minds were put to work on problems for which no military textbooks of the past offered answers, but the work did not advance to the satisfaction of those who were watching over it. The freshly trained Soviet scientists and technicians, eager, devoted, serious though they were, needed the guiding hand of more experienced older men. Few of the latter had escaped the latest party purge and the renewed persecution of intellectuals. Stalin's speech, clearing the intellectuals of suspicion of disloyalty, brought them back into prominence.

The sky army of the future, even if its men were excellently trained and equipped, would be of little use if it suffered losses on its way down from the skies. The parachute was of supreme importance. When the parachute material was discussed at conferences, Fedor's name was frequently mentioned. They had few men as knowledgeable as he was about the texture of fabrics. But they could not call upon him to assist them; he had been put out of circulation on higher orders. No one would dare question those orders. Stalin's speech was a godsend.

Fedor gave himself wholeheartedly and wholemindedly to his new job. He had gone through years of hard work with little physical comfort, and the last year had dug deep into his resources of mind and spirit; but he worked now without sparing himself, giving every ounce of his remaining strength. He was driven by an urgency which stemmed partly from his age—he had to hurry if he was to achieve results—and partly from the constantly repeated official slogan: "The Soviet Union is racing against time."

At the time he was called back to work, he was given a pep talk, though he hardly needed one to induce him to take the job. He was told that the Soviet Union was in danger, that the rest of the world had one aim alone—to wipe the only Socialist country off the earth. He was told that the Soviet Union was in the same mortal danger it had been in during the years of its infancy. He was told that every tractor, every piece of ammunition, every new machine, every item of national defense, built then, built immediately, that very minute, added a brick to the impregnable wall which the Soviet Union had to present to the world when the attack came. On the speed of their work depended Russia's very existence. No speed was too great in that case, said Fedor, said thousands of Fedors, said hundreds of thousands of Fedors, said millions of Fedors.

Fedor was given a free hand in his work, and the Personnel Department was ordered to let him alone. Still even though absorbed in his work to the point of oblivion, he was conscious of the presence of a watchful eye. Papers disappeared from locked drawers and as mysteriously reappeared. At meetings where most confidential matters were discussed, men whom Fedor didn't know were present and stenographers he had never seen took notes. A faint click of the telephone announced the presence of an unknown listener. Well, as long as it didn't interfere with his work!

One day an unannounced visitor walked into his office and introduced himself as the liaison man between the GPU and the plant. This was the first time Fedor had talked to a member of the dreaded GPU who openly disclosed his identity. In the past they had come to him in the guises of engineers, secretaries, personnel workers, or shop stewards. Fedor had to overcome an unpleasant stir in his stomach and a slight tendency to stutter before the conversation could go smoothly.

The GPU man, Ilya Gromov, was in his middle thirties, slightly built, with prematurely graying hair, a scar on his left cheek, and a nervous twitch around his lips. Gromov was used to the impression he made on people when he introduced himself as a member of the GPU. With a cigarette, a smile, and a few words about the beautiful Indian summer they were having, he managed to put Fedor at ease.

"There is no special reason why I came to see you, comrade Gavrilov . . ." The suaveness and exaggerated quietness of Gromov's tone were also the results of the uneasiness with which he was usually met.

"You probably understand, comrade Gavrilov, that a project like yours is not without interest for us, and that my commissar gives its activities great attention. I would even say that your project happens to be his favorite child . . . and"—here he showed a grin composed of studied embarrassment and genuine mockery—"you must be aware that this interest expresses itself in certain ways. Well, to put it in plain words, it will be simpler for all concerned if you and I get together regularly, and I see and hear directly from you how things are. Mind you, this is by no means a control over you. Oh, not at all. It would be very wrong if you saw it that way. It is only because, as I said, we are so very much interested in this project. And if at any time you feel that things aren't going exactly the way you think they should, if there is anything, anything at all, you want to have cleared out of your way—let me know. Never hesitate to call upon me for help. There are always ways and means to help, you know, always."

His grin was now openly mocking, without any pretense.

This is the way a cat would look and talk playing with a mouse if they had human ways, thought Fedor.

It looked as if everything that had to be said was said, and Gromov got up to go.

"Oh, by the way," he turned back from the door, "you have a brother in Paris, haven't you?"

Fedor nodded. His lips tightened. A cramp in the pit of his stomach made him bend over. Was the shadow of Pavel, a White émigré in Paris, going to destroy his life now? Out of fear, he had stopped corresponding with him long ago. Was this the new "down" Ludmilla never ceased to dread?

Gromov cast a quick glance at Fedor and seemed to be satisfied with the effect of his words.

"He is married to Nazarov's daughter, Zena, isn't he?"

Fedor nodded again, and the blood left his face. Here it came! How could he have believed that life had started anew for him? Gromov leisurely lit a cigarette and offered one to Fedor. Fedor's fingers shook as he reached for the cigarette. As if unaware of the agony he was causing, Gromov continued in a cordial and light tone:

"Well, then, that means, dear comrade Gavrilov, that we are in some way connected, you and I. Not too closely, to be sure, but still . . ."

He was talking now in a natural conversational tone. But years of experience had taught him the never-failing effect of pause in sapping the nerves of his victims, and pauses had become a part of his way of speaking. Never let a man relax too long! He paused, watching Fedor's fingers torturing the unused cigarette.

"Zena has a sister Vera, hasn't she? Vera was married to Michel Dolinin, wasn't she? He was killed fighting us?"

Must all the shadows of the past come out at once? Fedor kept nodding his head waiting to be butchered. But Gromov had had enough. One had to be careful with the older men, he decided. Their hearts weren't so steady, and he really wanted no harm done to Fedor. The visit had been meant to be a perfectly friendly visit; he had had no sinister intentions at all. The cat-and-mouse game had somehow crept into it out of sheer habit.

"As you well know, comrade Gavrilov, Vera has two daughters. Kira is married to Maxim Nazarov. But I wonder whether anyone in the family knows to whom Katya is married. Do you, for instance, know?"

Fedor shook his head. He had hardly ever seen Katya in his life, had not heard her name mentioned for many years, and had never given her a thought. What was the man driving at? Gromov laughed and rubbed his hands.

"Could you guess to whom she is married? Well, she is married to me, she is married to me. What do you say to that?"

Gromov was so pleased with Fedor's dumfounded expression that he gleefully beat his knees with his hands.

"I knew it would surprise you, I knew! What do you say, eh? We are relatives, aren't we?"

Now that Fedor studied Gromov's face closely he had a vague recollection of having seen that face before. Where?

"I saw Katya for the first time long ago," continued Gromov, "about ten years ago it was. She wasn't much more than a little girl then. She came to visit her grandmother, Kseniya Nazarov . . . I lived in the house then."

Of course! Now Fedor had it. He had seen him only once but he recalled it now. Gromov had been one of Natasha's "lame ducks," people she befriended, looked after when they were sick, sat with when they were lonely. Gromov had been working for the Cheka then; Natasha had helped him fight down the nightmares that tortured him during his attacks. Soon after Fedor saw him he had left the house, and no one in the family had ever heard of him again.

Once, shortly before an attack, Gromov had been sitting in Natasha's room when Katya came in on one of her rare visits. She was about sixteen then. It was summer and she had been wearing a white dress, white shoes, and a white ribbon tied around her blonde curls. With her white skin, blue eyes and artless smile, she had seemed to Gromov like an apparition from heaven.

That night his brain rocked between red and white, white and red. Between the apparition of a white angel and the red floods of blood. Out of long-forgotten days came the soft hands of a mother, the white dresses and merry smiles of sisters; came whiteness, the whiteness of snowy table linen, of flowers, of candles in a church. It was being pushed back by the sound of screams and shots, by the black filth and red blood of the Civil War and of the Cheka dungeons.

Shortly after Katya's visit, Gromov's attacks became so bad that he went into a hospital. There, in his nightmares, the girl in white beckoned to him, disappeared when he tried to reach her. He yelled and struggled—he had to get to the girl, she was his salvation from the red blood, and the nurses had to tie him to his bed. After he was well enough to return to his work and to normal life, he rarely saw blood in his dreams. But when he did, the girl in white appeared and her whiteness banished the red. In time her features became blurred, and he was not sure he remembered them.

Years later, in the spring of 1929, a year and a half before he made his call on Fedor, he saw the name of Katya Dolinin, on a list of inmates of a lumber camp in the Far North who were being sent back to Moscow for release. Gromov stared at the name in utter disbelief. It couldn't be she! He couldn't see his apparition in white, the girl whose delicate beauty had haunted his dreams, in the pitiless inferno which, as he well knew, was a prisoner's lumber camp in the Far North. But even in the darkish police picture he recognized her; and looking at the picture, he knew that he had never forgotten her, and that his salvation was still in her.

He read Katya's dossier closely. Unimportant as she was to the authorities, few details of her years in the North were omitted from the reports. The GPU worked well! Katya went to the camp as the accomplice of the well-known thief, Nikolka Heartbreak. She seemed to be passionately devoted to him. Gradually, under the conditions of camp life, she changed into a woman who, conscious of the effect of her beauty on men, used her body in payment for services— comfort, clothes, food, warmth—as easily and naturally as people paid for them with money. Gromov smiled. Katya's past made no difference to him. Her future would be his. She would want no services from anyone else.

He wrote out an order to send Katya Dolinin to him when she arrived in Moscow. This was not an unusual thing to do. Few victims of the GPU won complete freedom after their release, for they were good material as informants on former associates—political or criminal. The dread of falling again into the GPU net made them compliant. A young beautiful woman like Katya could hardly expect to be forgotten by the GPU after her release. The order that Gromov signed was a casual routine matter to his subordinates.

But Katya, in later years, could never feel that there had been anything casual about the matter at all. A casual routine matter—that sudden miraculous change from the filthy, crowded, rat-infested barracks of the prison camp, where the cold ate at her bones, to the luxury and warmth and spacious comfort of Gromov's apartment? A casual matter, for one who had always been terrified of the unknown, the unfamiliar, to be relieved overnight of panicky uncertainty about her future and enveloped in the security of her life as Gromov's wife? A casual, routine matter . . . Oh, no; if she was Gromov's salvation, he had most surely been hers.

Looking back, Katya could always recall every detail of that swift bewildering transition. She would see herself on the train again, as it crawled through the night toward Moscow, her face pressed to the window. There wasn't much she could see in the darkness, but she couldn't sleep, and she couldn't stand the sight of the snoring bodies, ugly in their relaxed abandonment, mouths open, limbs twisted together, heads resting on bellies, legs, backs, wherever they found a place to rest. Tears from the smoke of the locomotive, from the stinging tobacco of the guards, prickled behind Katya's eyes. She rubbed her eyes, and her hands felt rough. She looked at them. They were bad, rough and red, but not so bad as they had been during the first months in camp. Then they had been covered with cuts, bruises and calluses, always bleeding. Then she had been loading wood all day long, from early morning till late evening. That was before she had learned how to escape from work—the easiest thing in the world! Besides, she had still had Nikolka. But somehow life had pushed itself between them, with its persistent call for food, for warmth, for shelter. That was what made her so afraid of life now. How could she ever get those things for herself, when even Nikolka had failed? Wasn't he the one who, step by step, had taught her how to get from men what she needed, he who once had been ready to kill any man who looked at her? Would she have to get them again in the same way?

The high spires of Moscow's churches were seen in the morning fog. Katya crossed herself and started her morning toilet. There was no way to get out of the compartment over all the bodies, and there probably was no water in the car anyway. She spat on a corner of her grayish crumpled handkerchief and rubbed her face and as much of her neck as showed above her blouse, then wet her handkerchief again and rubbed under her armpits. She couldn't stand the pungent smell of her own perspiration. With a broken sidecomb, she tugged at her curls, first going through them with her fingers to untangle them, until she got them as fluffy as unwashed sooty hair could be. Then she took from her bundle the greatest treasure of all. Over nothing else had she watched so carefully as over this old battered powder box with a piece of lipstick in it. There was not much powder left and the lipstick could only be used by smearing the remnants of it on her finger. But it was real powder and real lipstick. She tucked her blouse tightly under her skirt, cleaned under her nails with a piece of cardboard, and tied a red kerchief around her head, mindful not to spoil the effect of the hair encircling her face. Finally, she threw the coat around her shoulders, and was ready for Moscow.

Huddled together, unwashed, unkempt, the group of women prisoners stood on the station platform. Katya kept as far away from them as the guards would let her. Men turned their heads to have another look at her, and she smiled defiantly with her eyes and red lips, and wrapped the coat tighter around her body. The guards were ready with the truck and the group was led away.

In the prison yard there was another wait, and from behind window bars Katya heard the familiar calls and invitations. A prison official whispered with the guards and they pointed out Katya to him. One of the guards disappeared behind a door and returned with a prison matron.

"Prisoner Katya Dolinin," the guard called out, and, forgetting her defiant smile, Katya stepped forward, her eyes anxious, and fearful. "Follow her," the guard ordered curtly. The matron led her through endless halls to a narrow corridor. The air grew hotter as they approached the corridor. A moist cloud poured out from under a door.

A bathhouse! Katya could not control her joy. She forgot even to be afraid. Who cared what happened as long as she got a bath! When had she last had a bath? She couldn't call a bath the few buckets of cold water the fifty women would get once in a long long while. And never any soap, and never any hot water.

The matron opened the door and pointed wordlessly to a bench. Yes, this was a real bath, with a bench to sit on, and for undressing. She threw off her filthy clothes. The matron, still without a word, pointed to the door from under which thick clouds of steam were coming, and Katya went through. It was not a room, it was paradise!

Katya could never remember how long she stayed in the bath. It probably was not more than an hour but it seemed days to her. She scratched her scalp with her nails till it hurt. She wouldn't mind the pain, if only she got the creeping things out of it. Again and again she soaped her hair with the cake of real soap, and reveled in the foam which, black at first, had gradually become snowy white. She soaped and rinsed her body at least a dozen times. She looked at her glowing body, its womanliness restored, the womanliness that had been so outrageously, so indignantly debased from lack of soap, water, and sanitary comforts, and, exhausted, lay down on the bench and let the hot steam envelop and caress her. No, she couldn't waste time that way. She soaped herself again and stood again under the shower and poured more buckets of hot water over her body.

The matron knocked at the door:

"Enough!"

Regretfully, Katya left the bath. Her own clothes were gone and in their place was a pile of fresh underwear and a clean gray cotton dress. The sight of them reconciled her to having left the bathhouse. To have every stitch on her body clean—for the first time in three years! The underwear she had taken to the camp she had washed to shreds in cold soapless water, and in the midst of all that filth and the cold one forgot all about clean things anyway. The matron reappeared with a glass of tea and two thick slices of black bread. The tea was hot and sweet, and the bread was fresh. Katya did not waste a crumb of the beautiful bread.

"Want to sleep?" The matron's voice was grudging and mean.

Did she want to sleep? She lay down on the hard bench and covered herself with the coat. She was not really conscious of covering herself with the coat; she was asleep before that.

In her sleep Katya was on the train again. The train was rocking, rocking more and more till it was almost impossible to hold on. The rocking must stop, she would fall out, there was nothing to hold on to. But the rocking did not stop, and Katya felt her body flying in the air.

"Get up! Get up! Get up!" the wheels were screaming. Now the wheels took on a human voice.

"Get up! Get up!" The human voice was screaming right into her ear.

Katya opened her eyes. The matron was shaking her roughly:

"Get up! Get up!"

Even the unpleasant old woman could not take away from Katya the blissful voluptuous sensation of having a clean body and clean clothes. Her hair was dry now and she combed it till it crackled, and admired its sheen in the mirror. They gray dress was not too becoming but it was clean, and the mirror told Katya that it did not detract from the pink, fresh look her bath and sleep had given her.

Through the same long halls, the matron brought Katya back to the yard where an armed guard took over and led her to another building where the windows had no iron bars and were high and clean. Again Katya walked through many long halls. But these halls were wide and carpeted, they had glass doors every few steps, and an armed guard standing at each door. Katya's guard showed their passes many times before they reached the room where they were going. It was an office with desks and secretaries. The guard turned to talk to one of the secretaries.

Katya's fears returned. What was it all about? What were they going to do to her? Her knees shook when a door opened and she was told to go in. She had not seen the door before. It really was not a door; it was part of the wall, and nothing betrayed the room behind that wall. It was a high-ceilinged room with deep soft rugs and well-polished furniture. A large dark desk stood near the window. Why was she here? She had heard many stories of tortures and third-degree questioning in this building. But why in this beautiful room? And why she? She was nothing but the former sweetheart of a common thief. She was not even a political . . .

"Sit down," a voice came from behind the desk.

She sat down on the edge of a chair, her eyes down, her knees now shaking violently.

"Don't be afraid of me, I am not going to harm you . . . ever."

Katya raised her eyes and looked questioningly at the man who had spoken those extraordinary words. What she saw made her heart stop pounding. She was on familiar ground, pleasantly at home under a man's admiring eyes. So that's what it was! But who was he? And how had he known of her existence? She was not frightened any more. She looked at him, her blue shining eyes holding out under the burning stare of his.

The girl in white! Even in that drab gray she was the girl in white who had saved his sanity. To touch her! To open her lips and drink her! To hold her! He pressed his fingers into the upholstery of his chair. He must get hold of himself and go slowly.

Katya had completely recovered, and while Gromov was fighting down his excitement, she looked at him appraisingly. Not very much to look at. He was slight and rather colorless. But there was a fire in his eyes which had promise . . . Among the many things Katya had found out about men was that there was no relation between their lovemaking and their looks. Anyway, what difference did that make to her? She was not a romantic girl any more: she gave her body not for love but for what she could get for it. People paid with whatever they had: she paid with her body. Some men had cheated her. They took the payment and did not deliver. But every one of them had been eager to accept the payment. There was no mistake about this man either. Well, she was ready to pay. What would she get for it?

Gromov was still staring at her. What should he say? How should he approach her? He had erased her past. The woman he was looking at was to him the symbol of purity and goodness, and he wanted to worship her. How could he say it to her?

"You are surprised, aren't you? I had prepared a story to explain it, but . . . I want to tell you the truth."

Katya did not expect to take seriously whatever he was going to tell her. Men had all kinds of approaches. The end was always the same, whatever their approach. This one seemed to be having a hard time working himself up. Well, if he needed to tell a story for that, it was all right with her. But when Gromov started to talk, Katya's eyes opened wide. Natasha, grandmother Kseniya, the white dress, the last white dress she ever wore. . . . No, this was not just a story. And the man was not working himself up; he was pleading for her love! The fool, the wonderful fool! Didn't he know she didn't have to be pleaded with? A promise of food and shelter would do. And he sounded so serious, so touchingly serious. Her heart softened. No one had ever talked to her like this. What could she do to thank him for talking to her this way? Even though his promises would probably never be kept, she must thank him for talking this way. She knew only one way of saying thank you; nobody ever wanted any other thanks from her.

She stood up and reached out her arms to him. More gratitude welled up in her. He didn't throw her on a couch as she had expected. He didn't tear buttons and he didn't hurt her to satisfy his desire quickly. He took her hands, and he had tears in his eyes. He held her gently in his arms when their lips touched. And the kiss was not a quick preliminary to the next step. It was a long tender kiss. She felt how strongly his body was longing for her but he only kissed her hands gently, finger after finger, again and again, worshiping her as no man had ever done.

"Katya, will you marry me . . . my wife? Will you, Katya?"

It was easy for Ilya Gromov, high in the hierarchy of the GPU, to write off as dismissed the case of Katya Dolinin and it was easy for him to take an immediate vacation. He was going with his bride to the beautiful Caucasian mountain retreat which the GPU had built for its members on the shores of the Black Sea. During the two days he needed to prepare for the trip, Katya went to visit her mother. It was late afternoon. Vera sat at the window using the last light of day for her solitaire. She was so absorbed by it that she did not hear Katya open the door. Katya flung a bag with sweets on the table and ran to her. Vera did not recognize her in the dark room.

"Who is it? Who? Who are you?" Vera's voice was high and stinging, and Katya drew back. In the camp she used to dream of friendly voices, and the one she heard most often was the melodious silvery voice of her mother when she and Kira were children.

"It's me, Katya, your daughter."

"What are you doing here? I didn't know they ever let people out of jail."

That was all. Vera did not make a move toward Katya, and Katya remained standing in the middle of the room, her eyes full of sudden tears. She had dreamed so often of coming home!

"Well, take your things off, don't stand there like a pillar. It's too early to make a light. Your eyes are young; you can see well enough without light. If you want food, you'll have to wait. They are in the kitchen now."

The way she said "they" gave Katya a chill. How could anyone nurse so much hatred for so many years? Her heart overflowed again with gratitude for Gromov. If not for him this was where she would have to live, with a mother consumed with hatred. Even for her, her own daughter, whom she hadn't seen for three years, she had only a voice rasping with anger.

"And what do you intend to do with yourself? Don't get the idea that you can count on me. The few trifles you left me are gone. I can hardly take care of myself, so don't you expect anything from me. And don't expect anything from your dear sister; she doesn't even know she has a mother. Don't expect anything from anybody."

Katya made a move to the door.

"If you want to wash up, use the basin here. I never go to the bathroom, so I won't have to clean it. You don't expect me to clean for the whole damned bunch of them."

Katya was aghast. No language could shock her any longer. But Mother! Vera mistook Katya's horrified expression.

"Oh, you can use the toilet. Do you think I gave that up, too? Unfortunately, I can't."

Katya left as quickly as she could. Before she left, she made another attempt to break through the armor of her mother's bitterness, to put her arms around her, but Vera pushed her away. She did not ask why Katya had come, where she was going, what she was going to do with herself. Katya started to tell her but Vera would not let her.

"I don't care . . . as long as you take care of yourself and don't depend on me."

Katya would have felt better if her mother had even made some claim on her; but apparently she wanted only to be left alone.

That evening Katya knelt before Gromov and kissed his hands. Thanks to him, thanks only to him, she did not have to stay with her mother. She could not have stayed there anyway; she would have walked the streets and gone with the first man who wanted her. And there would have been a second man . . . a third . . . a fourth . . . and then jail again. She did not know how to work, there wasn't a thing she could do. Instead she was safe and warm and loved, and she slept in a soft bed with clean sheets and warm blankets. And she was clean, every bit of her body was clean from head to foot, and she wore a clean nightgown. Before she fell asleep, Katya tried to tell Gromov what she felt. "Never, never shall I forget what you've done for me . . ."

It was late in the season and there were few people in the GPU sanatorium where Gromov took his wife. They had the privacy they wanted. Gromov moved about slowly and spoke softly. Life seemed a dream from which he was afraid a brusque move or word might waken him. He would have been happy enough simply to give himself wholly to Katya and to have her near him. But he had more than that. She clung to him. She did not want to let him out of her sight or out of her arms. She clung to him because it was unbelievably good to be protected. She clung to him because of the gratitude she felt, and she clung to him because of the physical enjoyment he gave her. His slight body was strong in love.

After the month in the Caucasus, Katya found herself the mistress of a real home. A real home was something she had not had since she was fourteen. Gromov's apartment was in the new wing of the GPU building. It had a bedroom, a dining room, a study-living room, a bathroom, a toilet, a kitchen, and a pantry, and they shared it with no one. It also had mahogany furniture and Oriental rugs and fine china and silver. It also had a cook who met Katya with grim suspicion. Was the new mistress going to watch over the ration books and the accounts? Gromov had never done that. But it seemed that Katya was only too ready to close both eyes and both ears, and the household was left in complete charge of the cook, to everybody's satisfaction.

A life of dreamlike unreality began for Katya, a life she had not known existed in Soviet Russia. She did not believe it at first when Gromov told her:

"Remember, Katya, my angel, anything you want . . . just say so. There is nothing, nothing at all you have to deny yourself."

She tried it out. She wanted pure silk for a dress, she wanted patent leather shoes; she got them. She wanted an eiderdown comforter; she got it. She wanted linen sheets and a damask tablecloth; she got them. She wanted knitting wool and silk yarn for embroidery; she got them. She wanted a piano, she wanted a victrola with plenty of records, she wanted an original painting in the living room. She got everything she wanted. She never asked Gromov where he got things that had not been available in stores for many years; she was not interested in the why and how of things as long as she got them.

Had Katya asked, Gromov would hardly have disclosed to her the secret of the well-guarded GPU storerooms. To the treasures from czarist palaces and princely mansions brought there during the first turbulent days of the revolution new riches were added every day. The confiscated possessions of people who were arrested and exiled, besides the harvest of the customs officials, found their way there. The GPU watched the Soviet borders carefully not only to prevent foreign enemies from coming into the country but also to prevent luxuries from a decaying bourgeois world to corrupt the morals of the Soviet citizens. Silk stockings, records, delicacies, cameras, or any other gifts sent by friends abroad rarely reached those for whom they were intended. They were kept safe in the storehouses till asked for by the deserving few or sent to a commission store to be sold mostly to foreigners.

Few government leaders used the privilege of eating from gold plates or covering their wives' legs with pure silk. They were hard-working simple people and so were their women. Typewriters and fountain pens were the treasures they chiefly coveted. But to the disgust of many an old revolutionary fighter, the power and glamour of the GPU and army worked like a magnet on the pretty young women for whom good clothes and good meals today meant more than the Socialist millennium. The top GPU and army men became the storerooms' best customers.

Katya met some of the young wives of Gromov's colleagues, and they initiated her into the secrets of the best beauty parlor, the best dressmaker, the best dancing teacher, the best shoemaker, and all the other "bests." With all this Katya was enchanted and her days were pleasantly full. Almost from the first, however, she had cherished a particular desire, which finally was fulfilled a few days after Gromov told Fedor of their marriage, when she played hostess at a family dinner. Her mother refused to come. Maxim, Kira, Peter, Natasha, Fedor, and Ludmilla all were there. For two days Katya had Gromov's car at her disposal. Back and forth the chauffeur drove her and the cook to the well-supplied GPU store until there was no space in the kitchen for any more bags of food. Katya helped the cook marinate, fry, and bake. She felt well recompensed for her efforts by the startled looks on her visitors' faces.

"Come, come, don't stand there as if your feet were glued to the floor!" Laughing, Katya pulled Maxim into the dining room. One after another, the others followed and stood, stunned by the bright lights, the luxuriously set table, and the rich smells of the food. In the winter of 1930, not one of them had seen anything of the kind for a long time. It took several toasts in vodka and their hosts' spirited energy to help them recover.

They sat around the table eating and talking about Afinogenov's latest play, Leonov's much-discussed book, and that new amazing musical genius, the youthful Shostakovich. The guests seemed to be at ease—that is, if one did not observe them too closely. But Peter noticed, with a little stab of pity, how hard Natasha tried to hide her red chapped hands under the shawl she wore, ostensibly for warmth, but actually to conceal the shabbiness of the only dress she possessed. Her eyes seemed fascinated by a bowl of sugar standing in front of her. Neither of them had seen a bowl filled with sugar for years, and he wondered if she was thinking of their own empty cupboard.

Ludmilla's thoughts had gone back twenty-five years to the first dinner party she gave for the family. There had been Anton, Vera, Michel, Zena, Pavel, Fedor's mother, the young officers. Kira and Katya had been babies then, Maxim an enthusiastic youngster, Vera, Moscow's belle. What had they been talking about then? The war with Japan, the czar's injustices, their hopes for a free happier Russia. They had said what they thought openly, though it was dangerous, though there were people present who could betray them. Now around this table they were not talking openly about things that really mattered to them. Now they were afraid—afraid of their host, of the GPU-man Gromov.

Gromov kept filling the plates and the glasses, calling for toasts, laughing loudly at every hint of anything to laugh at, and he saw to it that there was never a pause in the conversation. Katya seconded him. The wine went to her head almost as strongly as the feeling that she was on top of life. Didn't she have the strongest arm to lean on, wasn't she the one who would never again have anything to fear in life. Maxim, Kira, Ludmilla, Natasha—in the past, who had she been, the silly little girl, compared to them. And now they were sitting around her table; she was their hostess. She loved them all, she loved everybody, she loved the whole world.

Her gaiety and her warm care for her guests were genuine. But it was with a great sigh of relief that her departing guests heard the guard lock the front door behind them.

"Never," swore Maxim, "never again will I set foot in this building. Neither my wife's sister nor the devil himself will ever drag me here again."

"Don't be so sure of that, Maxim," Kira teased. "Have you forgotten that another wing of this building has rooms for unwilling guests?"

"Ah, so that's how badly you want to get rid of me? Now, here, get your punishment! Get it, get it, get it!"

Every snowball was a hit. Kira struck back. Peter joined them. Even Natasha couldn't hold back. The cold strong air, the sparkling snow, and above all the relief of being out of the GPU house made them feel sportive. Ludmilla laughed out loud when the soft snow covered her face. Fedor couldn't remember when he had heard her laugh last. They all kissed saying good-by, laughing because of their disheveled locks and wet faces, and because for a moment life had become young again. They were sure that this time they would definitely keep the promise they had so often made to one another in the past and always broken—to meet often.

## CHAPTER 27
## *Natasha and Peter*

THE newspaper Peter used as a shade over the lamp shifted and the light fell on Natasha's sleeping face. All evening the newspaper had kept slipping and Peter patiently kept fixing it. This time, instead of shading the light, he turned it out and closing his eyes leaned back in the chair. What was the use of going on? His eyes were burning from lack of sleep. The drawings before him filled him with disgust. He could not improve them, he hated them. How could he improve on work that he hated? If only he could get his hands into the trunk that stood in the corner. Covered with a Paisley shawl, the trunk served as a settee and his old plans were buried there under rags and junk. No, better to forget about those plans—someone might see them. And he must, he must watch his step now, for who knew what would be declared wrong tomorrow or in the next hour? Better to do nothing at all on his own, only what someone above told him to do, even if it meant designing things that nauseated him.

All the bitterness Peter felt showed in his smile. As if being careful had ever helped him before. If it had, would they still be living in this hole? Every time he had raised his head in hope, he had been knocked down again. No, being careful would not do him much good but at least he might escape too much harm.

Peter went to bed without taking off his clothes. Only two hours were left before the new day but sleep would not come. He was thinking of those old plans in the trunk and with the thought of them came back pages of the past years. The time after Natasha's reinstatement four years ago. He hadn't shown himself a great hero in those days. He had been scared, plain scared, his head deep in the sand. He'd wanted to work, he'd wanted to be with his family, that's all he'd wanted. Then when it was all over and he was sure they were out of danger he'd lifted his head again. The sky had seemed clear. His work was highly praised; Natasha graduated and got a job as a textile engineer, and they'd started hoping again for some improvement in their life. They were still suffocating in their two crowded rooms. An evening at home had been little joy. The children did not let them live; they did not let the children live.

On the strength of his position, they'd been entitled to better quarters, more food, more clothing, and if he hadn't dreaded the thought of the inevitable investigation he'd have put in an application. Good thing he'd been such a coward, as it turned out. But it was the last thing in the world he'd expected, having the government reject those plans for the new apartment houses. The months of work they'd put in on them! And they'd followed instructions to the letter!

Peter stared into the dark, painfully remembering the violent attacks in the press that had immediately followed the rejection. Denunciation upon renunciation had been showered on them for "loss of revolutionary vigilance," for "succumbing to bourgeois influence," for "ignoring the new joyful spirit of the country." "Enemies have wormed themselves in . . ." newspaper editorials said. "Instead of the beautiful houses they used to build for the bourgeoisie, these hirelings of capitalism think their ugly boxes are good enough for the proletariat. . . . They turned their eyes away from beauty and gave us ugliness . . ." The "ugly boxes" were the modern straight-lined buildings of which the young Soviet architects were proud. And "ugly boxes" became the refrain of the attack. The contracts with the foreign architects were canceled and they too were attacked as counterrevolutionaries who had misused their profession to undermine the morale of the proletariat.

Peter's name was singled out among those accused of sabotaging the true taste of the Soviet workers. He was no longer trusted to work independently. Incompetents, equipped with vulgar taste and obsolete textbooks, stood behind him and gave him orders. He was told to forget everything he had ever done or dreamed about before. He was told to paste Greek goddesses, laughing fauns and nymphs, and columns on buildings under construction wherever space could be found for them. The same figures and columns which were meant to symbolize the new joyful life of the proletariat had to be added to the finished and half-finished plans of new houses. Peter soon realized, however, that he and his comrades were not the only victims of the new party line that followed Stalin's momentous pronouncement that the First Five-Year Plan was a success and that "life had become joyous and gay."

Peter had an old friend, a painter, who in 1929, at the beginning of the plan, had been attacked in the press because of his inability to adjust himself quickly enough to the change of line; he had still been painting a woman with her hands in her lap doing nothing, or a sunset without a working figure embellishing it. When the line changed again in 1932 and Peter's work was pronounced all wrong, this same painter was under attack once more, and his paintings were not allowed to be exhibited. He complained to Peter:

"I would rather do anything now than paint. You know I love to paint faces, any faces, there are no dull faces for me. Every face has something to say, and I don't know of anything more exciting than to get this something out. I can't paint a face now. All they want me to show is a stupid empty smile and lots of teeth. Where do they get all those teeth? I never thought people had that many teeth, and all of them made to measure, big, white, square . . . at least that is what I am supposed to paint."

Woe to the musicians who could not forget quickly enough that somewhere still lurked sadness and tragedy; who did not remember that all life had become "gay and joyful." Anathema on the heads of theater producers, educators, philosophers, poets who still took the revolution seriously, who still believed that a revolution created new forms of art, new ways of living, of loving, of thinking, and who still groped and experimented. Threaten them, attack them, ridicule them, do anything to silence them if they don't conform! Down with doubt, discussion, wisdom, analysis! Long live silk dresses, permanent waves, ice-cream cones, open-air cafés, dancing classes, parades, new pictures of the Leader, new marching songs, and conformity, mediocrity, piece-work, speed-up work, Greek columns and smiles, smiles and Greek columns! The Leader had spoken!

Peter bit his nails and suppressed a moan. He must not wake Natasha. She couldn't help him, nobody could help him. Besides, she didn't agree with him. She thought there were many reasons to be happy now. How could she understand him? How could anyone understand him? He'd be laughed at if he tried to tell what hurt him. He would have laughed too if he were, say, a bookkeeper, or a machinist, or a miner, and an architect had come to him and said that he was ready to kill himself because he was forced to design new lavatories with Greek columns for the Park of Culture and Rest. And would they care if he told them that this was a monstrosity which could drive a man to insanity, that these lavatories were squat and dumpy, rising only a few feet above the ground, and that a Greek column had to be taller than a few feet. Ah, what was the use? The hideous lavatories with the fat Greek columns were probably not worse than the other monstrosities he had to help build. But for some reason these lavatories hurt him most of all.

An hour more, and they would be getting up. At least, Natasha did not have to jump out of bed now at dawn to stand in line for milk and bread. There were no lines, no ration books, there was enough to eat in this blessed year of 1934; they had enough wood, the children had warm clothes. That was why Natasha was so grateful. She couldn't get over the new food stores, and being treated in the stores like a human being, and taking purchases home in neatly tied packages. Peter remembered the day when she first brought home a can of paint and matching yarn for her new stockings. She was as pleased as though the world revolution had arrived. It was the day the newspapers announced the Soviet-French pact. It was hard for him to swallow the way the editorials lauded the French government, which up till then had been called reactionary, corrupt, and worthless. On the day Laval arived in Moscow and was feted as a loved brother and friend, Peter had an argument about it with Natasha.

"Weren't we always told that the duty of a French worker in case of war was to rise in arms against his bourgeois government and overthrow it?" he'd asked.

"Certainly," Natasha had agreed. "What else should he do? Fight on the side of his government, his archenemy, against other soldiers who are his brothers in class?"

"Right! But don't you see he can't do this any more? His archenemy, the French government, is our friend now. The French worker can't rise against a friend of the Soviet Union, can he? He will have to support his government, even if it means killing his brothers."

"Oh, Peter, can't you stop your eternal doubting and questioning?" Natasha had been impatient. "Where will it get you? Why don't you have more trust? Our government is fulfilling every promise made us. It tells us to have a little more patience and all our hardships will be over. Hardships are ending. Don't you see they are ending? So why don't you have faith that everything else will be worked out for our good?"

"But what about the French worker? What about his good?" Peter had persisted.

Natasha had shaken her head in despair over his stubbornness.

That was all she saw—that he was stubborn. Every discussion ended the same way. Natasha had one answer to everything. Whatever the Soviet government did could only be for the welfare of the people. Those on top were devoted to the interests of the people; they should be trusted. There was no use arguing with Natasha. She had completely relinquished her right to think and to form her own opinion. She, who in the past had so firmly denounced any attempt to introduce a material incentive for serving the Soviet state, saw nothing wrong in the money prizes being distributed right and left for speed-up work. She saw nothing wrong in anything. She was completely taken in by those confounded cans of paint and the abundance of food and the many new movies and the Children's Park and the magnificent subway that was being built. Those who supplied her with these things had her complete confidence.

Thinking about it, Peter was getting angrier and angrier. Didn't Natasha see what was happening to them? How small and smug they were getting! She had cried when many years ago she'd been teased about her starched curtains and asked why she didn't get a canary for her room. A canary! The symbol of the contemptible, petty bourgeois life! How insulted Natasha had felt then. Yesterday all the papers had printed the picture of a worker's new apartment. It showed rooms filled with doilies and frills, a bed covered with a fancy bedspread, heavy, dust-catching furniture and hangings, and a cage with a canary! Even the *Pravda* editorial had a kind word for the coziness which a canary added to a room. Natasha had looked at the picture and said dreamily:

"A day will soon come when everyone will live in an apartment like that. It's been worth all our sacrifices."

Why remind her that they had expected from the revolution much more than doilies and a canary?

The alarm clock went off and interrupted Peter's brooding. The day began. As usual, Volik had the floor at breakfast; he always woke up full of energy. He was talking about what their teacher had said yesterday:

". . . and, she said, you must be thankful day and night that you are Soviet children. There are no happier people in this world than the Soviet peoples, she said. Outside of the Soviet Union life is one long nightmare for those who are not rich capitalists, it is a life, she said, with never any pleasure and never any rest . . ."

Peter ignored Natasha's under-the-table nudges. "And she didn't mention anything good at all, nothing at all? Are you sure?"

"Of course not, father. What could she mention? Ah, you know it yourself, father." Volik knowingly winked at Peter. "You can't

fool me, you're just teasing me. You know as well as the teacher does"
—Volik was full of fire and gestures—"how workers are exploited out
there and have no protection at all, that women are treated like
slaves, and that children don't go to school, they are too poor, they
have no shoes and they are always hungry."

"I was under the impression," persisted Peter, "that in some countries, for instance, England, America, Germany, they had trade unions
and even compulsory education for children. I thought that most
people there knew how to read and to write."

"Don't be ridiculous, father! Where did you get such funny notions?
You better not repeat them. You will make me ashamed of you, my
own father saying such things!"

The conversation got lost in the rush of packing lunches and hurry-
ing off to school and work.

Had Peter seen Natasha's face on her way to work, he would have
been surprised and probably pleased. She looked scared and lost, as
she sometimes used to look in the days when she still dared to admit
that something had shaken the building of her faith. Now she would
never admit to Peter that the building was not all the solid rock she
pretended it was. And she avoided admitting it to herself. She repeated to herself so often what was being constantly told them, that
everything they had hoped for was coming true and that it was all
coming true in exactly the way they had hoped, that most of the
time she sincerely believed it.

She usually succeeded in quickly pushing out of her mind whatever
might soften the solid rock. That morning it wasn't easy. She told
herself that Volik's teacher was right, that her children were lucky to
be growing up in the Soviet Union, in the land of a bright future, and
that they must always be conscious of how lucky they were. But . . .
must they be told lies about the outside world? There were, of course,
many places in the world where there was exploitation, poverty,
oppression. But were workers defenseless in every other country?
Women were not slaves everywhere else in the world. Children went
to school in all civilized countries. Why couldn't Soviet children be
told the truth? Would that diminish their pride and faith in the
Soviet Union? Natasha detested lies, and that was sheer lying, however she tried to understand and explain it. Why should Volik grow
up as if he were a man from Mars, with no idea of what went on in
the world? Her Volik, her Maya, and all the other Voliks and Mayas.

What should she do? Talk to the teacher? Now she was being
ridiculous. Funny, that was exactly what Volik had told his father—
Don't be ridiculous! She knew perfectly well the teachers didn't say
anything on their own. If those were their orders, there was nothing

any mother or anyone else could do about it. Volik was happy and satisfied. To him the Soviet government, the Communist party, and its Leader were on a pedestal, high above anything else in this world. Any word coming from them was sacred truth. Anyone doubting that word was a traitor and an enemy. Volik had great faith in his future. And he was right! Natasha agreed with him in that. Even if there were trade unions and compulsory education in some capitalist countries, no one could deny that no child could look so confidently into the future as a Soviet child. But . . . why lies? Wasn't the truth about the Soviet Union good enough to enable them to stand any truth about the outside world? Why lies? They hadn't lied in the beginning.

There she was, back again where she didn't want to be; it was too hard to silence the questions. Natasha remembered well what they had been taught then. Yes, we have made the revolution, they were told; in this we are ahead of the whole world. But for centuries we have been behind while the other countries have been marching ahead. We have to catch up with them. And they were also told in what way the others were ahead and what Soviet Russia had to catch up with. They were told about trade unions and schools and health centers and low infant mortality in advanced capitalist countries. They were told that they had a great deal to learn from Austria, Scandinavia, England, Germany, America, France. They were told to study well whatever good there was anywhere in the world, and then to perfect it in Soviet Russia. And when they had done it and shown the world a country that had combined in itself the good of the whole world and that it had provided its people with happiness and satisfaction, who could doubt that all other countries would follow their example? That was what they had been taught in the beginning, and Natasha's heart beat faster when she recalled how inspiring that vision had been. Why had they been urged to find out the truth about the achievements and progress of the outside world then, and why must they be told lies now? Why?

This was a bad day for Natasha. Besides working as an engineer in the Trekhgorka Textile Plant, she also conducted there two afternoons a week classes for the women workers. This was one of her class days. She had prepared a special program for that afternoon, because it was March 8, the Women's International Day. The inspector of adult courses sat for a few moments in her class; afterwards he called her in for a talk. The talk was short.

"We've had complaints about you again, Natasha," he said. "The women say your language is much too difficult for them to understand. You must adjust yourself to them."

"I am using the simplest possible language," Natasha protested. "You wouldn't want me to speak ungrammatically."

"I don't care how you speak as long as the women understand you. That will be all."

On her way home from work Natasha recalled this and was furious. Had she for years polished her language in school only to forget everything now? Hadn't their idea been to bring the masses of people to a higher level of education, to raise them to the standard of the more fortunate, educated people? It certainly had not been to proletarianize the language, as so many did now, by bad grammar and profanity. Hadn't Lenin urged them to achieve a mastery of the Russian language? His language was certainly clean and clear. There was no cheapness and vulgarity in it, and certainly no attempt to stoop to a lower level.

As she approached their house Natasha's thoughts were interrupted by the children playing in front of it. Their games were rough and seemed to Natasha to involve a great deal of shoving, knocking down, and name calling. Volik was one of the noisiest. He saw Natasha, grinned, but did not pause in his play, which was sitting astride a smaller boy, boxing the boy's ears, and shouting at the top of his voice.

It was a rough way to play on the whole, but, Natasha thought, it was better so. What good would it do him to be sensitive and quiet like Maya? Volik was happier the way he was, taking everything in his stride, never worrying about anything. Why should he? Weren't there enough people to do his worrying for him? There was Stalin, who like a loving father watched over all Soviet children and cared for their needs. There were the Comsomol and Pioneer leaders, who were the representatives of the party—of Stalin. And there were the teachers, who carried out what Stalin thought was best for the children. With his whole heart Volik meant it when with his classmates he recited in unison, "Thank you, comrade Stalin, for a happy childhood!" Stalin was the sun that shone over his, Volik's, life, and under the cover of this sun there was nothing in the world for him to fear or to worry about.

Natasha knew that as dear to Volik as Stalin was Lenin. Volik cut out every picture he saw of Lenin in a newspaper or magazine, and collected them all. He had many times visited Lenin's mausoleum, standing in line for hours. Natasha smiled, remembering Volik's rebellion against his name, which was a diminutive of Lenin's name, Vladimir. That was when he had been very little, and when he had had constantly to hear, "Have you forgotten what your name stands for? Don't you know what you owe to this name?" He had heard it when he wouldn't take his afternoon nap in the kindergarten, when he tore his pants, when he refused to eat, when he cried because his mother wasn't at home. It did not help at all that the many thousands of other little Voliks and Volodyas had to bear it too. And then, when on Lenin's memorial day their kindergarten teacher read to them about Lenin's childhood, and Volik discovered that as a boy Lenin too had torn his pants and fought with other boys and ignored meal- and bedtimes, it had endeared Lenin to his heart more than the most eulogistic words ever could. That day saw the beginning of his Lenin-worship.

Walking up the stairs, Natasha could hear Volik's voice, she could hear it in the room even though the windows were closed. It warmed her heart to listen to the clear, strong voice. The maid was setting the table for supper. They had an elderly woman now, Akimovna. Natasha would have preferred a young woman, but the young women either got married or went to work in factories. If only Akimovna wouldn't pray so much and mumble and grumble most of the time. Nothing was good now, she found; people were bad, food was bad, money was bad, the weather was bad. But despite her grumbling, her heart was warm and kind, and Natasha never had to worry about her neglecting the children—the trouble was that she was much too much devoted to them and never stopped worrying and fretting over them. When she first came it looked as if she would not stay; there was a never-ending quarrel between her and Volik. He insisted that there was no God, she would cross herself and call God's mercy on his head for saying such sinful words. Finally, Natasha persuaded Akimovna not to tell Volik that there was a God and made Volik promise not to argue with Akimovna that there was none. The children grew used to Akimovna's grumbling, and as long as she wasn't too insistent that they mind her everything went well.

Akimovna greeted Natasha with concern:

"Well, there you are, dear, cold and tired. The house is quiet now; why don't you stretch out till bedlam breaks loose again?"

Natasha thought the idea of stretching out was a good one, for in the evening they were all going to their district's Woman's Day celebration.

"Where is Maya?"

"Where should the little pigeon be? With the neighbors' children, playing. Don't you worry, she will be in soon enough. She will smell that Mother is home. That's it, cover your feet, close your eyes."

Little pigeon! Natasha liked the way Akimovna called Maya "little pigeon." It reminded her of her own childhood, of grandmother Kseniya, of other friendly people who had called her that. Maya needed warmth and tenderness. Life would be hard for her. She didn't take things as lightly as Volik did; she was easily hurt.

Natasha's heart began to beat fast, as it always did when she thought of the days when she and Maya were both very hurt. That had been two years ago. Since then she had learned to live with her pain, but the memory of the night that the note from that horrible woman fell out of Peter's pocket was still piercingly sharp.

The children had gone to bed. Peter was at a meeting and she was alone in the room mending his trousers when the note dropped out of a pocket. She picked it up and added it to the little pile of things she had emptied from the pockets. A casual glance at the note written on office stationery stopped her. What would the word "darling" be doing on an office memo? Startled, Natasha read the note. It was full of endearments, of reminders of shared intimacies, and it was signed "Your adoring Murka."

At first Natasha felt nothing but nauseating disgust at the vulgar tone of the letter. But then the hammer blow went down. So that was why Peter had left her alone at nights! And she had thought that he had finally come to his senses, that he had realized there was enough to bind the two of them without physical love. And while she'd been priding herself on their superior relationship, he was finding solace in orgies with that cheap, silly thing Murka! The way the girl wrote about their love, it must be orgies. It was not their own pure love! What would Murka know about their kind of love? Not she! Natasha's tears changed into angry sobs when she thought of the girl to whom Peter had turned. Natasha knew her. She was a secretary in Peter's office, and stood out among the other girls because of her frizzy blonde hair with a baby bow in it, her china-blue doll's eyes, and her tight clothes which undressed rather than dressed her plump little figure. That he had chosen a woman like that was what made it so terrible!

If only it were someone else! But Natasha couldn't lie, not even now. That was not true; she was only trying to fool herself. Someone else would have been just as terrible. It was not because Peter had chosen the vulgar stupid Murka but because he had another woman at all. Natasha had sometimes told herself that someday this would have to happen, that normal men and women must have physical love, that if Peter went away from her it wouldn't be his fault. But now that the moment had arrived, she found that neither her mind nor her heart was ready to accept it. Forgetting about the children, the neighbors, Akimovna, Natasha threw herself down on the couch and gave way to violent, shuddering sobs. It was long before midnight; the apartment was noisy with many voices, and the neighbors did not hear her. Volik was a sound sleeper. But, as she learned the next day to her dismay, Maya had heard her and watched her, terror-stricken, too frightened to move or call out. And until Maya fell asleep from exhaustion, she must have witnessed, without understanding, at least part of the scene that followed when Peter came home.

Natasha heard his step on the stair and, by the time he walked into the room, she was almost calm. Only her hands betrayed her; they shook uncontrollably as she held out the note. Peter glanced at it and his face went white. Then swiftly he crossed over and sat down beside her on the couch, and held her hands tightly.

"It is out now. I am sorry, believe me, Natasha, that it came to you this way."

"It is the end of us, Peter, isn't it?" She struggled to keep her voice even.

"What are you talking about? This has nothing to do with you and me, nothing at all."

"So it is not true?" She was still very quiet.

"It is not true that this is the end of us, Natasha; but the rest is true."

"You are not going to leave us . . . and go live with her?"

"Of course, I am not going to leave you. Here, with you and the children, is where I belong and where I want to be. The other thing has nothing to do with us, I assure you. If sleeping together were all you and I had in common we would have been separated long ago. I haven't made human nature the way it is but neither can I change it or go against it. I tried hard to be faithful to you—not that I believe in any of this nonsense about being faithful. But I knew it would hurt you and I didn't want to hurt you. Natasha, you are not a child. You know the facts of life; don't close your eyes to them. Neither Murka nor any other woman could have come close to me if my body had been satisfied. Sometimes it was not only the hunger of my body that made me go there. I relax there. You know I never can really relax here. Please, Natasha, listen even if it hurts; I want you to know the truth. Murka leaves my soul and my mind empty but she is one of those women who believes in catering to a man. It may be old-fashioned, but it does a man good to have someone take his tastes and whims seriously, look up to him, laugh at his silly jokes. You never did. Oh, I know, I know—women are men's equals today—they too work and all that. I know, Natasha dear, but this doesn't change the fact that nature has made man the stronger and woman the softer partner. I don't ask you to forgive me, Natasha. I don't feel like a criminal and I don't feel that I have to be forgiven. Do you understand, Natasha?"

Natasha did not say anything. It was good to have Peter caress her hands and to hear him tell her how important she was to him, and that he was not going away from her. She reasoned with herself. What right did she have to make a scene and interfere with Peter? What about the freedom they had decided was to be theirs, to live their personal lives as they wanted to? But neither Peter's reassuring words nor her own reasoning could take away the smarting pain that the image of Peter in Murka's arms gave her. She was all mixed up. Two Natashas were fighting within her. One was a primitive Natasha, who wanted to claw, to scream, to pull hair. The other was Natasha the Communist, the new woman, the believer in freedom in marriage, the rejecter of enforced chains. Which was the real Natasha? Was it the woman who now threw herself at Peter's feet and begged:

"Peter, my love, my only one, Peter, don't ever go to this woman again . . . don't ever go to any woman again! Please, Peter, promise me, promise me that you never again will touch another woman."

The other Natasha, the new woman, pulled her back and shouted, Shame! shame! shame! But she didn't care. She wanted Peter's promise! Peter wouldn't promise.

"Natasha, come to your senses! Maybe I'll never touch Murka or another woman in my life. Maybe. But I don't know, and I refuse to lie. I cannot promise. Don't torment yourself, Natasha, and don't torment me. Often enough, these years, I have had to go against my feelings and my convictions. I've lied, I've been insincere. I was forced to if I wanted to survive, if I wanted you and the children to survive. Keeping something away from you so as not to hurt you was not lying. But to promise you something I know I am not sure of would be lying. Please, Natasha, don't force me to do it. Let me keep at least this one part of me clean. It is very important to me. Natasha, dear, please understand."

Peter's voice shook with the urgency of his feeling. He held Natasha close and kissed her face and throat with kisses of passion. Her arms went around him. All fight and anger had gone out of her. She lay limp and soft in his arms, warm under his caresses. Her body was alive to him as it hadn't been for a long time. There were no more words. Out of bitter tears and heart pain came an interchange of love which left them exhausted and tender in each other's arms.

"Now, Peter," whispered Natasha in his ear, "now you can promise. Promise, do."

"Peter, why don't you say anything?" In the darkness Natasha tried to see his eyes. "Everything is good again, isn't it? Isn't it?"

"Of course, it is, darling, and I love you dearly. I always have. You are the dearest of all in the world. But don't torture yourself and me. I am not going to promise."

Natasha overslept the next morning, and Peter as well as the children had left when she woke up. A note was pinned to the pillow: "The world isn't going to end if you are late to work for once. Phone them that you were sick. Love you, darling. Your Peter." The "your" was underlined. The children had scrawled their signatures under the note. Yes, whatever happened, Peter belonged to her and the children, and to their life. All she had to do was not to think about that other thing. While she dressed, she listened for the end of the phone conversation in the hall, so that she could telephone the factory. It was unusual to be dressing alone in the room in the morning. She enjoyed it and took her time. She stood before the mirror and combed her hair. It was still thick and shiny, and the little curls still insisted on springing out to cover her forehead and ears. She wore her hair now in a becoming chignon. She couldn't be as negligent about her looks as she used to—not since the party encouraged everybody to look well dressed and attractive. She was pleased with her skin too. It was clear and white again, hardly any spots or wrinkles. It must be the better food they ate now. Eyes? Well, they usually were clearer; they showed last night's strain. Not to think, not to think . . .

The conversation in the hall was drawing to an end. Natasha listened to it with pleasure. A neighbor was ordering her groceries over the phone. Being able to order groceries over the phone was only one of the luxuries they enjoyed now. Natasha looked around. The rooms were small and crowded, it was true, but the walls were freshly painted; they had two new table lamps with large bulbs, a new mattress, a special table for the children.

Natasha telephoned the factory, hurried through her breakfast, and was off. During the day there was little time to think about anything except her work, but on the way home the last night's disturbing images troubled her again. She had almost succeeded in banishing them when she entered the house. A child was crying on their floor. Maya! Natasha found the little girl on Akimovna's lap, her eyes swollen, her body shaking with sobs.

Natasha threw her things on the floor, and knelt at Maya's side: "What is it, what is it, my child?"

Maya slid out of Akimovna's arms and clutched at Natasha.

"Father . . . you . . . Father . . ." That was all she could manage.

Akimovna's eyes were red too, as she raised a troubled face to Natasha.

"That's how she has carried on for hours now. Don't ask me anything, I wouldn't know. Better ask your precious Volik what it's all about. It was something he said that put her in this state, the poor lamb."

"Where is Volik? I didn't see him in the street."

"Where would he be? Probably in the yard in some mischief or other."

Volik was called in and from the children's incoherent story Natasha understood what had happened.

In the excitement of school, Maya had forgotten her mother's crying of the night before until, while she was chatting with Volik over their after-school snack, it suddenly came back to her. She had told Volik everything she could remember, how Mother cried, what Mother said, what Father said.

"What do you think was the matter?" she had asked him.

"What could have been the matter? Only one thing. Perfectly clear!" Volik had said with the confident assurance of one who knew the world well. "Father is in love with another woman and he is going to leave us and he is going to live with that other woman instead."

"Wha-a-at?" Maya had been immediately terrified.

"Sure, that's what it is, Father is going to be married to another wife now. It couldn't be anything else."

"Oh, no, Volik! No! No! That means Father isn't going to be our father any more."

"Now now, don't be a sissy, crying doesn't help."

Volik's voice had been loud and suspiciously gruff, but as he explained anxiously to his mother afterwards, he couldn't behave like a little girl even though he too thought it would be terrible if Father left them and married another wife. He had told Maya again not to be a sissy, then had dashed down the stairs and plunged into the first street fight he encountered.

Maya's unrestrained weeping had brought Akimovna in from the kitchen.

"My little pigeon, what is it? Have you eaten something bad? What is it, speak to me, my darling, what is it?"

"Father separate . . . Father is going to separate . . . I don't want Father to separate" was all Maya would say.

"What is this nonsense? What are you talking about? Your father is all whole. He was so this morning. Now, now, now, be quiet, little pigeon. Nobody is separating, everybody is all whole."

"No, no, no . . . Father is separating."

Akimovna had felt Maya's forehead. The child must be delirious. She had covered her with a blanket and rocked the sobbing child in her arms.

Natasha was unable to quiet Maya. "I want Father, I want Father," the child whimpered. Natasha looked anxiously at the clock. Peter would be home soon. He would reassure Maya. The promise he wouldn't give to his wife he would surely give to his child.

» 274 «

But Peter did not promise Maya anything. He covered her face with kisses, he held her tight in his arms and made her stop crying. Again and again he told her how much he adored her. But when she asked him in a voice that made Natasha's heart turn at the sound of adult agony in it:

"And you will never, never, never go away from us? Never?"

Peter said:

"My little darling, we are all of us together now, aren't we, you and Volik and Mother and I? Why think about anything else?"

"But I must think, father, I can't help thinking about it. Will we always all of us be together? Yes? Will we? Yes?"

Peter did not say yes. The exhausted child finally fell into a restless sleep. Natasha turned to Peter with a fury he had not suspected her capable of, but Peter remained adamant.

"I can't and I am not going to promise, Natasha," he said. "Not even to Maya. I thought you understood what I was trying to tell you last night. You remember what an apostle of truth I used to be? Life has made a liar and a hypocrite out of me. I may be all wrong in what I am doing—believe me, it would be much easier for me to say, 'Yes, I promise that I won't ever change my mind, that I won't ever touch another woman, that I will never go away from you'—but if I do, something will break in me. The last anchor to truth will be gone. Don't make me do it, Natasha."

In a few days Maya stopped asking Peter to tell her that he would never leave them. A child forgets easily, but Natasha never forgot the depth of Maya's hurt during those days. Her own hurt was buried deep. She never talked about it with Peter. He would come home late, or be away on a Sunday; he would be too gay or too sad; he would show passion, or he wouldn't show any. Natasha doubted and worried, but did not ask any questions; she knew there would never be any answer except "I am not going to promise."

More exhausted by the pain of recollection than by her day in the factory, Natasha at length fell asleep on the couch. But when she opened her eyes half an hour later she had no other thought in her mind than the Woman's Day celebration in the evening.

She would have liked a bath first, even a cold bath, but she couldn't get into the bathroom. Their day was tomorrow: today was the Vlassovs'. Grandma Vlassov was guarding the door to the bathroom lest anyone get to her precious hot water.

"Go along with you, go along," Natasha heard her chasing someone away. "You think it's for you I heated the stove, it's for you I used up my wood? On with you . . . don't stand there . . . I wouldn't let you in, it's my day!"

"But, grandma Vlassova," pleaded an unhappy voice, "it's a holiday tonight and we are going to the meeting. You know I haven't got a basin and you wouldn't want the children to go to the club unwashed."

Poor Grunya! Natasha felt sorry for her. If they weren't so terribly crowded themselves she would call Grunya and her children in to wash up. But the family would be home any minute and there was not much free space in the small bedroom where their washstand stood. She had better hurry her own washing now before the others came. Natasha was in a holiday mood. Next to May 1 and November 7, this was her biggest holiday. The International Woman's Day! All over the world women knew about this day but only in their own Socialist country were women permitted to celebrate it openly and joyously. That morning the *Pravda* editorial had said so. Today she wouldn't let anybody or anything spoil her mood. Not even if Peter, as he so often did, found something to grumble about. What a pity she couldn't make him see things the way she saw them. But it wouldn't last long now. In not more than two, three years, maybe even in one year, everything in their life would be so perfect that Peter wouldn't find anything to criticize.

By the time Maya came home, Natasha was all ready, wearing the new dress she had bought last year, her first new dress in many years. It was a plain navy-blue woolen dress with a shiny pink dickey. Natasha disliked the dickey, but at the time she bought the dress there had been little to choose from. The saleswoman had cleared her throat and let loose a torrent of words:

"My dear comrade, I am sure you don't want to be out of tune with the times. We must forget our sad, dark years when a plain somber attire was in place; it expressed our mood then. But the times have changed, we live now in gay, joyful times, and how are we to show it? In the way we look, my dear comrade, in our garments, in a good-looking hair-do, in manicured nails. Take the dress, it is a pretty dress, wear it, and proclaim through it that you have joined in the general chorus of joy and gratitude."

Who knew? Maybe the saleswoman was right. Maya, when she came in, was enchanted.

"Oh, mother, how beautiful you look! Your dress is so pretty! Please let me touch it, I will be careful."

Maya caressed the cheap pink rayon with the tips of her fingers. Maybe the dress wasn't so ugly after all, or maybe the poor child had never seen anything really pretty in all her life. Oh, never mind! Nothing, nothing was going to affect her holiday spirit!

"Quick, Maya, let's get busy! So Volik and Father can wash up."

More water was fetched from the kitchen, and Maya got a thorough scrubbing. Akimovna had washed and ironed Maya's Pioneer outfit, the white blouse and navy-blue skirt. As she always did on holidays, Natasha had bought new Pioneer ties for the children. With cheeks red from the cold water and soap, with red ribbons in her pigtails, her new flaming red tie, her eyes shining in anticipation of the big evening, Maya danced before her mother and Akimovna and demanded that they admire her. Natasha was touched. Maya was not often gay and playful.

Whistling and stamping his feet, Volik came running up the stairs. He was next at the washstand. When he emerged from the room, his head still wet and not one hair out of place, in a fresh white blouse, the new red Pioneer tie, pressed trousers held tight by a belt with a well-polished buckle, his shoes polished to their original brown color, he radiated cleanliness. He was unusually quiet as if to make his behavior fit this shining personality. Everything conspired to give him a festive feeling: His mother in her magnificent dress, Maya just like that model Pioneer poster in school, Akimovna all dressed up too, the table covered with a white tablecloth.

"Read to us, mother." Volik thought that under the circumstances this was the most dignified way to spend the time waiting for Father. At least this way one was sure that the crease in the pants and the part in the hair would stay in place.

All three were so absorbed in their favorite book, *Little Brothers*, that they knew Peter was in the room only when he put his arms around them.

"Don't move, don't move, let me look at you," he said. "In the old days, if Christ had had a sister, they would have called it, 'The Mother of God with Her Children'; today they would call it 'A Soviet Family.' Children, children, why can't it be March eighth every day? What a pleasure to look at you and what a pleasure to touch you without getting mud or paint or sticky candy all over me. Don't tell me, I know. I know I am late, I know I am to hurry, I know everything. It won't take me long, not if Mother helps me. Come, Natasha! My, you look fine! The dress makes you look like a young girl. Look, look, children, your mother is blushing!" Peter laughed and Natasha's happiness was complete.

Peter's face was in and out of the basin:

"Know what happened? I am more disappointed than you are. I really looked forward to going with you and the children. But what do you think the secretary did? Went and got sick . . . and now I have to deliver the speech at the women's meeting. And if you think I know what to tell them, you're mistaken. I think our women live a hell of a hard life today."

Peter, drying his face, noticed that Natasha's eyes had clouded. Oh!

He mustn't talk that way today; Natasha took her Woman's Day very seriously and she was sure women were having a wonderful life and that they ought to be very thankful for it. Well, that was all right with him and, since he had to say so at the meeting anyway, he might just as well forget his own opinion. He tried to make amends.

"Not that they don't have lots of advantages, dear; of course, they have. Now, be a good girl. While I shave take a few notes for me, I mean on the advantages. What would you start with? Equality with men in jobs, in education, then nurseries, care of pregnant mothers. Fine, fine, go on . . . Oh, boy, will I give them a speech! Krupskaya herself couldn't outdo me! Now, now, Natasha, don't look hurt. I mean it, I really mean it, I will make a wonderful speech, an outstanding speech. I will be thinking of you and my words will drip with feeling and sweetness. I mean it, Natasha, please smile again, you smiled before. Come, smile."

The dickey got slightly crushed but Peter made Natasha smile again.

There was so much excitement in the air that the children easily got over their disappointment that their father was not going with them. Dinner was a quick affair. The dishes were left for later. Peter kissed them tenderly and left them standing in front of the house. They were waiting for the neighbors so that they all could march to the meeting together. Groups of men, women, and children were moving from other houses in the direction of the big club hall where the meeting would take place. Soon their group was moving too. Someone broke into a song; others joined in.

The hall was almost full when they got there. The walls and ceiling were covered with red bunting, streamers, banners, portraits of leaders, posters, slogans, paper flowers, evergreens, paper lanterns. Calls and greetings flew back and forth through the hall. Volik and Maya went to sit with the other school children for whom the first rows were reserved. Watching them take their places, Natasha derived intense pleasure from the flower garden of scrubbed, smiling faces, white blouses, red Pioneer ties, and from the sound of their excited ringing voices. These children would never know trouble; the way the country was moving ahead now, by the time they grew up there wouldn't be even a pebble on their path, it would all be straight and smooth. How unimportant all those things Peter found fault with.

Ah, there they came onto the stage, the leaders of the district, their best men and women. Natasha stood up with the rest, applauding and cheering. Next to her sat a woman whom Natasha knew slightly. The woman's husband was a hero of the Civil War and active in the party. He was pensioned, but to supplement the small pension he did odd jobs here and there. There he was, sitting on the stage, one of the main speakers. The woman was a skinny mouselike person with a haggard face and toilworn hands. They lived in the next house and many times Natasha had tried to induce her to join their club activities, or participate in an outing or other neighborhood affairs.

"I have no time for that," the woman would say in a listless voice.

Now, too, she sat listless, showing no interest even when her own husband got up to make his speech. Everybody else was enthusiastic about her husband's speech and about the other speeches; they loved and they applauded the singer and the violinist and the comedians and the acrobats. But Natasha's neighbor kept her hands folded in her lap with never a sign of life in her faded tired eyes. Thrilled as Natasha was, her spirit was dampened whenever she looked at her neighbor. After the end of the meeting Natasha, in sudden determination, followed her and, without any preliminaries, asked what was wrong and whether she could help. The woman looked at her without answering, and Natasha repeated both question and offer. The woman must have seen something in Natasha's face that reassured her, for she started talking.

She had four small children, she told Natasha, and a paralyzed grandmother. Her husband liked to drink and most of the money he earned never found its way home. Their rooms were dark and damp, in a semibasement. It was bad for the children, for her too. They all coughed. Twice the children had been sent to sanatoriums; they looked fine when they came back, she said, but soon they were sick again. She left the house only to go shopping. Who would clean after Grandmother? The old woman was constantly soiling her bed. And who would take care of the children when she was away? They couldn't leave them anywhere. Nurseries and kindergartens belonged to some factory or institution, and their father had no steady work in one fixed place. Life was hard.

"Do you mean to say that you find no improvement in your life over the old?"

The woman was silent for a moment, then she again looked at Natasha. And again that look must have reassured her.

"I'll tell you about last night." She spoke slowly, in the way of people who spoke seldom. "He came home angry, scolded me, scolded the children and slapped them—they were all over the place, he said. He scolded at Grandmother—she groaned too loud, he said. 'Look at yourself,' he shouted at me; 'you look like a witch. Your hands, your hair—you look like an old hag!' He used bad language and cursed right there in front of the children. He cursed me and the new ways. It was much better in the old days, he said. I had started on a pile of the children's clothes to be washed for today—we don't have many changes for them—and he yelled at me to put it aside and to help him with 'that damned speech,' as he called it, the speech you just heard him make. You see, I went to school for four years and I can write better than he. Do you think my heart was in the speech? With his yelling and cursing it was hard to find words about how much better it is for women now than before. You can see that, can't you? While they were saying such pretty words there on the stage, I couldn't help thinking of the children, of Grandmother, of the darkness of our lives, of the dishes piled up, of the mountains of dirty clothes, of the way he had prepared the words you all believed . . ."

Natasha's holiday spirit was jolted, but only for a short moment. What of it? She knew they had already reached paradise. Of course, many lives were still hard and miserable. Of course, much had yet to be done. Why get upset over one sad case? Natasha knew a remedy—her old remedy; more work; greater efforts to make life better. But first of all, those children must be placed in a sanatorium and kept there till the family got a better place to live in. A bed must be found in a hospital for the grandmother. And the party would have to tell the man that unless he changed his personal behavior he would be exposed and disgraced before his comrades. No, she was not going to get discouraged over one instance of evil. It could be improved, it must be improved, and she would see to it that it was. The holiday spirit flooded her again; her faith and her readiness to work and to sacrifice were firm.

CHAPTER 2 8
*Maxim and Kira*

STAMPING his feet and shaking his shoulders and head to get the snow off, Maxim called through the hall door:
"Ready, dear?"

"Ready!"

He unbuttoned and took off his fur-lined coat, fur cap, and woolen mittens. Kira was putting on lipstick before the mirror.

"Kira, Kira, how many times have I told you to wait till I come home?"

"All right, all right, no harm done, this one is no trouble."

Kira wiped off the lipstick and offered her lips to Maxim.

She once had had a lipstick which gave her trouble. She had paid a lot of money for it at a commission shop, an American lipstick with the word "Kissproof" on it. She had been in the habit then of wiping off her lipstick before she entered the factory library where she worked. But that new lipstick refused to come off and all day long she had felt the reproachful looks of the factory women. Today, of course, it wouldn't matter. That had been some years ago. Today almost everybody wore lipstick.

"Didn't you say you were ready?" asked Maxim, releasing Kira.

"Yes, I said I was ready and I am ready."

"Is this the way you are going, with braids around your head?"

"Uh-huh, that's the way I'm going, with braids around my head."

"Didn't you go to the hairdresser? Don't you usually go before a party?"

"Not any more, I hate them; I hate hairdressers!"

"Since when, my dear? And why so violent about it?"

"I hate those silly women, our Soviet Pompadours! I can't stand their stupid jabbering."

"Nobody forces you to go to the fancy beauty parlors, there are plenty of others."

"I hate the others too. I hate every one of them. But let's go now, we don't want to be late."

They were going to a banquet which concluded a convention on the new industrial giant projects. It was a beautiful, clear evening, and they sent the chauffeur away. Arm in arm they walked along the boulevard lined by trees with snow.

"You want to know why I hate beauty parlors? You'd hate them too. Use your imagination. Kolkhoz women come in, with healthy red faces and calloused hands. You should see the beauticians go at them; they torture the poor women's faces with facials and packs, cover their broken nails with deep red varnish, and squeeze one ruble after another out of them. But I think I hate most the posters with slogans on the walls. It's those slogans that make the foolish women feel that if, like their old masters, they can sit in a chair and let a made-up doll serve them, they have achieved socialism and that they are the masters now. And I, fool that I am, I used to let them torture my hair and face because I too was caught by the slogans. I was beginning to believe that beauty parlors were a symbol of our 'happy and joyous' life, and that having them meant having socialism. No more, not me. My kind of socialism and happiness doesn't need permanent waves and polished nails. What do you say, Maxim?"

They were approaching the banquet hall.

"What do you want me to say? Defend beauty parlors? I don't

give a damn about them. If they make our women happy, all right, let them stay; if not—to hell with them! You object to their being used as symbols of our Socialist success? So are sausages being used, talking movies, dial telephones, cellophane wrapping, aspirin tablets. Everything we produce is being shouted about as a unique product of socialism, as if no one else on earth ever eats sausages or swallows aspirin. You know I feel the way you do, I don't like it a bit. But it really isn't very important, Kira, believe me. What is important, is this —look here . . ."

They were now inside the building. The foyer had been converted into an exhibit. Stands with charts and maps, plaster models of power stations and plants, samples of industrial and agricultural machinery were surrounded by eager spectators. In less than five years, a nation which in the past had little to do with anything mechanical had become obsessed with whatever was driven by power. People had fallen in love with machines. The delegates to the conference and their guests stood now before the charts and models, worshiping them and believing in them with the same faith with which their ancestors a thousand years ago had worshiped and believed in fire and clay idols. Many of those models and charts had been born as a result of weeks and months of meetings under Maxim's leadership. How could he worry about beauty parlors or anything else when they had achieved all that and when they had all those magnificent people there who had built those things and who were going to go on and on building more?

For Maxim, the evening was worth all the worries and troubles in the world, and much more. It was good to talk to and drink with the men who had done it all. They had done it at great sacrifices. No money could pay for the years of tragic errors and tragic accidents, in the waterless bare wilderness far from civilization and comfort, amidst squalor and filth. Their sacrifices had borne rich fruit. They could celebrate now, and they were certainly celebrating. By the time the official speeches and official toasts were finished, tongues were entirely on their own. Everybody talked loudly, laughed. Some cried; that was their way of being very happy and very drunk.

When the celebration was over they stood for a long time in the street making sentimental farewell speeches and repeating them over and over again. They stamped their feet and clapped their arms to keep warm. Maxim and Kira returned home along the boulevard again. Soft snow was still falling. It seemed fairy-like, the way people moved noiselessly as if on wings, and the way everything gray and shabby had become beautiful under the glistening white cover. Several

Red Army men and their girls walked abreast ahead of them, their arms interlocked, and singing. Maxim and Kira fell into step.

"They are beautiful, these new songs, very beautiful," said Kira, "and it is good to march to their tune. But don't you find them somewhat tailored, too much made to order? Stalin said that our country was young, that our life was gay and joyous, so the tunemakers got busy and turned out dozens of songs about the country being young and gay and joyous. Stalin said that no one will ever beat the Red Army, and dozens of songs are repeating his words."

"I liked our Civil War songs. Remember them, Kira? They were heart-gripping, those songs. Remember the one about Partisans throwing themselves onto barbed wire so that their comrades could use their dead bodies to get over? And the one about the Comsomol sending his last good-by to his beloved when the Whites surrounded him? They were sad, those songs, they tore at your heart, but they were very real, nobody ordered them."

"It's all right for songs to be sad. A real song always has something sad, unless it's a marching song. But all songs can't be marching songs as they are now. After all, what do we want to sing about in songs? What we are longing for—our hopes, our loves, our memories. This must have some sadness, it can't all be loud and gay. I don't believe we are going to abolish sadness in human souls just because we are building factories and bridges and canals and grain elevators. They were built thousands of years ago too. . . ."

Maxim let Kira talk. He knew that when she had something on her mind she had to have it out, and he loved to listen to her.

"When you look back, you see that the very best in music, writing, painting, was created out of sadness, out of doubt and soul searching. Are we going to give up everything except what Stalin tells us to sing and write about? We will be lost if we do, lost, despite all our new factories and bridges."

"I know how you feel, Kira dear. I know it well. I wish I could say you are wrong . . ." His voice sounded sad, not at all as it had earlier in the evening.

I'm doing it again, Kira thought. Why do I have to bring up things that make us both sad? Why can't I let Maxim alone and not spoil his fun? She rubbed her face on his fur collar and laughed.

"Never mind the songs, Maxim! Wasn't it fun this evening? I was afraid I would be bored among engineers and economists and learned people using big words about things that are beyond me. But I wasn't, really not, not a bit. And I understood all the speeches. Yes, yes, I did, and don't you dare contradict me!"

She had Maxim smiling again, and everything was all right. At home, they helped each other shake off the snow, and while Maxim put away their clothes she hurried into the kitchen to prepare tea. It didn't take long to prepare tea in that kitchen. Kira served it sitting on a low stool at Maxim's feet. They had had a huge meal at the banquet, fish, soup, roast goose, a rich cake, but Maxim always found room for a glass of tea with lemon, and strawberry preserve. It was warm and very tranquil in the room. There was no traffic in the quiet sleepy street. The new houses for the chosen few were never built on noisy thoroughfares. A heavy entrance door with a double lock separated them from the outside world, and nothing from inside the house ever disturbed their quiet retreat. Far away was the time when, day and night, the lives of dozens of other people seeped into their room. They sat in silence, as they often did, enjoying the peace and the feeling of being together. Kira was the first to get up.

"Time for bed, Maxim. Don't expect to sleep late tomorrow morning; I won't let you. I have everything ready, so we can leave early. The car will be here not later than eight. Come, darling, I don't want you to be sleepy tomorrow."

Tomorrow was Sunday, and whenever the weather permitted, they drove out to Serebriani Bor. There, about an hour's drive from Moscow, the same chosen few had their cottages amidst birches and pines, near the river. Maxim's was a frame house with intricate wood carvings on doors and shutters, with most of the luxurious furnishings of the former owner, a Moscow millionaire merchant, intact.

Kira had protested at each of the steps that had led them to their present way of life, a life in which the best services, the best food, the best clothing, the best transportation, the best vacations were at their disposal. But they had been living that kind of life for some time, and she had become used to it. Only once in a while now did the old rebel who hated inequality flare up.

One occasion for rebellion had occurred when Maxim was appointed to a commission to investigate complaints about unsanitary conditions in food stores. Maxim counted on Kira's help, for he knew nothing about the food store situation. But neither did Kira, it seemed. Neither did their domestic help, Polya. It was long since any of them had set foot inside an ordinary food store. Their friends and their friends' maids were in the same position—they knew only the special store for top government officials. Polya was sent on a tour of the neighborhood food stores, and on the basis of her findings Maxim wrote his report.

Kira had been disturbed by the incident. She had not realized to what extent they had lost touch with ordinary people and ordinary life. Maxim associated with the outside world through secretaries and assistants. He was still making inspiring speeches about the "necessity of sacrifices," about "every one of them putting his shoulder to the wheel," and he was sincere about it. But their experience with the food inspection made Kira wonder whether these had not become mere words without content.

Kira had again been perturbed during the weeks following the conference of the Helpmates of the Captains of Industry, which she helped to organize. "Our husbands have successfully built the foundation of a happier life," said the women in their call to the conference, "now let us, the wives of the Captains, help this happier life materialize." From all over the country women, many of whom had spent years of hardship and loneliness in the deserts and wildernesses, assembled in Moscow. Sergo Ordzhonikidze, their husbands' boss, the commissar of heavy industry, in his warm human way took up their cause. He helped them arrange their conference and together with Stalin attended the sessions. Many moving words were said at the conference, endless pictures taken with Stalin, working plans laid out and appeals sent to all Soviet women. Housewives, who for the first time in many years could enjoy leisure from worry over food and children's shoes, were asked now to give up this leisure. They were asked to become patrons of factory kitchens, workers' and students' dormitories, nurseries, schools, motherless homes. They were asked to give their knowledge and experience to make life better. Kira made the speech calling for volunteers. She was an impressive figure. Tall, very dark, her eyes sparkled with the excitement of the moment and of having Stalin sitting right behind her, her teeth flashed in a smile when applause interrupted her words, and her large graceful hands stretched out in a picturesque gesture in an appeal for help. The response was immediate and spectacular.

A former opera singer who had given up her career to follow her husband to Magnitogorsk was the first to speak up. "I shall sing again," she said, "but only to bring music to the homes and schools of the new city I have seen born in the steppe, and," she added, "that is not all. You see, before I became a singer, I was a peasant girl. I still know how to raise chickens. I give you here my solemn promise, and I will keep the promise, that in a year we shall have a modern poultry farm."

Cheers and applause greeted her words.

"I too shall give you a solemn promise!" a former dancer declared. "I too shall return to my art and dance again, but not on a Moscow, Leningrad, or Kiev stage. No, I shall dance in the shadow of the Urals, I shall teach dancing to the children of those who chose to live like primitive man, without electric lights and comforts, so that future generations would have more electric lights and comforts. But I too will say, this is not all. I too grew up on a farm. I don't know how to raise chickens but I can grow flowers. And I promise you that in a year our schools and homes will have gardens where no flower gardens ever grew before."

More cheers and applause and handshakes with the leaders. This followed every speaker who pledged to do her part in beautifying life. Some were modest pledges. One woman promised to see that the restaurant tables in her husband's plant were always covered with clean tablecloths. Another promised to "liquidate" flies in the homes of their settlement; she would buy gauze for the windows with her own money. One woman promised to share her ability in laundering, another was good at sewing, she would teach others, but, she added:

"I want them to learn more than that, I want them to learn to choose a gay pretty print, to cut a dress so that it will please the eye."

And "I will teach our women to air their rooms regularly" . . . "I will teach the children piano" . . . "I will teach swimming" . . . "I will hike with the children" . . .

The wives of military leaders, of scientists, writers, teachers, actors followed the example of the wives of industrial leaders, and called conferences too. After her great success at the first conference Kira was much in demand as a speaker. She performed at first with unlimited enthusiasm, but her enthusiasm wore off when it became apparent that "wives" felt it simply a fashionable duty to organize, to make speeches, and to promise to beautify the lives of their husbands' less fortunate colleagues and employees. The pictures with Stalin, the interviews for the press, the repetitious speeches became an established routine, a far cry in spirit from the genuine spontaneity of their first conference. To Kira's disgust, some of the women were obviously interested solely in publicity for themselves and their husbands, in the medals that could be got if they pushed themselves far enough into the limelight. Suppose she should be accused of pushing herself into the limelight? The thought was disquieting and she decided that she would rather quit. Thereafter she refused all invitations to appear in public. The medal Stalin presented to the leaders of the "wives," she put away and never wore, though she was one of the first to receive it. It was not a medal she was after.

Wanting to do concrete work, she was given the task of visiting workers' homes to see what could be done to improve them. Here, also, her initial zeal soon wore off. Too often she was met with suspicion. What had she come for? The very suggestion that she was in any way superior to the women she visited outraged her. But what about the undeniable fact that she came from a comfortable new apartment, that she was dressed in a warm fur coat, that she ate excellent food and occupied the best seats at theaters and concerts? And what about the equally undeniable fact that the homes she inspected were crowded and unhealthful? The people were not properly dressed and their food should have been better. When she got home she would rage against the inequality and cry in her helplessness to change it and in her disgust at her role of lady-patron.

Although she relinquished this work too, she did not give up the idea that fired her: even more than before she wanted to use her leisure to do something practically helpful for those who still lacked so greatly the privileges she enjoyed. Maxim offered her an idea. Factory libraries were understaffed. Why not volunteer her services to improve them? He knew exactly which ones needed help. That was something she could do well, a job in which she could be useful without being patronizing. She seized the idea, and spent much of her time at it, well satisfied with the results. Some of the libraries were open on Sundays but Kira always kept her Sundays for Maxim. There was nothing in the world worth a day with him.

They got up early on the Sunday morning after the banquet, as Kira had planned. The sky was still covered with a light-pink mist when they left in the car for Serebriani Bor. Shortly Maxim leaned forward and spoke to the chauffeur.

"You shouldn't have turned here," he told the man. "You should have gone straight ahead."

"It's all right, dear," Kira said. "I have to pick up something at Natasha's."

A small bundled-up figure waited in the doorway of Natasha's house. When the car stopped, the little figure dashed forward straight into Kira's arms.

"Aunt Kira, Aunt Kira, oh, Uncle Maxim, Uncle Maxim, . . ." Maya was overwhelmed with the joy of being in the car with them and of going out with them to the cottage. There was plenty of room in the car but Maxim drew Maya onto his lap and there she settled with a deep contented sigh.

"So that's what you had to pick up at Natasha's!" Maxim was beaming. "You and your surprises! I thought we were to pick up something worth while, something to eat or to drink. And look what we got instead. A useless bundle!"

Maya laughed, a happy laugh. She had before her a whole long heavenly day and night with Kira and Maxim in Serebriani Bor. It was warm in the cottage when they arrived there, the wood crackled in both stoves, and the house was filled with the smell of baking. A couple who lived rent free in one of the bedrooms had taken care of that. It wasn't long before Maxim and Maya, equipped with shovels, went out to clear the sidewalk. Maya was soon doubled over with laughter. Could it really be that every time Maxim had a shovelful of snow to throw into the ditch the sun blinded his eyes so that he mistook her for the ditch? From the house Kira heard Maya laugh and she wished Natasha could be there to hear it. Natasha always complained that Maya laughed so seldom, that she was much too serious for her age.

Until Maxim went upstairs for his afternoon nap, Maya did not stop laughing for a moment. While he was asleep, she found a book to read. But the book lay unread on her lap while she looked through the window at the sun playing on the snow. Sooner or later, every time she was with Kira and Maxim, she would begin to wonder why things couldn't be the same in her home. Why didn't her mother laugh like Kira? Maya loved Kira's loud laughter, which rang through the house and made everyone feel light and good. And why didn't Mother muss up Father's hair the way Kira did Maxim's? He would make believe he was angry when she did it, but his eyes smiled and he would kiss her hands. Maya was sure her father would like it too. Once Maya did muss his hair and he laughed and he mussed her hair up too and they both had a good time. And once Maya put Mother's hand on Father's hair, but Mother just let it rest there and went on talking about something serious, and nobody laughed. Of course, her mother was wonderful, Maya was sure of that, she was the best person in the world, but she would be even nicer if she weren't always serious. Sometimes Maya wanted to say something light or funny but then she would look at her mother, and not say it, and go quietly into her corner to read or do her homework. If she were like Volik it would be different. He didn't need someone else to be gay with. He didn't care how Mother looked; he just went ahead and said and did funny things by himself. But she, Maya, couldn't do it. She needed someone to start being gay; then she could be gay too. With Maxim and Kira it was easy.

Ah, Uncle Maxim was up! Maya pelted up the stairs—she was going to be the first to mess up his hair! Kira raced after her, but Maya was first. She didn't get very far, though. Maxim knew her ticklish spot and fought back. Kira got into the fight too. Maya shrieked with laughter.

"Off with you, off with both of you!" Maxim pushed them both off the bed. They fell on the floor, and then of course they all had to laugh some more.

Afterwards came that wonderful hour, the tea hour. Maxim carried in the samovar. Here they always drank tea from a samovar, because they had plenty of time. The tea table was attractively set with things Maya liked to eat. She knew that the pretty teaspoons and china, the silver dishes for sugar and cream, and the tea towels embroidered with red and black roosters had once belonged to her great-grandmother Kseniya. When Kira first told her how this great-grandmother used to live, Maya said:

"Then she was a bourgeois, wasn't she? Doesn't that make me and you a bourgeois too? And that is very bad, isn't it?" and her eyes were frightened.

"No, no, darling, certainly not!" Kira was quick to soothe the child's fears. "Some of our greatest leaders had rich parents or grandparents. That doesn't make them bad people."

The child certainly got frightened easily, Kira thought. If only she were hers, she'd quickly cure her of it.

After tea and a walk in the glow of the late afternoon sun, they returned home for another of Maya's favorite hours. When she came to think of it, every hour in this house was really her favorite hour. Now she curled up on the bear rug ready to listen to the grownups talk. This was the hour for visitors, for neighbors from Serebriani Bor, for guests from town. Kira played the piano; someone had brought a violin. There was playing, and there was singing, and there were funny stories. Kira wouldn't let anyone start serious talk; she'd shake her head and laugh:

"No, no. Not today. You have a whole week for that. Today let's be merry."

And they were. Maya did not know how long they were merry. When she opened her eyes she was lying undressed in her bed. That always happened! Why did she have to fall asleep in the midst of such good fun? Had she known the pleasure she was giving Kira and Maxim by falling asleep on the rug, she would not have minded it. To carry her to bed, to undress her, to tuck her in, and to sit at her bed holding hands and behaving as if she were their own little girl—that was for them the best hour in a day filled with pleasant hours.

Next morning, driving back to Moscow, the three sat silent in the car. After a while Maxim bestirred himself.

"Now, now, you women, what's the matter with you? Don't pull such long faces! You wouldn't want to spend your lives throwing snowballs and doing nothing! There's work to be done and plenty of it, isn't there? And at the end of every week there is a Sunday, and I don't see why Maya can't come out with us next Sunday and every Sunday. And Volik should come out too, and Natasha, and Peter . . ."

Maxim said that every time on their way back to town, and it helped, it cheered them up, but it never worked. Natasha did not see much of Maya during the week and it was hard to let her go away every Sunday. Natasha herself had to spend part of her Sunday doing chores for which there was no time on weekdays. Volik had his Pioneer Palace with its sport clubs and workshops, and nothing on earth could compete with the enjoyment he was getting there. And Peter—for him Sunday was the only day he could stay in bed till mealtime. And afterwards there would be a walk with Natasha, a movie together, or a visit with friends. And on some Sundays Peter would go away for a few hours, and Natasha would not ask him where he went. It might be that he wanted to walk by himself, or that he wanted to talk to a friend about things which did not interest Natasha. It might also be that . . . It was no good thinking about it. Natasha would not ask and Peter would not say. So there it was, and Maya continued to be the only one to spend an occasional Sunday in Serebriani Bor.

A month later, however, there was a day, rather an evening, when all of them, Natasha, Peter, Volik, and Maya, came to Serebriani Bor. With Kira's permission, Volik brought his friend Mishka and Maya brought another little girl named Sonya. Ludmilla and Fedor were there, and Ilya Gromov and Katya came with their four-year-old daughter, Tanya. Colleagues of Maxim came with their wives, and so did their Serebriani Bor neighbors. They all got together for the New Year's celebration. It was Maxim's idea to give the coming of the year 1936 a grand welcome. It would be something worth celebrating: it was going to be a glorious year, the best they had ever had. That there were plenty of difficult spots still ahead, Maxim knew, but there was so much to rejoice about that it was easy to forget the inevitable hardships. Stalin's new constitution alone could make Maxim forget all troubles, past and present. It was not the kind of constitution that someone on top writes out and hands down. No, not their new constitution! At least a hundred people sat with Stalin and discussed and thought over and talked over every word of it—teachers, workers, artists, scientists, even plain housewives. It was the best constitution the world had ever seen. It promised every man and woman all the freedoms; it promised jobs, education, vacations, security in old age and sickness. What more could one want? Yes, Maxim thought, they had an excellent reason to celebrate the arrival of the new year.

The other adults felt the same way, and the children had a special reason for celebrating. A week ago an incredible thing had happened. The Christmas tree under its new name of a New Year's tree was again permitted by the authorities. It was more than permitted. It had become unpatriotic, anti-Soviet, counterrevolutionary not to decorate a tree for New Year's. As a child Kira had adored Christmas trees, it was one of the few things from the old days that she missed. But when it was suddenly forced on them, out of the blue, by an article in the newspaper, she rebelled.

"No, no, and no! I am not going to have one for our celebration!" she cried when Maxim suggested it. "It's a disgrace how even you accept this business of ordering us around as though we were innocent babes or damned fools! Yes, yes, I love a Christmas tree, I have always loved one, even when I was not permitted to have one, but no one is going to order me to have one now!"

Her rebellion did not last more than a day. She never could resist any change for very long, and this time it was harder than usual to resist. The whole city seemed to thrill to the "New Year's trees." Newspapers, radio, posters on the walls appealed to the citizens to do their duty and decorate a New Year's tree. Factories vied with one another in offering their trucks to bring trees to the city. Communist Youth leaders made eloquent speeches in factories and schools.

"No one without a New Year's tree!" they urged. "What is good for the children of the bourgeoisie is good for our children! Only enemies of the people want to deprive the children of the proletariat of their well-deserved joy!"

It was easy to be eloquent at meetings. It was harder for the Soviet Youth leaders to supply their schools and clubs with festively decorated trees. There was nothing to decorate them with and, besides, what did they know about decorating trees? They were too young. They held whispered conversations with their grandmothers, who were triumphant; it was a long time since young people had asked them for advice.

Once Kira had succumbed and decided to have a New Year's tree, she had to have a very wonderful tree, the kind her family used to have in her childhood. At the market she found just the tree she wanted, and set out in search of decorations. The streets were black with people on the same errand. Hardware stores, electrical shops, upholstery stores, not to mention department and toy stores, were besieged with people looking for something suitable to hang on a tree. Figures out of an era long dead appeared at street corners selling wax angels and old Christmas tree decorations. Kira bought all of these she could find, but it was only a few. How could she decorate her beautiful tree with these few pitiful trifles? She went home discouraged. The sign ELEVATOR OUT OF ORDER met her eyes and made her utter some unladylike words. That happened often, but why did it have to happen today, when she was dead tired from walking? She started to walk up the five flights. On the third floor she stopped to catch her breath and blessed the broken-down elevator! What a find! At the American correspondent's door lay the usual heap of boxes and papers. Again she blessed something she had always been furious about—the foreigner's complete disregard of his neighbors.

She knew that children rummaged among the things the American threw out into the hall and that many adults were not averse to poking in the debris. Empty cans, discarded rags, wrapping paper and string were the most sought-after articles. Now Kira rummaged too, quickly so as not to be caught at it. She held her breath at the riches she found. The torn and crumpled Christmas wrapping paper was still beautiful. Kira had never seen anything like it—wrapping paper with angels on it, with Christmas trees and red berries and pine branches. And many kinds of string—green, blue, red, even gold and silver. Even the boxes had angels and berries and green branches on them. How rich America must be! And the broken tree decorations in a box—the American might think them worthless but not she!

Now home, quick! It would be fun to have the children do the cutting and pasting. Kira phoned them. Volik answered and before she could say a word he cried out:

"Aunt Kira, Aunt Kira! Know what? They gave us ideas about things for the tree, lots of ideas! I have them all. . . . Where? In my head, of course! Can I bring them? Ha-ha-ha! No, I am not going to leave my head behind. . . . Maya says she wants to come too, and Mishka is here, he wants to come too . . . What's that? Wait, Maya is saying something. . . . She says she wants to bring Sonya too. . . . All right. We'll be over soon."

Kira spread her treasures on the floor. She hesitated over the wire clothes hanger. She could well use that. They had a few hangers made of rough wood, full of splinters which were bad for the clothes and bad for the hands. The wire hanger was smooth. The foreigner's maid once boasted that her mistress's closet was full of silk-covered hangers. In America, she said, the wire hangers came back with clothes from the cleaners and her mistress wouldn't think of using them. And then the maid said that her mistress hung only one dress on each hanger. How rich, how rich they must be! Well, Kira would let the children decide. If they could use the hanger for decorating, she would let them have it.

The children stood at the door, their mouths open.

"Aunt Kira, where did you get all this?" Volik's voice was stern and his eyes worried.

Kira told them and Volik's face lighted.

"And I thought . . ." He didn't have to finish. Kira knew what he had thought—that she had begged the foreigner for it, that she had humiliated herself before him and showed him how poor the Russians were. Volik would rather have died than admit this to a foreigner who was rich only because he came from a country where people got rich by exploiting the poor.

The fate of the hanger was quickly decided.

"Look, look, Mishka! We've got it! A piece of wire, of real wire! I never thought we would find one!" Volik jumped with joy. Among the plans he had in his head one called for wire which, submerged in a chemical, became effervescent and made the best decorations. With a sigh, Kira saw her beautiful hanger bent by the boys into a five-cornered Soviet star. The chemical part of it was to be done by Mishka's father, who was a chemist. Now for the cutting and pasting! Weren't they fortunate! There were even bits of silver paper which everybody dreamed about but nobody had. There was a great deal of discussion over the shapes of the decorations. The boys wanted them big, with lots of meaning and expressive of Soviet ideas. Maya wanted them to be just pretty. Kira settled it by dividing everything and letting each do what he wanted.

Maxim found them on the floor, faces and hands dirty, eyes sparkling, all four talking at the same time. It was time for supper, but Kira did not have the heart to interrupt the children and send them home. She telephoned Natasha that they were staying for supper, and sent the maid down for more cold cuts. Kira prepared an appetizing-looking platter of meat, cheese, cucumbers and tomatoes, surrounded by glasses of milk. The children ate fast, in a hurry to return to their work. Even Maya today found no time for her usual regret that at home the food was never served so attractively as at Kira's. Later in the evening Peter and Natasha came to take the children home.

"The children must go, really they must, it is very late," insisted Natasha soon after they arrived.

But Peter and Maxim were as reluctant to be torn away as the children were. Maxim was making a snowman and a witch, and Peter was cutting out little houses complete with fences around them. On the entrance of one of his houses Peter pasted "R. H. Macy & Co." which he cut from a gift box.

"What does it mean?" asked the children.

"It's an American name, it must be some man . . ."

"Who could he be?" wondered Maya.

"Most probably a banker, a big capitalist banker who exploits poor people," declared Volik.

"You think he could be a Fascist?"

"Most probably so" was Volik's authoritative answer.

"Will you get ready to come now?" Natasha was getting very impatient.

"Please, please, mother, don't let us quit yet, please."

"Let them be, Natasha, let them enjoy their fun. This is their first tree."

"But they have school tomorrow, they will be tired, they must be in bed on time."

Kira felt it was useless to plead with Natasha for the children. Natasha did not seem to be aware of the gaiety and excitement created by the glittering things the children were making. She was only worried because it was late, because it was past their bedtime. Had Natasha forgotten how she used to beg her grandparents to let her stay up when something special was going on—and that Anton and Kseniya had always let her?

The children got up from the floor and held a whispered conversation in a corner. What was it? A conspiracy? A call to rebellion? Not that, Kira hoped. She did not want an unpleasant scene, and Natasha wouldn't give in anyway.

She called to them gaily. "What do you say, children, didn't we do a splendid job? We are almost ready. You all come tomorrow. We'll finish it and pack it all in boxes ready to put into the car to take out to Serebriani Bor. How about it?"

The children whispered some more and pushed Maya into the middle of the room. Maya blushed, caught her breath, and said very quickly:

"Aunt Kira, Uncle Maxim, could Mishka and Sonya come with us to celebrate New Year's, now that they have helped us? Could they, yes?"

Ah, so that was it! Kira opened her arms wide and embraced all four of them.

"Of course, of course! How silly of me, I never thought of it! Of course, you two come along, and what a time we'll have!"

A time indeed! The children had never before experienced the thrill of opening packages marked with their own names—real presents of skates and books and shoes and mittens and water colors and skiing caps and fancy notebooks. Besides the toys and decorations which the children had helped prepare, the tree was hung with shiny tangerines, candies, nuts, red-cheeked apples, homemade cookies shaped like toys and animals.

Under cover of the joyous noise and excitement of opening the packages and admiring the tree, Ludmilla stole away into a corner. Fedor followed her. It was forty years since they had had their first Christmas tree together. Without saying it, each knew the word that was in the other's mind. "Remember? . . ." Yes, they both remembered many happy Christmases together, some quiet, with just the two of them, others spent with friends, joyous holidays resounding with laughter and singing. Always there was a tall Christmas tree, glittering in white and silver—that was how Ludmilla liked her tree. And she always wore a white dress with a silver sash and silver tinsel in her hair. It was long since they had thought about their old Christmases; it was long since they had thought about their past at all. Life was simpler if all one thought about was the present and maybe a few hours ahead. Ludmilla had one thought only—to make Fedor comfortable. His heart was bad, and after two fainting spells in the office, he was given permission to work with his secretary and assistants at home. Ludmilla saw to it that they did not overburden him.

Since Fedor had been working at home, little of the outside world had penetrated to them. His assistants never mentioned the tensions and conflicts of the office or the occasional arrests of colleagues. They discussed nothing but the practical work of the project which, conceived five years ago, had reached enormous proportions. Most particularly, they never mentioned the reasons for the tremendous preparations for an airborne army, the war clouds over the world—for they would not, if they could help it, disturb the serenity of those two kind, white-haired people. Life was smooth and quiet for Fedor and Ludmilla now, and even Ludmilla was no longer fearful of a new down in their lives.

The children were left to play with their new toys and one after another the adults joined Fedor and Ludmilla. Maxim fought away the memories which the sight of the two sitting hand in hand in the corner stirred in him. That was the way they sat at that last Christmas celebration at home before the revolution, with his mother the sweet friendly hostess. Away with it! Why should he think of the past? The present was good enough for him! Certainly worth drinking a toast to! Maxim made a long speech on their Socialist achievements, on their hopes and their wonderful future. Everybody drank politely.

"No, no, no!" protested Maxim. "This isn't the way to drink today! What have we been fighting and hoping and living for? Just for that, for what we are getting now. And you behave as if this were a year like any other old year! Ah, you, wake up! Come to life! Let's drink to the children! May no clouds ever darken their sky! Bottoms up!"

Many more toasts followed. The speeches became shorter, the drinks tasted better. Even Natasha's pale cheeks had a pink glow in them, accentuated by the vivid pink dickey of her dress. Katya also wore a dark dress with pink trimmings. But hers was of real silk, and the pink was a delicate pastel shade. She wore patent leather shoes with very high heels and pure silk stockings. When Katya walked one could hear the rustle of a silk petticoat. Maxim was so full of boisterous life that not even Ilya Gromov, who always affected him like a bucket of ice-cold water, could dampen his spirits tonight. After all—who was he? The GPU? So what? The constitution would clip the GPU's wings. No more going around terrifying people, no more grabbing them at three in the morning and sending them away nobody knew where. No more, no, sir! Maxim felt definitely wonderful and laughed looking at Gromov.

And Gromov laughed looking at Maxim. Gromov felt good too. He had twelve hard months behind him. There had been no moment of relaxation since the day in December, 1934, when Kirov was shot and Stalin, in reprisal for the death of an old friend, ordered the GPU to weed out anyone suspected of having a disloyal thought in his head. They did a good job. The jails were full, so were labor camps. No one could complain now about the lack of men for road building or ditch digging in the far north, in Siberia, or in Turkestan. Thank heaven, the last few weeks there'd been a lull; few people were arrested. The new constitution might prove to be a good thing. He would not, Gromov decided, mind a change at all, for the GPU too. They had enough of a job to guard the borders, and there were plenty of working hands in the camps, even if they never arrested another person. And if things changed, maybe a day would come when Maxim would treat him as he treated Peter or any other man who did not belong to the GPU. That day might not be far ahead—look at Maxim laughing at him!

Gromov walked over to Maxim, his glass full, and the two men drank and slapped each other on the backs and laughed loudly. It was wonderful the way everybody loved everybody on this New Year's Eve!

The Gromovs had brought a large box which Katya said they would open later. Now she was opening it and told everybody to look away. "And no peeking till I tell you!"

They heard the present before they saw it. They heard Katya wind a victrola and then a romantic heart-stirring tango come out of it. This was Moscow's latest craze. A foreign record, and a tango at that! People paid hundreds of rubles to get one. The Gromovs had been generous in their present. Another tango followed the first, then a fox-trot, and more fox-trots, and then came the most coveted of all records. No price was too high for these, for the nostalgic songs sung by the famous White émigré singer Vertinski in the cafés of Paris, Berlin, and Shanghai. "Decadent" and "degenerate" these songs were officially called and they were strictly forbidden to the ordinary Soviet citizen. But coming from Gromov himself, they could be fully enjoyed without worry about their origin and without fear of punishment.

They must all be starved for a change from the dry formal stuff they were fed on, Ludmilla reflected, studying the absorbed faces of the others. How could they otherwise listen with such rapt pleasure to those affected words and that honeyed music dripping with false sentimentalism. Even Maxim seemed subdued and listened with his eyes closed.

Natasha was fighting with herself. These songs were bad, wrong, they were condemned by the authorities, they were not their—Soviet —songs. She must not like them. Katya should never have brought them here; she could not have got them in any good way. Natasha struggled, but she couldn't help it—she enjoyed the songs; they caressed and warmed her, and they tugged at her heart. Now Katya was playing a tango again. Peter hummed it softly. Amazing how quickly he picked up the tune, Natasha thought. She hadn't known he had that talent. Peter got up:

"Kira, will you take over from Katya? I will try my luck."

He walked over to Katya. He put his arm around her, and they swayed gracefully to the tantalizing strains of the tango. Natasha had discovered another talent in Peter! She had no idea that he could do that kind of dance. She asked him about it when he sat down.

"There's nothing to it," he said casually, "anybody can tango. All you need is a musical ear. Want to try?"

It seemed she had no musical ear because she couldn't dance the tango. Peter danced with Kira. Kira did better than Natasha but could not match Katya. He danced with Katya again.

"I heard you tell Natasha that anybody can dance a tango," she said with a twinkle. "Don't tell me you never tangoed before. You may fool Natasha but you can't fool me. Confess now."

Animated as Peter was by the wine, the sensuous music, and the seducing perfume of the pretty woman in his arms, he would not let himself be caught off guard. He laughed but he did not confess. That was a close thing though with Natasha, he thought ruefully. Murka had this record too; he'd almost betrayed himself by humming it.

Peter didn't have to say anything; Katya knew the answer. She knew it from the way he smiled to her, from the way he held her, much closer than the dance required. She liked him. She would enjoy seeing him and dancing with him again; but she'd have to leave it at that. She must be careful. Ilya must never find out that he and his tired body, worn out by nights of work and the never-slackening tension in the GPU did not satisfy her any more. But there were more discreet ways of finding pleasure than in an affair with Natasha's husband, charming as he was. Some of Ilya's colleagues had pleasant retreats for this purpose, and with them there was no fear of being indiscreet or unpleasantly surprised. Not for anything in the world would she want to hurt Ilya. What he didn't know didn't hurt him; but here, under his eyes, she had better watch her step. So it might be as well to stop dancing altogether. Peter was drawing her still closer and his lips brushed her hair. It was getting very exciting, and it was hard to interrupt the dance.

"Once more," Peter begged, "let's have one more."

"No, please, let me go."

Reluctantly he let her go. She might be right, after all. Better not to go too far. Marital infidelity was frowned upon by the party these days, and a family scandal was considered almost as bad as political heresy.

They did not dance together any more.

"A waltz, a waltz!" demanded Maxim, and made everybody dance, even Fedor and Ludmilla and the children. They danced a waltz and a polka and a one-step, and a waltz again, and some more polkas, with a lot of stepping on feet, getting in one another's way, laughing and shouting, Maxim laughing and shouting loudest of all.

The clock struck midnight. Happy New Year! Happy New Year! A kiss! a toast all around!

The children could hardly keep their eyes open. Natasha worried:

"How on earth are they going to get up tomorrow? The New Year's school celebration starts at eleven in the morning."

"I have an idea!" said Maxim. "How about putting them to bed upstairs? There's room for all of them."

"But . . ." protested Natasha feebly.

"Keep out of this! I won't let anything interfere tonight . . . anything," said Maxim and began to carry out his idea immediately. In a few minutes the children were asleep and the party continued. Maxim stood in the middle of the room, his hair tousled, his face hot, and conducted the singing with wild gesticulations. They sang till they were hoarse, they sang all the songs they knew, old and new, sad and gay, love songs and martial songs. When there were no songs left to sing, they danced again, folk dances, with stamping, whistling, and whooping.

"Ah, good, good, good" was all Maxim could say when he finally gave up and fell exhausted into a chair. More food had been set out on the table, and once more they ate and drank.

The Gromovs whispered and slipped out of the room to go upstairs and get Tanya ready for the trip home. The child had slept peacefully through the noise, and did not move when Katya wrapped her up and Gromov took her in his arms to carry her to the car. His little jewel! What was Maxim's toast? "Let's drink to the children! May no clouds ever darken their sky!" Ilya Gromov was sure of that! Their lives were going to be cloudless and soft. Their parents were seeing to that.

Katya pressed her lips to Tanya's warm pink brow and made a gesture of brushing something away over her head. On their way to Serebriani Bor they had stopped at Vera's. Katya had hoped that if she tried once more she might persuade her mother to come with them. Since Tanya's birth the hard crust around Vera's heart had shown a crack. When she looked at the child her eyes lost their steely hardness and something like a smile showed fleetingly around her mouth. Katya thought that, since the child was going with them, Vera might be coaxed to join them. But when Katya suggested it, Vera got very angry. To her, the Bolsheviks, Maxim and Natasha, were still the murderers of her husband and son and the happy old life, while Kira, Fedor, and Ludmilla were their accomplices. She burst into violent language when Katya offered the argument:

"But, mother, we are lighting a Christmas tree—"

"Keep your wicked mouth shut, you wretched creature! Don't you dare use that holy word for your devilry! How can you let the innocent eyes of the child watch your fiendish celebration? I curse you, do you hear! Curses on all of you . . . curses . . . curses . . ."

Katya, used to her mother's abuse, had paid no attention. But now, recalling her mother's curses, and being superstitious and slightly drunk, she made the sign of chasing away evil from her child's head. Could her mother have included the child in her curse?

One after another the guests left, but not before Maxim had embraced each of them and repeated many times in the fullness of his heart:

"Oh, children, children, wasn't it wonderful? Never let us forget this night! Remember my words—our troubles are over forever; this is the beginning of a new life for us, of a wonderful beautiful life!"

"The beginning of a wonderful beautiful life" were the last words in Maxim's mind before he fell asleep on January 1, 1936.

# Part Three

## 1936-1942

CHAPTER 29

*Maxim and Kira*

"FOOL, fool, fool that I was!" Maxim, lying in bed, listening to singing youngsters in the street, thought of their 1936 New Year celebration. Less than two years had passed but it seemed more than two centuries. He had been completely drunk then, drunk with the hopes he saw already fulfilled, with the "beginning of a wonderful beautiful life . . ." Fool, fool, fool! And he had kept on being drunk for many months afterwards, not letting any shadow darken his pink cloud. Old comrades in exile? The GPU still the all-powerful dreaded master? The Leader deified, idolized, eulogized, flattered to nausea? These pricks were nothing, really nothing in the light of the one and only thing that mattered. And that was that they had reached the end of their tortuous road. The road ahead of them had been straight and clear and easy, with the word C-O-N-S-T-I-T-U-T-I-O-N spelled all over it. Who bothered about a few pebbles on the road? Fool, fool, fool!

He might have been a fool, but he had really believed that for the first time in many years he was going to be a man again, an individual, with all the rights and considerations an individual was entitled to; that he was going to be again Maxim Nazarov, and not one of a faceless mass chained to somebody's iron will, not a mere cog in a merciless machine. He had believed it. Nothing could shake his belief.

Even Kira, who had a way of disturbing him with her questioning, did not bother him then. She had been bubbling over herself. She had no longer needed his help when troubled by doubts; she had had enough faith to help herself. She had even got over that nasty abortion business all by herself. That was a nasty business. Kira had almost exploded with indignation when the draft of the new abortion law was published. It prohibited abortions under penalty of severe punishment. Kira had once told him that if she were able to have children she would never think of having an abortion; she would rather have a dozen children. But, she said, women should have the right to decide for themselves whether they wanted children and how many. She had always been so proud that Soviet women had this right, which was being taken away from them at the same time that they were given a new constitution promising them all rights. But Kira's indignation quickly changed to elation when they were told that as yet there was only a draft of a law. Women—and men too—were to speak up and say whether they liked the new law or not, and on their opinion would depend the decision. Maxim saw little of Kira then. She was all over town, getting petitions, signatures, urging everyone to write letters to editors, helping editors sort the letters, speaking at women's meetings, calling on them to use their right to decide what they wanted and to let their voices be heard loudly.

"I really don't have to work so hard," Kira had told Maxim, "there is no doubt about what the women want. They want better housing, more nurseries, safer birth control; they want children, they want more children, but they don't want the right to have abortions taken away from them. What I am after, to tell you the truth, is to have our voices drown out the few who came out for the law. You know whom I mean, the usual lickspittles with their oily fawning! They don't realize, the fools, that their time is over, that the tune has changed. They still think they must scream, 'Hail, hail!' to anything the Kremlin puts on paper. The fools don't know that now the Kremlin wants to hear what real people say, not slaves. I am not worrying, we are millions, many millions, we can't lose out against a handful."

Kira was badly upset when she heard over the radio that the new abortion law had been accepted. The thunder of millions of voices, indignant, protesting, pleading voices, had after all been drowned out by voices of a few servile bootlickers. She had cried all that night. Maxim had stayed up with her and consoled her, but he was deeply disturbed too. Could it be a warning that the constitution did not mean all it promised?

But other things were happening then, good things, which had even made Kira forget her disappointment over the new law. The good things had been improvements in every phase of the people's lives, in the genuine gaiety and high spirits, in the general loosening of the tension under which they had lived for so long. People were filled with hope and faith and they showed it in the way they spent their leisure.

Like everybody else, Maxim and Kira went to the theater and to concerts more often than they had ever gone before. They spent evenings in the National Café or in the Metropole, where they ate an elaborate supper, met friends, and danced to a jazz orchestra. Even Maxim learned to dance modern dances. He couldn't lag behind everybody else, Kira insisted, and she had her way. He took a few lessons. It was not much of an effort for him, since three times a week a dancing teacher came to his office in the evening. Taking dancing lessons had become as obligatory as attending classes in political science.

Kira had been right. Everybody danced, young and old, high school students and white-haired, world-renowned university professors. Some felt easy on the dance floor but others, like Maxim, at first were hesitant about dancing under the crowd's appraising eyes. Gradually he had relaxed, stopped counting his ones and twos and threes in an audible whisper. On warm evenings they sat in open-air cafés under gay colorful umbrellas, or they went to the Park of Culture, where they listened to music and tried their skill in sports and games. They usually wound up after a tour of the many dance pavilions with folk dancing. Sometimes they just strolled among the magnificent flower beds. Oh, yes, they had wonderful times during those few months after their New Year's celebration. He had never had so much fun in his life. He had never had any time in his life for fun. Fool, fool, fool, he had thought it would last forever!

And then . . . Ah, why think, why not try to fall asleep? Maxim turned over and pulled the blanket over his head. Useless! He couldn't sleep. It wasn't the singing of the youngsters in the street that kept him awake. It was what always kept him awake now—him and Kira and thousands of thousands in their beds at home or on boards in a prison cell. It was always with terror that Maxim thought of a prison cell. Why was it that of all the horrible things that had happened to people this last year a prison cell should seem to him the most horrible of all? Weren't the trials and the executions of old Bolsheviks more horrible? And the liquidation of those who had built up the country's industry in endless suffering and agony? Their being branded as traitors, saboteurs, and spies? The deadly fear in people, the fear to speak, to think, to confide in a friend, in a son, in a wife? Yes, all this was horrible. But to Maxim nothing was so horrible as that old comrades, the men and women who had filled the czarist jails, were occupying the same jails now. Perhaps some of them were in the same cells they had been in twenty years ago. Maxim could scream when he thought of this. Almost everyone he knew had been shot or was in jail. The few who weren't, like himself, waited for their turn. When would it come?

There was a time, in the very beginning of the purge, in the fall of 1936, when he told himself that something must have happened to justify it, that the men involved must have committed unforgivable crimes. But as more people were arrested it became harder to believe this. He knew many of the men. Their loyalty to the Soviet Union was, like his, above any other loyalty on earth. But hard as it was he had forced himself to believe that they must have been guilty of something. If he had let himself think that they were completely innocent he would have had to think that Stalin was wrong, that the motives behind the purge were other than what the people were told. Those were very dangerous thoughts to have. As long as he possibly could, Maxim chased those thoughts from his mind. He kept telling himself that there must be things he didn't know and therefore didn't understand, that Stalin's reasons for keeping the truth from the people were good reasons. He must have patience and wait.

Maxim had waited. And every day more people were arrested and more were shot or exiled. And every day the papers printed more tales of espionage here and sabotage there, of willful railroad accidents here and willful poisoning of Red Army men there, of men selling the Soviet Union to the Nazis and the Japanese, of men plotting for years to kill Stalin. And those who were exposed as spies and saboteurs and plotters were the same men whose praise the papers had sung in the past. Men known, loved, and revered by all. Men with proud Orders of Lenin on their breasts; men whose portraits adorned Soviet schools and homes; men whose names were given to the cities in which they had been born, to factories they had built, to colleges whose science they had enriched, to streets, theaters, parks. Every day apartments became empty in the houses where the liquidated leaders of industry, party, science, education had lived. Stunned, ghostlike men were led away in the middle of the night; desperate women and children were dispossessed in daylight.

Maxim turned over heavily in the bed. Life had become a diabolical puppet show, and the puppets were live men. He was there, he wasn't there, he was up, he was down, he was alive, he was dead. Yesterday a man had sat at his desk, signing papers, speaking over the telephone, going home in the evening to his wife and children, and today there was a seal over his door, and the man was gone, gone, gone, no one knew where he was gone. Yesterday a familiar voice had answered a phone, the same voice which had answered this phone for weeks, months, maybe years, and today a stranger asked, "Who is there? Who, did you say? Repeat the name . . ." and one could almost feel the eagerness with which an invisible hand wrote out a name, another fish caught in the net!

In the beginning of the purge, he had constantly reminded himself that this was not the first time their high hopes had crashed. And every time they had recovered their hopes and regained their faith, but he couldn't say that any longer. It was unbelievably ghastly this time. It had never been so ghastly before—and to have come right on top of their most dazzling hopes! And it didn't help to say to himself that this was not the end, it couldn't be the end, not with what they had achieved, not with the magnificent work they were doing and planned to do.

Nothing helped him with the million weights he had on his body, on his mind. When he had to make a step, sign a paper, make a phone call, dictate a letter, the weights were there, they held his hand, his head, his feet. He'd fight and fight the weights until he could sign his name or make the call, but what a coward he was while he did it, how his body trembled and sweated. It was really his mind that trembled and sweated, his mind, which knew well that there was no escape this time. No escape for him and no escape for anyone else. It had reached out to everyone now, no, that wasn't true, not to everyone, but to all those whose memory could reach back to the glorious days of the revolution. Even some of those who tried to erase the memory of their past and who prostrated themselves before the Leader had not escaped. Only those who didn't remember the revolution could hope to escape. They were young, they had not known Lenin; to them Stalin's word was God's word, Stalin could trust them to follow him in anything.

Why? Why? Why did this horror have to happen? If only he could find an answer. Suppose Stalin had discovered that a few were disloyal. Disloyal to what? To whom? To Stalin personally, to the Soviet Union, to the revolution? Never, never to the Soviet Union and the revolution. These men were his, Maxim's, kind of men. The revolution was their child, they would have died defending it. Disloyal to Stalin? What did that mean? That they disliked some of the things Stalin did? But Stalin was doing lots of things, all kinds of things, one very different from another. He changed overnight, and called bad today what he had called good yesterday, and what had been good yesterday was a crime today. Stalin changed the party line all the time, and Maxim himself had not liked many of the changes. Did that make him disloyal to the Soviet Union and the revolution? Never!

They used to disagree with what Lenin did or said, and they told him so to his face. What would have happened if Lenin had called them disloyal because of that and punished them? What would they, good Bolsheviks, have done? They would have denounced Lenin as an unworthy leader and would have followed other leaders, men who served only the revolution and did not demand personal allegiance. Yes, that's what they would have done then. And now? Now they were being butchered one after another by a man who had put himself in the place of God Almighty, who had made himself invincible and irremovable through terror, threats, murders, through his bloody GPU henchmen. What should they do? What could they do? For where was there anyone to go against Stalin? Would the youngsters, whose minds he had poisoned by rewriting history for them, by falsifying the past? Whose characters he had killed by destroying decency and truth in them, by filling them with deceit and lies, lies, nothing but lies? Or people like himself, bereft of all human dignity and courage, cowed into silence and obedience by a threat of brutal reprisal? No, there was no one to raise a voice or a hand to save them from a tyrant.

But maybe he was not a tyrant? As he had so often before, Maxim clutched at the hope that maybe there was a good reason behind all this cruelty. No man on earth could kill off in cold blood his old comrades and personal friends, and cover the whole country with an iron blanket of fear which sealed lips and minds. There must, there had to be a good reason for doing so and there must be a good reason for not telling them the truth. Maybe—maybe it was because the outside world mustn't know the truth? Maybe something in the outside world was the cause of it, something that for the time being had to be kept secret? Didn't he, didn't they all, know that the whole world was lying in wait for a breach in the Soviet dike, waiting to fall upon the Soviet Union and destroy it? Could it be that?

For a moment Maxim clung desperately to that possibility. If that was the reason, if the fate of the Soviet Union was at stake, then everything could be justified. Could it, Maxim, could it? Even the murder of the Old Guard, the leaders of the revolution, the soiling of their good names? And if the fate of the Soviet Union was really at stake, why not say so? Every man, woman, and child would rise to defend it. If the Soviet Union was in danger, did it stave off the danger to liquidate its best people, the most patriotic, the most loyal? To disorganize and weaken the Red Army by killing off its generals, to disorganize and weaken the industry and the party, their minds and their hearts? And if there was danger from abroad, why destroy the foreign Communists in the Soviet Union—the Poles, Germans, Finns, Austrians, Bulgarians, Yugoslavs, who came to their Soviet fatherland to seek sanctuary from persecution? It was an open secret that the foreign Communists rotted in graves and in jails along with their Soviet comrades. And it was an open secret that the few who remained free had betrayed their comrades, had forgotten that there was a No or a Maybe in the human vocabulary and licked the dust at the Leader's feet. No, this was no way to fight off danger from abroad. That certainly was not the reason for Stalin's murderous purge.

Maxim turned from side to side in torment. What had turned the courageous fighters of the past into the cowards they were today? When had they started to go wrong? Was it when, in their eagerness to build good tractors, turbines, guns, they gave all they had to the improvement of those tractors, turbines, and guns and forgot about improving themselves? It was long since he or anyone he knew had worried about their souls. Once upon a time they used to worry and talk about the human being, about making a fine new Soviet species of human being. There was a lot of talk about the human being now too, a lot of it, but it wasn't the kind of talk he was thinking of. Now every word was artificial. It came from the top in slogans and resolutions, not from the hearts of the people. Yes, it was their own sin; in their fanatical efforts to build up the country they had stopped improving themselves, and that was why it had been easy to make them cowardly and submissive. But that still didn't explain the purge. Now, suppose he was right and Stalin was all wrong? Suppose Stalin was committing the greatest crime on earth, suppose Stalin was ruining the Soviet Union? Again there would be the question, how could they stop him? What should their next step be? Speak up? What good would that do? They wouldn't be permitted to finish the first sentence; they would be dragged off and shot with or without a mock trial. All that would come out of the attempt would be another clean name sullied in the eyes of the young generation, another useful, good life ended, and endless agony and tears for another family.

Family . . . Maxim's heart contracted when he looked at Kira. What had become of his girl, the big girl with the quick, warm smile and the cheerful "Very simple"? She hadn't smiled for a long time. There were deep shadows around the eyes which he guessed were now staring into the darkness. Night after night she lay with her eyes wide open, without moving, without saying a word. They had stopped exchanging their thoughts. He refused to listen to her fierce bitter accusations against Stalin. He could not listen. He could not lie to her and defend the purge—and he must not agree with her. Even silence would have meant agreement. When—it was not an IF any more—they would come for him, Kira might be called to testify against him; and who knew what means they would use to make her talk. The less she would be able to say about his thoughts, the better for her. This silence between them was very painful, but he must keep silent for her own protection, for her, the one he loved above everything else in the world. But not above his Soviet land. Even for her sake, he would never betray it— not that there would ever be any need; Kira was as true to the Soviet Union as he was. But like him, she did not see Stalin as its symbol. That, however, had nothing to do with her loyalty to the Soviet Union.

Again Maxim's thoughts reverted to the past. If he went very slowly, if he thought very clearly, perhaps he could figure out how it had begun, understand why it had happened at all. Fear had first come long ago, in 1927 when Trotsky had to go and his friends were exiled, when the GPU turned its whip on the party. Fear was with them when the Five-Year Plan was introduced and when no one was permitted to oppose it, when defendants started to say things at trials which everybody knew were lies, when the GPU whip cracked down at every hint of disagreement, and when good men began to be called "enemies of the people," "traitors to the revolution." Maxim knew of this fear, he had felt it himself, but he had been able to silence it with the enthusiasm and excitement of the plan and the industrial growth of the country, with the first signs that their great hopes were being fulfilled.

That was their sin. They should never have permitted these fears to be drowned by the ear-splitting fanfare about dangers from outside and achievements inside. They should have protested against the terror and the fear when there was still time to do so. They should have understood it better. He could see it all clearly now, now when it was too late to do anything. Now fear had become part of their very being, it had made them shivery and uncertain inside. Now anything could be done with them, anything Stalin wanted. There was no one to say a word against him. Stalin had started to scheme long ago. He prepared the field well with his fanfare of screaming words and slogans and abusive smears and character assassinations. He knew that someday they would be softened up enough to be putty in his hands. He knew it years ago when he first started to feed them small doses of fear, increasing them a bit at a time so that they wouldn't resent too much what was being done to them.

With a nostalgia that burned him with its pain, Maxim thought back to the years when they had known no fear of death, no fear of anyone above them, but only fear of losing the fight. He went further back, to the years before the revolution. They had had no fear then either. They hated the czar but they did not fear him. They hated the police but they did not fear them. And they were not afraid to talk, to exchange opinions, to discuss. Money was collected for families of czarist victims, documents forged and hideouts provided for fugitives from the police, and it was done by people who were not revolutionists.

The kindness and helpfulness of people in those days seemed incredible to Maxim when he thought of today's miserable victims. It seemed fantastic for him to be comparing czarist days with today and favoring the first. And it seemed fantastic, suddenly, to hear Kira speaking as if she had read his thoughts. She must have been speaking for some time, but the first words he heard were:

". . . and remember, Maxim, how Fedor's house and purse were always open to you and your friends? Who would dare open a door, a purse, a heart today? I know. You were fugitives from an enemy police, you were fighting the czar. But, Maxim, don't you see, the victims of today are also victims of an enemy police, they are victims of an enemy of ours. . . . Don't stop me now, Maxim, I've kept silent long enough. I can't keep silent any longer, at least not with you. No one hears us, let's be frank as we used to be. I can't go on living with you as a stranger. Let us be close again, please. Tell me, I must know it, tell me, not with your tongue alone, but with what is deep, deep down in you—was Marshal Tukhachevski a traitor? Has Rakovski sold himself for money? Was Krestinski a traitor, Bukharin? You knew them, you admired them. Were they traitors, were they? Answer me . . . you must answer me!"

No, he mustn't answer. Kira was unable to lie. The GPU would know if she hid something from them.

"What are you talking about, Kira? You don't believe that they would otherwise be accused—"

"Yes, yes, I do, and so do you. I know you do. Maxim, for the sake of whatever is sacred to you in our life, talk to me . . . talk to me, don't lie any more, it will kill our life."

Maxim didn't say anything but he didn't protest, and Kira knew that she had won.

"Maxim dearest, I want you to understand me. It is not that I mind suffering. Remember, I never complained when life was really very hard for me. I bore the hardships with pride. I would be ready to spend every minute of my life the way I lived then, freezing, starving, working like an ox. The body, the physical part of me, was exhausted and often desperate. But my heart was singing a hymn of the future, I wore a crown on my head when I dragged the garbage down to the dump, when I carried water up the broken stairs, when we walked twenty miles for a bag of potatoes with our toes sticking out in the snow, when we spent our free days helping to dig and to build. We drive in cars now, we are well dressed and well fed, but there is no pride in me, no dignity, and no hope, not an ounce of it. And I am frightened, Maxim, I am terribly frightened."

Maxim still did not say anything. But he held Kira close and stroked her hair.

"Maxim, I can't go on like this. It's all wrong, wrong, wrong. You know it too, don't you?"

His answer was a gentle kiss on her cheek.

"Then why don't we do something, Maxim? Why don't we at least try? Remember how you stormed and fought when things were wrong? When the GPU wanted you to fire your assistants and take instead the men they sent you, you didn't care whether you lost your job or your head, you threw the men out. They threatened you and your answer was 'I need efficient people around me, and I am the one to choose the people.' You went to Stalin, and you won. And remember nineteen-twenty-nine when they put you in charge of getting foreign currency, and you found out that the GPU was arresting dentists who had gold needed for their work, and Jews who got dollars from American relatives? You almost choked with rage when you heard about it and how horribly they grilled them to make them give up their gold and their dollars. Remember what you did? You resigned on the spot, and wrote a long, indignant letter about it. I typed it for you. I used to be so proud of you. I was never afraid, I didn't mind your risking your neck, your position, I loved you for it. Maxim, come back to yourself, be the old Maxim again, fight for what's right. Maxim, Maxim . . ."

Tears were running down her cheeks, he could feel them on his hands. What could he say? Of course, he remembered his old fights against inefficiency, meanness, red tape, bootlicking. Even if he wanted to he couldn't forget them. Those pygmies he had fought wouldn't let him forget it. Kira didn't know that they had crawled out of their holes like bugs, their old jealousies and piques well preserved throughout the years. They had done so every time there was a purge, and after it was over they had crawled back to nurse in bitterness a new failure. But today was their day, this time they wouldn't have to crawl back. Life was theirs and theirs only.

"Kira, listen to me, listen well. I am beaten. There were times before when it looked as if I were beaten. I was not then; I am now. I am all burned out inside. It isn't my fault, it is that times have changed so. Courage is not a trump today, Kira. Cowardice and meekness are . . ."

He was silent again, lost in his thoughts. Maybe, if he hadn't got into the administration, if he had chosen to work with his hands, not with his brains, he might have escaped this nightmare. Or if he had become a doctor, a scientist, if he had never joined the party . . . No, that wasn't true. It wouldn't have changed a thing. He would never have escaped the nightmare whatever he was doing, if he had kept his brains, his conscience, his moral sense. Everywhere heads were rolling, rolling, rolling, physicians' heads, teachers', workers', actors', engineers', writers'. No one was safe; there was no escape for those who remembered. Wherever his thoughts wandered, they always came back to that. These days it was a crime to remember—and a misfortune.

Kira was shaking him.

"Maxim, Maxim, you frighten me, why don't you say something? I don't think I can stand it. Maxim dear, can't we go away? Anywhere, I don't care where, as long as we get away from here."

"Go where, my dear?"

"Couldn't we go abroad, Maxim? Everybody abroad isn't our enemy. Aren't there some people who are for us?"

"For whom? For us? For the Soviet Union? Of course, there are such people. But who would we be? Fugitives from the Soviet Union. They wouldn't want to be our friends. If they are Communists they have to believe what Stalin tells them, and in Stalin's eyes we would be enemies. Foreign Communists are as cowed and silenced as we are here. As to the others, you know that the others were always our enemies; I wouldn't ever want them to be my friends."

"But there must be some place in the world we could go, some place where we could find people to whom our revolution is still important, to whom human freedom is important, decency, truth?"

"Don't be a child, Kira. Today those words have no meaning anywhere within reach of Stalin's arm. And, besides, how can we think of going abroad when we can't go to another city in the Soviet Union without permission? You know that. We can't move without a passport. No, dearest," he spoke softly into her hair, "we can't get away anywhere."

Kira stuck to her idea.

"But, Maxim, people are being sent abroad to work all the time. Couldn't we be sent?"

"They wouldn't send me abroad while the purge was on. Every one of our men was recalled from abroad—and every one of them has disappeared. They send young men now . . . some of them are good men, good engineers, good economists, good financiers. And their minds are what they should be these days, obedient, unquestioning. No, Kira, they wouldn't send old Bolsheviks like me. And if they would, I wouldn't go because I would have to leave you here. One member of the family always has to remain behind. You understand? No, dear, there is no place for us anywhere in the world but here. We are trapped. Our borders are sealed tight, only a bird or a rabbit could get through."

And after another silence:

"What do you want me to do, Kira? Be heroic, shout out what I feel? I want that myself. I should like to be courageous once more. I could be. But only once . . . You know that some have been shot without trials and confessions, though it would have been very helpful to have everyone confess. You know why, don't you? Because they felt the way I do now. Once more they wanted to be courageous and real human beings. They refused to lie. Suppose I do it too? And then what? Face the firing squad of my own comrades, and be no more? Not to live, not to be close together as we are now? Kira, Kira, what shall I do, what do you want me to do?"

Quick and steady came the answer:

"To live, I want you to live. Let me help you . . . in my own way."

If she was to help Maxim, Kira decided the next morning, first of all she must stop brooding in his presence. She must be serene and calm when he was at home. This was much easier to decide than to do, for there was little serenity in her. The old values by which she had judged and understood things in the past were no longer valid. One's acts were no longer dictated by common sense or by a feeling of duty or integrity. There was nothing now about which she could say "Very simple!" Nothing was simple any more. People did not even talk the way they used to. At best one was met with half-words, half-sentences, hints, evasions, but most often silence. Not long ago in the streetcars, on buses, in the beautiful new subway that was their crowning pride, Kira had seldom failed to fall into conversation with another passenger or to laugh over a joke or share the general indignation over a drunkard or a rude passenger. She kept silent now. She was unsure of herself and she did not trust anyone.

Kira needed more free time to carry out her plans to help Maxim. She would have liked to give up her library work in the factory for which she had volunteered four years earlier during the "Wives'" campaign. But she was afraid to mention it lest someone thought it was wrong of her to stop. Working in the library had become agony to her. Ten years earlier she had given up a library job in protest against a censorship which she thought was wrong and silly. How naïve she had been! The censorship they'd had then was liberality itself compared to what they had now. The present censorship began suddenly in the midst of that wonderful period of relaxation and plenty, which had also been reflected in the bookshelves. They had never before had such an array of luxury editions, richly illustrated and bound, of foreign translations, of reprints of classics, of travel books, poems, adventures for juveniles. The blow fell after the first trials in the fall of 1936. Kira's favorite foreign authors, first André Gide and then John Dos Passos, were proclaimed enemies. Their books were destroyed, and librarians and teachers of foreign literature were told to forget their names. Then lists came to the library, new lists every day. Hundreds of books were forbidden. And afterwards party officials and GPU agents came to inspect the books on the shelves, and it was an unfortunate librarian on whose shelves they found a forbidden book. The lists grew so long and there were so many forbidden books that one occasional visit of an inspector was not enough. The library set aside space and a desk for the new addition to its staff—the official censor. During the book purge ten years before, Kira had occasionally argued with the "purgers" and had even once or twice won a point.

But one did not talk with the purgers now. They had many different lists and many different printed orders, and they went about their work according to these orders. Some books were completely eliminated. In others, an introduction or a photograph or a few pages were taken out. In some, a line here and there mentioning a name crossed out. It was a heartbreak to watch them destroy or butcher irreplaceable volumes: books on the Soviet civil war, biographies of old Bolsheviks, priceless books on Lenin, what histories of the Red Army had remained after Trotsky's name was wiped off the pages of Soviet literature and history books ten years ago. The great truth about the years of the Bolshevik revolution was being destroyed forever. Never could it be restored. One after another, the men who had made those years glorious were being swallowed by the insatiable purge. Their pictures, their very names were being obliterated, and nothing but dust or shameless lies would remain of men who should have gone down in history as heroes. A page, the most valiant page of the revolution, was being mercilessly torn out of history, and she, a librarian, a custodian of history, had to stand by helpless.

A conversation she once had with Maxim often came back to Kira. She had been complaining to him about something she thought was wrong.

"You mustn't get upset every time something is not right," Maxim had said. "You can't expect socialism to descend on us from the skies, all ready made and lovely. It takes long years of work and struggle. Remember that we are building socialism with pain and tears and, yes, plenty of mistakes, and that we have to build it with whatever bricks we have at hand. There are good bricks and there are bad bricks. We have to use them all. In the end, when the building is ready, it won't matter . . ."

"I'm not so sure about it," she said. "I wonder whether it wouldn't be better to slow up a bit, and look over the bricks and throw out the bad ones. I wonder whether the bad bricks won't show someday, whether a good building shouldn't be built with good bricks only."

"There is no time left for selecting the bricks, Kira. We are in a great hurry, we must finish our building, a strong building which no enemy can ever destroy."

Could she then have been right about the bricks? Could a good building be built with bad material, with lies and murder? And what good was the best building in the world if the people who were to live in it were destroyed?

Kira did not ask these questions when Maxim was with her. He must see a calm face and hear a calm voice. Pursuing her new program, she bought herself a new dress. She frequented the beauty parlor again; had a permanent wave and wore dark-red polish on her nails.

She planned to give a party. Some people had been giving parties all along, and Kira loathed the very thought of them. Parties amidst executions and arrests! Now she understood why people were giving parties and going to parties; it was a way of showing that they had nothing to worry about, that their conscience was clear and untroubled.

Now Kira was doing it too. Her first party was a great success. Maxim was drunk enough to dance his favorite folk dances as exuberantly as ever. Who could ever suspect him of dangerous thoughts? Kira gave more parties and often invited Maxim's colleagues for dinner and accepted invitations to their homes. For some of them she had nothing but contempt. They were little men with little souls, but they were the men who now sat firmly in the saddle. Kira was friendly with them, she praised their wives, praised their children, their food, their jokes. Her voice was always gay, her smile big, and the ideas she expressed bristled with quotations from the morning paper. And always pinned on her breast shone three medals: the one from Stalin for her services at the "Wives'" conference, the second for her Civilian Defense activities, the third for excellent marksmanship. Only a highly patriotic, loyal person who had nothing in the world to fear could speak, laugh, and look as she did.

The strain of the constant lying and pretending was hard to bear. At moments, Kira burned with shame for her words and smiles and acts. At moments, she wasn't sure that even the hope of saving Maxim was worth such shame.

One evening after supper, when she and Maxim were sitting and reading quietly, the doorbell rang. Maxim's mouth tightened at the corners. Kira opened the door. There stood Natasha, her face drawn and wretched. Peter! . . . had they arrested Peter? And Natasha dragging behind her the trail of Peter's fate to Maxim. With chattering teeth, Kira forced herself to ask:

"How are things?"

"All right, the children are well; Peter has a meeting tonight."

Ah-h-h! Kira wanted to dance with relief! But Peter might still be arrested, and, anyway, if Natasha had come to talk and disturb Maxim, she, Kira, was going to see to it that there would be no talking, no questions, no anything.

"Come in, Natasha, come in; why don't you come in? We are glad to see you."

Kira's voice was much too bright and loud. Natasha couldn't understand it. How could she sound so gay? Didn't she know that Maxim was one of the very few left in the Planning Commission and that the purge there was still going on?

"You came just in time, Natasha, we were getting ready to go see a movie, a new movie, a musical. Maxim came home tired, he wants to relax, don't you, Maxim? It's supposed to be something very special, I am sure you will like it, Natasha. You will join us, yes?" Kira talked very fast, eager to make Natasha understand that there was no use expecting to talk things over, that there would be no talking things over, period.

Natasha understood:

"Thank you, Kira, but I can't stay. I just happened to be in the neighborhood."

Maxim couldn't stand Natasha's eyes:

"Stay a while, Natasha, you can't be in such a hurry."

"We could go out together, Natasha, and walk part of the way together. But we really must go now, Maxim, we shall be late."

"I don't think I can wait, I must go right now . . . Thanks, anyway. Good-by, Kira, good-by, Maxim."

Natasha was gone. Maxim sat with his head in his hands. Kira bit her lips so as not to cry.

"Was it necessary, Kira?" Maxim asked wearily. "Such a silly lie about a movie. Natasha knew it was a lie. Must we be cruel too? Isn't it bad enough to be hypocrites?"

Afterwards Kira went cold with shame every time she thought of that evening. Natasha must have suffered before she decided to come to them. If you went these days to talk to a friend, it meant that your heart would burst if you didn't. And she had turned her away. Natasha! Her own cousin, Maxim's favorite niece! God, to what depths of baseness had they sunk to give up friendship, to give up every gleam of human feeling—was it worth it?

No, no, we mustn't go on with this, Kira would decide, it is dishonest, it is mean, it is cowardly. Nothing is worth being mean and cowardly. Better die . . . Die? But I don't want Maxim to die. I don't want him to die, and I don't want him to go to prison. I want Maxim to live, to live here, with me. That is worth everything on earth. Yes, I'll go on lying, deceiving, betraying friends. Anything to keep Maxim with me . . .

All their nights had started in the same way. For over a year the hour when the cars started to come down the street, a little after one, they stood at the window looking out. They never went to bed before then. They stood this way one evening several weeks after Natasha's visit. The purge had slowed down. Lately, two or three nights in succession no car had come down the street at all.

"Come, dear, it is late."

"Wait, Kira, I hear a car, let's wait till it passes."

The car slowed down as it approached their house, and their hearts slowed down too. With an ugly screech, the car stopped in front of their house. Shadows were seen behind the curtained windows in the house across the street.

"No, no, no, Maxim, it can't be . . ."

"Of course not, my dear. We're not the only ones who live in this house. This isn't the first time they've come to the house."

That was true. More than once Maxim and Kira had stood holding their breath, clutching at each other's arms, listening to the steps. And so great was their relief when the steps went by their door that their ears and hearts were closed to what was going on behind the doors at which the knock was heard.

Now the steps were right behind their door, but they had been there before, on their way to other doors. The steps stopped at their door, but they had stopped before too, verifying a name, an apartment number. They would be on their way in a moment, of course, they would. They always had gone on before.

But this time they did not. They knocked at this door, at their door. Kira threw herself on Maxim's breast and held on to him with arms turned to steel. The knock was getting louder.

"Let me go, Kira, don't make it worse." Maxim used all his strength to free himself.

Three men entered the apartment. One remained at the door, his hand on his pistol.

"Citizen Maxim Nazarov? And this is your wife? How many rooms? Anyone else living here? Your age? Occupation? Party member?" The GPU officer sat down at the table and opened his note-book. He was very young but his voice and ways betrayed an excellent training. He missed no psychological trick to paralyze his victim with the feeling of helplessness and hopelessness. Maxim was not even frightened. He was only helpless and hopeless. He answered one question after another in a meek, limp voice. The officer was looking over a pile of papers his assistant had taken from Maxim's desk. On top of the pile was the new edition of the Soviet Constitution, a tiny, red volume with gilt edges. Maxim straightened himself and raised his head:

"Have you the right, according to the constitution, to enter a citizen's apartment and search his belongings? Aren't we protected by the constitution against it?"

The officer laughed, a cynical, short laugh.

"You yourself don't believe what you say, Nazarov."

Maxim was again meek and resigned. But now he was also frightened. He had hoped against hope that it might be only a house search, that perhaps his name was connected with someone who had been arrested, and they had come to verify something. But when the officer dropped even the "citizen," not to mention "comrade," and called him plain Nazarov, Maxim knew that this was the end. Only an enemy of the people forfeited the right to be called citizen.

They searched the apartment thoroughly. Not one sheet of paper, not one book, not one piece of furniture, of clothing, of houseware, of bedding escaped their scrutiny. Everything was turned over, looked over, ripped apart, broken open if necessary. The catch was not rich. A few old letters, a few unimportant books. Two months earlier Maxim had burned most of his library and records which he had been collecting for over thirty years. The search was over.

"Get dressed," was the order.

"Where are you taking him?" These were the first words Kira spoke. Throughout the search she had stood close to Maxim, holding his hands, patting them, warming them with her breath.

The man smiled. The cruelty of his smile did not fit the friendliness of his tone:

"You have nothing to fear. If your husband is innocent, you will have him back very soon. You don't think we would harm him if he was innocent, do you?"

He looked straight into her eyes as if warning her not to think so.

"Can I give him something to take along?"

"No need for that, he will have everything he needs. It really seems to me that you don't trust us, as if you think we mistreat people." He laughed his short laugh.

Kira too felt thoroughly hopeless and helpless. She helped Maxim dress, wound the woolen shawl around his neck, and stuck a toothbrush and a cake of soap into his pocket.

"Good-by, dearest." Maxim's voice was choking but he smiled at her. "Good-by, my love, good-by, my big girl."

Don't weaken now, don't make it harder for him!

"Good-by, Maxim, my dearest. You'll be back soon, and everything will be as it always was with us. Yes, my dear, you'll be back soon, very soon . . ."

They held each other in their arms and smiled through tears.

"Time to go!"

KIRA stood behind the door, which almost struck her in the face as it closed. She stood for a long time, a still dark silent figure. Then she moved away from the door and sat down by the kitchen table. She sat for many hours, without moving. It was daylight when a knock at the door roused her out of her stupor. Another knock. How long had the knocking been going on? Were they coming for her now? She was ready, oh, how ready she was to go where they had taken Maxim.

Kira walked to the door shuffling her feet, with no strength to raise them from the floor. A neighbor whom Kira knew stood at the door, a woman named Lydia. They used to see a great deal of each other until Kira decided that Maxim must be kept away from anyone who could endanger him. And Lydia could endanger him. Her husband had been one of the first to be arrested in this house and Lydia was not a safe person to associate with. Kira even stopped greeting her. And now Lydia was here, saying comforting words, something about hot tea, about sleep, about offering her help. And there was no resentment in Lydia's voice because Kira had ignored her in her misery, no triumph over Kira's misery; only plain compassion, only plain old-fashioned human kindheartedness. Kira threw her arms on the kitchen table, and bitter sobs tore out of her throat. When she calmed herself, Lydia had hot tea and a slice of buttered bread ready for her.

Lydia was talking but Kira did not get the meaning of the words. Her mind was blank.

". . . that's what you must do, see? Don't you think I am right?"

Lydia gave up. Well, Kira would soon get over the first shock, and come to herself; they all had to.

"I think I want to go out now," Kira said in a dull voice.

Lydia laughed.

"Don't try to fool me, you want to be left alone. All right, dear, I'll go. But remember you have friends here, we will help you."

Again Kira sat alone at the kitchen table. And again many hours went by until she heard a knock at the door. It was Lydia, with two other neighbors. Kira had worked with them in the same Civilian Defense unit, and they had all got their medals for marksmanship at the same time. One of the two women had dropped out several months before, the other only recently. No one could remain active in the Civilian Defense if a member of the family was arrested. Lydia was busy at the stove heating a bowl of soup she had brought. She forced Kira to eat it.

"I know it isn't easy to eat, the throat is all tight and you can't swallow. I know it, we all know it. But you can't afford to lose your strength, you need it. Don't you understand that you have a lot to do now?"

The women talked, and listening to them, Kira learned that the families of the arrested had developed their own routine of life. They lived behind a wall which separated them from those untouched by the purge. The wall opened only to let in a new victim of the purge. Now that Kira was a victim too, those who were still safe would erect a wall against her. The women initiated her into the ways of life on this side of the wall.

First of all, they said, she must pull herself together. There was no time to indulge in her unhappiness.

". . . that is a luxury; forget about it," they told her.

The House Committee had to be officially informed. Not that they didn't know, but they expected Kira to come to them. Maxim's office had to be informed too, the sooner the better. If she was lucky, they would give her his last salary. Some officers did that. But of course the most important thing of all was to find out where they had taken him. Prisons varied; some were better than others. In some they would let her send him food and a blanket, maybe even underwear and money. In others they wouldn't permit a thing. This was a matter of luck. They instructed her in detail how to go about finding out which prison Maxim was in.

Before doing this, Kira decided on some steps of her own. After all, she didn't know what the other husbands had done, but she knew that Maxim was innocent. Only she had known his private thoughts. So he really couldn't be accused of anything serious, and most probably it would be cleared up very soon. They would let him come home, maybe even give him a vacation to make up for the anguish they had caused him. The women might be right in the cases of their husbands, but not in Maxim's. All she had to do now was to see some of his influential friends, some of his colleagues, those she had been associating with lately. She would know how to explain everything to them, and in no time everything would be cleared up. Kira was all hope again.

But not one door opened to her, not one phone call went beyond a junior secretary in the office, and the receiver was banged down when she called the men at home. Not a soul on the other side of the wall was ready to listen or to help. The wives and mothers on her side did not blame Kira for not having followed their advice and for having first tried her own way. She would come around, they knew. They had done the same things in the beginning. They too knew that their men were innocent. They too were sure that this one and that one would help. Hadn't they been intimate friends for years? Hadn't they worked and danced and spent vacations together? Hadn't they celebrated weddings and birthdays together, and gone to funerals together? Hadn't they helped one another in need and rejoiced together over successes? But by a stroke of magic the past had suddenly vanished as if it had never been. They were shunned; old friends did not recognize them in the street, letters came back unopened.

Few, very few were the stories of an old friend who had the courage to give shelter or share food with an outcast. And his or her name could only be whispered in strictest confidence. It was too dangerous these days to possess a heart. Kira never heard a word of blame from her new friends. They all felt guilty. When they were on the safe side of the wall, they had been deaf and dumb too.

She was doing now what the more experienced women told her to do. She notified the House Committee officially and informed Maxim's office, and she started on the tortuous road which hundreds of thousands were treading. She went from prison to prison and each time stood in a line reaching far into the deep snow outside. In every waiting room there was a small window with opaque glass and with such a narrow opening that nothing but a heap of papers and a hand could be seen through it. Kira would lower her head to reach the opening with her lips and with a faint voice she would whisper Maxim's name.

"Louder, louder, you don't expect me to hear anything with that infernal noise out there?"

"Out there" reigned an oppressive silence interrupted only by a low whisper or by tears which could not be suppressed.

"Maxim Nazarov," Kira would repeat in the same faint voice. Even after weeks she invariably lost her voice and nerve when she approached the window. Her heart beating furiously, her hands clenched, she would watch the clerk's hands go through papers.

"Not here! Next!"

Sometimes Kira could not find the strength to move away.

"Not here, I told you! Move away! Next!"

Once despair overtook her. She suddenly lost all hope of ever finding Maxim, and burst into tears at the window.

"Now, now, don't take on so," a plain-looking woman in a coarse gray shawl comforted her. "Never lose hope. Look at me, last spring they took my husband away, he is a mechanic. For sabotage, they said, he broke a machine, they said, purposely. The liars, he who loved his machine more than he loved his own children. And they didn't tell me where they took him, and the children keep crying and asking, and what am I to tell them? But I don't lose hope. Look here," she pointed to the line of people with bundles standing at another window, "look at them. I know some of those people, they stood right here with me, for many weeks and many months. But now they have moved into that line, and they bring things for the prisoners, and someday you and I will be standing in that line too."

That was what Kira lived for now—for the day when she would be standing in that other line with a bundle for Maxim. She had forgotten her dream that he would be free soon. All she now wanted was to hear, "Yes, he is here . . ." and to get into that other line, into the line with the bundles. It was long since Kira had prayed, but she prayed now. She didn't know to whom she prayed but she folded her hands as she had as a child and asked to be permitted to stand soon in that line with the bundles and never to be in the third line, in the line of horror. That line was for people who were summoned by the GPU. They came to hear that a husband had been sent to Siberia, or a daughter to the hospital, or that a trial was set for a certain day, or . . . a death announced.

At home the neighbors listened to Kira's accounts of her search, tried to comfort her, and urged her to dispose of her belongings before the GPU got hold of them.

"Sell them as quickly as you can, sell all you can. Any day they may come and tell you to get out, and there will not be much they will let you take along. And how long do you think you will call the Serebriani Bor cottage your own? Get hold of everything you have there before it is too late."

At first Kira refused to think of selling anything. But she had no money at all. Maxim's office did not give her anything, and she did not want to work now when she needed every minute of the day to look for Maxim. It was like tearing out a part of herself to sell anything, for everything was associated in her mind with Maxim. After long uncertainty, she decided to sell one of their two complete sets of Lenin. Her shock was great when a secondhand bookshop, which less than two years ago would have been ready to pay any amount for a complete set of Lenin, refused even to look at her books.

"Look at our shelves, judge for yourself," said the store manager.

"You think they could hold another set? We have at least two dozen of them."

At home her friends explained it to her:

"Books were the first thing we sold. That's what we were all rich in, books. And what books were we rich in? Lenin, Marx, Engels. In the beginning the stores were glad to take our Lenins and Marxes. We had at least that advantage over you, the latecomers."

Kira had better luck with their records. She easily sold every one of them. It wasn't bad to sell records, she told herself. Records were impersonal. After records, a tablecloth, bedsheets, her new winter coat, and a warm blanket found their way to the special shops opened to take care of people like Kira.

She also listened to the advice of her neighbors and sold whatever she could carry out of the Serebriani Bor cottage. But there was one piece of advice they gave her that it made her sick even to listen to.

". . . it's no use for our kind even to try to apply for a decent job. The first question they ask you is 'Is anyone in your family an enemy of the people?' You answer, of course, with a no because you don't believe in his being an enemy of the people. But they finally get around you and make you say yes. Then they say good-by to you, and you say good-by to the job. Now, if you are serious, Kira, about getting a job later, when you find Maxim, you'd better make up your mind right now, because there will be no job for you unless you want to divorce him."

Kira was flabbergasted. "What! Divorce Maxim! I'd rather die."

"Well, my dear, it's up to you. I only told you how things are. And, after all, it's not a real divorce. He'll understand. If he is ever free again, nothing will keep you apart. Others have done it too."

"But doesn't that mean I could never write to him, never send him anything, not even a sign of love?"

"Of course, it does. But what choice do they leave you?"

The woman who was speaking had divorced her husband. Kira knew that she had never stopped loving him. But with a child to take care of she had been faced with the choice of getting a job at the price of a divorce or remaining the wife of an enemy of the people, in which case she could not have supported her child and would have risked losing it to a government institution. Both choices had been equally heartbreaking. She chose the divorce. But Kira had no child; she would never have to make that choice. She would rather starve to death when she had nothing left to sell, she said fiercely, than think for one moment of divorcing Maxim.

Every day it became harder for Kira to believe that after hearing so many times "No, he is not here," she would ever hear another answer. But one day the fingers of the invisible person behind the window, stopped at one paper and the invisible person said, "Yes, he is here. Your day is Tuesday, on the wall you will find the list of things you can bring him, be here at ten in the morning, not one minute later. Next!" She didn't hear a word he said after "Yes, he is here." There was a ringing in her ears that drowned out his words. But others in the line heard. A woman repeated what he said three times before she realized that Kira did not understand what she was saying. She wrote out the day and hour on a slip of paper and also copied for Kira the items from the list on the wall.

"And now, my dear, go home. Tuesday is almost a week off. Take a rest, you seem to be done in. You found your husband, your calvary is over, mine is not."

The woman tied Kira's shawl around her neck and buttoned her coat.

"Don't forget to put your gloves on, the wind is very cold" were her last words to Kira. Later at home Kira thought of the woman. She mustn't forget to thank her. Who was she? Kira had never seen her before, and she never saw her again. But for a long time Kira remembered the stranger's kindness.

She had found Maxim! Twice during the following week Kira went to the dingy prison on the very outskirts of Moscow and stood looking at the prison walls. Nothing but the walls could be seen from the street, and the lines of the many hundreds of waiting people. Behind which wall was Maxim? How was he? Had they given him a blanket, a pillow, a towel? It didn't look as if they had; those items were on the list of things she was to bring. She stood in the biting icy wind and her tears froze on her cheeks. She saw Maxim starved and frozen on a hard bench or on the floor, his clothes crumpled and filthy, desperate, maybe feverish and sick. Her poor darling! There was nothing in the world, not even the most excruciating thing, she would not do to ease his suffering. And here she stood, a few yards away from him, completely useless to him. From no one in power, whether it was the clerk at the GPU window or the almighty Stalin, could she expect a flicker of sympathy, nothing but cruel inhuman indifference.

But she never failed to find understanding and sympathy among those who were on her side of the wall. When she brought home the news that she had found Maxim, her neighbors' excitement moved her to tears. And like the unknown woman in the prison office, they urged her to take a rest.

"There is nothing for you to do now but to prepare the things. There isn't much to prepare, there isn't much they let you take to him. Rest now, you need it. You don't look any too well."

Did she really look so bad? Kira looked into the mirror, something she hadn't done since Maxim had been gone. No wonder they all said she must have a rest! Her dark smooth skin was swarthy and flabby. The deep lines around the mouth, the wrinkles on her face and neck made her look like an old woman. The luster of the hair was gone. Kira wondered how the flour had got into it, and then realized that it was a gray strain. Even the shape of her face had changed. The wide forehead seemed wider, and the oval chin thinner, and the whole looked frightening and ugly. But worst of all were the eyes—sunken empty dark holes, with gray shadows around them. Two months had done that to her!

Kira turned away from the mirror. There was no time to think about her looks. The parcel for Maxim was the only thing that mattered.

"Be sure," the women had said, "to wrap everything you send him in a towel or a handkerchief. Make it look like real wrapping, then the guards will let it go through, and your husband will have some extra things."

How could she rest? She had to figure out what to get for Maxim, how to prepare it, how to pack it. A week wasn't too long for that, not if she wanted to do it the right away. For food she could prepare hard-boiled eggs, meat patties, tomatoes, rolls, cheese, and she would wrap it all in napkins. Napkins were even better than handkerchiefs. The underwear she would put into his favorite towel; the one she had embroidered for him. The blanket and pillow would go into pillow cases. Kira washed and ironed the napkins, towel, and pillow cases with special care, only remembering at the very last moment to crumple them well to make them look like rags used for wrapping. When she shopped for the food she went from store to store, choosing the best of the best she could find.

The trip to the prison usually took not more than an hour but Kira left the house before seven. She had to let several crowded street-cars go by before she could force her way into one with the heavy bundle. The snow was deep and the streetcar moved slowly. The two blocks from the streetcar to the prison took her quite a while. It was not easy to wade through the snow. It was lucky that in her impatience she had left the house so early because by the time she reached the prison yard it was after nine. The yard was black with people. Weary figures stamped their feet in the snow and blew on fingers numb with cold.

Why did they look at her with such strange looks? Kira could not understand.

"My, woman, but you are late!" the guard greeted her, adding her name to his list. Her number was 376.

"How can I be late? It is hardly after nine. I was told to be here at ten."

"All right, have it your way. They'll tell you." With a disdainful look at the waiting crowd, the guard disappeared into the warmth of the sentry box.

"What did he mean?" Kira asked.

"Where did you come from? When were you born?"

"But this is my first time here, I really don't know anything." Kira almost cried.

A man took pity on her:

"It's true, admission is at ten. But these beasts should have told you that they never let all of us in. We never know how many they will let in. All we know is that those who come early have more chance. I was here at three in the morning, and do you think I was the first? Seventy-five were here before me."

"So . . . they may not let me go in?"

"Unless a miracle has happened and it's all been changed over night, I can assure you they won't. And I can assure you that many of us will drag these bundles back."

"No, no, that can't be. They told me . . . they promised me . . ."

The man was losing patience with Kira.

"Where do you think you are? And who do you think you are? And who do you think they think you are? They told you! They promised you! Forget it."

"Leave her alone!" A woman tugged at his sleeve. "Don't torture her, she will find out soon enough," she added under her breath, and then turned to Kira: "Don't you listen to him, you never can tell, things may have changed; they may let you in."

"Don't stand like that, move your feet; they will freeze," someone advised Kira, but she had no strength to move her feet.

Suppose they didn't let her in? Suppose Maxim could have had all this and he was not going to have it because she'd stayed home in a warm room instead of coming here on time as the others had? Would he ever forgive her, would she ever forgive herself? Maxim dear, it isn't my fault! I didn't know! I really didn't know.

"For God's sake, woman, are you crazy? Wipe your tears! Your cheeks are all white, they are frozen." Somebody's hands rubbed snow on her cheeks. Kira didn't care; she wanted to freeze, she wanted to freeze to death!

A tremor went through the waiting crowd. The gate opened and two guards, one with a list in his hands, came out. There was complete silence. Only the heavy steam from their quick sharp breathing betrayed the tenseness of the people waiting for the verdict. The guards took their time. They lingered over the business of lighting their cigarettes and exchanged a few words which they seemed to find very funny. A man unable to stand the tension any longer murmured, "Beasts, devils!"

"For God's sake, shut up! You'll ruin us all!" whispered those who heard him. They knew well what would happen if one of them lost patience. It had happened before. Every one of them would be sent home immediately, and any number of Tuesdays, as many as pleased the prison authorities, would be taken away from them.

The guards seemed to be ready for them now. The one with the list started to call out numbers going down the list from number one. From time to time they skipped a number and someone in the crowd moaned.

"Two hundred eighty! That's all for today!" the guard with the list called out and disappeared behind the gate.

"The rest go home!" called out the second guard. "And move fast, we don't want any of you around!"

He let the lucky 280 go in and slammed the gate with a loud bang. It was a very definite, a final bang.

Over a hundred people remained outside the gates. Now they could put down their bundles, it didn't matter if they got wet, there was a whole week to dry or replace their contents. They sat on their bundles, desperate, crying, cursing. One of the women, whose number was skipped, sat wringing her hands and wailing:

"They must have killed him, they must have killed him! They always let me in before! They must have killed him!"

A very young girl, almost a child, also one of the earlier numbers, sat next to Kira, pale and trembling.

"I envy you, I really envy you," she said to Kira. "They didn't let you in because you came late, you had a very late number, there is nothing for you to worry about. But me! There can be one reason only for me, my mother is dead. Or they sent her to the north or to Siberia. She might as well be dead, she is sick, she is very sick . . ."

The girl could not control herself. She wept silently, heartbreakingly. Kira put her arm around the girl's shoulder. For the first time since Maxim's arrest she forgot her own sorrow. But what could she tell her? Could anything console the child?

"Now, dear, never lose hope." She was suddenly saying words others had been saying to her. "How would your mother feel if she saw you in this state? There could be so many reasons for their not letting you in. There could be simply an error. Errors happen all the time, you know it yourself. And who knows, maybe right now, at this very minute, your mother's case is being reviewed and she may be free soon. You have heard of cases like that, haven't you?"

"She's right, she's right," said a tall elderly man in a fur cap. Kira had never heard of such a case and she was sure that neither had the man. "No use, child, killing yourself over something you don't even know is true. And that goes for you too," he turned now to the woman who was still crying "They must have killed him!"

"But why, why," asked the young girl, "why don't they let us all in?"

"The prison office," volunteered somebody, "wasn't built for that many people."

"But don't they know it by this time? Why let so many come when they know they won't let us in?"

"Now, now, my dear," said the tall elderly man, "don't tell me that you haven't learned better during the year I've seen you around. It's only one of the ways they use to torment us. Why do you think the guards start smoking their cigarettes the minute they come out with the list? They could have finished them inside. They have done it every time I have been here, and I've been here many, many times. And let me tell you something: Don't ever look for the reasons they let you in one Tuesday and don't let you in on another Tuesday. There were plenty of Tuesdays they didn't call my number out. Sometimes they didn't let me in for weeks at a stretch, but I came back here every Tuesday. And then one day they started letting me in again. Now I put everything in a laundry bag, and they let me have the bag after my son takes out the things, and he always manages to scribble a few words on it. And from his messages I know that he was in there all the time they wouldn't let me in."

If this had happened to him it could happen to all of them. Their bundles seemed to be a little lighter now, and their limbs did not feel quite so cold.

Kira also took home with her a spark of this hope, but it did not last long. It went out the moment she began to unpack the things she had prepared for Maxim. She was in the midst of her desolate task when a shrill ring of the doorbell made her jump. She wiped her tears. That couldn't be the neighbors—they would knock gently, they would never scare her like that.

Kira opened the door and stepped aside to let in three uniformed men, the chairman of the House Committee, and a janitor. The chairman had always been full of smiles and compliments for Kira. Wasn't Maxim one of his most important tenants? Maxim's position and Kira's flashing smile had got sinks repaired and defective bulbs replaced without a minute's delay. But now the chairman had no friendly smile or compliment for Kira. His ruddy face was yellowish and his eyes avoided hers. He was sick at his stomach. He hated his job now, the job which until a year ago had been to him, a former grocery salesman, the culmination of his dreams. This was not the first time he had been forced to do what he was doing now and every time he died a million deaths. To witness and to affix his signature to a notice that threw perfectly good people out of their homes was a ghastly thing to do. However, nothing short of losing his mind would make him say so out loud. He had a wife and three children. For their sakes, he had to go on being a scoundrel. He had to say: "Yes, comrade, this is she, the wife of the . . . man in question. Yes, comrade, all this belongs to them. Yes, comrade, she lives here all alone."

"All alone in this nice, big apartment? With all those nice things? Don't you think, my dear citizeness, that it is a bit too good for you? And don't you think it would be very interesting to find out how you got it all?"

The sneering tone and smile of the GPU officer made Kira flare up:

"The government gave us everything you see here, there isn't a thing we got in any devious way. And my husband has not been pronounced guilty of anything yet. He may come back any day."

"He may? That's very interesting. Now, let's see"—the officer was sitting on a corner of the couch—Maxim's favorite corner—opening his briefcase. "I have something here which may contradict slightly what you said. Where is it? Ah, here we have it. 'Maxim Nazarov, never having broken with his bourgeois past . . . used the position into which he wormed his way . . . in order to enrich himself.'"

"It's not true, it's a lie!" Kira's lips were white. "That's the last thing you can say! Maxim never wanted any of it, neither did I, we never wanted it, never!"

"Is that so? Very, very interesting. So you didn't want anything at all? It was all forced on you. I am in a truly difficult position, am I not? Whom am I to believe? But enough of the comedy now! You didn't seriously believe that I would take your word against this document, did you? Let's get down to business, and without any interference from you, you understand?"

He called to the chairman and the two soldiers who were watching with completely impassive faces. They went from room to room, writing out an inventory of every object in the apartment. The half-unpacked parcel for Maxim was in the officer's way, and he kicked it aside with his foot. The contents spilled out on the floor and rolled under the couch. For the first time in her life Kira felt that it would be easy for her to kill a man.

The inventory was finished.

"That's all. Sign here." The chairman signed, and after him the janitor. "Now you . . ." The officer pushed the pen into Kira's hand.

"What is this? What am I signing?" She did not realize what it was all about.

"Nothing much. Only that this is what we found in the apartment."

"And then what?"

"What do you mean, then what? You aren't here to ask questions. You are only to answer questions and to do what you are told to do. Now sign here."

But Kira had not finished with her questions.

"But what are you going to do with this list of my belongings?"

The officer laughed. "Listen to that! Her belongings! Your husband got them while he was plotting against the people. They don't belong to you, they belong to the people. Will you sign now? Or . . ."

He did not have to finish his threat. Kira took the pen and signed her name. Once again she was overcome by the feeling of utterly hopeless paralysis. A blade of grass does not fight a hurricane, she thought. What was that? What was the man saying?

". . . at six o'clock sharp you will get it."

"What will I get at six o'clock?"

"How do you like that? Here I am talking to her and she stands there dreaming. At six o'clock you will get the address of the place where you are to live, and you are to go there without wasting a minute. This apartment is not yours after six o'clock. Did you hear me this time? And don't take anything with you that is marked on this list. Don't try to cheat, you can't cheat us."

They were ready to leave now. The officer was pleased. This job had been completed quickly and well, without the usual scenes and hysterics. He had three more jobs to do today. The two soldiers looked as indifferent when they left as they had when they came. They were peasant boys fresh from the village, who had little feeling about what they were doing. They didn't like tears and screams, and it was good that they had none here; otherwise the job did not bother them. Why should it? It was only right to punish men who were traitors, and it was only right for their families to suffer too. When kulaks were liquidated in their villages seven years ago, the families were punished too. Why shouldn't the city people be punished the same way?

They had all gone and it was quiet in the apartment, quiet as death. It was one o'clock. At six she would leave. It would have been a great relief to lose herself in despair now, to throw herself on the floor, to cry and to tear her hair. But not once during the next hours did Kira allow herself to break down. Not when she told the neighbors what happened in the prison yard and later in the apartment. Not when, with their help, she gathered together the little she was permitted to keep. By six o'clock she was ready, boxes tied, the suitcase locked. She walked through the rooms, touching the furniture, the walls, the books, the curtains. Her lips moved in a little whisper!

"I am saying good-by only to them, Maxim. This is not a good-by to us, Maxim, to you and to me. This is only a page of our life, of our life together, yours and mine. We will have other beds and we will have other books, my dear, this is not important, believe me, Maxim, don't feel bad if you hear about it. This is not the end of us, Maxim, of you and me."

Kira's head was high and her eyes dry when two GPU soldiers came for her. The soldiers refused to say where they were taking her.

"You'll see when you get there," they said curtly.

The soldiers put out the lights in the apartment, they tightened the water taps, made sure that all windows were securely closed, and pulled the shades down. This was routine work for them, they had done it many times before. Then they sealed the apartment with a double seal.

After a long drive the truck stopped in a neighborhood familiar to Kira. It was not far from where Maxim had lived for many years, first alone and then with her. The streets were poorly lit here, and it was some time before the soldiers found the right house. It was exactly like the one Kira and Maxim had lived in—dingy and dilapidated, with broken stairs and a nauseating smell.

The soldiers helped to carry Kira's belongings to the third, the top floor. There was no light on that floor, but the men had a flashlight. There were several doors.

"How the hell are we to know which one it is!"

One of the doors opened and a slim young girl looked out. At the sight of the uniforms she began to tremble violently.

"What do you want, what do you want? Did you bring news?" she asked in a terrified voice.

"Nothing to get excited about. There is nothing we want from you. All we want is to find that empty room we are looking for and beat it to supper. That's all."

The girl pointed to the door next to her room. Yes, that must be it, the key fitted.

"That's all now, here you are, in your new cozy little home. It isn't exactly like the one you had, but . . ." The soldier looked around—his comrade was out in the hall—and continued in a low voice: "Times change, don't lose heart." The other soldier was back now and his voice became loud and gruff again: "This is good enough for your kind . . . too good even."

The soldiers left; Kira felt terribly alone, with a cold desolate emptiness inside. Who else lived here besides that frightened young creature next door? Kira looked through the window. The one dim lantern threw little light and she could not see much. But what she saw sent a rush of warm life through her. This was near the prison! This was almost around the corner from the prison! Maxim! Maxim! Somehow she would find a way to let him know how close she was to him.

Kira was alive now, planning eagerly for the next Tuesday and for all the other Tuesdays. Never again would she wait till morning to go there; she would be there before midnight, and even a heart of stone would not turn her away! She began to sort out her meager belongings. First of all, of course, Maxim's things. She had been ready to kill the officer when he kicked the bundle with his foot; now she could bless him. The contents had rolled under the couch, where his men had already looked, and so the things had remained there untouched. Otherwise, they would probably have put the underwear, the pillow, and the blanket on their list. Well, the food would not be any good by Tuesday—she would have to eat it herself. She would prepare fresh food for next Tuesday.

Money was a problem—there wasn't much in her purse, and now she had nothing, nothing at all to sell. She would have to look for a job. They wouldn't let her work in a library, of course, but she would do anything, sweep the streets, wash public toilets, anything, to have money to buy food for Maxim. Even the wife of a prisoner could be trusted with that kind of work. But what about the Tuesdays? How could she go to work and have her Tuesdays? How? Kira felt nothing now but a terrible headache from the question hammering in her head, and the empty feeling in her stomach. Was there a way of making tea? Where was the kitchen? No, she would rather do without hot tea than go out now and face people. The sound of a toilet being flushed across the hall from her room solved another important problem.

Kira ate the food she had prepared for Maxim. There was no need to keep her tears back now and she let them come. In tears she spread out a sheet and blanket on the narrow, hard cot, in tears she undressed, and in tears she fell asleep. When she opened her eyes the dinginess of the room in daylight shocked her. Last night darkness had hid the filthy window, the cracked floors and peeling walls. Once long, long ago she had moved into such a room and she had transformed it into a paradise. But where would she find the will and the energy to do anything in this room? Life was no life without Maxim. She had no desire to get up, to get washed, to meet her new neighbors, to go into a strange kitchen. Something was scratching at the door. Kira opened it a slit.

"Let me in, please," said a thin soft voice.

It was the frightened girl next door. She came in dressed for the street, in a glistening black raincoat, striking in its elegance and for the fact that it was out of season. The girl must have been used to having people wondering about her unusual outfit.

"That's all I have to wear," she immediately explained, "this and a summer coat which I wear under it. My father gave it to me." She swallowed deeply and then went on in a quick, breathless voice: "I came to tell you that if you don't want to go into the kitchen, you can make tea in my room. I have a kerosene burner, I left everything for you on the table, here is the key. I know how you feel. I came here the way you came. If you need something, look around in my room, help yourself to anything you want. I must rush now, I'll see you in the evening."

She turned back from the door:

"Oh, yes, they are not bad in this house. There are some like us, you will meet them tonight."

Kira stood at the window watching the girl cross the street. A pathetic, skinny thing, hardly more than seventeen. What suffering the child must have gone through to understand other people's feelings so well!

In the evening Kira learned that her name was Nina Glavko. Kira knew about her father, who had been one of the Soviet Union's finest diplomats abroad. He was also one of the men Maxim had once spoken of who was executed without trial and without a confession. There were rumors that in prison he behaved like a hero, that he demanded to see his old friend Stalin, to hear from Stalin personally why he was accused of crimes Stalin knew he had not committed. When he was told to sign a fabricated confession, he cried out loud, for other prisoners to hear him, that they were all victims of a counterrevolutionary plot, that Stalin and his clique had betrayed the revolution.

". . . we read about his execution in the papers," Nina told Kira, "nobody told us anything before that. Mother and I were going from prison to prison, from one official to another—no one said anything to us until we read it in the papers. Mother—" Nina needed all her strength to go on—"mother lost her mind that day. They . . . they had to put her in a strait jacket and carry her away. You see, she and Father loved each other very very much. And so I was left alone, and they brought me here one evening just the way they brought you here last night. I work in a factory, and once a week I visit Mother."

Later Nina introduced Kira to two women and a man who lived in the house, who were also on their side of the wall. With their help and advice Kira solved her job problem. There were all kinds of factories in the neighborhood where they needed women for unskilled work, they told her.

"They don't pay much, but what can you expect? And look for one where they work seven days a week and where you can pick the day you want to have free. Most people want a Sunday but you want your Tuesday, so you ask for Tuesday. They're short of workers, and they don't care who you are and what day you want free."

Two days later Kira started to work in a factory six days a week, Tuesdays free. Every Monday after work she shopped, prepared Maxim's parcel, slept for two hours, and at midnight was on her way to prison. She was lucky. For two whole months there was only once that they didn't let her deliver her package.

Life moved in a slow rhythm of monotonous work, of suppers with Nina, of Tuesdays. Kira often cried when she was alone, but hunger had to be stilled, stockings mended, clothes washed, news exchanged with new friends in this house and old friends from her former home. And there were hours when the daily tasks or sympathy for other victims dulled her own pain a little. There was an evening in the early spring when the snow on the ground was melting under the first rain, and Kira came home wet and chilled. As she neared the house she was almost thrown off her feet by someone running out. The glistening, black raincoat!

"Nina, Nina, where are you going? Nina! Wait for me, Nina!"

Nina certainly heard her, but she didn't stop. Kira ran after her as fast as she could but the rain blinded her eyes and she had to pause for a moment. Now Nina was too far away; she could never catch her. With her eyes, Kira followed the glistening raincoat till Nina was out of sight. Then she turned back with a worried heart. The neighbors were waiting for her. Less than half an hour ago Nina had come home from her weekly visit to the hospital. Her shoes were soaked through, and the water was running in streams from her uncovered head. She must have walked all the distance. Her eyes were wild, so was her voice.

"She is dead," Nina had told them hysterically. "She died from an injection, they say. But I know that they did it purposely. They wanted her to die. They always said it was a nuisance to bother about her, about a useless life, they said. A useless life! My mother, my beautiful, my wonderful mother they called a useless life. They showed me a body. They said it was my mother. Of course, it was not my mother at all. This was not my beautiful wonderful mother. It was the body of an old, ugly hag. They killed my mother, they killed her just as they killed my father."

Then she had run out of the house. That was all. What should they do now? Tell the police? Nina would not want the police to look for her. All night long they sat up, waiting, hoping. The next day the *Evening Moscow* had a short item: "The body of a young, unidentified girl clad in a black raincoat of obviously foreign origin was washed up on the bank of the Moscow River. She must have slipped and fallen into the river during last night's rainstorm."

For a while the tedious rhythm of life was disturbed but it soon resumed its slow and uniform beat. Kira got into the habit of praying every night before falling asleep. She still did not know to whom she was praying and very often she did not know what to pray for. Should she pray for Maxim to do anything they want him to do? To admit to crimes he had never committed, to sign confessions he had never made? And then what? Others had lied and betrayed their faith because they had lost this faith or because they hoped to save themselves or their families. They had signed forged confessions, they had testified to their guilt at trials, and they had lost their lives anyway.

Soon Kira knew that Maxim had not weakened and that he had not confessed to something he never did. She knew it because he was condemned without a trial. Much would have been made of a trial at which a man of Maxim's reputation confessed to having been a traitor. Fortunately for Maxim, by the time his case was taken up the purge had lost its initial fury and fewer shots were heard at night in prison yards. He was sent to the arctic to work in a labor camp. Once in two months he was permitted to exchange a letter with Kira, once in three months he was permitted to receive a package.

Kira continued to work in the box factory. She ate, she slept, she cleaned her room, she talked to fellow workers in the factory and to neighbors in the house. But she was really alive only when it was time to expect a letter from Maxim and when it was time for her to write a letter or send him a package. The intervals were desperately long, and sometimes it was almost beyond Kira's strength to get out of bed in the morning or to drag her feet out of the way of a racing car. "Maxim needs you!" set her feet in motion again.

NATASHA rarely admitted to herself that she had any doubts about the purge. When she did, she quickly dismissed such heretical thoughts. Of course, the purge was necessary and just. Of course, Stalin was right. How else should he have dealt with men whom he had trusted and who betrayed him? Of course, some innocents had suffered. There was no time to sift out the half-guilty and the innocent. A spreading cancer of betrayal and sabotage had started to grow on the Soviet body. It had to be cut out so drastically and totally that no trace of the disease would be left and no weakness remain to which it could ever return. Nevertheless, on certain days when she heard of families torn apart, of children taken away from parents, of children forced to testify against their parents, it was hard for Natasha to silence the doubts.

And then there was one day when nothing she said to herself helped, when she couldn't carry her doubts alone any more and she had to talk to someone. She couldn't talk to Peter. He was very violent about the purge. He saw no justice or necessity in it. He saw nothing in it but brutal ruthlessness. The last time she had tried to argue with Peter she said:

"But we must destroy those who are plotting."

"You believe in this mythical plot?" he cried out. "I don't and never will! What proof have they given us? Find me one real, factual bit of proof. You can't! Words they give us, many empty words; lies they give us, but never proof! And if there was a plot, that still doesn't justify the killing and destroying of our best people. Stalin's life is certainly not so precious as Lenin's was, even you will not say that! And when that woman wounded Lenin in nineteen-eighteen, did thousands and thousands have to pay with their lives? Thousands of good loyal Communists! But Stalin—never, never will I forgive him, and I will never forgive him for what he is doing to decent, truthful, kind, human beings like you. He has made you wallow in cruelty, in lies, he has made you betray every decent feeling, he makes you worship a god who is a sheer demon."

"Stop, Peter, stop! I am not going to listen to you, I must not listen to you." Natasha closed her ears.

"Of course, you must not. And I know why. You are afraid to listen to me because your conscience tells you that you must run to the GPU to denounce me. And it is only that one tiny spark of decency they haven't succeeded in extinguishing which keeps you from it. Go, Natasha, go, run, tell them what your husband said; others have done it before you. I should like nothing better. They will shoot me then, and I should prefer death to living in this morass of hypocrisy and barbarism."

Of course, it was Natasha's duty to inform the GPU. But Peter must have been right about that last spark of decency in her. She did not do what many husbands and wives and children had done. Peter was sick, she kept telling herself, he was not responsible for what he was saying. He didn't understand; he would when he got well and calmed down. One did not report a sick man. But they never again discussed the purge. They mentioned the names of those who disappeared and those who took their places, but they exchanged no opinions. It was better that way.

On the day when Natasha could no longer carry her doubts alone, she had learned in the morning that the director, his assistants, the chief engineers, the head bookkeeper, the party secretary, and everyone else who had a responsible position in the plant where she worked had been arrested during the night. There were no doubts in her mind about these people. She had worked with them for four years; she had seen their selfless devotion and loyalty. For the plant, they had neglected their personal lives and their families. Every success of the plant—and there had been many brilliant successes—had been due only to their efforts. Prizes and orders and the official thanks of the government had been showered on them time and again. Editorials had been written in their praise. Twice Stalin had invited plant representatives to the Kremlin. And now—in a few hours—their record was wiped out and they were arrested.

When Natasha came to work, some of the rooms were already sealed, in others the search was still going on. Papers were strewn on the floor, secret formulas, annual reports, estimates for the future.

By noon a new director had come. He immediately called a meeting of the staff. He was a big powerful-looking man with a red fleshy face. A man of his build and face should have had a loud strong voice and a self-confident bearing. But his voice was much too thin and weak for his bulk, his eyes did not look straight at the people he was addressing, and his fingers kept twisting at his coat buttons. He consulted a typewritten text as he talked, and from time to time turned for approval to the GPU men who sat at his side.

". . . vicious saboteurs . . . serpents whom in his kindness our beloved Leader had nursed at his heart . . . sinister monsters with black souls

. . . strove to destroy our efforts. . . . But the deluded scoundrels, the mad dogs, the fiends, the scum of the earth . . . they miscalculated, they blundered, they bungled, and . . . they failed. The never-tiring eye of our beloved Leader, his stout indomitable heart detected and stopped the thieves, the sharks . . ."

He stopped to wipe his brow.

"Comrades, right here, among you, among honest simple Soviet workers, into the heart of this plant, the cunning enemy had thrust his deadly claws. But our beloved Leader in his great wisdom cut off the claws before they could tear out the very heart of this plant. The plant is saved, comrades, and it is up to you now to clean out whatever remnants of the vicious work of the wreckers still linger in your midst. I trust that with the help of these our comrades"—he pointed to the GPU men—"every trace of sabotage will be brought to light. You all must help, and help right now, without any delay. Everything else will have to wait."

All work stopped in the plant. The day was spent answering the questions of the GPU men who called in reinforcements. In teams of three they went from department to department, from shop to shop, interrogating every member of the staff, every worker, and every cleaning woman, returning to the same people for more interrogation.

Natasha was shaken. She had often read in the papers the kind of speech she heard their new director deliver. Each time she had believed every word and been horrified anew by the number of saboteurs who had succeeded in infiltrating into key positions. Now, for the first time, she could not accept the official accusations. Nothing could convince her that even one of the people arrested during the night was a saboteur.

Natasha was waiting for her turn to be questioned. She would hide nothing, she had nothing to hide. She had never seen any sign of sabotage in their plant, and she was going to say so. She had all prepared in her mind what she was going to say. But the first question fired at her was: "When did you first discover the sabotage in the plant?"

Three pairs of eyes watched her, three hands held pencils and paper ready. The way the question was put made it hard for Natasha to say what she had prepared. And suddenly she understood that a truthful answer was not important to these men at all; all they wanted from her was proof to substantiate their accusations. If she didn't answer the way they expected her to answer, they would question her own loyalty, they would build up a case against her as they had against the others. No, no, not that.

She heard herself saying words that had nothing to do with those she had intended to say:

"My job is a little job. All I do is inspect dyeing of materials. I had no access to anything else, just to that, and so"—this was terribly hard to get out—"I never had any occasion to observe the sabotage."

"The criminals kept the loyal engineers away from real work, they prevented them from having any insight into what was going on . . ." The interrogator was reading aloud Natasha's testimony the way he was putting it down on paper.

No, no, no, that's not true. It is only that we were each assigned to a certain job, but they would have let me see anything I wanted to. These words sounded so loud in Natasha's head that she thought she was saying them. She was not.

"Now, comrade engineer, can't you recall any instance when in your job, in dyeing materials, there was damage or waste or loss? Wasn't there any, ever?"

"Of course, there was." Natasha's heart sank when she saw how quickly the three pencils went down to write this, and how not one of them took down her next words. "There always is in this kind of work."

"Well, then, tell us all about the damage, waste, and losses. Tell us every instance you recall. Dig into your memory, look up the books, take your time, but be sure to tell us everything!"

Natasha made use of their permission to take her time. She kept turning the pages of her reports though she knew the exact page and line on which losses were reported. She needed the time. She was trying to find words to explain that their losses were smaller than the losses in any other plant; that their figures on losses were their greatest pride; that because of these figures they had won all the government honors and prizes; that no plant in the world worked without some losses. She must tell them that. In the name of the truth she must do it, and try to save the men who were so unjustly accused.

"We want only figures, nothing interests us but the figures," they stopped her every time she made an attempt to explain the figures.

Finally they warned her: "What are you trying to do, comrade engineer? Justify sabotage? Be careful."

When they had finished with her, they shook hands, thanking her: "You did your duty well, you gave us ample proof that these men who were entrusted with the sacred task of serving our Soviet Union, used this trust to try to destroy us."

For once Natasha was not in a hurry to go home. It would take only a very small thing, she knew, to make her break down, and if she broke down, Peter would know how she felt and never again could she present to him that front of solid rock. Right now her rock had turned to soft sand, and the sand was running out fast. She could not stand it; she had to talk to someone. Maxim would help her, she thought. He was wise and strong, and he had known all the top men in the plant—indeed, it was at conferences with Maxim that they had been working out their plans. Maxim had visited the plant several times, and had always been full of praise for the efficiency with which it was run. Maxim would help her understand, as he always had in the past.

But this time he did not, he did not even want to hear what she had to say. True, it was Kira who said that they were going to see a movie, it was Kira who saw to it that there was no talking. But had Maxim wanted to, they could have talked. He did not want to. Natasha saw it in his eyes. She wanted to cry when she thought of Maxim's eyes. Timorous uncertain eyes they were. Where could she hope to find strength, if Maxim, that tower of strength, had lost his?

Natasha pleaded sickness when she got home, went straight to bed and pretended to fall asleep. The next day she was promoted to the job of one of the men who had been arrested. She was now to supervise the entire dyeing process of the plant. This new job scared her. It was a far more responsible position than any she had ever held until then.

"Only through perfect results in your work, without any errors, without any losses, can you prove your loyalty and can you restore the damage done by the cunning minds of the enemies."

With these words the new director sent her and the others to their work. The threat in his words was not lost on Natasha. She gave herself completely to mastering her new job. She could not afford an error. The very word "error" had ceased to exist. Crime, sabotage, counterrevolution, wrecking, treason—these were the new words for the most insignificant errors. It was a nerve-racking and backbreaking task, but Natasha did not mind that part of it. It was even a help in keeping her mind empty of unwelcome thoughts.

The new job relieved her of her classes in the factory school, and she was glad about that for she dreaded the kind of questions her pupils might ask her. With her family and the other workers in the factory, the only people she ever saw now, she avoided any conversation except on immediate everyday problems. Her old curiosity about people was completely gone. She did not want to know what was going on in other people's minds and lives; she was eager not to know.

After a period of intense work and no thought, Natasha began to recover her composure, at least on the surface. But events made it hard for her to keep this hard-won skin-thin placidity.

Once reading his evening paper Peter suddenly cried out: "Look, Natasha, look at this!"

It was an obituary of Fedor Gavrilov, full of praise for his work, for the devotion of this former class enemy to the cause of the people. The obituary was signed by the highest dignitaries of the state.

"I am glad he died this way," said Peter, "I was worried about him. Everyone of any importance has been cleaned out of the Textile Trust, especially in Fedor's department where they work exclusively for defense. They were accused of selling secrets to Hitler. It's a good thing Fedor died before it touched him."

"Oh, Peter, he would never have been touched, a man of his age, near seventy."

Peter knew very well that age was no protection, but argument with Natasha was something he carefully avoided. He did not say anything, and Natasha continued:

"Poor, poor Ludmilla! To outlive Fedor, and to be alone at her age! I must go to see her; I am sure she needs help."

Natasha did not have to go to see Ludmilla. The next morning the papers brought a belated announcement:

"With great grief the Textile Trust announces the death of one of its outstanding experts, Fedor Gavrilov, and of his wife, Ludmilla Gavrilov. The burial took place on . . ." The date was a week ago.

Natasha was glad it had happened like that; it was better than either of them remaining alone. She wanted, though, to know the details of their death. The neighbors she asked about it sounded very mysterious but would not give her any information. They did give her, however, the address of the woman who had helped Ludmilla with her housework. The woman was happy to pour out the story to someone whom she knew as a distant relative of her dead masters:

"The master's old assistants stopped coming, so did the secretaries. New ones came, and I heard the master say to the mistress that he couldn't work with new people, that he wasn't even sure they were real engineers, he thought they were sent to spy on him. Then they didn't come either, no one came, no one telephoned, no salary was sent to him, as if he was dead. He was very nervous, and his heart was getting worse and worse. The mistress worried into a shadow of herself. Two weeks ago a man appeared in the house, he asked neighbors questions about the master, and we saw him at all times watching our windows. I heard the master say that he was much too old and sick to stand an arrest and that the mistress would die when they took him away. And one afternoon the mistress sent me on an errand. She saw to it that I was well bundled up, it was a cold day, she gave me her warm gloves. But how was I to know? She was always so sweet to me. When I returned, it was dark in their bedroom, I thought they went to bed early. In the middle of the night, the bell rang once, again and again. The master's sleep was very light, but no sound came from their bedroom. I opened the door, and four men were there. They were loud. 'Sh-sh,' I said to them, 'you'll wake them.' They pushed me aside. 'But that's what we came for, to wake them,' they said. I cried and followed them into the bedroom . . ."

The woman stopped; her face had a deadly pallor. Her hands were icy.

"I don't know much what happened afterwards. I fainted, so did one of the men. On the bed they were lying, the masters, their throats cut, the bed soaked with blood. He still held the razor. For four days they let them lie there, their deaths were kept secret, I was not to tell anyone anything, nothing was done about a burial. If you ask me, they didn't know whether to make a traitor or a hero out of the master; after a week they must have decided for a hero. That's the way they buried the master."

It might have been hard for Natasha to recover from this shock if a few days afterwards their monthly meeting devoted to Loyalist Spain had not absorbed her emotions and quieted again the imps of doubts that danced in her head. Natasha was chairman of the committee through which the plant's workers sent relief regularly to Spain. These meetings had always been a great inspiration to Natasha, but this time she dreaded it, afraid that in her present state of mind she might not find the right words. When she was called upon to speak she was unable to begin and her eyes wandered around the rows as if appealing for help. And she found the help. It was in the great number of people who had turned out in a blinding blizzard, in the gay reds of the women's kerchiefs and of the Pioneer ties, in the Soviet and Spanish flags hanging over the platform, in the beautiful faces of the Spanish children who were their guests that night, in the pile of the month's donations—clothing, food, medical supplies, toys. Natasha looked at the people and the gifts, and she saw thousands and thousands of gatherings like theirs, in every Soviet town, in every Soviet village. Yes, wherever Soviet people lived they got together to help their fighting brothers and sisters in Spain. Names of Spanish rivers and plains, of Spanish cities and of Spanish leaders had become familiar to all of them. In every home, with hearts beating with pride or sorrow, they followed the Spanish struggle on maps of Spain.

Yes, Natasha found all the help she needed, and her speech was eloquent and heart-warming.

". . . they are fighting our fight," she ended, "let us show them that we know it and that we are thankful to them. Let us spare no effort to help them, comrades! And now it is up to you to decide what more we should do to help. You tell me, and together we will carry out whatever you say."

Natasha sat down. How easy it was to speak. Why had she been so afraid before? She found the answer to that in the words of a woman in the audience.

"Dear comrades," the woman said, "you all heard that we are asked to decide what more we should do to help our Spanish friends. What have we done until now? We have brought our modest gifts and we have given one day's wages a month. Let us give double of what we gave before, comrades! Let us give two days, and those of us who can afford it, those who have no children, let those of us give more, three days, four days."

Her words were drowned in applause, cheering, and loud "Hear, hear! Bravo! Good for you!"

Natasha knew then why it had been so easy for her to speak. The woman's proposal, like Natasha's own speech, came out of her heart; no one had decided it for her beforehand. Only at Spanish meetings these days did the chairman come without prepared resolutions and decisions, and was the audience asked to decide for itself what it wanted to do. Here, at these meetings for Spain, and only here, still existed a genuine spontaneous spirit, and only here Natasha felt a breath of the free participation of their early meetings. There was no organized cheering, nobody felt obliged to burst into applause at the mention of certain words or names. The words that called forth the loudest and most enthusiastic acclaim that evening were words they didn't even understand because there was no one to translate what the Spanish girl was saying. It did not matter to them what she was saying, this tall slim child with the beautiful black eyes and the soft husky voice. She was Spain to them, and in her person they expressed their love and their solidarity with Spain.

By the time the meeting was over, Natasha stood again on solid ground.

Natasha's expressive face made it difficult for her to conceal her feelings; Peter was always aware when she was troubled by doubts. Had he thought that no doubt ever entered her mind or that the official, stale phrases were always holy truth to her he would have turned away from her. Knowing what he knew about Natasha, he felt protective toward her. He was, he believed, the stronger of the two. He had started out in life with the same ideals and the same gods that she had started with. He gradually saw his ideals soiled and his gods tumbled from their pedestal. This brought him deep despair but he had the strength to admit to himself that his gods had tumbled. Natasha saw and knew everything he did. But when she admitted to herself that something was wrong with her gods she did not have the strength to go on, so she simply refused to admit it. He was able to face the bitter truth and go on living with open eyes, at times even enjoying life. Natasha could not. If it were possible for him to talk to her about it he would say to her:

"We started out to do something magnificent. We have failed in our first effort. We have achieved some of the physical, of the material things we dreamed about. But we have failed in everything else. There have been other failures of new ideas in history, but these ideas were not lost; they came back again later. So let us call our failure only a setback. Maybe not we, maybe it will be our children or their children who will come back, and they will finish what we started to do. The flame we have lit is not dead. Its sparks are alive all over the world. Maybe the next step will be made in another country. Maybe the people there will have learned a lesson from our failure, and they will not betray the human element as we did in our foolishness. They will not turn their backs on morality and principles, as we did. Or maybe the next step will again be ours, and we will be more sensible then and will succeed. But whatever happens, our dreams are not dead, Natasha, they are only postponed, they will come back to life again some day."

If only they could talk again about their old dreams. He would have helped her face the truth without too much pain. He did not want her to be hurt. Neither her reluctance as a wife nor her extreme seriousness, which at times chilled him, nor their mental estrangement could destroy the image of the girl of sixteen years ago, the lovely girl with the white skin and dark truthful eyes. He blamed life because of what it had done to her integrity. His heart was full of compassionate warmth for her.

But there were moments when pity was pushed out of his heart by anger, when sparks from the anger an inanimate object aroused in him would fly out and burn Natasha.

The inanimate object which he detested was an ugly, black contraption sticking out from the wall. It was the loudspeaker of the official radio: "our instrument of torture" Peter called it. Peter had violently objected to its installation. He wanted to wait till he could buy a radio on which he was free to listen to programs of his own choosing. But the official radio was one of those bounties which the authorities so kindly forced upon the population. Natasha would have considered it highly unpatriotic to refuse to have it installed. For months it had been hammered into them that nowhere in the world except in the Socialist Fatherland would a government be interested in supplying its people with loudspeakers.

There was no escape from this blessing. If their own wasn't on, the neighbors' were going at full blast. There was no way of tuning them down or softening the harshness of the tone. Their rooms were constantly filled with music Peter didn't care to hear, with news and exasperatingly boring speeches which he had read or heard already, with no less boring lectures on irrigation in Kazakstan or the flora in North Siberia. He was resentful of the accursed thing on any day, but his hate of it was reserved for special days. That was when the proceedings of the purge trials were being reported or a speech by Stalin was being rebroadcast. No matter how many times Stalin's speech had been printed in the press or heard over the radio, when it was rebroadcast everyone listened. At least, everyone's radio was on. It would not have looked proper if one's radio was silent at such a momentous hour. This could have aroused grave suspicions. Let there be no doubt about their loyalty! Millions of homes presented the same picture, the picture that drove Peter to his flashes of anger at Natasha. They would put away newspapers, books, sewing, washing, cleaning, and sit around the radio. Stalin's voice with its monotonous unmelodious inflections, his butchering of the Russian language with poor accent and poor style, his way of building his speeches on a sly asking and answering of questions grated upon Peter's nerves. Natasha would not move throughout the speech, no matter how long it lasted. Neither would her grandmother have moved while a priest conducted a church service!

This was bad enough. But listening to the trials was a million times worse. To hear Bukharin or Rakovski or any of the others who had been the gods of his youth called traitor and spy was almost impossible to stand. He sat with his eyes closed. He was afraid that if he looked at Natasha, listening with an eager intensity and nodding her head in approval at the abusive invectives being thrown at her former idols, he could never forgive her.

During the nightmarish days of the purge Peter often marveled at the workings of the human mind. Events of an indescribable horror were taking place. Events which should have torn their very lives out at the roots. Events which should have frozen their blood and made them lose their minds. Instead of that, movies, theaters, amusement parks, and cafés were filled to capacity. Fashion stores did a flourishing business. Vacation trains to the South were overcrowded. Poets attracted huge audiences to their recitals, young people kissed on park benches, housewives cooked and scrubbed with their usual devotion. The first shipment of bananas and grapefruit stirred Moscow and inspired editorials in the daily press. Children played and yelled in the streets undisturbed by the plight of their playmates who had to testify against their fathers before the fathers were shot.

The life of Peter's own family had not changed. They ate, they slept, they laughed, they tried to dress decently and to keep healthy. He himself was aroused or disturbed only for short moments at a time. The only change he found in himself was that he was much more interested now in the details of their everyday life. He had never cared much before what they were going to have for dinner or what new acquisitions Natasha had made for the house, not even what marks the children brought home from school. He had never before spent so much time with his children, drawing for them, reading with them. It became a family habit to read items from the newspapers together in the evening. Fortunately the press now provided plenty of interesting material to talk about. North Pole expeditions, spectacular parachute jumps, women fliers lost in the taiga, the longest ski trip ever made—from Siberia to Moscow; a constant stream of visiting Ukrainian beet growers, Donbas miners, Kazak dancers, White Sea fishermen, Uzbek cotton planters, Caucasian horsemen, and a succession of music, theater, movie, and dance festivals took up much of the newspaper space. The visitors were entertained with great pomp in the Kremlin, so were the heroes of the North Pole, the fliers, and the sportsmen. The descriptions of their talks with Stalin and their pictures with him did not leave much room for anything else in the press between the trials. During the trials, of course, the press was devoted entirely to them. The few Soviet leaders who died a natural death during those days, the celebration of Pushkin's centennial, the birthday of the poet Rustaveli, Stalin's fellow Georgian who had lived a thousand years earlier, the revival of a rusty old poem about the warrior-prince Igor, the anniversaries of the births and deaths of the czarist generals Suvorov and Kutuzov, all this rated many pages in the newspapers. This was a real blessing and it helped make Peter's evenings at home with his family peaceful and entertaining. He could easily be forgiven for having overlooked among the great hullabaloo over the glamorous beet growers and General Suvorov's upright character an item about British Prime Minister Chamberlain's trip to Munich or the tragic defeats of the Spanish Loyalists. It could not have been so very important anyway. If it were, they would have been told so. Peter saw in all this a purposeful design to keep his mind and all the other Peters' minds well occupied and clear of unnecessary thought. Peter did not object to this design. In the purge he had lost the last feeble capacity to object or protest even inside himself. It was better for him this way, it was quieter and safer.

In the fall of 1938, two years after the purge had started, the press was still reporting occasional arrests, acts of sabotage, executions. These occasional items seemed like a ripple on still waters after the storm of the Big Purge. Anniversaries of czarist patriots, prominent visitors to the Kremlin, and spectacular sports and art events were still being prominently displayed in the press. They still supplied enough topics for Peter and Natasha when they read the papers together in the evening and helped them avoid subjects which might arouse an unwelcome discussion. They never mentioned the new, severe punishments for being late at school and work, or the cutting down of vacations for pregnant women and nursing mothers, and many other items which occupied their minds a great deal. They did not discuss even the subject closest to them all at the present moment —the new shortages—after the one conversation they had about it.

"No wonder food is scarce again," said Natasha, "stores empty, no shoes, no textiles. What with the enemies and saboteurs who have wrecked the industry—"

"Natasha, use your logic. Didn't the shortages start after these people were arrested? Whatever we had in plenty we had while they were heading our industries; things began to disappear after they disappeared."

Peter immediately regretted his words. He should never have said them. Even if Natasha agreed with him, she would have to argue that he was wrong. As for himself, he was better off neither thinking nor talking about this. And, what was much more important to him, Volik was listening, and Peter knew that he had to be very careful in Volik's presence. Peter always felt Volik's watchful eye on him when he said anything "political." Things were fine as long as they stayed in the technical field. There Peter had Volik's complete confidence and respect.

Volik was almost fifteen now and, being a model Pioneer, he hoped to be admitted next year to the Comsomol. His behavior had to be above reproach and one of the first rules of such behavior was a never-relenting vigilance. The enemy is everywhere, he was being daily reminded in his Pioneer press and at his Pioneer meetings; his ways are clever and cunning. He may be hiding in your own family, in your school, even in your Pioneer organization; always remember to keep your eyes and ears open. No word is insignificant, no deed is unimportant. Watch—and report!

His mother was all right—Volik was sure of her—but he was not completely sure of his father. Being a good engineer or a good architect was not enough. Many of them had proved to be traitors. And there was more to it than that. The traitors had chosen these professions because they gave them a good chance for sabotage. This had been emphasized in many editorials in the *Pioneer Pravda*. Their Comsomol leader had said it too and he told them how to make sure that everyone they knew was of absolutely unquestionable loyalty. He gave them a few questions to ask people—for instance, could there be any loyalty higher than the loyalty to Stalin and the Soviet state? Or, would you hesitate to report a member of your family if you doubted the loyalty of that member? Or, did you ever question the guilt of the purged? There were several more. His mother answered every one of them in the right way. His father first laughed and didn't want to answer them at all, and even after Volik insisted he still did not give any straight answers. Next day Volik brought home from school and hung on the wall a poster showing a huge Soviet worker fighting with a many-headed and many-armed hydra. The poster read: "No Pity! No Mercy! Cut off the enemy's thousand heads and thousand arms!"

The crudeness and ugliness of the poster made Peter shudder but he forced himself to smile at it and even to nod approval to Volik. What was the difference? You wanted to live or you didn't want to live. And if you wanted to live you did what was needed to live. And what was needed just then was to keep nodding approval. Peter was very tired and he wanted to have his peace. If saying yes would keep him alive and keep peace, he was ready always to say yes. He had learned how even the slightest no could disturb his peace. He once mentioned waiting for a long time in the rain for a streetcar, which brought an angry retort from Volik: "Would you rather be an American and be unemployed and have to sleep on a filthy subway floor in New York?" Another time Peter's comment on the toughness of the roast made Volik even angrier: "If you were a starving Polish peasant you would be mighty happy to eat any meat at all!" Volik was in the midst of his course on the state of the world outside the Soviet Union. He knew without any doubt that everything in that world was of an unrelieved hopeless black as contrasted to the pure cloudless white that was the Soviet Union. The slightest criticism of things Soviet showed lack of appreciation for what they were privileged to enjoy, and was sheer blasphemy to Volik.

Peter was careful. Only seldom did he forget himself and arouse Volik's suspicion or anger. It was easy with Maya. With her Peter could relax. The questions she asked and the things she was interested in had little to do with any ideologies, Soviet or capitalist. She would sit quiet for hours on the window sill and then suddenly say:

"Look, Mother, look, Father . . . First it was pink, just a tiny little bit pink, then it got more pink, then it was red, then the red turned into purple, and the purple turned into a dark blue, and now the stars begin to come out. It is so beautiful, I could cry."

Or she would draw animals and flowers of the wildest forms and colors. She also drew houses. She always drew them low and rambling, hidden among trees, with open porches running along all four walls.

"I don't want to live in a city. I'd like to live among flowers and trees and birds and animals, but only small animals, I don't like big animals, they frighten me. And only when it is very very cold will I sleep inside. I will sleep on the porches. I will have a bed on each porch and I will move from one bed to another, with the moon, with the stars, with the clouds . . ."

Maya delighted Peter with her fantastic drawings and her dreams. They worried and disturbed Natasha. Why couldn't Maya be like the other girls? Why did she have to draw those ridiculous nonexistent things and refuse to make posters for the school and the Pioneers? At home she recited so nicely, but she refused to take part in any Pioneer affairs. It is true, there she could not well recite the old-fashioned sentimental verses she preferred—but why should she prefer them? When Natasha pressed Maya to do what other children did, Maya begged her:

"Please, Mother, don't make me do what I don't want to do. I don't do anything bad to anybody, do I? I like to stay home, by myself, I like it when it is quiet. They make so much noise at the Pioneers, they don't talk, they shout, they scream, it hurts my ears the way they scream. I know I could never get up in front of them and make a speech or recite, I know I couldn't, why should I try? I don't want to do it."

Even if Natasha had been willing to let Maya alone, the school and the Pioneers were not. They complained that "Maya was not active enough," that "Maya's spirit was not the right Soviet spirit," that "Maya chose the wrong friends." Most complaints were about the "wrong friends." Maya could not stand loud, self-assertive children, and sought out the shy, the quiet ones. It so happened that most of these belonged to purged families. They were children who, after the shock of a parent's disappearance, did not find their way back to a carefree, noisy, active life.

Natasha was annoyed by the many complaints.

"Must you pick your friends from families who are under suspicion?" she once asked with an anger to which Maya was not accustomed. "Aren't there enough children from the right kind of homes?"

Maya's big brown eyes were full of reproach.

"But I don't feel sorry for them, and I do feel sorry for the others. Don't you pity them, Mother, don't you? They are very unhappy; wouldn't you try to be nice to them to make them feel better? Why should I be friends with those who don't need me, who are happy without me?"

Natasha had nothing to reply to that. All she knew was that Maya did not behave the way other children did, that she was different from the others, that it was bad to be different from others, and that the school and Pioneers did not like it. To be different meant to arouse suspicion. Even Maya's own brother was suspicious of her:

"Any other kid would be happy if I were to take her along to the Pioneer Palace, but no, not she. She wouldn't think of it, it is too noisy for her, she says. Why do you think she's that way, Mother? You think she doesn't like what we are doing, Mother?"

Oh, no, he must not think that of Maya. In his zeal he might get her into trouble.

"How can you say such a ridiculous thing, Volik? Of course, Maya loves everything the Pioneers are doing, but you know how girls are."

"Don't make me laugh, Mother, you don't know our girls. They put us boys to shame the way they can go on marching or making speeches without ever getting tired. Most of our cell leaders are girls. Oh, no, it couldn't be that."

"All right, then let's say some girls and even some boys are that way, shy, embarrassed to talk, happiest when they are alone."

"Sure, Mother, I know that kind. But there is always something wrong with them; with their families, rather."

To Natasha's relief, Volik was very busy with his own life. An outstanding Pioneer, an outstanding student and athlete, he had much too little time to worry about his sister—or his father.

With life settling back after the purge, the fear of contact with the wrong people was loosening its grip. The moment had come, Natasha thought, to find out what had happened to some of those she had lost sight of lately. Most of all she wanted to know about Kira. The papers had announced the name of Maxim's successor. That meant Maxim's arrest. No other news about Maxim was reported. Was he alive? What had happened to Kira? For many months Natasha was afraid to get in touch with her. Now she felt it was safe to telephone Maxim's apartment. She did it from a pay station. A strange woman's voice answered. "Who is there? Whom do you want?" The fear of the purge was still alive in Natasha. She ran out of the booth as fast as she could in case the call was being traced.

Ilya Gromov had been arrested in the spring of 1937 when his chief, the head of the GPU, the feared and hated Yagoda, was arrested. His execution had been announced later, together with the execution of several other prominent GPU members. When Peter read of it, he had said:

"I never liked Gromov and I don't think he was a spy, but if innocents are to die, let it be men like Yagoda and Gromov. On their hands is the blood of many innocents. . . . I wonder," he added, "whether the thousands whom Yagoda sent to jail are going to be freed. If he was a traitor all these years, the people whom he sentenced must have been good people."

Natasha hoped to have more success in finding out about Katya and her child. Tanya must be six years old now. She had been a beautiful baby. An old loyalty stirred in Natasha. The child was grandmother Kseniya's great-grandchild, just as her own children were. The least she could do would be to find out what had happened to the child. How? Through Vera? It was long since Natasha had last heard about Vera from a gossiping neighbor. These past years one did not do much gossiping with neighbors and certainly not about people like Vera. And it was long since Natasha had last seen Vera's gaunt black figure with eyes staring straight ahead, not looking at anyone. Natasha was never certain whether Vera recognized her—there was never a word or a sign.

Through an old neighbor in Vera's house Natasha found the dressmaker who worked for Katya and who used to stay in her apartment for weeks at a time. She knew all about Katya and Vera. She did not like to be rushed and told the story in more detail than Natasha cared to hear.

"... of course Katya, the poor soul, got bored. Who could blame her for it? Young and beautiful as she is. She wanted to talk about a new dress or her new hair-do, and even among their women she couldn't find many she could talk to about the things she cared for. . . . It wasn't so bad as long as her husband had more time for her. That was before that accursed day Kirov was assassinated. Stalin and Yagoda left immediately for Leningrad to investigate, and Ilya was on their train. He was away for eight days, and when he came back he was never the same again. Even in bed, she told me, he was not the same. He didn't care about her the way he used to, and he was always worried. . . . And one day he almost knocked her down. I heard him scream: 'It's a lie, it's a lie! Don't dare say it again! It's none of your business!' She told me later what it was all about. She'd never asked him any questions about his affairs, but that day somebody told her that Kirov was not shot at all the way the papers said. The man who shot him was not a Trotskyite who did it to hurt the government but a man whose wife Kirov took for himself. Now, this was something Katya was really interested in and she wanted to know more. After all, why does a woman have a husband close to such an affair if she can't find out more about it? But he just screamed at her. She got angry then, and asked him more questions, just in spite. Was it true, she asked him, what people said about Stalin's ordering a hundred innocent men shot who happened to be in the Leningrad prison when Kirov was killed? And was it true that terrible things were happening before the prison, like mothers of the young men killing themselves? This time, she said, he didn't say a word. He didn't get mad at her for asking. He just sat with his head in his hands while she asked her questions.

"She carried on like mad when they came for him. I think it was mostly because she was afraid. She was terribly afraid. . . . Now, I have seen other wives in the same boat. Going around as I do, I have seen plenty of them but I never saw anyone so afraid of being put in prison. . . . 'You aren't going to take me away too? You aren't going to do anything to me? You will not put me in prison?' Imagine worrying about herself being in prison when her man might be shot. And you wouldn't believe it, she was making eyes at the man who was in charge of Ilya's arrest. He was very important, Ilya being so important himself. 'Oh, what will I do now? Oh, how will I live? Oh, who will take care of me and my child?' Oh, oh, oh, it was, and I, I, I! And grabbing at the man's hands and letting her robe open and show her breasts. Well, she certainly got what she was after. It wasn't more than a week after poor Ilya was put to death that she moved into the man's house. She is his wife now, and she gets from him all she got from Ilya. She certainly has a soft life."

"And Tanya?"

"He didn't want the child. I heard him say so. You would think a mother would at least put up a fight for her child. Not Katya, not she. She gave the child to her mother."

"What? Tanya lives with her grandmother in the old house?"

"Oh, no, not there. They live near the town of Klin. They wouldn't let the old woman stay in Moscow. She was one of the 'undesirable elements' they sent out of Moscow. If you ask me, they wanted the old woman's room, and that was a good excuse to get rid of her. Katya sends her money and things, and has visited them there. Tanya goes to school . . ."

"But isn't it very bad for her to live with such an embittered old woman as Vera?"

"Vera may be embittered with you and me, but she certainly isn't with Tanya. She worships the ground the child walks on. The child has done something to her. Vera learned how to talk again, even to smile, at least to the child. Tanya is a happy little girl."

CHAPTER 32

*Natasha and Kira*

KIRA came home hot and tired from work on a summer evening in 1941. A week ago she had received one of Maxim's regular letters with the usual, "Am well . . . received your last package . . . hope you are in good health . . ." Over the few words that followed Kira had cried bitterly. "If you can get permission, send a candle in the next package. The evenings are long here." Kira knew enough about the place where Maxim was to understand that not only the evenings but most of the days were dark there too. She knew that they had no light and heat in the closely packed barracks. It was his asking for things like a candle, a comb, a nailfile, bedbug powder, a spool of thread, a salve against sores, things she seldom could send him, that always made her cry heartbrokenly. Modest as his requests were, she either could not get permission to send them or they were unobtainable in Moscow. In what filth and destitution Maxim must be living.

Today for the third time she had tried to get permission to send him the candle. But again the clerk told her that if a candle was found in the package, Maxim would be deprived of the privilege of receiving packages. She should be happy, the clerk added, that she could send him anything at all; not many were so lucky.

With a heavy heart Kira climbed to her room, careful not to fall on the rickety stairs. A letter was sticking in her door. Except for letters from Maxim, Kira never got any letters, and his next letter was not due for many weeks. It was a fat envelope made of wrapping paper, the kind they had all learned to make again since envelopes, like all other goods, had once more disappeared from the stores. It was obvious that the person who wrote the address had tried to disguise the handwriting. The postal stamp was Moscow. Kira tore the envelope open. At the sight of what fell out of it she turned deathly white and her breath came quick and loud. Kira locked the door and turned off the light. The window would give her enough light. No one must know that she was at home; she had to be alone now.

Kira spread before her bits of paper covered with Maxim's handwriting. They were of many shapes, some torn off pieces of wrapping paper, others margins from a newspaper page, two were envelopes in which she had mailed her letters to him. They were written with a thick unsharpened pencil. Only words written with the pencil freshly moistened were easy to read, the others were hardly decipherable. Parts of it looked like a diary, other parts like letters to her. Kira had heard that by bribing the guards or by throwing an envelope out of a train on their way to a new place, prisoners had sometimes managed to get word through to their families. Kira had never dared hope for that kind of luck. Now she held such a letter in her hands! She didn't read it immediately; she cried shakenly and kissed the dirty and crumpled pieces of paper. God knew where Maxim had had to hide them! Finally she dried her eyes and, sitting on the window sill, began to read:

". . . the main thing is to use every effort to remain a human being, not to turn into a beast. Some comrades have lost all human characteristics. Good comrades, very good comrades. One must not blame them. It is very hard to be always hungry. It is only the thought of the guard's club that often gives me the strength to go on breaking the frozen ground. . . . I don't want to die yet. . . . Not as long as there is still hope of seeing my wife someday . . . hope that maybe someday I will be a human being again, not the hungry filthy half-frozen ragged beast I am today.

". . . I wish we could talk again as real people talk, not bark one at another as we do now. Everybody distrusts everybody else. . . . I know that my being here is a tragic mistake but why is Samoilov here, Kuragin, Steinberg, Maskalov? Maybe there was something in their past which justifies their being here . . . They make me feel that they are not sure I am here without a good reason. Why are we this way? Why not talk like comrades and try to understand the calamity that has befallen all of us?

". . . When I was young we used to read good books in czarist prisons, we studied science and languages and politics: prisons were like a university. Young people learned to think in prison. . . . We have no books here, no newspapers, nothing to read. . . . We were comrades then, there was respect and friendship among us. We despised the stoolpigeons planted by the police and we made life hell for them. We have stoolpigeons in our midst now, we know it, but it is hard for us to recognize them. . . . We are not comrades now, we are not sure who our enemy is, we don't know even whom to call an enemy, we all feel differently. And we feel differently about stoolpigeons. We don't even know whether to call them stoolpigeons. . . . Aren't they after all the servants of the Soviet government, isn't this still our government? . . ."

Kira found it hard to decipher Maxim's scribbling. He must have been writing in most uncomfortable positions, with nothing suitable to put the paper on. Words were wide apart, sometimes one written on top of the other, as if the writer could not see in the dark what he was writing. With great difficulty Kira was able to read almost every word of the first few notes. She had them in chronological order, Maxim put a date on each. But try as she could, there was no way to make out all his writing after January, 1940.

"... It is a thought to make a man insane. It can't be true what they say. They must have all lost their minds. But there are so many of them, and they come from different places at different times, and they all say the same things ... old Jews with long white beards, why should they lie? And the Polish children, they say the same thing, they couldn't all have gone crazy in the same way. . . .

"... Kira, Kira, I need you, help me to understand. I am afraid I am losing my mind. How can I remain sane if what they say is true? Tell me, tell me, Kira, it isn't true! Tell me that Stalin never signed a pact with Hitler! Wouldn't we have laughed ... wouldn't we have rushed the lunatic who said it to an insane asylum?

"... I called Kasimir a liar when he first told me ... he had clippings hidden in the lining of his cap, where he keeps his murdered wife's picture. There it was, Stalin and Molotov smiling at Ribbentrop, Molotov's own words about blood friendship with Hitler. . . . Kira, Kira, I can't stand it, I don't believe in anything any more. If this is possible, then everything is possible, there is nothing sacred.

"... since the Poles came, the guards sometimes give us papers to read; they know that the Poles told us. I don't understand the papers. We were always told there was no greater beast than Hitler. What has changed this? What has made Roosevelt become worse than Hitler? And the British? They are at war with Hitler, we are friends with Hitler. No, no, no, I must be insane . . .

"If any one of us remains sane it will be a miracle. The Jews— the wretched creatures, it turns one's heart to look at them. Simon is only twenty. He told me how they fled when the Germans came. They fled to meet their saviors, the Red Army . . . Communists among them, Socialists, workers, peasants, intellectuals, Poles and Jews . . . death was nothing to them as long as they didn't fall into Nazi hands. Their saviors met them with bayonets and bullets, many were killed . . . they were herded into cages . . . Thousands died on their way to Siberia, most of their women and children died, hunger and cold . . . saw them die, saw them being thrown out of the train by Soviet soldiers . . . lost one another, children, parents, husbands, wives.

"... when they told me about Finland, I was so ashamed I could have cried. A giant attacks a fly! The mighty giant fights a tiny neighbor . . . so proud when we gave Finland its independence, Lenin insisted on it, he didn't want any of the booty grabbed by czars.

". . . death would be merciful. To have lost everything, all hope, all faith, to have lost the Soviet dream . . . moans, crying at night, desperate hating faces . . . a stinking body covered with lice, nothing decent left inside or outside. . . . Kira, do you understand it all? Answer me, help me . . ."

More words followed, but not even by holding the candle so close that it almost burned the paper could she bring out a single letter. Maxim's tears had effaced every trace of them . . . Until morning, until the hour when it was time to get dressed and go to the factory, Kira sat over the miserable scraps of paper. She did not cry anymore. She was dry eyed and quiet now. She hid the papers well, washed her face, and went to work.

"I have a headache . . . the heat got me . . ." she told the women who worked near her, and they let her alone.

What should she do now? There was no way of letting Maxim know that she had received his letter, no way of sending him a comforting word. The next letter to him could not be sent for six weeks, and anyway she could give him no hint that she had received his—never must the prison camp censor suspect that she had heard from Maxim outside his official letters. But suppose she could have written him a real letter and told him all she knew? Could she answer any of his questions? What could she say? She didn't understand anything herself. She had never realized so clearly as now, shaken out of her somnolent existence by Maxim, how little she had been concerned with anything beyond Maxim, his letters, her packages to him. The pact, the partition of Poland, the attack on Finland, all these events she had taken as they came along, without thinking much about them. It was empty and lifeless inside her since Maxim had been gone, nothing excited her, nothing was important enough to worry about.

Now she wanted to think and to understand. Maxim expected her to know the answers, he expected her to be interested and to understand. She could not fail him. But how was she to inform herself? Through whom? Her coworkers? They talked only about the petty occurrences in the factory or about their difficulties in shopping.

Was there anyone else she could talk to? Even with her comrades in misery, in the old house and in her present home, Kira had never discussed anything that did not have some bearing on their imprisoned relatives. People seemed to have lost the ability to exchange real thoughts.

Then Kira had an idea. Natasha! Peter! Natasha must have forgiven her for turning her away three years ago. She must have understood the reason for it. Yes, she would go to them—they wouldn't turn her away. Anyway, they were the only people she could think of and she was going to talk to them.

Kira went to them straight from work. She was right—Natasha had forgiven her. Natasha threw her arms around her, hugged her and kissed her, and they both cried a little. Maya looked at Kira with wide eyes. That poorly dressed oldish woman couldn't be her beautiful laughing aunt Kira! Kira turned to Maya and her eyes too opened wide. That lovely tall girl, with dark dreamy eyes, with two long braids and Natasha's white skin—was that the little Maya whom she and Maxim liked to think of as their own child? What a tall girl she was, tall for her fifteen years. Kira smiled at Maya, and then Maya knew; no one else could smile the way her aunt Kira smiled—that wide big smile, which even now, on the tearstained thin face, made Maya think of sunshine. Kira pressed Maya close.

"Maya, my little darling," she whispered.

No one could have brought back Kira's lost happiness with Maxim so vividly as Maya. She must pull herself together. She had not come here to go to pieces over memories of the past.

Kira shook hands with Peter, who greeted her warmly. Only Volik remained aloof. He said a quiet "Good evening" and stood watching the others. Natasha caught his watchful look. She quickly checked her tears and her excitement.

"Straight from work, Kira?" She made her voice sound matter-of-fact, as if there was nothing unusual about Kira's coming. "Working in a factory, you say? What kind of factory? How are things there? Tell us all about it. We'd love to hear. . . . Is your factory on the Red Banner list or on the Turtle one? We hope on the first, don't we, Volik?"

So that's what it was! Kira understood now what had made Natasha suddenly change from the sincere warm welcome to this artificial chatter. It was Volik! Volik with the Comsomol pin in his lapel, eyeing them sharply.

Maybe she shouldn't have come at all. Maybe she should say now that she happened to be passing by and dropped in for a minute, just as Natasha had, three years before. As if he had read her thoughts, Peter took the shopping bag out of her hands, and made her sit down near the open window:

"This will cool you off, it's hot tonight. How about some tea, Natasha? It's nice the children are home, so we can have a cozy evening together. Come, Maya, come Volik, sit down, tell Aunt Kira what you have been doing. Don't you think they have grown big and strong? Show her your muscles, Volik."

Apparently they really wanted her to stay. Natasha looked flushed and pleased as she prepared the tea things. Maya helped her. Peter went on with his small talk until Volik, clearing his throat, said:

"I must go now . . . I have a meeting."

"No, really? What a pity! And I was so glad we were all going to be together tonight. Can't you stay, Volik? Are you sure? It will not be the same if you go."

Kira could clearly hear in Peter's voice that he had known all along that Volik was going to a meeting. What was going on? Why was Peter so very eager to prove to Volik that he was sorry to see him leave them? Wasn't he overdoing it? Wouldn't Volik notice it as she noticed it? No, Volik did not. He took his father's assurances seriously. And if his father wanted him to stay it meant that they had nothing to hide. It was going to be just an ordinary family visit, nothing suspicious. Relieved, Volik said good-by to Kira, poked Maya, and kissed Natasha good night. With Volik gone, Natasha dropped all pretense of being interested in Kira's factory, and showered her with eager questions:

"What happened to Maxim? Alive? In Siberia? And you—how are you getting along? Where do you live? Do you need help? . . ."

This was not Natasha the stern party member in whose presence Kira had at times felt slightly subdued. Natasha's voice was warm and affectionate, and it was easy for Kira to talk the way she had hoped she could talk to them. She talked, she told them everything her heart was full of, but she didn't get the answers she was looking for. Natasha was silent, her head buried in her hands, while Kira talked. Peter admitted he did not know any answers.

"What do I know, how can I explain anything? I am as bewildered as you are, as we all are." Peter stopped. He couldn't see Natasha's face, it was hidden. Was she going to jump up and forbid him to express his "heretical thoughts" in her presence, as she had done before? No, she only buried her head deeper in her hands and said nothing. Peter went on:

"I often wonder what other people think. I wish I knew. Nobody says anything except what is in the papers. Has anything remained alive in people? I suppose many are cynical, they are not fooled, but they play the game, they know what happens if you don't play the game. Many, I suppose, are sincere, and, like our own Volik, believe that Stalin is the wisest man on earth and that we are the chosen people because we are privileged to live under his protective arm. It has been hammered into our heads long enough. . . . Don't try, Kira, to understand, nobody can. We don't know the facts, we don't know anything. Don't ask questions. If you are told that Hitler is your friend or that all Slavs are your blood brothers, accept it, don't ask questions."

Kira was not too disappointed about not getting her answers. Simply to be able to talk about Maxim, to tell someone what happened in the past three years, was an indescribable relief. She could have stayed on and on. But Natasha suddenly got up and, her face flushed and nervous, she began to urge Kira to leave:

"You'd better go; I don't want Volik to find you here—he may become suspicious."

"Now, now, Natasha, don't exaggerate." Peter did not want to hurt Kira by this sudden dismissal. "It is very early yet; even Volik couldn't find anything wrong."

"It's better for Kira to go now," Natasha insisted, "and, besides," she added, averting her eyes from Peter's, "I feel like having some fresh air. I'll walk with Kira to the subway. Don't wait up if I am late, Peter, I may want to sit on the boulevard; it is cool there."

Natasha was fidgety and impatient, obviously in a great hurry to leave. Was she really worried about Volik's finding them in the midst of an only too obviously interrupted conversation? Peter doubted it. Natasha always found the right tone with Volik; he never suspected her. What was it, then? Was she going to hurt Kira? Peter doubted that too. Natasha linked arms with Kira even before they went out the door.

They were hardly out of Peter's hearing when Natasha, shaking violently, said:

"You don't know what you did to me tonight, Kira! I thought I had forgotten how a real human voice sounds, a voice which speaks from the heart, the way you spoke. I thought I had forgotten that I once had such a voice too. I still have it, Kira, I found it tonight."

"But you have Peter. Don't you talk with him the way I talked with Maxim?"

They sat on a bench under a linden tree, on the boulevard across from Ludmilla's former home. Again Natasha buried her face in her hands and it was with difficulty that Kira could hear her words:

"No, I don't. We haven't talked that way for many years. He doesn't know what goes on in me, I don't know what goes on in him. Don't you see, I am a party member, my heart and my soul are not my own, not my husband's, they belong to the party. If I talked to Peter, if I permitted myself to listen to his doubts or let him suspect my doubts —I could not have remained a faithful party member . . . And I wanted so much to remain one . . . I am afraid I am not . . ."

Natasha lifted her head and clung to Kira with both hands.

"Let me talk, will you, Kira? I must talk. I know, you came to us so we could help you. But I need help myself, you must help me, you must let me talk. I can't stand it any longer. Will you let me talk, will you?"

Natasha's voice was trembling and her hands felt feverish. Kira put her arm protectively around Natasha's shoulder. "Of course, Natasha, I will, of course."

"I don't even know where to start. Don't mind if my words jump around; there is so much I want to get out, and I don't know how to talk any more. It was words that first began to disturb me—the same words we heard twenty years ago. Then they sounded fresh and young, and they were very exciting. But when you hear the same words for twenty years, they don't sound fresh and young any more. I heard them on all occasions, big and small, in print, in speeches, on the radio, and they began to sound stale to me, formal, empty, false, ossified. I forced myself not to feel that way; I really wanted to take the words religiously as I used to take them in the past. It was hard, Kira, very hard, and I fought very hard. I kept lying to myself and convincing myself that I believed in them. And you know when I definitely knew that I was lying to myself? It was on the day when the papers printed the news about the pact. It hit me like a blow. Peter got all white and pressed his lips together to show me that he was not going to talk about it. We didn't talk—we never talk about things that hurt us. In our plant they called a meeting: to explain the pact, they said. I was very glad about it; I'm sure the others were too. Everybody looked bewildered, but nobody said a word. We had an important speaker from the Central Committee. I sat in the first row; I didn't want to miss a single word, I wanted to understand. And you know, Kira, what he said? I still remember it, I don't think I'll ever forget it. He said, '. . . the great wisdom of our beloved Leader has saved us once more from disaster. . . . Again his genius reached out in time and cut off the claws which an enemy thrust out to destroy the Soviet fatherland. . . . Let us thank him, let us tell him of our feelings for him, of our eternal loyalty to him, to our Beloved Great Stalin!' Not a single word to explain why we had to make a deal with Fascists! And you should have heard the applause, and the shouts 'Long Live Stalin!' The applause would have lasted indefinitely but the speaker was in a hurry. He cut it short and pulled a resolution out of his pocket. It was a repetition of what he had just said. We adopted it unanimously and he left even while we still had our hands in the air—every one of us, for of course no one had the courage not to vote. Oh, Kira, I can't tell you how I felt. I was so let down, so humiliated. To treat us like a herd of stupid sheep, sheep who weren't supposed to know anything, only to follow . . ."

A man sat down on their bench. Natasha waited till he left before she went on:

"Oh, Kira, how I began to hate words! I couldn't hear them, I couldn't read them any more without my nerves twitching and jumping. And all the time having to be silent about it, never to betray my feelings. But once I almost betrayed myself. You know when it was? At that big celebration in the Bolshoi Theater after the last elections. I got three tickets and I took the children along. They were all there, our leaders—Stalin, Beria, Andreyev, Zhdanov, Molotov, Bulganov, Malenkov. It was the first time the children had seen them so close, and Volik was almost sick with excitement at breathing the same air. He kept looking at the boxes with a worship on his face I had never seen before. I looked at the boxes too and my heart almost burst with pain. Remember who used to sit in those boxes? Remember Bukharin, and that twinkle in his eyes? And Karakhan? He used to make women's hearts flutter. And Radek, who always tried to look as wild as he could? And Tukhachevski? Sokolnikev? Mezhlauk? Kamenev? Serebryakov? Ossinski? Krylenko? Petrovski? Krestinski? . . . Oh, Kira, I could hardly hide my pain. And at that moment I realized for the first time that I had been deceiving myself, that deep inside I had never for one minute believed that any of those men were traitors. For one moment I felt good—that was when we got up and sang the 'International.' But then the speeches began, and the words began, words, words, words, which I had heard thousands of times before and which grated on my nerves so that I had to hold onto my seat. And I wondered if the speakers really believed in what they said or were they deceiving themselves and us when they exclaimed, ' . . . our great Soviet democracy, the only, the greatest democracy on earth . . . where else do people live our kind of life, our happy and carefree life? . . . The rest of the world is decaying in the blackest hopeless misery. . . . And who is the one to whom we owe it all, every moment of our wonderful happy rich lives? Who but our precious . . .' And the applause thundered even before the speaker mentioned the name. I began to lose control of myself. What happened next was even worse. You remember the old actress Polonskaya? She was middle-aged when we were children. They dragged her out to speak. And there she stood, in an old-fashioned stiff court robe, glittering with pearls and diamonds, the ones she got from the czar and the grand dukes, her bosom heaving and her voice shaking with old age and false emotions. She held out her hands to the audience and gushed: 'My dear dear friends, it was the happiest day of my life when I was given the greatest privilege of all—to vote in the district which had the honor to elect Him, Him whom we all love, adore, worship, Him, the immortal Stalin!' And she talked about the miserable days of the past, of the hunger, of the secret police and jails full . . . Imagine her, who was a friend of the czar and swam in luxury! It was then that something in me revolted and I decided to make an end to my lying and deceiving. I was going to tell my children that it was all false, that the old woman didn't mean a word she said, that no one had meant a word they'd said, and that I was going to tell them the real truth. But when I looked at them, what did I see? Maya's eyes were swimming in tears, she was so touched by Polonskaya's clowning. Volik was manfully controlling his emotions but I could see how deeply he was impressed. And I knew I couldn't say a word to them, I couldn't destroy their lives, I had to continue to lie and to see them grow up in a world of lies . . ."

For a long time Natasha sat silent, staring at her hands. When she started to talk again it was as if she was continuing her thinking out loud:

"It was only Volik with whom I had to be careful not to betray my real feelings. Not with Maya. Maya, as you must have seen tonight, is not interested in politics. Volik really worries me, Kira. Suppose he finds out how I feel? What happens then? Anything. It would make little difference to him that I am his mother, that he is my only, my adored son. He is above all a member of the Comsomol, his loyalty is to the party, not to me. I ought to understand—didn't I feel the same way? Volik is a wonderful boy. He is lively, he is quick, good-looking, clear-eyed. His body is the body of a young athlete. He has great physical courage and he has won competitions in parachuting and ski jumping. But you see, Kira, all I can think of are physical qualities. Has Volik got any moral courage? I don't know. His marks are excellent at school. But has he real intelligence, the kind that makes for great thinkers, great writers? I don't know. Volik has no way of showing this. He has no way of showing any of his own feelings or own thinking. Don't you see, Kira, in his whole young life Volik has never yet been confronted with a choice between two alternatives. The choice has always been made for him. He has always been told what he should think or do. He has never known anything else in his life. To him this is the only possible, the only right way to live—to have everything decided for him by the Leader, by the party, who know best, much better than he, what's good for him and for everybody else. He accepts this willingly, even with joy. He wouldn't know how to behave if he were on his own, if he had to make his own choice. They are like that, the young people. They are healthy, strong, self-confident zealots. They are capable ambitious students, they are fearless in their readiness to follow. They make good doctors, good scientists, good technicians, good athletes . . . Are they hard, are they soft? Who knows. I've heard them get very sentimental and I've seen them full of cold brutal fury. But it was always something they were told to get sentimental or furious about. I never saw Volik or any of his friends really impulsive. Young as Volik is, he has hated many different enemies already. Today he hates the Americans and English as fiercely as he hated the Nazis only a while ago and when he says 'democracies' he says it with the same sneer he used to have for Hitler.

"You are not bored, Kira, are you? But, you see, when I talk about Volik I am really telling you how I feel. I haven't talked for many years, as I told you. Now, Volik, he talks freely and loudly. All the young people talk that way. They have nothing to fear from their words. They couldn't say anything wrong. Nothing they say comes out of their own minds; they couldn't possibly make a mistake. I miss so much the spirit of adventure in Volik. I had so much of it when I was young. Once we talked about travels in faraway lands. 'Me? Go abroad?' snapped Volik. 'Am I crazy? Why should I ever want to go away from here? Isn't this good enough for me?' ... He is so lively, and still at times he seems like an automaton to me. Oh, Kira, a mother shouldn't look at a son with such critical eyes! But Volik to me is the symbol of what has become of our youth: automatons, strong healthy automatons who are gay and happy, but who are not real live people.

"Look around, Kira. How many really exciting interesting people do you know today? The kind Maxim and my mother, for instance, were? None, I am sure. Nobody stands out above the crowd, everybody merges into the crowd. Do we have writers who inspire us, writers like Gorki, Chekhov, Andreyev, who each had such a strong individual personality? Our writers now are automatons too, they follow the party line, as we all do. Remember, Kira, the books we loved? Remember Tolstoi's women, Turgenev's? Do you know any unusual women now? Our women are pale, gray inside; like parrots, they repeat words they hear. Look at me, Kira. I used to be a fighter; so were many women in our youth. But do you see any fighters now? Krupskaya, Kollontai, they are the products of the old days. Where are such women today? ... Take grandmother Kseniya, first subdued by her father, then by her husband—she still had a character, a personality all her own. Remember grandfather Anton? Cut out of stone. ... We live according to prescriptions, how can we develop real characters, strong personalities?"

Wearily Natasha leaned her head against Kira's shoulder.

"Yes, you are right," Kira said softly. "I know, Natasha, that you did not have much respect for my parents. I can't blame you for it; I myself despised their views and their ways. But even they were individuals, they were colorful, not the pale shadows life has made of you and me and Maxim."

When they parted they said good-by with a long embrace.

Natasha's step was quick and light as she walked home. Peter heard it on the stairs. She walked like the young Natasha, as she had in the days when there was no burden on her heart, when she rushed home every day breathless with enthusiasm. There was no breathless enthusiasm on the face of Natasha when she came into the room now. But there was serenity in her eyes, they held again that look which had always made people trust her and feel that never could a girl with such eyes utter an untruth or do a wrong. Natasha walked over to Peter with outstretched arms. On her way home she had decided to tell him, You were right all along, I was wrong. But she did not have to say it. He held her close:

"All right, all right, Natasha dear. I knew you would come back to me someday."

They did not say much. Natasha, weak after the feverish rush of emotions in her talk with Kira, put her arms around Peter tightly, smiled through tears.

"I am home again, Peter, I am home with you, I am here to stay with you. I feel as if I'd been away from you many years."

"You understand me now, Natasha, don't you? On the surface, live as you have till now, deceive and lie—we have to—but inside keep honest. Don't fight the good in you, Natasha, don't destroy it, my darling. Someday we will again be able to follow our conscience."

They were close to each other, happy in having found each other again, happy in a silence full of understanding and nearness.

CHAPTER 33
*War!*

THERE was little silence in their lives a few days later. Neither was there in the life of anyone in Russia or of anyone anywhere else. Radios, telegraph lines, telephone wires, ship signals, sirens, horsemen, alarm bells, and just plain frightened citizens spread the news to the shores of the White and Black seas, to the farthest Siberian outpost, to the Caucasian mountaineers, and to the newly Sovietized Polish villages. The Nazi hordes had descended on the Soviet land! Hitler had broken the pact and gone to war against the Soviet Union!

For many years the Soviet people had been told that someday there would be a war between their Socialist country and the capitalist world. They had been told that their many privations were necessary because of that future war. They had built up an industry such as no other country had ever built in so short a time. They had built up an army which, though weakened through the purge, was still the most powerful Russia had ever possessed. They had built up a nation of men, women, and children ready to defend their country to the last breath. It was true, they had also been told that they did not have much to fear. Who could ever have forgotten Stalin's words, words which had become their Holy Gospel:

"We want not one foot of foreign soil, but we will not give up an inch of our own soil."

No, they had not had much to fear with such a promise from Stalin. And they had not had much to fear since the pact with Hitler—repugnant though it was—had made them safe from an outside attack and had kept them out of the war in which the capitalist world was engaged. It had been necessary to prepare and to be ready but it was good to know that it was being done only as a precaution. Stalin's promises were always good, the people could rely upon him.

But something had gone wrong, and in one dreadful second all the promises and all the safety were blown away. Foreign soldiers marched on Soviet soil. Foreign planes covered the Soviet sky and the thunder of foreign heavy guns deafened Soviet ears. But Soviet minds, conditioned to blind obedience, did not ask questions at any time and certainly not when their country was invaded. Amidst the confusion and blunderings of a criminal unpreparedness, under the blows of the furious Nazi onslaught, with many Red Army commanders new and inexperienced, with whole factories and important transportation junctions falling into enemy hands, with casualties and prisoners mounting into hundreds of thousands wherever battles were fought, with towns and villages being burned by either retreating friends or advancing foes, with despair and fear spreading over the land—the people, the little people, were each performing their quiet heroic deeds in this great national debacle.

Ravaging and burning, the German Army moved closer and closer to Moscow. Endless processions of trains, cars, trucks, boats, horse carts carried away the fortunate ones who were permitted to leave the endangered city. School children were being evacuated to safety with their teachers and their school equipment. Jews, who were tortured and murdered wherever the Germans moved in, were being evacuated too. Factories, hospitals, libraries, scientific institutions, museums, theaters were leaving, taking along their staffs with their families, their machinery, exhibits, books, carloads of Stalin's portraits, laboratories, scenery, beds, food.

Two people in Kira's house were among those evacuated. Not, of course, people whose relatives were enemies of the people. Kira was still working in the box factory, and after work she helped dig defense ditches around Moscow. Air alarms sounded, Germans flew over the city and dropped incendiary bombs. But Kira and the others who worked with her did not quit work to flee to safety. They would not have quit, even if they had had the choice, for they did not want to see Moscow fall into German hands. But they had no choice. They were not supposed to run away. Their lives were not precious lives. There were millions and millions of other expendables in prisons and in labor camps. Who cared if some of them were killed? The security squads worked overtime and daily brought in many more expendables. Yes, those who dug the Moscow defense ditches were heroes. They dug under enemy fire. Foreign reporters sang hymns to their heroism, and the world press printed their songs.

Kira stood to her knees in mud. Cars passed on the highway, cars filled with people and their belongings, including pets, dogs, cats, birds. Kira watched them. If not for the purge, she would have been one of them, the wife of an important man, one of the Soviet aristocracy, fleeing from danger and leaving the plain people behind. Would she have thought then that it was unjust and contrary to Soviet principles? But would . . . would it all have happened, would the war have happened? Maybe not. That's what Peter had said when she saw him last. He had said that never, never could the pact with Hitler have been signed, if not for the purge. If the men who had been purged were alive, they would never have let it happen. And if not for the pact, how could Hitler have started the war? He could never have done it if he had not Stalin's assurance that Germany's eastern frontier was safe from Russian attack, that he did not have to fear a second front on the east. That was what Peter had said. And Maxim? What would he have said? Would she ever know that? They told her that she could not send him letters and packages now, and that she could expect no letters from him. Men and trains were needed for more important things than letters from criminals, they said.

The shovel sank easily into ground, soaked by several days of rain, but the wet clumps of soil slid back off the shovel. It was hard to make any progress. Carefully, Kira held the shovel so that the soil should not fall back into the ditch again. She was terribly tired. She had a whole day's work in the factory behind her. It was a long week, for they had no Sundays now; they were making containers for shells. And after work she had to dig. Of course, she wanted to dig. She wanted to defend Moscow, she was ready to work day and night to defend Moscow from the Nazis. If only she weren't made to feel such an outcast, someone who had to be watched lest she betray Moscow to the Germans. Before thrusting her shovel back into the ground Kira stopped for a moment to straighten her aching back.

The news of the war finally reached the bleak Siberian tundra that was Maxim's home. Some of the prisoners who had spent many years in that hell, their hearts embittered with hatred, did not care what the outcome of the war would be. One even said, "Let them get a licking, a good bloody . . . licking!" Nothing could make any difference any more; their lives were shattered beyond repair.

But men like Maxim felt differently. They did not look very human, either, with their wild hair, rag-covered sickly bodies, eyes feverish from hunger and watery from disease, their gums toothless from scurvy. But they were still able to rise above their own depravity. Human feelings were still alive in them, and new hopes stirred.

Deep down in the quarry, Maxim leaned on his pickax and let his thoughts wander. He was far, far away. He was in Moscow. He saw himself, head high, marching in a demonstration. Moscow must be full of marching people today. He saw himself speaking at a meeting, his heart aching with love for the Soviet land. He was too old to fight but he was not too old to double, to triple his efforts to work for victory and he appealed to all men too old to fight to do the same. Oh, how much he could still do, how much he would do! He leaned more heavily on the pickax, a dreamy smile on his face . . .

"Eh, you, get going, you loafer, get going! I'll show you." With his heavy boot, the guard knocked the pickax out from under Maxim's arm. Maxim fell, his face and head hitting the ground with a loud thud.

"Get up now, get up! Back to work!"

The guard kept kicking Maxim until he got to his feet. All day long, while working, Maxim wiped his face until by the end of the day streams of blood and tears had colored his filthy sleeve a muddy pink.

A few days after the beginning of the war Peter, Natasha, and the children were separated. Natasha was sent to Sverdlovsk with the Chemical Department of her plant. Peter remained in Moscow to work on Moscow's defense plans. When the plans were completed he, too, was transferred to Sverdlovsk. They lived on the outskirts of town, on a muddy unpaved street, in a one-story wooden shanty without plumbing. Their Moscow rooms seemed like a paradise of comfort by contrast. But this was not important now, since they were seldom at home. They worked day and night. Cots were put up in factories, laboratories, and offices, and there were many days when Peter and Natasha did not see each other.

Maya was not far away. Her school had been evacuated to a village in the same part of the Urals, which had become one of the main centers of wartime Russia. Every school girl was assigned a war job, and Maya's job was reading to wounded soldiers in a nearby hospital. She spent every moment after school in the hospital. All reading for soldiers had to be approved by the authorities but, fortunately for Maya, her beloved old poets and writers, frowned upon before, were all in great favor now. Noble sentiments, sweetness, nostalgic love sonnets —these were the order of the day; they were fashionable again. Girls like Maya were fashionable again, girls who blushed easily and who did not use rude words, the "Turgenev women," as they used to call them in the old days. Unless the conductor's baton changed its direction again, Maya's parents need not worry about her now. Maya could be herself and no Comsomol leader would come to them and complain that their daughter was not in tune with the times. For once Maya fitted into a party line.

Volik was in an officers' training camp. They seldom heard from him. There was no time for him to write and the transportation lines were too overtaxed to take sufficient care of private mails. Once Volik had a three-day furlough. These were days full of anxiety. Moscow was out of danger but in the west and in the south the Nazi armies kept rolling, laying waste the land and covering it with blood. Plants, dams, and buildings, representing years of selfless sacrifices and proud dreams, were blown into dust in a few hours. And there was no end in sight. Official bulletins were noncommittal. People comforted one another with words of hope, but deep in their hearts they were not too sure about the outcome.

But Volik was sure. It never entered his mind that there could be more than one outcome—complete Soviet victory over Hitler. As to the present defeats, well, they were not really defeats. The Red Army was retreating in order to lure the Germans deep inland, where soon, any day now, they would be surrounded and destroyed. The terrific casualties? Well, the figures were grossly exaggerated, Volik said; there were too many people, anyway, who always insisted on magnifying troubles—worthless crackpots they were. It was better not to repeat their lies.

Peter felt very close to his son, to the handsome youth in the Red Army uniform. They were sharing a great moment, when all the pettiness and deceit and fear which had poisoned their lives had to give way to one common hope and one common desire—the victory of the Soviet Union. But Volik's first words killed any desire Peter had to talk openly with his son. He had been stupid to think that he could share with Volik the thoughts he confided to Natasha last night:

" . . . you know how little I was ready to dance to Stalin's tune? But still less am I ready to cringe before the memory of czarist old generals or of old bandits like Khmelnitski. . . . We are fighting the Nazis the way we fought all our wars, against the Kaiser, against Napoleon, against the Turks, Swedes, Tartars . . . Doesn't Stalin trust us to fight well under Soviet slogans? Fatherland War, we call this war, just as we did in eighteen-twelve! Holy Russia, we say again, instead of the Soviet Union! Why is Churchill suddenly our dearest friend? American bankers and industrialists have become our best friends. . . . We are dripping with love for democracies whom we hated only a short while ago."

"Ah, Peter, what difference does it make what we say now? The main thing is to win the war. And, Peter, I do believe that things will be different after the war; this terrific suffering must change things, life will be freer, better."

"You are right, Natasha. It really doesn't matter what we say now as long as we win. But just the same, I for one would much rather fight under Lenin's banner than the banner of Peter the Great."

These were thoughts he could share with Natasha, as he could all his thoughts now, but not with Volik, not after Volik's first words:

" . . . so until we are old enough to be sent to the front, we are assigned to security duty. Oh, Father, this is so terribly exciting! Now more than ever we must be vigilant. It is better to destroy thousands of innocent suspects than let one criminal escape. These three days are my furlough but they told us that no days should be wasted now, that we could do some work on our furlough, and I wonder whether you and Mother couldn't help me. Have you ever heard anything suspicious around here? Like people saying that the war will bring changes? Or that maybe the war could have been prevented, that someone has made mistakes, or any such things? Have you?"

His parents assured him that they hadn't but that they would certainly let him know if they did. Natasha held her son's hands, she smiled at him and embraced him, but said little to him. Neither did Peter. They let Volik talk. He was full of tales about his comrades, wonderful guys all. Every one of them, of course, above any suspicion. But, still, they were told that even with each other they should be vigilant.

". . . and some are peasants, real peasants, their fathers can neither read nor write, and the boys are going to be officers just the way I am. Now, tell me, where else in the world could the son of a peasant be an officer?"

Volik was brimming full of "Where else?" "Just wait till the right moment comes . . ." was the tenor of his conversation. "The world hasn't seen the bloody lashing we'll give them. Stalin will know when the right moment comes."

The German attack found Vera and her granddaughter Tanya in the village of Lavrovka about ten miles from Klin. This village was the favorite summer spot of Klin families. A shallow stream ran through it, the delight of children, and it was surrounded by dense woods. This was the second summer Vera had brought Tanya here but there were few people who had heard her voice and still fewer who had seen her smile. Her voice and her smile were reserved for Tanya. The ten-year-old child, with her blue sparkling eyes, golden curls, silvery laugh and graceful body, was the image of Vera as she had been fifty years before. Tanya was proof to Vera that that past was a reality and not a dream. Tanya wore coarse clothes and shoes like the other girls, she cared nothing about her hair or skin, she was as godless as the rest and repeated ugly words she heard others use. But what was odious and sinful in everybody else was not so in Tanya. Nothing in Tanya seemed wrong to Vera.

Vera had no interest in the war news until the lightning advance of the Germans suddenly brought Lavrovka into threatening proximity to the war zone. And one day they were there, on the main street of the village. They came with such speed that the men and the younger women hardly had time to escape to the woods. It grew deadly quiet overnight. The streets were deserted, and there was no sound of human voices, laughter or singing. With the Germans came an elderly Russian, Nikita. He had left Russia in 1919 and had lived in Germany ever since. He helped the Germans, he snooped around, asked questions about the Partisans, saw to it that the Germans had enough food and fuel and that their orders were promptly carried out. His face was full of glee when disobedience or a disrespectful word about his masters brought the culprits into the Gestapo's hands.

The house in which Vera lived was given to a German major. Vera and Tanya slept on the floor of the dark drafty shed. Vera had to wait on the German officers who had their meals and spent the evenings with the major. When she first saw their smart tight-fitting uniforms and heard their sharp commanding voices, it touched long-forgotten chords in her. She felt no contempt or hatred for them, and they aroused no terror in her, as they did in the other villagers. They seemed to her much more civilized than the peasants with whom life had thrown her and for whom she had never felt anything but contempt. Through Nikita's hints, she discovered that a few other villagers felt about the Germans as she did. Nikita had quickly recognized in Vera a kindred soul but he dared not treat her better than he treated the rest of the villagers, and he could not risk being seen talking to her. The Partisans worked well, and well-aimed bullets frequently found their way into traitors' bodies. They had spared him because they knew that the Germans would exact a cruel price for his death. But here and there he found an occasion to drop a few words and Vera caught other whispered comments.

"It couldn't be much worse under the Germans . . . they couldn't behave so badly as the Communists say they do."

"The Germans will at least let one use the products of his own labors."

"I was a prisoner in Germany in the last war, I wish our peasants lived the way German peasants do."

Despite her agreement, Vera felt no closer to those people than to the other villagers. They were all nothing but filthy peasants. It is true, the Germans did not treat her much better than cattle, but then they did not know who she was; they thought she was one of the peasants. Silently she moved around and did her work, waiting for the day when she could disclose herself to the Germans and be a lady again and be a human being again. When they learned who she was they would take her and Tanya to civilized Germany, where decent people were respected and where the mob knew its rightful place.

Tanya worried her. With their fishing poles, with baskets for berries and mushrooms, the village youngsters started out early every morning and returned at night. They were always excited and always whispering in corners. And Tanya, of course, was with them. What were they up to? Vera hated the idea of the child's roaming the woods which were full of dangerous Partisans, and spending her days with those rough ill-mannered children. But Tanya wouldn't listen to her. Luckily, however, the Germans patrolled the woods, which made it much safer for Tanya to play there.

One day the loud screams of a child followed by two shots were heard in the woods. When the children returned in the evening, Tanya was not with them. They did not know what had happened to her. They were all far one from another when they heard the screams and the shots. From the children's frightened words, Vera understood one thing: the purpose of their daily excursion to the woods was to get messages and food to the Partisans. It was all clear to her then; the Partisans had tortured and killed Tanya.

Vera knew just what she would do. She would tell the Germans who she was, what the Partisans had done to her grandchild, and that the village children could show the Germans where the Partisans hid. She washed herself, combed her hair, and put on a clean dress. She had to look as much of a lady as possible. She half opened the door to the major's room. The Germans were having a gay party; they were drunk and laughing loudly at the story one of the officers, a middle-aged man with a red brutal face, was telling them. Vera listened. She remembered enough of her German to understand him, and what she heard froze her to the floor.

". . . the little fool thought I wanted her berries . . . 'Take them, take them,' she kept pushing the basket to me. I knocked it out of her hands. 'What do you want?' she cried. 'What do you want? I have nothing else to give you.' 'Oh yes, you have,' I said, 'and what you have . . .'"

The officers laughed loud in appreciation.

"She got really scared. She started to run away. I had a stick in my hands, and I threw it after her, and she tripped and I had her where I wanted her. God, did she kick! And she scratched and she bit me, I am all black and blue. You wouldn't think a child her age would have so much strength. It didn't help her much, though, not for long anyway. I didn't intend to but I had to silence her, she screamed so."

Encouraged by the others' laughter he added more details and they bellowed till their faces were purple.

"The old woman will never know what happened to that brat of hers; I threw the body into the thicket."

Those were the last words Vera heard. With death in her eyes and her heart, she went back to the shed and took an ax. Quietly she turned the handle to open the door to the major's room. Her hand was pulled away and the door was closed again. Strong hands drew her back and took the ax out of her hands.

A man's voice whispered, "Sh-sh, not a word, follow us."

She did not know who the men were, where they were taking her. They walked the length of the village, keeping close to the houses as people always did those days so that they could disappear quickly into a doorway at the sight of a German patrol.

In a hut at the very end of the village, a door opened to let Vera and the men in. There were many people in the room; the men were bareheaded, the women had tearstained faces, and some of them were kneeling before the bench under the icons. A body covered with a man's coat was lying on the bench. Someone lifted the coat and with a cry Vera sank to her knees. Tanya's body was black with bruises and dried blood, and her little dress was bloody and torn to shreds.

"The Partisans brought her down from the woods. They found her near their hideout. He will pay for it, the beast," Vera heard someone say.

All night long Vera stayed beside Tanya's body. The golden curls were tangled and muddy, and the face, the innocent sweet face, was a tortured grimace of horror with a torn mouth and a hole over one eye. All night long people came and went. They bent low over Tanya, they knelt and said a prayer, they touched Vera's hand and whispered comforting words to her.

The morning found Vera still on her knees, her head resting on Tanya's body. And this was the way the German patrol found her on their morning inspection tour. A heavy boot rolled Vera to the floor.

"Whose body is it? Who is responsible for it?" shouted the sergeant.

The villagers were ordered into the market place for questioning. How did the body get to the village? The major appeared on the scene. All the bitterness, the suppressed violence, the pent-up pain and hatred of a quarter of a century was in the word Vera spat at him when he passed her: "Murderer!" Again strong friendly hands drew her quickly back into the crowd.

The major spun around.

"Who said that? Who? Who? . . . I will give you five minutes to tell me. If in five minutes I do not know who it was, every tenth one of you will be shot."

Vera made a move to get out of the crowd, but they held her back.

"Keep still," they whispered to her. "Let them shoot all of us, it doesn't matter. They must learn that we stand together. Don't you dare open your mouth!"

Vera looked at them, unbelieving. She had despised them, yet they were ready to die for her! In a daze she took her place with the others when the major ordered them to form a wide circle around him and his soldiers.

"Well, the five minutes are over. Let me see, where shall I start? Who should be the lucky first one? Here! No . . . let me see . . . Here! But then, why not here?"

He was turning around, pointing here and there, all smiles, pleased with the good idea he had. Nikita was jumping around near him, showing his appreciation for the major's excellent sense of humor.

"Well, let's say we start here." The major pointed to a boy of twelve. Vera looked at the boy's mother, who paled and clutched at her son's hand but showed no weakening in her eyes. Vera made a move toward the woman. Those around her again whispered fiercely to her to keep quiet, and they held her firmly, so that she should not betray herself. Furtive eyes began to count the tenth, and faces whitened and grew tense and terrible.

"I really don't know why I should make it the tenth. I think the eighth would be much more fun," said the major, and with enjoyment watched the counting glances. The peasants noticed him, and, their eyes turning neither to the right nor to the left, looked straight into his face while he continued:

"No, I don't want eight either. Well, Karl, what is your favorite number? Say any number you like. Well, which shall it be?"

Karl, a very young soldier, his face not less pale and tense than the Russians' faces, murmured something unintelligible in a choked voice which he couldn't control. The major turned to another soldier, who seemed to be more receptive to a good joke.

"Seven is my lucky number, Herr Major!" he cheerfully announced.

"Good enough for me, seven it shall be!" was the major's final decision.

Soft murmurs were heard in the crowd:

"Glory be to the Lord! . . . God Almighty, bless Your children! . . . Forgive our sins . . . For Mother Russia, for Holy Mother Russia . . ."

The boy who was the first to be shot clenched his fist in the anti-Fascist salute and his lips shaped words:

"For our Fatherland, for Soviet Russia!"

Throughout the endless minutes in the market place, Vera had been listening to something within herself. She knew now that life was not all ugliness. She knew that if she lived she would not forget that. She knew she would not forget those brave faces, the warm smiles they had the strength to give her, the friendly eyes of the Jewish doctor, the frightened childish eyes of the young German soldier . . .

A sense of warmth flowing through her was loosening the long-tightened muscles of her heart. A faint smile was moving up to her eyes. Vera was one of the sevenths. . . .

It was May 5, 1942.

*Set in Linotype Granjon*
*Format by A. W. Rushmore*
*Manufactured by The Haddon Craftsmen*
*Published by* HARPER & BROTHERS
*New York and London*